THE RITUAL

The Ritual

By

David Rhodes

Bookstand Publishing
www.BookstandPublishing.com
www.cyberread.com

Published by
Bookstand Publishing
Division of CyberRead, Inc.
Houston, TX 77079
1977_2

Cover design by Thad Rhodes

Copyright © 2002 by **DAVID RHODES**
All rights reserved. No part of this publication may be reproduced or transmitted in any form or by any means, electronic or mechanical, including photocopy, recording, or any information storage and retrieval system, without permission in writing from the copyright owner.

ISBN 1-58909-334-8

Printed in the United States of America

Watch for these other titles coming soon by

David Rhodes

Risen

Door 13

ACKNOWLEDGEMENTS

This book is for Rocio Molina for saving my life and believing in me.

You raise me higher and give me strength.
I love you with all my heart.

I would like to give special thanks to my father, author Rawlins Rhodes for his support and kind words. I'm proud of you, Dad.

Also, a special thanks to Thad Rhodes for his gifted artistry.

Table of Contents

Part 1. Cain

Part 2. The Gathering

Part 3. The Book

Part 4. The Night of Cain

PART 1
CAIN

1

The town never saw him coming, never knew that such things as what he could do existed. However, there would come a time when most would embrace him into their lives.

He rolled into town on a hot July afternoon, dragging a dust cloud behind him from a black mint condition '77 Cadillac. The glaring sun gleamed off chrome, metal, and glass as he pulled up to the pumps at Zeb's station and turned off the engine. The dust suddenly lost its forward momentum, swirling and settling back to the ground around the car. Ants infested the sticky remains of a melted ice cream bar that someone had discarded next to one of the pumps.

The old man limped out to the car, wiping his hands on his greasy coveralls. He didn't want to get a smudge on this beauty, no sir. The windows were tinted so dark, they almost matched the car. He leaned over next to the driver's side window, and rapped a couple fingers on the glass. He could see his reflection as clear as a mirror, his old baseball cap tilted sideways over his white bearded face.

The electric motor whirred as the window lowered, and a burst of cold air hit Zeb in the face like a breath of Old Man Winter himself. The man in the car had jet-black hair, and sported a pair of reflector sunglasses. Zeb thought it odd that he was even *dressed* in black, and on such a sweltering day, too, but with that air conditioning, you could wear a damn *parka* and stay cool.

"That AC feels mighty good, mister. That's some ride you got there. A real beaut," Zeb said, looking the car over from one end to the other.

The man removed his shades, and grinned. "Why, thanks, old timer. It's my pride and joy." The man's eyes were the sharpest

2

blue Zeb had ever seen, and when he grinned, Zeb got the feeling this one could bite your head off.

"'76, right?"

"Close. Real close. '77. You know your cars pretty well, don't you?" the man asked.

"Yes sir. Been workin' on cars ever since the Big One. WWII, that is. That's how I got my limp. Damn shrapnel in the knee. Ain't no good for anything, but I can still work on the cars, yup. So I tell ya, I'm someone who can *really* appreciate a ride like this one, yes sir. Been workin' on 'em for years."

"That's amazing. I guess I can trust you, then, to check the oil, huh? Go ahead and fill it up, too."

"Yes sir, right away," Zeb said, and popped open the large hood. He pulled the dipstick out, and wiped it clean. He noticed smoke coming out of the open window, and chanced a peek around the edge of the hood. The man had his shades back on, and a cigarette hanging out of one side of his mouth. And even though he was wearing the shades, Zeb could *feel* him looking right at him.

Damn fool, Zeb thought, *gonna blow us from here to Kingdom Come.*

He though about mentioning it to the man, but somehow thought it wouldn't be a good idea.

He shut the hood gently (didn't want to slam the hood on this beauty), pulled out a dirty red bandana and wiped the front of it off, then wiped the beads of sweat off his forehead. It was getting *damn* hot today, hotter by the minute.

As if reading his thoughts, the man said, "Real scorcher, today, isn't it?"

Zeb stuffed his bandana into his back pocket, and wondered over to the window. "Yes sir, gets hotter every summer, seems." He limped to the rear of the car, opened the gas port, and unscrewed the gas cap. The air around the port was slightly distorted as hot fumes escaped, and once again Zeb found himself thinking about how that one cigarette could blow his station sky high. Sweat was running down his face now, and he again pulled out the bandana, wiped it off, and returned it to his back pocket.

Real scorcher today, isn't it?

Zeb took the nozzle from the pump, and flicked the lever over. The numbers rolled to zero like a slot machine; he never could afford to get the new digital pumps, but in a town as small as this one, there really wasn't much of a need. And Zeb made sure these pumps worked just fine, yes sir, never had a problem with them at all.

He pushed the nozzle into the port, set the automatic shut-off on the handle, and limped back over to the window. The smell of cigarette smoke was strong. Zeb was an ex-smoker himself, but he didn't think he'd smelled anything as rich as this. *Damn things must be deadly,* he thought.

"She's fillin' up now, and your oil's just fine. Anything else I can get for ya' today?" he asked, accidentally sucking in a lungful of that killer smoke. He pulled out the bandana again; it was warm and moist in his hand, and he used it again to wipe his face. Beads of sweat were forming like dew in his beard, and dripping onto the dusty ground.

"Well, now that you mention it, an ice cold drink sounds really good right about now," he said. "You know, something to take the edge off this heat." He grinned at Zeb, and Zeb smiled weakly back, revealing a set of stained and crooked choppers.

"Why, Yes sir, I've got the coldest pop in town right inside. Got cold beer, too, if you're thirsty for that. Just a minute, let me get this gas." He went to the back of the car and grabbed the nozzle. He would stop it before any gas could spill on this baby, yes sir, and then he would get a cold drink for this guy, and one for himself as well. The heat was feeding his thirst, and he downright *needed* a cold one right now. If he didn't wash the dust back soon, he would be choking on it.

And damn if he could remember a day as hot as this one. Large wet circles were forming under his armpits, and his whole body was damp in his overalls.

He heard the gas rushing to the top and released the automatic shut-off. He squeezed off a few more squirts to top it off, returned the nozzle to the pump, took the cap out of his pocket and screwed it back on, and shut the lid. Then he pulled out the bandana, which was practically soaked by now, and swabbed his face. If he didn't get a drink soon, he was going to dry up and blow away. He saw heat waves rising off the ground, and his eyes watered, squinting closed. His head was spinning, and damn if he hadn't felt heat like *this* in years.

He limped over to the driver side window, squinting at the man sitting behind the wheel. The man snubbed out his cigarette in the ashtray, and looked up at Zeb, who was staring at him, momentarily lost in his own thoughts.

"How about that drink, old timer?"

4

Zeb could think of nothing better; if he didn't get something down his throat right now, he was absolutely going to pass out. He could almost feel the heat waves shimmering around him.

"Oh, yeah. Come right on in, mister. Looks like I'll be needin' one m'self," Zeb said, heading for the office, which was connected to the one tiny bay where he occasionally worked on cars, and sometimes even tractors. After all, this *was* farm country, and he *was* the best mechanic in town.

He pulled open the smudged glass door, and savored the cool air from the window mount air conditioner in the office as it flowed like liquid past his face. He held the door for the stranger, and then followed him inside. The place smelled of oil and stale cigarette smoke. A small table stood in one corner, heaped with tattered magazines, and flanked by two chairs. He stopped for a moment at the counter next to the old cash register, and leaned against it, closing his eyes and soaking in the cool air.

"You all right, old timer?" the man dressed in black asked. Even his boots were black, and shined like mirrors.

"Yeah, I'm alright, yes sir. Just a little hot today," Zeb said. He went over to the cooler, and slid open one of the doors. "What'll ya' have, mister?"

The man looked over at the cooler, and pondered its contents for a moment.

"Hmmm. You know, an ice cold beer would go down really good right about now," he said, taking off his sunglasses and smiling.

Zeb looked into his cold blue eyes, and was taken aback by their sharpness, their unnatural color. *Must be contacts,* he thought, *everyone's wearin' 'em nowadays.*

"You musta' been reading my mind, mister, because that's exactly what I was thinkin'." He tossed a beer over to the man, who caught it with one hand. Zeb popped his open, and foam bubbled out of the top. He slurped down the foam, and then took four humungous swallows before setting the can down on the oil stained counter. Foam ran down one side of his beard, and he swiped it off with the sleeve of his coveralls.

"I don't believe I caught your name," Zeb said.

"That's because I never told you," the man said. He popped open his beer and took a couple of swigs, closing his eyes and savoring the taste. For a moment the only sound in the room was the hum of the air conditioner. Then he opened his eyes, and set his can down next to Zeb's. He leaned back against the counter, propping his elbows up on the ancient top.

The air conditioner clicked, and stopped running altogether.

"Well, I'll be damned," Zeb said, and went over to it and started pushing buttons. "Ain't never had a problem with it before." He went back to his beer, downed it in several gulps, and tossed the empty can into a trash barrel behind the counter. He limped over to the cooler for another can.

"Gonna grab m'self another. You want one?"

"No thanks, I'm great." The man seemed to be suddenly lost in his own thoughts.

The office that was once pleasantly cool began to turn warm, then hot, in the space of several seconds. The man didn't seem to notice; he just stared out the window, and swigged off his beer.

Real scorcher....

Zeb opened the beer and took a couple of swallows.

Then the *real* heat hit him, surrounding him like a blanket of fire.

He dropped the beer on the floor, and flecks of foam sprayed out across the large front windows. Sweat poured down his face, soaking into his clothing. His collar felt like it was choking him, and he struggled to get air, searing hot air that burned as it entered his lungs. He clawed at his collar, trying to loosen it, and ogled at the man leaning against the counter.

He was watching Zeb with mild amusement, not a drop of sweat on him.

"Who are you?" Zeb gasped. He tried to grab the zipper on the front of his coveralls, but he instantly let go when the hot metal burned his fingers.

"That all depends on you, my friend," he said. "I can be your best friend, or I can be your worst enemy. I'm going to be here a long, long time, and you are going to do exactly as I tell you." He grinned at Zeb.

"Are we going to be friends, Zeb?"

Zeb's face was turning bright red, and his eyes were watery with hot tears that rolled down his face and mixed with the runnels of sweat.

"Yeah," he said, more hissing than speaking. "Friends."

The heat left as swiftly as it came, and Zeb plopped down into one of the chairs in the corner, gulping in great breaths of the cooler air. Normal color slowly returned to his face. He sat gasping, staring up at the man, afraid to say anything.

"So we have an agreement, then?" the man asked.

"Yeah, yeah...yes sir."

The air conditioner gave a loud *click!* and hummed to life, blowing deliciously cool air into the room. Zeb jumped up and stood in front of it with his eyes closed, savoring every molecule of cool air as it blew onto his face. He had never felt anything so good in his life.

"Alright, then. That road out front there," he said, motioning through the front windows. "Is that the only road in and out of town?"

Zeb turned around, letting the cool air blast the back of his head. "Yes sir, that there's the only way in and out. I pretty much see ever' one that comes and goes. I see 'em or I hear 'em. I got my little room in the back. No use wastin' all that money livin' in town."

Zeb had the feeling that the more he yakked, the more information he offered to this stranger, the safer he was. He was still trembling, but the man had a smile on his face now, so he was able to exercise a little control.

"Good. *Very* good. You're being most cooperative, Zebediah. I think we're going to be great friends. So tell me, is there a *lot* of traffic?"

"Oh, hell no. Mostly just the farmers headin' out with loads of corn. This ain't much of a town, mister, mostly just farms. We don't get many outsiders here."

"You know, I was hoping you'd say that. So here's what I want you to do. You're going to let me know if you see any outsiders come down this road. Or anybody out of the ordinary for that matter. Also any late night activity, because who's going to be hauling corn in the middle of the night, huh?" His face went somber again, and Zeb felt a chill shiver up his spine.

"Yes sir, ain't no one gonna haul corn in the middle of the night," Zeb said, and he hesitated for a moment, looking down at his oily work boots.

"What is it, old man?" the man asked, slightly irritated.

"Well, sir," Zeb said, his voice shaking, "I was wonderin', um...how am I supposed to get a hold of you? I mean, I don't even know your name." He looked up at the man, and was relieved to see him grinning at him.

"Relax, Zeb. I'm not going to hurt you anymore, just as long as we stay friends. Tell me, is there a church in town?"

"Yes sir, it's just a little one, but it serves its purpose, I s'pose."

"Well, that's where you'll be able to find me. Now, how do I get there?"

Zeb pointed out toward the dusty road in front of the station. "Ya' just follow that road into town, and it'll take ya' right smack down Main Street. Then ya' go left, and head on up to Church Street. Ya' can't miss it. Real old church, that one is."

The man walked right up the Zeb. Zeb cringed, but forced himself to look right into his eyes. The blues of his eyes were like ice, and Zeb again felt as if he were looking not only at the outside of him, but the inside.

"Zeb, you've been a big help. I hope we remain friends for a long time." He pulled his wallet out of his back pocket, unfolded it, and pulled out two twenties, which he laid on the counter next to the register.

"Keep the change, old timer."

He pushed open the office door, then looked over his shoulder.

"By the way, the name's Cain. Remember it."

Zeb watched him stroll out to his Cadillac in the bright afternoon sun. He opened the driver's side door, and then stood looking at Zeb for a moment. Zeb felt that familiar chill in his spine. Cain put on his sunglasses, got into the car, and drove away toward the direction of town, raising a plume of dust behind the car.

Zeb sat down in one of the chairs and looked at the thumb and forefinger of his right hand; there was a small red blister on the tip of both, tiny reminders of this sudden, bizarre visitation.

"God help us all," he said.

2

Cain cruised slowly down the dirt lane, taking in the surroundings, *studying* the surroundings. Straight ahead of him a large wooded area rose up, bright green with summer foliage, and beyond that, undulating hills as far as the eye could see.

The lane curved to the right, and took on a northeasterly direction straight into town. He pulled over and got out of the car. The dust cloud billowed around him, and then began to settle. The black Caddy was getting a fine layer of dust. He walked to the front of the car, boots crunching on the gravel, and surveyed the scene before him.

To anybody else, it would have been a beautiful scene, indeed; to him, it was a place to hide, a place to commit his vile acts, a place to play. The town was very small, and most of the buildings were either partially or totally obscured by the massive oaks that lined the streets and bordered cornfields. The surrounding countryside was dotted with farms, with huge silos and barns dominating the landscape. It brought back memories of his childhood in rural Iowa, and of the farm where he grew up. It hadn't been a real *working* farm; his grandfather had left it to his father, who sold off most of the animals and farm equipment to pay off the back taxes on the place. All that were left were some chickens, a couple of dogs (there were, of course, several stray cats and always a horde of kittens running around), and some rusted hulks of old farm equipment. Those were the days when he was young and still innocent, a boy full of endless energy, who, at age fourteen, would witness something that would change his whole outlook on life.

Lucas lay awake in bed, staring at the square of moonlight stretched across the floor. The whole house was dead silent; his parents were already asleep, and his little brother Jake lay snoring in the other twin bed across the room. He hated sharing his room (naturally, he considered it his room because he was older, and tougher) with his brother, but Jake was afraid of the dark, and had too hard a time sleeping alone. Now, Jake was nine, and was still in his room, and probably would be until they were both old farts in wheel chairs.

There came a soft tapping on the window, and Lucas got out of bed, went over and peered through the glass. His friend Clay was outside motioning for him to come out. Clay's father owned a farm just down the way, a real working farm, and sometimes Lucas felt bad for his friend because of all the hard work that came with living on a farm. Mr. Pederson always said that the key to a good and prosperous life was hard work and a clean soul.

Lucas thought he was just plain nuts.

Lucas raised the window, and stuck his head outside. The cool summer breeze brought the smell of freshly cut hay and manure. Crickets chirruped crazily from their hiding places.

"C'mon, I got it," Clay whispered.

"Just a minute," Lucas said, and padded over to the bedroom door. He opened it with the ease of a burglar, and made a quick check of the hall. All was dark and quiet. He went over to his brother's bed; a small nightlight was plugged into the wall next to Jake, and it bathed his sleeping countenance in dim yellow light.

Lucas was already dressed, so he pulled on his sneakers and climbed out the window, closing it to just a crack. They ran over to their secret place behind the barn, where they had stacked old lumber in two piles, leaving a gap in the center where they could sit unseen.

They sat against the splintery wood of the barn, above them a full moon glowing brightly on a blanket of stars. Clay pulled a wad of paper towels out of his jeans pocket and unfolded it, revealing a small mound of pipe tobacco.

"How did you get it?" Lucas asked, taking in its strong aroma.

"Heck, he leaves it layin' around everywhere. I could probably take the whole thing, and he wouldn't notice," Clay said. He stuck his hand in a hole in the end of one of the lumber piles, and brought out the pipe he and Lucas had fashioned from a hollowed out piece of corn cob, and a length of branch from a bush next to Lucas's house that they had discovered to be naturally hollow long before thoughts of making a pipe had ever entered their minds.

Clay jammed some of the tobacco into their makeshift pipe, and then pulled out some stick matches from his other jeans pocket. He handed the pipe to Lucas.

"You ready?" he asked, his face looking odd and very serious in the moonlight, as if by this grown-up act they had become two different people altogether. The pipe felt alien in Lucas's hand, and he was glad for the dark so Clay couldn't see his hand shaking from the anxiety and paranoia he felt at that moment. He half expected his father to jump around the corner at any moment and yell, "Aha! So this is what you're up to!"

"Ready," he said, and he tried to block the paranoid thoughts from his mind as Clay struck a match on the side of the barn and held it to the pipe.

Lucas drew slowly, letting the smoke puff out the side of his mouth. The flavor was very rich, very adult, and he felt some of the paranoia slipping away from him. He handed the pipe to Clay, who looked into the bowl at the glowing cherry inside, and then stuck it into his own mouth and drew deeply.

He inhaled some of the thick smoke, and instantly went into a coughing fit.

"Shhhh! We're gonna get caught. Don't inhale it, you dork!" Lucas said. "Cover your mouth!"

Clay handed the pipe back to Lucas, stood up, and paced back and forth, taking in huge gulps of the night air until his choking subsided.

"That stuff is strong!" he declared, his voice slightly wavering.

Lucas drew again on the pipe, taking care not to inhale, and blew smoke up into the air. The full moon and the stars seemed to dance, and take on a life of their own. His head felt light, like a balloon on a string swaying in the wind. He stood up and handed the pipe to Clay.

"Do you feel different?" he asked, smiling widely. He didn't know what, but it seemed something very significant was happening, as if this secret ritual was changing their very lives.

"Yeah, I feel weird," Clay said. "I'll bet this is what they mean by 'getting high'."

They both stared up at the stars, feeling the earth spinning beneath their feet.

Clay started to puff some more, and Lucas noticed small, flickering lights in the woods north of their position. He stared for a moment, thinking it was a side effect of the smoke, but he soon realized the lights were real, and he tapped Clay on the shoulder and pointed.

"What's that?" he asked in an urgent whisper, and Clay looked over toward the woods.

"I don't-" he said, and after a moment, "What is that?"

"C'mon, let's see," Lucas said, and rammed his finger into the pipe, trying to douse it. He burned his finger a couple of times *(would have a small blister on the tip of it the next day), and stashed the pipe in its secret place in the lumber pile.*

They ran across a dirt field toward the woods, heads still spinning and floating from the tobacco. As they drew closer, they hunkered down, and crept slowly to the tree line. From here they could see figures moving around through the trees, some bearing torches. The deep voice of a man reached their ears in bits and pieces; it was impossible to discern what he was saying, so the boys crept a little closer. And then they saw something that made their eyes want to pop out of their heads.

A naked woman was laying on her back on top of a huge boulder in the middle of a clearing.

The boys looked at each other through the shadowy darkness of the trees, and then turned their attention back to the woman. They had been there before, during their daytime explorations, had even stood on the boulder, but they never had a clue it could be used for this. She seemed to be asleep. Her arms hung limply, and her head lolled to one side, her brown hair fanned out behind her on the rock. Lucas could see her breasts, the puff of hair between her legs, and he looked over at Clay for some kind of acknowledgement that he, too, had seen it, but Clay was too busy gawking.

He could see the figures plainly now, and he realized why Clay was staring so intently at the seen before him. The figures all wore black robes, with hoods pulled over their heads. They formed a rough circle around the boulder. The one with the deep voice stood at the head of the woman, one arm extended out over her, his other arm cradling the book from which he was reading something aloud which made no sense at all to the boys.

Lucas counted the figures - there were thirteen.

Witches, *he thought*, these guys are witches!

He looked over at Clay again, and this time Clay looked back, his eyes wide with fear. The figures started to chant, and when the boys looked back toward the clearing, the man with the deep voice was standing to the side of the boulder, facing directly toward them, and he had both hands poised above the woman.

A green swirling mist formed in the air around her.

The woman's body jerked, and she half raised her head and gazed dreamily at the haze rising up in front of her, and then she fell limp again. She blinked, and tears sprang from her eyes, glistening in the torchlight.

Lucas's heart pounded; he knew the woman was going to die, and he was frozen like a deer caught in the headlights of a car. He dared not make a sound.

The figures were still chanting, and the man with the deep voice removed his hood. Even from their position, Lucas could see his dark, piercing eyes. His long black hair spilled out from inside the hood. He raised his arms and called out in that strange language. The hairs pricked up on the back of Lucas's neck and arms. Sweat dripped down his face, and now his heart pounded so hard, he thought it would burst right from his chest.

Lucas thought he felt the ground rumble.

He looked over at Clay, and saw that he had his head lowered, as if trying to block out what he saw in the clearing. A moment later his back hitched up and he retched, and to Lucas, that one little sound seemed magnified a hundred times in the quiet of the woods.

The sound reached the clearing, where all the figures turned and peered into the trees. The boys could hear low murmurs. The longhaired man glared through the darkness where they hid, and his eyes seemed to fix on Lucas.

"There!" he called out, pointing toward the boys.

A thought raced through Lucas's mind: Damn tobacco! He got sick from that blasted tobacco!

All of the figures had entered the trees, and were headed in their direction. They were close, but they hadn't yet seen the boys. Their feet crashed through the undergrowth, drawing closer, and Lucas could hear them talking amongst themselves, could see their imperceptible faces under the hoods in the flickering torchlight.

Lucas grabbed Clay's arm and hissed, "Run!"

They still had time to avoid being caught, and Lucas knew better than to run toward home. The very thought of these people knowing where he lived made him shiver. He pulled Clay along as he crept to his right, working his way to the far side of the clearing. The longhaired man was still standing next to the woman, cradling the open book with one arm. A single torch was stuck in the ground next to the boulder. The greenish mist had vanished, and Lucas saw the woman again raise her head and look around, tears on her face.

"You ok?" Lucas whispered, and Clay nodded his head in the dim.

"Yeah. The smoke...I couldn't help it. Made me sicker than a dog. I'm just a little...little dizzy, now," he whispered back, and Lucas could smell puke on his breath. "Where we going?"

"*Away from my place. We'll sneak back later, after we lose 'em. If my old man finds out I'm out here, he'll kill me.*"

They had worked their way almost all the way around to the other side of the clearing when they heard someone's voice echoing through the woods. They laid down flat on their stomachs in the thick undergrowth of ivy, and surveyed the scene. In the darkness of the woods on the opposite side they saw torches moving among the trees.

"*Keep looking,*" the man in the clearing called, and he placed the book on the boulder next to the woman, pulled the remaining torch out of the ground, and struck out for the woods.

The voices began to grow distant. The clearing was now bathed only in moonlight, but Lucas could still see the naked form of the woman, a site that would simultaneously haunt and arouse him for years to come.

He saw something else, too.

"*Come on,*" Clay said, tugging at Lucas's shirt, "*let's get out of here!*"

"*Hang on,*" Lucas said. He got up and went for the tree line at the edge of the clearing.

"*Lucas!*" Clay watched as Lucas's form all but vanished in the darkness.

Lucas hunkered down behind a tree next to the clearing. He could still see torches moving like fireflies in the dark beyond the other side of the clearing. Crouching, he scurried over to the boulder and ducked behind it. He ogled at the woman, and was half tempted to reach up and touch one of her breasts. Instead, he reached up and grasped the book with both hands, and the woman turned her head and looked down at him.

"*Help me,*" she said, her voice barely a whisper. Her words came slowly and deliberately, as if it took every ounce of effort to speak those two tiny words.

"*I…*" Lucas began, and then he heard someone returning to the clearing. "*I'm sorry,*" he said, "*Run! Get up and run if you can!*" He snatched up the book, and scurried straight back to the trees, trying to keep the boulder between him and whoever might be looking. He ran back to where he left Clay, who was still there, hiding behind a tree, eyes wide in the gloom.

"*Go, go, go!*" Lucas said, and they both took off into the shadows. They dodged trees and jumped over deadfalls, and when they were absolutely winded, they stopped. They bent over, taking great breaths, not quite able to talk. Lucas had a stitch in his side *that throbbed with every breath, and he held a hand against it while he caught his breath. The woods were silent, and the full moon cast an eerie glow over everything.*

An angry scream pierced the silence.

They looked in the distance toward the clearing, but could see nothing save for the torches, which were now just tiny lights floating around in the dark.

Another deep, angry scream echoed into the night, a long, drawn out scream that changed into a wailing, then into outright howling. Lucas felt goose bumps raise on his arms. He had heard coyotes before, but never anything like this.

The clearing began to glow green, like the mist they had seen before, only this was much brighter, emanating out from a central source, splashing green light everywhere. Lucas thought he heard someone yell something, but they were too far away to tell for sure. Then the light blinked out. They stood motionless, listening for anything out of the ordinary, but hearing nothing but the soft hush of the wind through the trees.

Something roared, like an animal caught in a trap, something wild, unnatural.

The boys stared wide-eyed at each other, Lucas clutching the book to his chest. The torch lights in the distant clearing began to bounce frantically around like molecules, and Lucas undoubtedly heard screams this time, fragmented and confused, and he suddenly wanted to get as far away from this place as humanly possible.

Just before they ran, they heard that inhuman, gargled roar, and after that all they heard was their own heartbeats drumming in their ears.

They hid in a cornfield several miles away for what seemed like hours. The moon crept across a black sky sprinkled with stars, and the corn swayed in the whispering breeze. The only other sound was an occasional flapping of wings, like a sheet on a clothesline on a windy day.

"Those guys were devil worshippers, Lucas," Clay said. "If they find us, we're dead."

"We'll have to sneak back around the long way, and we'll have to do it soon. My dad gets up early," Lucas said.

"Your dad! My dad gets up before the sun, remember?"

"Oh yeah, we better get back."

Lucas rubbed his hand over the book's cover; it felt rough, as if it were fashioned from leather. When he opened it, the pages seemed to crackle from age, and he somehow knew that this book was very, very old. The writing was illegible in the dark, but he could tell that is wasn't English. And there were drawings, but they, too, were illegible.

"You're crazy for taking that," Clay said. "I'll bet that thing is evil. Why'd you take it, anyway?"

Lucas thought for a minute. "I don't know, I just wanted it, I guess. Pretty crazy, huh?"

"Yeah, pretty crazy."

Lucas didn't want to tell his friend the absolute truth; that he was drawn to the book, that he had to have it, almost as if he were meant *to have it. He had risked his life for this book, and he would make sure that it never left his possession.*

The wind whispered softly through his hair, and it brought the smell of freshly cut hay, manure, and honeysuckle. Sparrows chirped and sang in the golden summer sun, and bumblebees hovered lazily through the daisies and dandelions that were scattered in the tall grass bordering the dirt lane.

"Perfect," he muttered, and climbed back into his Caddy. He started the engine, cranked up the AC, and headed into Oak Junction.

3

As Cain drew near town, the dirt and dust gave way to blacktop, the Caddy's tires humming quietly along the smoother surface. He drove slowly, trying to get a feel for his new home, and he decided that the residents here ought to get a feel for *him*. He let his dark influence emanate outward like a radar, and he could almost *see* what people nearby were doing, could *hear* some of what they were saying. Yes, he was definitely going to let the people of Oak Junction get a feel for him. A slight smile crossed his lips.

The Caddy inched past Nate's Diner, its reflection following it along in the diner's front windows. The waitress behind the counter was pouring coffee for one of the locals who had stopped in for lunch, and stopped mid-pour to watch the black Cadillac slide by out on Main Street.

Hal Winder, a local farmer and regular at Nate's, sat at the counter with a hot ham and cheese sandwich and a cup of coffee in front of him. It was his favorite lunch, and he often told Nate jokingly that if he ever stopped serving his hot ham and cheese sandwiches, he would lose one satisfied customer.

Of course, most people in town knew that wasn't altogether true; it was pretty much common knowledge that Hal had it in for the busty redhead behind the counter, but he was just too afraid to do anything about it. After all, he was a farmer, not a lover, and after his wife had passed on, he really had no clue how to deal with women.

Even Betty herself knew, could tell by the way he looked at her, and acted around her (not to mention all the talk that had reached her ears), and she thought it was downright cute the way he was always giving her attention. And she *did* like the man, but she was also old fashioned, and a little stubborn. She wasn't about to make the first move, no, she would leave that up to him.

He took a bite out of his sandwich, and looked over at Betty. She had a coffee pot in one hand, and seemed occupied with something outside the diner. He started chewing, and felt something odd in his mouth. He stopped chewing, a puzzled look on his face.

Something *moved* in his mouth.

He spat the wad of chewed sandwich onto his plate, and looked at it suspiciously. It moved, and then a large roach burrowed out of the mass, and seemed to regard Hal for a moment, its antennae twitching from side to side. Then it dashed across the counter and disappeared on the other side.

"Oh, shit!" Hal declared, covering his mouth and rushing for the men's room. The sound of Hal throwing up reached everyone in the diner, and some kept right on eating, while others put down their food, and started laying money down on the counter.

It would be a long time before Hal would eat another hot ham and cheese.

On the next block over, Cain passed the tiny newspaper office, The Grove Reporter - it used to be a fix-it shop until Freddy Martin died of a heart attack back in '92. It sat empty for a few years, and then the local librarian, a young man by the name of Jonathon Mott bought it for a steal from relatives of Martin. He began producing a weekly publication with a very low circulation, but he seemed to gain a lot of satisfaction from it, and actually gave away a lot of his stock.

A sign that read **CLOSED** hung in the glass of the front entrance.

Directly next door was Frandsen's Hardware, and Cain noticed two old men sitting on a wooden bench in front of the store. Cain thought: *How pitiful, to be old and useless, to just sit and wait for death to come.*

Oak Junction's two oldest residents, Jaspar Hendricks and Hank Tooley sat on the bench soaking up precious sunlight, occasionally jawing it up over some menial bit of news making the rounds through town. It always was a mystery to the residents of Oak Junction how these two became such close friends. Jaspar was a retired accountant who once had an office in Arlidge, and Hank owned a farm in Oak Junction that was now run by his eldest son. Jaspar had never married, and Hank's wife was in a nursing home in Arlidge (Oak Junction was just too small to support a nursing home, or a school for that matter - all of that was in Arlidge, about ten miles south of Oak Junction), so the two of them spent their days keeping each other company.

Hank wore overalls and a sweaty tee shirt, and he seemed to fit perfectly into the mold of the town. With Jaspar, however, old habits died hard. He always wore the same clothing, hand-medowns from his days as an accountant. Hank always teased him about the fact that all he needed was a pocket protector to complete the ensemble, but Jaspar was never amused. After all, a pocket protector *had* been as much a part of his wardrobe as shirt, slacks, and underwear. But try telling *that* to Hank.

Jaspar wore an old short sleeve dress shirt and black slacks that had seen much better days, and he had one leg crossed over the other, exposing a black sock that was pushed down to a scuffed dress shoe, and a skinny shin that was covered with white hair and age spots. His balding head followed the Cadillac with the tinted windows as it floated by.

"Now there goes something you don't see everyday," Jaspar said, and he suddenly felt something wet and warm on his face.

"No kiddin'," Hank said, looking sideways over at Jaspar. "That's one nice...Jesus, Jaspar, look at yourself!"

But Jaspar had already noticed. Blood poured from his nose, and onto his shirt, and he looked down at himself with his arms out in front of him as if he couldn't comprehend what was going on.

Hank pulled a hanky out of his back pocket. "Lean your head back before you bleed to death, Jaspar." Jaspar tilted his head back, and Hank began to wipe the blood off of his face, neck, and shirt. "What happened?"

"How should *I* know? I was just watching that Cadillac..." He lifted his head and looked down the street. The car had vanished. "Well, it's gone now," he said.

"Looks like the bleedin' stopped. We better go inside and get you cleaned up," Hank said. His knees snapped as he stood.

"Uh, yeah," Jaspar said, but he was still looking down the empty street.

Jenny White walked out of Grove Market and into the bright July sunshine, a paper sack filled with groceries under one arm, and her five year old daughter Ashley hanging onto the other. Jenny loved days like this; sunny and hot, hardly a cloud in the sky, birds singing in the trees that lined Broadway Street, and most of the other streets in town.

She paused to breath in some of the clean, fragrant air. It was redolent with hay and honeysuckle, and of course, this wouldn't have been farm country without the constant scent of manure lingering everywhere. But Jenny had lived here her whole life, and was quite used to that particular aroma, as were most of the other full time residents of the town.

"Come on, honey, let's go," she said, and then stopped short as a sparrow fell out of the branches of the tree closest to them. It lay on its back on the hot sidewalk, head twisted to one side. It twitched several times, and then lay still.

She looked up and saw a black Cadillac cruising down the street in front of them.

"Look, mommy, the birdie's hurt," Ashley said, and ran over to where it lay on the sidewalk.

"No, no honey," Jenny said, "don't touch it. They have bad, bad germs."

Ashley drew her hand back, making an O with her mouth, as if she were suddenly shocked at this new knowledge.

"Let's go, honey." Jenny grabbed her daughter's hand, and they started down the street toward home, where she would make dinner and wait for her husband to arrive home for dinner. She glanced over her shoulder, but the car was already gone.

Cain went west on Church Street, toward the edge of town, until it became West Church Street. The road curved southward and ended in a dead end next to a short expanse of empty field flanked by a vast field of corn.

It was here that the old stone and mortar structure had stood for many years, tenacious against the erosion of time. A small bell tower rose above the main structure (the bell had been replaced once, but the tower still served its purpose, ringing every Sunday morning, calling the faithful to the weekly sermons), and above that a steeple topped by a simple white cross that had been freshly painted and almost glowed in the sunlight.

Cain pulled up in front of the church and turned off the Caddy's engine. He got out of the car, and walked up onto the sidewalk. The sun reflected off his sunglasses as he looked up at the cross. There was a small but prim front lawn, with a small sign planted in the middle of it that read:

Fellowship Of God
Let God Embrace You
Welcome One and All

"Sounds like a invitation to me," he said, and went to the rear of the car. He opened the trunk, and lifted out a parcel wrapped in a black velvet cloth. He pulled back a few folds of cloth to reveal the front of a book. He ran his hand gently over the rough surface, and felt a static energy in the tips of his fingers. He breathed in deeply of its power, but not through his lungs; instead, he *absorbed* it into his very being, could feel something vast and powerful, something he controlled, and yet, something over which ultimately he had no control.

After witnessing the events in the clearing that night, and laying low in the middle of a cornfield for what seemed like hours (it was actually only about forty-five minutes), the boys managed to work their way home, ducking and hiding at every little noise. They finally reached the Cain farm, and Clay immediately went on his way to get home before his father awoke and discovered his absence.

Lucas slid his bedroom window up, and poked his head inside. He could see his brother's face in the dim yellow glow of the nightlight, could hear the slight snores, and he felt a wave of utter contempt for the boy wash over him.

He pictured holding a pillow over Jake's face to stop him from breathing...

It couldn't be possible, though, because he was still outside his bedroom window, the book tucked under one arm.

The book.

He had almost forgotten about the book. It felt warm to the touch, as if emanating an inner glow of its own. He would have to do something with the book; if he took it inside, a member of his family might find it, perhaps even his wimp of a brother, and then there would be Hell to pay.

He hurried back to his place behind the barn, and found a hole big enough for the book in the end of one of the lumber piles, and there he stashed it, safe from the probing eyes of the curious.

After climbing into his bedroom and taking off his clothes, he slid into bed and tried to sleep, but he found himself returning to the clearing in the woods, the naked woman on the boulder, the hooded figures, and the harsh man who seemed to be the owner of the book. All seemed to center around the book, as if it were at the heart of everything, He fell asleep thinking about the insane howling he and Clay had heard, almost a roar, and the sounds of people screaming.

That night he dreamt he was back in the clearing, and he was alone, save for the woman on the rock; he was standing right next to her, staring at her naked form in the moonlight. Her beauty hypnotized him. Her head, which was turned away from him, turned slowly toward him, and he could see the sheer terror in her eyes.

"Help…me…" she whispered.

There was a noise behind him in the woods, and he turned to see the longhaired man burst into the clearing, bearing a torch and a really pissed off expression on his face. Lucas tried to run, but he was frozen next to the rock. He flinched as the longhaired man ran past him to the boulder. He seemed not to notice Lucas at all.

"Where's my fucking book?" he screamed at the woman, lifting her up by the shoulders and shaking her. Her head lolled from side to side, and her breasts bounced and jiggled. She tried to speak, to say something, anything, but he let her drop, and her head smacked against the hard surface of the boulder. She fell unconscious, and Lucas saw a trickle of blood run down the side of the boulder and drip onto the hard packed dirt.

Other hooded figures entered the clearing, some bearing torches. Shadows danced and flickered obscenely on the tree line. Some of the figures removed their hoods, and he thought he recognized a couple of them, but he wasn't sure.

"We need to find the book!" the longhaired man screamed again, and he began to look desperately around the clearing. Some of the others followed suit. One man glanced at his watch, and said, "It's almost midnight, Master."

"I know, you fucking moron, I know! Just help me find the book!"

Lucas stood in the middle of the din, invisible to the participants of this particular dream.

The scene suddenly changed. People ran away from the clearing screaming, as an ungodly howl filled the night air, and Lucas saw the source of the howling above the clearing.

At first, it looked like a man with wings, but as it grew closer he realized it was no man, but some thing *he had never seen before. It had huge, leathery wings that flapped heavily in the air. It landed on the boulder, one clawed foot on either side of the woman. Its body was dark green, and covered with a clear slimy substance that dripped off its body in long thin tendrils. It had bright yellow eyes with vertical slits for pupils, and a curved horn on each side of its head. It opened its mouth and roared, a mouthful of needles glinting in the moonlight.*

It pressed one foot down on the woman's chest, reached down with both of its clawed hands, and tore her head from her body. It dropped the head on the dirt next to Lucas, and he looked away in horror.

With a great flapping of its wings, the beast rose into the air, and went after the fleeing figures in the woods. Lucas watched helplessly as one by one, the beast gathered the people up and brought them back to the clearing, where he would tear several limbs from their bodies and leave them bleeding to death as he went for more. People were moaning and crying out in agony, amidst it all the howling and screeching of the beast.

The carnage seemed to go on and on, and then Lucas happened to look down at the woman's head lying at his feet. The eyes were closed, and her tongue lolled out of the open mouth.

Then everything went quiet. Her eyes popped open, and Lucas tried to jump back, but couldn't. She looked right at Lucas.

"Help...me," she said, her voice echoing loudly in his head.

"Help...me...help...me..." Repeatedly, louder and louder.

He tried to cover his ears, but it only got louder. It got so loud that Lucas thought his head would explode, or he would simply go crazy, and be locked away in an asylum for the rest of his days.

Lucas awoke sitting up in his bed, clutching the sides of his head. He was drenched in sweat. His eyes probed around the room in desperation and terror; but there was only the soft glow of the night-light, and the monotonous snoring of his little brother.

He thought with sickening finality: It happened, it really happened, and it was all because of me. I have to get rid of that thing!

Later that morning, Lucas pulled the book from its hiding place in the lumber pile, and held it gingerly in his hands. The book was large, and very thick. It would take a while to get rid of it. He used a spade to dig a small pit in the ground, and then gathered small twigs and woodchips, and threw them into the pit. He produced a book of matches he'd taken from the utility drawer in the kitchen, pulled one out, and struck it. He held it to the wood until it burned his fingers, and then dropped it into pile, sticking his fingers in his mouth. He lit another, and held it on the same spot. This time the flame caught, and white smoke wisped up from the flames. He threw a few more dry branches on the fire, and watched it grow. His father was at work, and his mother inside the house, so he was pretty sure no one would notice the smoke.

When the flames were high enough, he set the book directly on the fire. The flames rose, as if fed by the book, and surrounded it in liquid motion. Lucas breathed a sigh of relief.

When the book sprang out of the fire.

It thudded in the dirt next to the pit, puffing out dust from underneath it. White curls of smoke rose from its cover, and then dissipated altogether. Lucas picked it up and stared at it; it was undamaged. Not a burn anywhere. No way, he thought, and dropped it back into the fire. This time, he threw more sticks on top of it to help stoke the fire.

Blue and yellow flames licked and crackled around the edges of the book, and for a moment all Lucas could see were the flames, and sparks lifting up into the smoke trail that twisted into the morning sky. He could feel the heat on his face as he waited in anticipation for the book to be reduced to ashes.

Again, it jumped out of the fire, thudding to the dirt. The wisps of smoke rising from its cover were blown away by a soundless gust of wind, and yet, Lucas felt no wind, could hear no sound, save for the crackling of the fire, which was not disturbed. The book popped open, and the pages fanned toward some predetermined spot, and then stopped altogether, leaving the book laying open on the ground.

Lucas hunkered down in front of the book and scanned the pages. On one page there was a diagram of the book itself, surrounded by different symbols he had never seen before. On the other page, a lot of writing in some language he could not decipher. The letters were familiar, but the way they were arranged was alien to him.

As he stared at the words, some of the letters seemed to blur and shift. He closed his eyes for a few seconds, and then opened them. The shifting of the letters had stopped. But he had a sense that the book was trying to tell him something, to give him a message, and part of that message was that it was futile to try to destroy it. Lucas closed it and picked it up. He didn't want to see the words, the shifting letters anymore, just wanted to figure out what to do with the book for the time being.

He studied it more closely. The cover was made of some kind of black leather, rough and undulating, with a crude skull embossed on the front in what looked like gold. He ran the fingers of his right hand over the cover. He felt, and even heard, a crisp static charge on his fingertips, like pulling apart two socks fresh from the dryer.

His fear of the book, of what it might be able to do, was lessening, and slowly being replaced by a timid curiosity, a cautious willingness to discover all of its dark secrets.

He dowsed the fire, scraping dirt over the top of it with his sneaker. He snuck into the dark confines of the barn. Dust motes circulated in the morning sunlight that streamed through cracks in the walls, holes in the roof. Once a center of activity, the barn was now used to store tools and old tires, and the rusted remains of an old International Harvester tractor that his grandfather had used when the farm had still been active. Now, all the tires were flat and cracked with age, and cancerous rust spots grew everywhere on its once bright green body. Half the engine had been removed, part-by-part, and all that remained was a rusted hulk of metal, plastic, and wires, bathed in a thick coat of ancient motor oil. Just seeing it brought back memories of when he and Clay used to play on it when they were much younger; he supposed Jake liked to play on it now, and to think of that gave him a weird sense of time, of things moving on and changing, only to repeat the process over and over again. Life was funny that way.

Between the two large rear tires was a hollowed out spot under the floorboards, another secret place that he and Clay had created, mainly for the thrill of having that secret knowledge all to themselves. They never really hid anything in there, but as Lucas had heard somewhere, there was a time and a place for everything, and now was the time, and here was the place.

He crawled under the tractor, brushed away dust and old strands of hay, and removed two loose floorboards. He inspected the hole to make sure that no mice had taken up residence there, and then set the book inside. After replacing the boards and spreading hay and dust over them to conceal the recent activity, he stood and brushed the dust off his hands and knees, and left the barn for the early morning sunlight.

Several days later, he would find two dead mice lying in the hole next to the book, and he found this strangely intriguing, so he left the two tiny bodies where they lay, and he would look at their decaying corpses every time he visited the book.

Of course, what he did not know at the time was that every *mouse under the barn was dead.*

4

Cain folded the cloth over the book, and strode up the narrow sidewalk to the church entrance. The walk was lined with meticulously placed marigolds in dark flowerbeds. He grasped a brass handle and pulled open one of the double doors. Cold air breathed out from the opening, and then he was inside, the door whispering shut behind him.

The air smelled of furniture oil and candle wax. At some point in time, someone had repaired most of the old plaster, and slapped on fresh paint as well. He approached the pulpit almost reverently. Standing against the wall behind it was a statue of Jesus on the Cross. Cain thought this odd, considering the size and financial stature of a small town like this one (Reverend Mott had purchased it with his own money from a statue and monument place in Arlidge, and was still making payments through the Almighty Convenient Installment Plan).

There was an open doorway to the right of the pulpit, and from somewhere beyond, Cain heard the shuffling of papers, the clearing of a throat. Through the doorway was a narrow hall leading to several rooms at the back of the church. Light spilled out into the hall from another open doorway, presumably the reverend's office.

When Reverend Mott looked up from his paperwork, Cain was standing in the doorway watching him.

"Oh, don't let me bother you," Cain said, leaning against the doorjamb.

Reverend Mott stood up, slightly startled at this sudden visitation, by a man dressed all in black, no less. It being Saturday and all, Mott himself had decided to go with jeans and a pullover shirt, a man of God in casual mode.

"It's no bother. Just working on tomorrow's sermon," Mott said, walking over to Cain and extending a hand. "Earl Mott. I'm the resident reverend here. And you are?"

"Cain. Lucas Cain. Pleased to meet you, Reverend," he said. He shook hands with Mott, and then stood studying the reverend, their hands still clasped together. He guessed the reverend at about forty-eight, forty-nine years old.

"What can I do for you, Mr. Cain?" Reverend Mott asked, trying to pull his hand away in an inconspicuous fashion.

Cain held fast to the reverend's hand; in fact, pulled him closer, almost face to face.

"Do you believe in Heaven and Hell, Reverend?" Cain asked.

Mott strained and pulled at his hand, but could not break Cain's grip.

"What kind of question is that? Of course I do. Now, will you please release my hand?"

"Let me show you something first, Reverend," Cain said with a snarl.

Reverend Mott no longer stood in his office, holding hands with a total stranger that now obviously meant to do him harm. He was in total darkness, total silence. Flames erupted with a *fwup!* all around him, and when he tried to move, they would burst forth and drive him back. The darkness was now filled with a sea of flames, and a sky of red. The flames began to close in on him, and a voice out of nowhere, *Cain's* voice, asked, "Have you ever wondered what your version of Hell would be like Reverend?"

"God will protect me from whatever harm you bestow upon me! Stop this foolishness now!" he yelled up toward the red sky. The flames were closer now, and the heat was unbearable. He was soaked in sweat.

"Run, Reverend, run. Run to save your silly little life!" the voice boomed.

The flames quickly closed in on him, and run he did; he panicked and dashed into the sea of fire, flames as far as the eye could see. Flames burned his hands and face, caught his clothes on fire, and burned every strand of hair from his head. He screamed in sheer agony as his skin blistered, then melted and slid boiling off of his body. He had just enough time to see his innards spill into the flames as he flowed into the fire.

"Bugs at the diner? What are you talking about, Hal?"

Deputy Mayfield looked up from his girlie magazine and listened in mild amusement as Sheriff Craven talked on the phone.

"Run that by me again...Well, what is it you expect me to do about it, Hal?...Alright, alright, I'll go have a talk with Nate...No, I won't mention your name...I'll let you know, Hal. Goodbye." Frank Craven hung up the phone, and sighed heavily. "That was Hal

Winder. Says there's bugs in the food over at Nate's. Almost ate one."

"Hell, I always knew the food there wasn't that good," Mayfield said, laughing out loud. Craven was not laughing. Mayfield dropped the comedy act. "You want me to go over there, Sheriff?"

"No, that's ok, Paul. Just stay here and man the phones. I'll just -"

The glass front door to the Sheriff's office swung open, and a man walked in with what looked like a large black sack over his shoulder. The office immediately filled with the inimitable smell of burnt cloth, and another smell that Mayfield didn't recognize. Craven, however, recognized it the second he smelled it. After bearing witness to bodies being pulled from a house fire, one never forgets the stench of scorched flesh.

With one big heave, Cain threw the burned corpse onto Deputy Mayfield's desk. Arms and legs flailed like a huge doll, scattering everything on his desk to the floor. Craven and Mayfield both jumped up, drew their revolvers, and pointed them at Cain. The burned, blackened corpse lay on Mayfield's desk, wisps of smoke still curling from its clothing and what used to be its skin.

"I think Reverend Mott's had a very bad day," Cain said, shaking his head sympathetically. "I think the heat was just too much for him."

"Put your hands up right now!" Craven demanded. At just over six feet tall, and two hundred and fifty pounds (a lot of that was hanging over his belt), he *expected* attention when he spoke. And he was now glaring at Cain with those same expectations in mind.

"I think you two need to put down your toys before you hurt someone."

"I'm not gonna tell you again, mister! Put your goddamn hands in the air!" The red was rising in Craven's cheeks, as it always did when he was pissed off. Paul always said it made him look cute. Craven never did appreciate Paul Mayfield's sense of humor.

"I can see we're going to have a problem here," Cain said, pacing back and forth.

Their guns began to waver, and they both felt something like invisible hands grasp their arms, and force them in different directions.

Facing each other.

Craven struggled to take control of his actions, sweat pouring down his flushed face as he tried to lower his weapon, which was now pointed directly at Mayfield's head. Likewise, Mayfield had his weapon pointed directly at Craven's head.

"I'm sorry, Sheriff, I can't help it," he said.

"I know, Paul, I know. What do you want, mister?"

Cain rubbed his chin in careful consideration. "First of all, let me ask you a question, Sheriff. Are you the only one in charge of this quaint little town?"

Craven's finger was growing dangerously sweaty on the trigger.

"I guess what I mean to say is, is there a mayor, or a town council, or anything like that I need to be aware of?"

"No, no," Craven said. The tone of his voice had taken a complete turn around, not necessarily out of fear of getting shot, but the growing realization that he was helpless against this man. An *unarmed* man, no less. "Oak Junction falls under the jurisdiction of District 12 out of Arlidge. All of our representation is there."

"I guess that leaves you and Deputy Fife here in charge, doesn't it, Sheriff?"

"Fuck you, man!" yelled Mayfield.

"Shut up, Paul! Let us go, mister, and we'll talk about this."

"Oh, we're going to talk, alright. And we're going to make one thing clear right now. I am in charge here. You work for me now."

Craven was silent for a moment. "I can't go along with that, mister."

Mayfield's gun fired, and Craven felt a bullet whiz by his head and slam into the wall behind him. Mayfield was wide-eyed and trembling with shock.

"Sh-sheriff, I didn't...."

"Ok, ok, mister, just let us go. You're in charge," Craven said.

Their arms fell limp, guns dangling at their sides.

"Gentleman, put your guns away, please," Cain said, "and the name isn't mister, it's Mr. Cain."

They holstered their guns, and stood uneasily, waiting for Cain to speak.

"I have now taken up residence in the church. Nice place, by the way. Now, this can be easy for everybody, or very, very difficult. I can inflict great harm on anyone who doesn't cooperate. Do you both believe that?"

They both nodded.

"Good. Very good. Because I will need you both to help convince everyone else in town, or else someone could get hurt. Understand?"

More nods.

"Mr. Cain, may I ask what it is you want from us, or what it is you want us to do?" Craven asked. He was so serious and businesslike in his query that Cain had to laugh.

"That will have to wait until morning, Sheriff. You and the deputy here will be at the church at nine a.m. sharp, in uniform. We're going to have a little meeting. Remember, Sheriff, I have no problem with killing someone. In fact, I quite enjoy it. And I will not hesitate, so no funny stuff. Are we clear on that?"

"Ok, mister...Mr. Cain, you'll have our complete cooperation, just please, don't hurt anybody." He held his hands up as if trying to calm Cain down. His own acquiescence nagged at him; he had never been controlled so easily before by anybody, had always run the show. But deep down, he knew there was no hope.

"Put your hands down, Sheriff, I'm not a lunatic. But you really don't want to piss me off. I will reward those who comply, though, and the rewards can be very nice. What would you like, Sheriff, money? Sex? Drugs? I can give you anything you want. Think about it, Sheriff. So, church in the morning?" he asked, looking back and forth between the men.

"We'll be there, Mr. Cain," Sheriff Craven said. He just didn't know what else to do but give in. And much to his dismay, he found himself thinking about what Cain had said.

What would you like, Sheriff, money? Sex? Drugs?

Cain casually walked up to Deputy Mayfield, and got so close to his face that Mayfield almost flinched. "And you, my friend. If you ever say 'fuck you' to me again, I will make you regret the day you were born."

Cain turned, and headed for the door.

"See you in the morning, gentleman," he said, then paused and turned. He waved at the corpse that still lay smoldering on Mayfield's desk. "Do whatever you want with that." Then he was gone, leaving the two men standing there like children who had just been scolded.

"What the hell are we gonna do, Sheriff?" Mayfield asked, watching the Cadillac pull away from the curb in front of the station.

"Were gonna do exactly as he says, Paul. Unless you have any better ideas?"

5

The sun rose the next morning into a cloudless sky, bringing the promise of another beautiful day in Oak Junction. It was a day that most people in town cherished, and counted among the many reasons why they lived there. The air was clean and clear, and so was the way of life. It was a far cry from the hustle and bustle of city life, and most folks preferred it that way. Even those who worked in the outlying cities like Arlidge and Greenview breathed easy after returning home from a day in the cement jungle.

The church bell began to ring from The Fellowship of God Church over on West Church Street. It was a beautiful sound, and beautiful way to start off Sunday, and people all over town put down his or her coffee and sweet roll, and either climbed into a car, or simply began walking to the church.

The church's double doors were propped open, and folks looked at each other questioningly; Reverend Mott had always been there to greet everyone, to shake hands, to chat with everyone on a first name basis. And while his absence did not go unnoticed, the parishioners greeted each other as they always did, and filed into the church to find a place to sit.

Jenny and Ashley White were among those attending church on this particular day (Harvey White was at home already nursing his first beer of the day, which is exactly why she attended church - it was probably the most peaceful time she had all week), Ashley wearing her frilly white dress with the pink trim, the one Jenny had bought for her just for special occasions (and getting out of the house was one of her *most* special occasions), and had later fought with Harvey over the ten dollars she had spent. Most of their extra money went for Harvey's alcohol, so spending money on anything like a new dress for his daughter was just plain *wasteful*.

Jenny wore jeans and a blue blouse, but in no way did she feel underdressed. The dress code here was wear whatever you have, and this was evident when you had a Sunday suit and black tie sitting next to jeans and a tee shirt.

Ashley tugged on her mother's shirt and pointed upward.

"Look, mommy. Where's the cross?" Jenny looked up, and saw that the cross was indeed gone. She thought: *That's funny. Why would he take the cross down?* And as soon as they entered the church, Ashley noticed something else missing, as well. "Mommy, Jesus is gone!" she exclaimed. A few heads turned at the sound of her voice, and there was some whispering. Jenny saw that the statue of Jesus *was* gone.

First the cross, now Jesus, she thought. *What is up with that?*

She bent down and whispered, "Yes, honey, Jesus isn't here right now."

Jaspar Hendricks was the last person to enter the church, as was usually the case, and he took his customary seat at the back, just in case he decided to take a little snooze during the sermon. And it wasn't *too* uncommon for Reverend Mott to raise his voice inconspicuously, one eye trained on the sleeping man.

The inside of the church was cool with the morning air, and people buzzed amongst themselves, waiting for Reverend Mott to appear. The bell ceased its ringing, and a moment later Paul Mayfield entered the room from the doorway that led to the narrow attic stairs, and the bell. He took a seat in a metal folding chair against the far wall, next to Sheriff Craven.

A hush fell over the gathering as Cain entered the room. He had traded his former attire for jeans and a black tee shirt, which was neatly tucked into his pants. He walked up to the pulpit, and scanned all the faces in the room.

"I would like to thank everyone for coming today," he said.

"Where's Reverend Mott?" somebody blurted out.

"Reverend Mott has been...detained. But he was kind enough to ask me if I could fill in for him today. I know those are hard shoes to fill, but I'll do my best. For those of you who don't already know me," he said, glancing over at the two uniformed men sitting against the wall, "my name is Cain. I'm going to be in town for a while, and I look forward to getting to know each and every one of you."

An old woman wearing a dress with a loud floral pattern raised her hand from the second row.

"You have a question?" Cain asked, flipping his long black hair back with one hand and cocking one eye.

"Well, yes, I do. What happened to the statue of Jesus? I always look forward to seeing it." There were a few murmurs of agreement in the room. "And just where *is* Reverend Mott? Is he sick?"

"Well, I'll tell you, Mrs...."

"The name's Gracie Miller. And I've been coming to this church for a long time."

"Well, Gracie, I just didn't think the statue went with the décor, you know? It just *had* to go. But, what an improvement, don't you think?"

"No, I do *not* think so, young man. I demand to know where the Reverend is!"

"The truth of the matter, Gracie, is…well, the good Reverend is just a little…dead." Cain's expression was one of false resignation. "It was only a matter of time."

A few gasps went through the crowd, and a large man in a tan polyester suit stood up from his place a few rows down, and said, "What the hell…excuse me, folks, what the heck are you talking about? If this is some kind of joke, we're not laughing, mister."

"That's Mr. Cain to you," Cain said, and a black shadow seemed to cross over his features.

"I don't care if it's Mr. President. I want to know what's going on here."

Sheriff Craven stood up and said calmly, "Sit down, Fred. Just sit down, and shut up."

Fred's wife tugged at his sleeve. "Sit down, Fred." He ignored her.

"No, Sheriff, I'm not gonna sit down until I get some answers. And you, you're asking for trouble, mister," he said, glaring at Cain.

"Fred, for your own good, sit your ass down and shut up," Craven said, glancing sideways over at Cain.

"Sheriff, that's enough," Cain said. "I'll take it from here."

"Yes sir, Mr. Cain." Sheriff Craven took his seat next to Deputy Mayfield, and Mayfield's mouth was open in utter bewilderment, bordering on contempt. Sheriff Craven had always been a man of good judgment, of good morals, and had always thought of others before him, but this, this was something new. Of course, the man had never been perfect, but this was a complete turn around of character.

"I'm not gonna tell you again, you fat fuck, it's *Mr.* Cain to you." This drew more gasps from the room, and a few people got up to leave. The double doors slammed shut, and one man tried to open one, but to no avail. "Go back to your seats," Cain said, baring his teeth. Those who had risen quietly returned to their places and sat down. Near the back, Jenny White was holding Ashley close, trying to comfort her, but Ashley's eyes were wide with wonder and fear.

"And you," he said to Fred Warren, who was now standing defiantly in the aisle, "you need to hold your tongue. Sit down, Sheriff." Sheriff Craven had once again risen, more out of habit than anything; when trouble arose, so did the sheriff. He cleared his throat and sat down.

"Are you going to put up with this, Sheriff? I guess I need to take care of this myself. How about you and me go outside, and talk about this…mister?"

"Fred, *please* sit down. We don't want any trouble, sir," Susan Warren said, addressing Cain.

Cain shook his head and said, "It's such a shame. Some people just have to learn things the hard way."

Fred Warren went to say something else, but stopped cold, as if it caught in his throat. He gagged and choked, and pushed his head forward, and for a moment it looked like the man was about to throw up. His mouth opened wide, and he retched, but instead of vomit spewing out, his tongue popped out. His eyes bulged from their sockets, his lips moved, trying to voice words that would not come.

"Fred!" Susan exclaimed, putting her hands to her cheeks.

His tongue began to *stretch* farther out of his mouth.

A woman screamed, and then cut it off by clutching her mouth.

A man's voice said, "Oh my God."

Jenny White held Ashley's face against her shoulder so she couldn't see what was happening, couldn't bear witness to this inhuman and illogical thing that was taking place before their very eyes.

"Mommy, I'm scared," Ashley said. "I wanna go home!"

"We will, honey, we will. Everything's going to be fine," Jenny whispered to her daughter; but the more she watched, the more she wondered herself if everything really *was* going to be all right.

Fred Warren's tongue had stretched impossibly long, a long pinkish thing that no longer resembled a tongue, but a long, thick rubber band being stretched to the limit. Fred whimpered and moaned, and dropped to his knees, clasping his hands together in a final plea for mercy.

The room grew silent, everyone watching horrified as Fred Warren gagged and moaned and whined, his tongue stretching even farther out of his mouth.

"I told you to hold your tongue," Cain said.

Fred Warren's tongue snapped free from his mouth, and fell to the floor a few feet in front of him. He screamed and covered his mouth, blood oozing between his fingers and dripping onto the polished wooden floor. He began rolling around, his screams muffled as his hand held tight over his mouth. Susan Warren began to sob uncontrollably, and a woman next to her put one arm around her, trying to comfort her.

Cain motioned at The Sheriff and Deputy. "Get him out of here. Now." He gazed at the people in front of him, and could hear their muffled, hysterical thoughts inside their troubled minds.

Craven stood up, but Mayfield hesitated. Craven grabbed his arm and pulled him up. They picked up Fred Warren, and dragged him screaming through the back hallway to the rear of the church. There, they deposited him outside, next to the statue of Jesus.

Craven was about to go back inside when Mayfield put his hands on his hips and said, "Hey, wait! Aren't we going to help him?"

"I don't think that would be a very good idea, Paul, considering the circumstances."

"You mean you're just going to give in, just like that?"

"Yes, Paul. Just like that. And I suggest you do the same. Now let's get inside."

Craven waited for Mayfield to go first, then followed him inside. Fred Warren lay writhing on the ground, bleeding to death through his fingers. Craven took one last peek at the man, and then shut the door behind him. Later, they would find him dead about thirty yards away in the field behind the church, the side of his face stuck in a pool of congealed blood.

"So, are there any more questions before I move on?" Cain asked the silent crowd of faces. He scanned the faces in the room, and locked eyes with Jenny White. She quickly looked away, holding Ashley close to her breast.

Sheriff Craven and Deputy Mayfield reappeared, and quietly took their seats.

"All right, then. Let's move on. My name is Cain. I would prefer to be called Mr. Cain. I have decided to make Oak Junction my home, because it is such a beautiful place to live. Ok, not really...I lied. I'm here because I want souls. I *need* souls. You see, a good friend of mine did me a favor a while back, and I'm repaying his kind gesture."

A man in the first row raised his hand, doing his best not to look too adamant.

"Now this is more like it. You have a question, sir."

"Y-yes, I do," the man stammered. "Are...are you the Devil?"

"Who I am, and where I come from, is not important. But, since you were so polite, no, I am not the Devil."

"But, sir...Mr. Cain...you said you wanted souls," the same man said. He looked as if he was about to be slapped in the face. Instead, Cain merely smiled at him.

"That's right, I want souls, and I will take them, one way or the other. But the souls aren't for me. Like I said, I'm repaying a favor. And that's all you need to know. I will take one soul a month, on a day chosen by myself. Anyone who stands in my way will most surely suffer, as you have obviously seen here today. Am I right, Sheriff?"

Sheriff Craven stood up and grimly faced the roomful of people. "He's right, folks. The best thing to do is just do what Mr. Cain says. I cannot guarantee your safety if you don't," Craven said, and sat down, the folding metal chair squeaking under his weight.

"Well put, Sheriff, very well put, indeed. Those of you thinking of running, or telling the authorities, just remember, you probably have friends or loved ones in town. You wouldn't want to see them get hurt, would you? Or would you? Human nature is so complex! But, no matter, I would find you anyway, and make you suffer like you have never suffered before. Like our friend with the loose tongue - no doubt he lying dead somewhere, a victim of his own stupidity." This last statement raised fresh sobs from Fred Warren's widow, and Cain stopped speaking, letting the sobs permeate the silence, and the minds of those present, so as to drive the sincerity of his message home.

"I just want you folks to live your lives as you always do." Cain began to pace back and forth in front of the room. "As for the souls, I'll leave that up to you. You can make it easy, or you can make it hard. I don't care where you get them, as long as it doesn't draw any attention to Oak Junction. Anyone who does that will seal his or her own fate. If you don't give me someone, I will be forced to choose on my own."

A few murmurs went through the room, and people looked around at each other as if already deciding who would be next.

"And you folks will show the good Sheriff here the same respect you would show me, is that understood?" Dumb nods.

"Ok. Tomorrow night is the full moon. That is when I will perform the ritual. Someone has already graciously volunteered for this very purpose, so you're off the hook for now. So, tomorrow night, you will all bring your friends and families to the field behind that old farmhouse on...help me out, Sheriff," he said, snapping his fingers several times.

"Old Farm Road. The old Willard farm."

"Right. Old Farm Road. Be there no later than eleven, or I might get a little angry. And you know what happens when I get angry, right? Or do you need another demonstration?"

Everyone shook his or her head, and there were a few "No, sirs," and a few "No, Mr. Cain," and even one "That won't be necessary, Mr. Cain."

"Good. *Very* good. I'm glad we're all in agreement. There is one more thing I would like to mention. There will be, let us say, patrols out and about, but you won't be harmed. That is, if you're good boys and girls." He chuckled good-naturedly. "As I told the Sheriff here, good behavior can reap good rewards. Think about it."

The double doors swung open, and half the parishioners almost jumped out of their skins. There were actually a few laughs among the group, and this made Cain smile; already, he was sinking his hooks into, if only just pricking the surface, a few weak souls. But he knew better than anyone that the first prick was all it took for greed and selfishness to take over. He was counting on it.

A square of sunlight spilled in from the doorway, and fresh summer air flowed in and seemed to bring the room back to reality.

"Now, you folks go home and enjoy your day," Cain said, and watched as everyone filed quietly from the church.

6

A full moon glowed against the splattering of stars, a faint aura surrounding it in soft, luminescent light; a moon that to lovers would have been romantic, to amateur astronomers would have been endearing and mysterious, to the average person, simply a beautiful side effect of nature. But tonight, it represented something different altogether.

Tonight, it represented something dark, a beacon calling the people of the town to an area of their minds that recalled all the old black and white B-movies they had watched as children, an area where the full moon meant vampires, werewolves, witches...evil. But this was no movie, this was reality, and pulses were racing with fear and confusion.

The old Willard place was a few miles out of town, toward the empty land and foothills to the north. The crowd that approached the field was filled with skeptics - spouses and family members and friends that had all listened to the bizarre tales told to them by the churchgoers, but were still convinced that there had to be a trick, a catch to the whole thing. And so, they tagged along as debunkers, assuring folks that this was some kind of ploy to perhaps swindle their money from them, leaving them penniless and feeling like the world's biggest fools.

They treaded over the old furrows of a long dead cornfield. Jenny was there, with her husband, Harvey, who was drunk, and tripping over his own feet, trying to keep up with her. She knew this would not be good, and had found a babysitter for Ashley. And as far as she was concerned, even the babysitter was too young to witness whatever spectacle Cain had dreamed up.

"Shlow down," Harvey said, grasping her arm. His thin fingers bit in a little too deep, and Jenny yanked her arm away.

"Damn, Harv, are you trying to break my arm?"

"Christ, do you always have to bitch about everything?" He said, stumbling again. She could smell the whiskey on his breath, and she turned away in disgust, rolling her eyes in the darkness.

Jaspar Hendricks and Hank Tooley trudged along through the field, Hank complaining the whole way about what a waste of time it was, and how he had to get up early for the morning's chores. "Just quit yer belly achin', and give it time," Jaspar said. "You'll see. I wasn't sleepin' in church yesterday."

Hal Winder, the man who now had a newfound hatred for roaches, walked alongside Betty Atwood and Nate Johnson, owner of the diner. Nate walked a short ways away from the other two - he was still pissed off at Hal for calling the sheriff and telling him there were roaches in his food.

Sheriff Craven had found no pesky bugs in the food, but that was still not good enough for Hal; now, he settled for just coffee, and ogling Betty.

Mike Frandsen, who ran the town's hardware store, was probably the biggest doubter of them all. He was down to earth, believed in the here and now, in what you could hold in the palm of your hand. He strode confidently over the dried soil, the sleeves of his blue work shirt rolled up, revealing large biceps that seemed to be the perfect compliment to his crew cut.

Ahead, a ring of tall torches glowed in the middle of the dark field. They tossed and flickered in the mellow night breeze. In the center of the ring, a thick post had been erected, its shadow wavering in the torchlight. Standing next to the post was Cain, expressionless and patient, his intense eyes watching the crowd gather around the ring of torches. Tucked under one arm was a bundle wrapped in black.

Behind Cain, and just out of site of the torchlight, were several more bodies, unrecognizable in the dim.

The churchgoers had managed to coax nearly half the town to show up, either in person, or by word of mouth. They easily persuaded the skeptics and debunkers, who were stoked and ready to turn this ruse into the biggest fiasco the town had ever seen.

The crowd gathered around, some going out of their way to get front positions for the show. Now Cain wore a sinister smile, for he knew there were disbelievers, people who would have to be *shown* just the way things were going to be.

Your souls are no longer your own, he thought.

Cain hushed the talkers and whisperers and rumor mongers by holding up his arms, and addressing the crowd with, "Can I get everyone's attention, please? Great, you're so kind. For those of you who don't know me, my name is Mr. Cain. And I am in charge of this town." He looked into the sea of faces and saw a few expressions of raw disbelief. Locals who could not fathom a longhaired stranger waltzing into town and taking it over, especially with a sheriff like Craven in town.

"I will now give the chance to anyone who would like to challenge my claim to enter this ring now." There were low mutters, and a voice said, "Who died and left you boss?"

This caused some scattered chuckling, and a young man in a tank top and Yankees cap stepped forward into the ring of light.

"Who said you could come into our town, and just take over?" he asked, pointing his finger at Cain. He swayed slightly from one too many long necks on the way over. "We don't even know you, mister."

"The name is Mr. Cain to you, asshole, and to answer your question, I did."

"You did what?" General laughter from the crowd.

"I did. *I* said I could just walk in here and take over. Now, stop pointing at me, and go back to your place before you get hurt."

"Oh, and like you're gonna make me?" the man said, again pointing at Cain.

Cain casually went up to him, and said, "Some people just have to learn the hard way." Before the man could react, Cain grabbed his wrist and said, "It's not polite to point, you know." He put the man's forefinger into his mouth and bit down. The man began to dance a little jig from foot to foot, and tried to pull his hand away, but to no avail. Cain bit down deeper, right next to the big knuckle on his hand, and the man's blood dribbled out of the corners of Cain's mouth.

Then Cain bit his finger off.

A gasp blew through the crowd like a stiff wind, and everyone stepped back a few feet.

Cain shoved the man backwards to the ground, whereupon he grabbed the short stub of his lost finger with his other hand, and began rolling around on the ground, yowling in pain.

Cain went to say something, and instead spat the finger onto the dirt at his feet. His lips were red with blood. "It's also not polite to talk with your mouth full. Excuse me." He bent down and picked the man up by his armpits. "I don't ever want to see your face again, unless you're ready to beg for forgiveness." He twirled the man around, and pushed him into the crowd, where he quickly disappeared, hunched over his wounded hand.

Cain pulled out a handkerchief and wiped off his mouth, tucked it back into his pocket, and then raised one arm and waved it in the air. "Would anyone else care to come forward, and voice an opinion?" he invited. Even the debunkers and the skeptics were mute at this last request. "Anyone? ....Ok, then. Now it's time to pay the piper, so to speak. Gentleman?"

There was a commotion at the back of the crowd, then two men broke through to the front; each had a tight grip on an arm of a bespectacled young man with a ponytail. He struggled to break free, but was no match for his captors.

Jenny was near the front of the crowd, and she thought she recognized the young man. She turned to Harvey, and said, "I think I've seen that guy before, Harv. Isn't he the librarian?"

"Shhhh! Shut up!" He watched Cain with bloodshot, unwavering eyes, the eyes of a child stricken with awe.

"Welcome, young man," Cain said, taking a bow.

"I demand to know what you want with me," the young man said. "*Why* was I put in jail? I've done nothing wrong! I want to speak to my father right now!" Some of the faces in the crowd looked guiltily away. The young man did not yet know that his father was dead. He *did* know, however, that he'd been at the library Sunday afternoon (he *was* the town librarian, after all, and he could go anytime he wished) when Sheriff Craven had picked him up and taken him to the jail, offering no explanation. The silence had been frightening, to say the least.

"I'm afraid that's quite impossible," Cain said, "but I guess it wouldn't do any harm to let you see your mother, now, would it? Sheriff, would you escort Mrs. Mott front and center, please?"

Three figures appeared from the dimness of the field directly behind Cain, growing more discernable as they came within range of the lighted circle. Torchlight flickered on Cain's features, and his shadow danced behind him on the soft dirt.

"Mom!" the young man yelled, and lurched forward. The two burly men holding him yanked him back and held fast. "What are you doing with my mother?" he cried.

"Shut him up," Cain said, with a wave of his arm. One of the men pulled out a red bandana, and gagged the young man.

Sheriff Craven entered the circle of torches, helping the good Reverend Mott's wife along, Deputy Mayfield following close behind. Evelyn Mott was gagged and handcuffed with her hands behind her back. She still wore her blue Sunday dress, the one she had been wearing when Craven had locked her up in a small conference room just down the hall from the cell where her son had spent the night.

"Sheriff, do your duty," Cain said. Craven unlocked one handcuff, stood Mrs. Mott with her back to the post, and then locked her hands together around the post.

Disbelief rose in the faces of the people watching, and their eyes grew wider with the fear that something very terrible was about to happen, something they had perhaps read about in books, or seen in one of those horror flicks they were always showing over in Arlidge. It was like a fear of the dark; they did not know what was there, what to expect, but they were nonetheless afraid of what lurked there.

Craven untied the gag from Mrs. Mott's mouth, and let it drop to the ground.

"Jonathon, get away, if you can!" she immediately burst out. "Your father's dead! They killed him! Run! Run while you can!"

Cain slapped her - slapped her *hard* - his hand connecting loudly against the side of her face. She let her head rest back against the post, a red handprint already appearing on her cheek. Jonathon screamed through his gag, and strained to free himself. His eyes welled up with tears, and his muffled cries were filled with desperation.

"How touching. How very touching," Cain said. "Now, we get to the good part. I must warn you, running away will only look bad on you. If you stay now, it will only get easier for you the next time. And there will always be a next time." He looked at the forlorn faces around him with his piercing eyes, and then walked to the edge of the circle, which was now empty, save for Mrs. Mott, who was leaning against the post in silent resignation.

Cain unwrapped the black velvet from the book and draped it over his shoulder.

Your souls…

"Now, you will meet *my* God," he said, and held the book out in front of him.

The book. It was all about the book.

His whole life seemed to center around the book, to almost thrive on it, and yet he still managed to keep its existence a secret. He had told Clay that he'd burned the book long ago, and they made a vow never to speak of it, especially after that terrible night in the woods.

But, he still had the book.

By the time he was sixteen, he was visiting the book everyday. He would sit in the dusty atmosphere of the barn, propped against one of the tractor's flat tires, and gaze wonderingly at the drawings, read the incomprehensible words. Something about the words seemed familiar to him, almost like a jumbled form of English.

The drawings, on the other hand, were something else altogether. There were beasts he had never seen before, and strange people being torn apart and eaten alive, men lying dead, their spirits drifting aimlessly. There were diagrams and charts; all accompanied by the same mixed up language.

There was one drawing, near the beginning of the book that drew his attention so strongly, so as to speak *to him. It was a drawing of a beast so wicked, so vile, that Lucas was almost sure it was real, or at least at one time had been real, and had something to do with the writing of the book. He would stare at the picture until his eyes hurt, but he could not look away. It was like looking at an old photograph of a long dead relative.*

But he did not need to understand the pictures, or the words for that matter, to know that the book was someday going to make him very powerful, indeed. He was already feeling its power course through him every time he touched it, and as time went on, could feel it linger on in his body and his thoughts for longer and longer periods of time. He grew confident, and confidence grew into arrogance.

His parents noticed the change in him, but he always kept them at bay. His little brother became frightened of him, even to the point of moving into his own room. Lucas was becoming a master of manipulation, and a master of deceit, and the older he got, the more he made it clear to his family not to invade his space. He would spend long hours in his room, thinking, making plans that seemed much more mature than his sixteen years. Thoughts of power, of control, of endless streams of money.

Thoughts of killing…

And then, there were the dreams. The horrible, horrible dreams which became less and less horrible, and more of an accepted realm that he seemed akin to. Dreams of fire and death. Dreams of demons torturing humans in a wasteland of human corpses as far as the eye could see.

And he dreamt of the demon from the picture. In his dreams, it was real. It seemed to beckon him with its mind, with its fiery red eyes. It spoke to him, as if conveying some message of importance, but he could never hear the words. Only silence. And yet, he knew the beast was calling him, telling him that his time was coming, his time of power, of his destiny. And his destiny was great.

As Lucas' initial fear of the book subsided and curiosity took over, he started to look for ways to unlock the secrets of the book. And since the subject was a book, there was no better place to look than the library. Lucas had managed to get his driver's license, and on weekends he could usually cajole his father into letting him take the pickup into town for a few hours (he actually told his father he was going to the library, and that was all the reassurance Mr. Cain needed).

Lucas wasn't familiar with the library system, had never been much of a reader, so at first the going was very slow. He searched the shelves for any material he could find about demons, witches, magic, and especially witchcraft. His memories of that night in the woods, the thirteen people wearing the dark cloaks with the hoods drawn over their faces, the naked woman on the boulder; this was a coven, thirteen being their number. And they were going to sacrifice the woman to the Devil.

At least he had gathered that much from what he had already read.

Then there was the book. Where did the book fit in? There were mentions of spell books, dark guides for casting spells of all types. And yet, it seemed that these books carried no real *power*, only the recipes to formulate the desired act, whether it be casting spells, or performing some type of ritual. And they all seemed to use the same symbol to represent their cause - the pentagram. In fact, these books and symbols were so widely published, so widespread, that to Lucas it seemed to dampen their authenticity. If these books were so remarkable in their secret knowledge, how come you could go to just about any bookstore around, or library for that matter, and pick one up for a song? Bookstores that also stocked comic books, and Shirley Temple videos, and books about how to take care of your pet. It just did not click right with him.

He knew this book was different, that it could not be found in any bookstore or library, but he had a feeling that a lot of people were nonetheless looking for it. It made him dizzy to think that he was the only person who knew where the book was hidden. But it was useless to him unless he could discover the secrets held within its covers. The book gnawed at and consumed him, drove him on toward whatever destination it had waiting for him.

One day during one of his Saturday excursions to the library, Lucas happened to walk past one of the computer stations the library had set up about twenty feet away from the checkout desk. He had never really paid much attention to the computers, had never used one, but something caught his eye, and he stopped to have a look.

A girl sat at one of the stations, studying the writing on the screen. She obviously was a student; a backpack lay on the carpet at her feet, and on the table before her a spiral notebook was open, into which she would occasionally scribble notations.

He watched with fascination as she used the mouse to scroll the pages in a seemingly endless stream of words.

Words....

He moved a little closer, and noticed that all the monitors had a little paper sign on top of them:

Remember!
 30 min. Time Limit
For Internet Use

The girl noticed him watching out of the corner of her eye. A slight smile crossed her face. A boy was watching her, so what? She caught boys watching her all the time. It was no big deal.

"Hi," she said, throwing a glance in his direction before returning to her screen.

"Hi," he said, and for a moment Lucas was at a loss for words. Then the gears in his head began to shift and turn. "Is that the internet?"

"Yeah, I'm doing an assignment for my English class. William Shakespeare."

"Is it very easy?" Lucas asked.

"William Shakespeare? Not really, it's a pain -"

"No, I mean the internet. Is it easy to do?"

"You mean, you've never been on the internet?" she asked.

"I don't own a computer," Lucas said, feigning embarrassment.

"Well, neither do I, you silly goose," she said, batting her eyes. "That's why I'm here."

Although Lucas was just playing her to get information, he actually was beginning to feel a little stupid for not thinking of this before. And his inadequacy with computers didn't help much, either.

"Yeah, right," he said. "So...how much does it cost?"

She laughed out loud. "It doesn't cost anything. It's free. Unless, of course, you need to print something out. That'll cost you a dime a copy, but hey, they've gotta make their money, too, I guess."

"Wow, that's cool. You can really print stuff out, huh?"

"Yeah, all you do is go like this," she moved the cursor up until it rested on print. "Then, you just click, and your copies come out over at the check-out."

"No kidding? Well, so how do you look stuff up?"

She touched the screen with her finger. "See that box? Notice how is says search right next to it? Just type in what you're looking for, and click on go. Pretty easy. And, if you don't know how to log on, just follow the instructions here," she said, pointing to the sheet that had been scotch taped to the table top, "and you'll be on in no time. Pretty cool, huh? You can do just about any...hey." The girl suddenly realized she was talking to herself. Lucas was already outside, climbing into his father's truck. He peeled out of the parking lot, and headed for home.

And the book.

7

Cain looked down at the book in his hands, torchlight reflecting off the gold skull on the front, and said, "Ic clypian eow Morgoroth, hlaford sceadu, ge-etan sawols, becuman don min offrung."

The people were silent; all eyes were glued to Cain and Evelyn Mott.

Cain said the words again, putting more emphasis on each word.

"*Ic clypian eow Morgoroth, hlaford sceadu, ge-etan sawols, becuman don min offrung!*"

The wind seemed to pick up some, and it tousled a lock of black hair across Cain's forehead. Then, the crowd began to mutter. Something was happening to the space around Mrs. Mott. The air itself was gaining color. A green haze formed around her, like a low-lying fog, and she raised her head and stared at it curiously, watching it shift and swirl around her feet and legs.

The ground began to rumble, as if somewhere nearby a train was coasting by. A great shadow, so dark that it stood out even under the cover of night, passed over the field as if a cloud was drifting swiftly overhead.

The ground directly in front of Mrs. Mott burst open, sending clods of dirt flying everywhere. It sounded like a grenade, and the crowd jumped back, most covering their ears.

And then *he* came out.

He popped out of the hole in front of Mrs. Mott, and bobbed up and down like a jack-in-the-box, stretching his thick, muscular arms out, and wiggling fingers that were long and thin and knotted with joints. His fingernails were black, and curled to little points at the ends, and they clicked as they struck each other.

Some of those in the crowd turned and fled, raw fear taking control of reason, blocking out all sense of the consequences that may befall them. One woman passed out in her husband's arms, while nearby a man fell to his knees, his hands locked in prayer. Most were rigid, like figures frozen in a photograph, unable to speak, or move, or even breath. The vision before them would not fully register with the part of their brain that differentiated being reality and fantasy; this was the two bound as one, and it left them transfixed with confusion and terror.

Cain fell to one knee and bowed his head.

"My master, my lord," he said, and looked up at his god.

The thing turned his head, and gazed upon Cain with fiery red eyes. A huge horn protruded from each side of his head, and curled around once before pointing forward. He had a bulbous nose, and when he drew his lips back, it revealed a maw filled with thick yellow teeth like needles, and several ropes of dark mucous stretched and wiggled between them as he opened his mouth wider. He towered above Mrs. Mott, although only his gray upper body was above ground. His lower body was one thick solid trunk that pulsed into the ground like an earthworm burrowing into its hole.

A few more fled as he turned his attention back to Mrs. Mott.

Your souls are no longer your own...

Mrs. Mott trembled uncontrollably as she lost control of her bladder, urine running down her legs and spotting the dirt.

Faster than a heartbeat he clasped the sides of her head with his spindly fingers, and sank, *anchored*, his fingernails into thick bone of her skull. She screamed in pain, and as she did, he lowered his face and opened his mouth to hers.

And he started to *eat* her soul.

Mrs. Mott's scream turned into a liquid gargling in her throat as the first wisps of her soul left her body. Then it came full force, out of her mouth, her eyes, and her nose, even her ears. It came together into one solid stream before being sucked into the other's mouth.

There was the *whoosh* of a strong wind, and yet, from where they stood there was nothing but the mellow night breeze. It was her soul, her clean spirit, a kind of smoky whiteness, followed by most of her bodily fluids, and as it drained from her body, her face and chest caved in on themselves.

Then, it was done. He pulled his fingers from her skull, and let her withered corpse collapse onto the ground, her arms, still handcuffed to the post, twisted and bent at odd angles.

Jonathon Mott screamed into his gag, heavy tears rolling down his cheeks. He tried to pull away, and almost succeeded. One of the men put a neck hold on him.

"Don't kill him, just get him out of here," Cain said, standing up. He held out the book reverently, as if it were made of glass. The men dragged Jonathon screaming and kicking through the crowd.

Cain's god regarded him once more, head cocked sideways, eyes filled with flame, and then he threw back his head and body, roaring into the night sky. He raised his arms above his head, and disappeared into the hole, every piece, every molecule, of displaced soil returned to its original place. It was as if he had never been there.

Mrs. Mott's crumpled corpse lay attached to the post like a deflated party doll.

Silence returned to the field, save for the sound of the breeze and the fanning of the torch flames. Sheriff Craven stood to one side, his mouth agape with wonder. If there had ever been any doubt in his mind, any reservation at all as to just how powerful and *real* Cain was, it was now totally wiped away. He had witnessed something that had filled him with wonder, with greed, with a whole new sense of being that he was now fully a part of. Witnessing that one act, he fell out of grace and into power, forsaking everyone, and everything he had once cared for.

And it felt *damned* good.

Cain seemed to sense this change in the Sheriff, because he turned and smiled slyly at him. The Sheriff nodded back. He then turned to address those who had remained, those who had also witnessed this bizarre spectacle without fleeing into the darkness.

Most had fear written on their faces, but some were awestruck; their faces showed a childish admiration, a *change* similar to what the Sheriff Craven was feeling. This was the beginning of their transformations, their inner renovations, the beginnings of a whole new world in which they would look at from a new point of view. One day very soon, their corruption would become absolute.

"Welcome to my world," he said, with a stony semblance of evil. "It is the world I have chosen, and it is the world you will choose, as well. Those of you who do not embrace it and follow its rule, will be consumed by it, and laid to waste. On the other hand, this world can be yours, to do with as you may. Good things await you. All you have to do is ask." He paused, and scanned over the pallid faces of his audience. "Go home, now. Go home and think. Talk to your loved ones. Kill your enemies. Live your lives the way *you* want to live your lives." He turned, and walked to the edge of the circle, wrapping the book up in its black velvet cloth.

Folks began to move away from the circle of flames, their heads hung in thought as they left for their homes, where they would deaden their fears with liquor or pills or smoke. Some would be celebrating. A few lingered on, unsure of what to do, apparently trying to gather enough courage to approach Cain in person.

Jenny White had tears in her eyes, and a great sorrow in her heart. Not only had she witnessed the murder of an innocent human being, a *friend*, no less, but also she had witnessed living proof that the evil she had only previously read about in fiction, or saw in the movies, was, in fact, *real*.

She loved Oak Junction, loved how peaceful and beautiful it was, a far cry from the crime and corruption of the big cities. And she had always accepted that the world was imperfect, a place where people killed people, pollution was eating away at the ozone, rivers ran contaminated with toxic chemicals; but these were *human* problems, mistakes made by common man. Still, the world had beauty, peace, and love, and this was the world as she had always known it.

Now, that vision had changed. The knowledge that such evil truly existed blackened her view of the world, spoiled whatever purity had remained for her in Oak Junction. The future was very uncertain.

As she turned to leave, she noticed the big wet patch on the front of Harvey's jeans.

"Good God, Harvey. You pissed your pants. Don't you think you need to change?" she asked.

Harvey just stood there, watching the courageous few as they walked toward the circle, and Cain. He had planned on going up there himself, but the sound of the ground exploding had caused him to loose his bladder, which had been brimming with the six or seven beers he'd drunk before coming out to see the ritual. He now sported a wet spot on his jeans, just to one side of his crotch.

"It was just an accident," he said, sounding surprisingly sober. "That damn explosion made me jump out of my skin."

"Let's go home, Harvey," Jenny said, and started walking off across the field, ancient corn stalks crunching under her feet.

A few people had reached Cain, and were speaking to him. One man actually reached out and *shook* Cain's hand. Harvey took one last look, and then stumbled after his wife.

The torches had long since been doused, and the field was engulfed in darkness. A lone figure worked its way toward the edge of the field. At the point where the field ended, and the tall weeds began, lay the body of an old man. The ritual had been too much for him, and he had struggled in the throes of a heart attack, making it this far before succumbing to death.

Hank Tooley lay on his side near the patchy weeds, one hand still clutching at his chest. His eyes stared straight ahead, now blank, lifeless. His tongue lolled from his open mouth. He wore his favorite attire - blue overalls and a tee shirt. No one had seen him go, no one had seen him die. Sometime during the whole thing, Jaspar had turned around to find his best friend gone. He assumed Hank had snuck on home sometime during the horrible goings-on.

But one person knew.

Cain bent down and picked up Hank's stiff, leathery hand. He held it in one hand, and patted the top with his other, as is saying goodbye to an old friend at a funeral.

"So sorry to see you go, old man. It's so sad to think that we live our lives always searching for something better, something more, and yet we are always pushing forward toward the inevitable end."

Hank listened quietly, staring out at nothing with his fading eyes and ashen face.

"And in the end, death always wins. From the moment of our birth it is there, waiting just on the other side of the door, waiting to pull us through to whatever awaits us on the other side."

Cain stood and looked at the corpse, the moon waning in the distance, the night wind whispering in his ear.

Lucas thought it too risky to remove the book from the barn, so he grabbed some paper and a pencil, and copied a few pages of the book. He occasionally would turn to the demon face near the beginning, stare at its twisted countenance, its ram-like horns.

This is not an animal, he thought, this is a king from another world.

He didn't know how, but he knew it to be true. And this leader, or king, could be your best friend, or your worst enemy, and he thought it was probably the latter in most cases.

Lucas took his pages into town, excited at the prospect of deciphering the book. On his first trip, however, he returned sorely disappointed. He had gone to the checkout desk and requested that he use the Internet. The librarian wrote the time and station number on a slip of paper, and handed it over to him.

"Please don't go over the thirty minutes, ok?" she asked.

"Sure, I'll watch the clock," Lucas said, and hurried over to station number 9. There were twelve in all, and most of them were being used. He looked up at the clock. It was 10:32 a.m.

It took him until 10:59 to figure out how to log on, even with the instructions taped firmly to the table in front of him. He looked up at the clock, and said, "Fuck!" An older man sitting at the next station over eyed him coldly. When he returned the tab of paper to the librarian at the desk, he practically had steam coming out of his ears.

"Was there a problem?" she asked, taking the tab of paper from him.

"Yes, there was a problem," he said coldly. "I used all my time trying to figure out how to log on to the friggin' thing." Lucas was truly pissed, but he knew that if he said 'fuck' in front of the librarian, he would probably never be allowed on the computers again.

"There are instructions posted on each table," she said, matter-of-factly.

"I know, I know," he said, cooling down a degree or two. "I've just never done it before. Can I have another thirty minutes?"

"I'm afraid that would be impossible right now." She nodded toward the computers, and Lucas followed her lead. All of the stations were indeed full, with the exception of the one he had just vacated, and she was already handing over a tab of paper to a man who had been waiting for his turn. The librarian must have noticed the frustration on Lucas' face; she smiled warmly at him, and said, "I'll tell you what, though, the next time you come back, just grab me, and I'll help you get logged on, and we'll get you going in no time."

Lucas noticed the line of people waiting for the computers. His anger was replaced with disappointment, but he felt he should at least be appreciative of the woman, especially if he was going to get anywhere with this.

"That's really nice of you. I will do that. I feel so dumb."

"Oh, don't feel dumb. Computers aren't the easiest things in the world to learn, believe me. It all takes time, and we're more than willing to help out."

"Alright, thanks a lot," Lucas said, and left. He drove home in silence, empty-handed, but not without hope. Things would fall into place, already were, and soon he would have answers. Maybe not right away, but soon. He would not stop until the secrets of the book were his.

Remembering the girl at the computer, Lucas stopped on the way home and bought a thick spiral notebook. This he would use for translation, a second version of the book written in English. He knew he would have to be careful with the notebook; alone, it would prove useless, but couple it with the book, and who knew what could be done.

Later, he went into the barn and pulled the book from its hiding place. The interior of the barn was dim compared to the bright afternoon light, but it was hot inside as the spring sun beat down on the world with the promise of a hot summer.

School would be out soon, and then he would have all the time in the world for the book. He thought about dropping out, but to do that now would mean trouble with his parents, and it would almost guarantee he would never be allowed to drive the truck again.

He sat and puzzled over the words. Some of them almost made sense, and yet, he could make no sense of it at all. He read the words, sometimes speaking them aloud, and every now and then he would get an odd feeling that he wasn't alone. That someone else was there, urging him on, pronouncing the words with him. This always led him back to the picture. It almost communicated with him, and it seemed to listen to him.

He heard a noise, and looked up - Clay was standing just inside the doorway watching him, his tanned face somber under his sun-bleached hair.

"I thought you said you got rid of that," he said.

"So I didn't. What's the big deal?" Lucas asked, setting the book down.

"Using our old hiding spot, huh?" Clay said, motioning toward the hole under the tractor. He thought for a moment, and said, "Do you remember that night, Luke? In the woods? When I look back now, I can't believe it. I just can't believe it. If those people had caught us, we would have been dead meat, don't you think?"

"But they didn't catch us. And they never will, because they're all dead now," Lucas said.

"How do you know that? You can't know that." Clay slowly shook his head.

"I know more than you think, Clay, so back off!" Lucas said, and a look crossed his features that Clay had never seen before. His eyes seemed to pierce into him.

"When you first took that damned book, I thought it was just a joke, you know? Just a crazy joke. I didn't think you'd get carried away with it. You don't call anymore, and every time I come over you're gone. It's like you're avoiding me. And now I know why. Is that what you want, Luke? You want me to go away, so you can be with your book?"

Lucas stood up and started to walk very slowly over the dust and hay covered floor toward Clay. His mouth was upturned with a half smile, a smile of utter confidence and strength. His sharp blue eyes glared unblinking straight into Clay's, and Clay could feel the hairs on the back of his neck rise.

Clay took a step back, but Lucas kept coming. He went right up to Clay's face and stopped.

"I want you to go away," he said, "...before you die."

For a second Clay saw in Lucas' face another, underlying countenance, one with terrible, twisted features. His blood pulsed in his ears. The air in the barn seemed to grow thin, and he found himself struggling for air.

"You're crazy...you're..." Clay sucked at the thinning air. "You're fuckin' nuts, man." He turned and staggered out into the hot sunlight, and bent over, putting his hands on his knees, drawing in deep breaths.

"Don't say a word, Clay."

He turned, and Lucas was standing in the doorway to the barn.

"Don't tell anyone, Clay, I'm warning you. You just don't know what you're dealing with. Just stay away, and don't say a word, that's all I ask." He went back into the barn, closing the big double doors behind him.

Later that evening, Lucas went to the clearing in the woods, as he had many times before. Although he had not seen any activity there since that night several years before, he could almost feel the presence of the people who died there. It was like a residue of their souls, lingering around like the smell of smoke long after a house has burned down.

He lay down on the boulder, on the very spot where the naked woman had laid that night, and stared at the stars.

8

Harvey White was the general manager of a small supermarket in Greenview, about seventeen miles north of Oak Junction. He had started out bagging groceries, mostly for the elderly locals, the ones who took up twenty minutes digging the $1.52 out of their coin purses, and spent even longer chatting with one of the two checkers that worked full time during the day.

Even back then Harvey was tipping the bottle pretty heavily, and when things got slow, he would run a dust mop across the floor, and then head to the back to clean the employee's bathroom and sneak out to his car to guzzle one of the cold beers he kept in the ice chest on the floor of the back seat. Then he would pop a couple of breath mints into his mouth and light a cigarette to hide the smell of the beer.

In those days, the owner of the store was acting as manager, and he and Harvey seemed to get along just fine. So fine, in fact, that Harvey often wondered if the boss wasn't juicing it up himself behind the closed door of his office.

Eventually, he got promoted to checker, which meant a raise in pay, but less time with the booze. As a result, when one of the local old timers got to babbling, it was all he could do to keep himself from reaching out and strangling someone.

This was also about the time he met Jenny, at a church dance in Arlidge, of all places (when you lived in this part of the state, you pretty much took what you could get), and had been dating her on a regular basis. She lived with her mother in Oak Junction, who back then was just beginning to succumb to the cancer that was spreading through her body.

So Harvey spent a lot of time at Jenny's house, where she could be close to her mother at all times. This suited Harvey just fine because it provided him with a place to sleep other than his parent's house in Greenview - they were on the verge of kicking him out for good - and it was the perfect place to do his drinking.

Jenny used to join him, looked up to him, even, because he was so cool with that beer in his hand. They would catch a buzz, and have sex on the couch, or in the bedroom, or hanging from the ceiling if they had wanted to; Jenny's mother was confined to her room, except maybe for a quick trip to the bathroom, and never posed a problem to their privacy.

Meanwhile, Harvey's boss was so impressed with his performance at the store that he decided to make Harvey manager so he could spend more time at home with the family. Harvey's eyes lit up when his boss took him into the office and pulled a fifth of whiskey out of a desk drawer, and poured them both a drink in paper cups to secure the deal. Excited as he was, Harvey hesitated, because he had never before dared to enter the sacred world of Having A Drink On the Job With Your Boss.

"Drink up, Harv," he had said. "You don't have to hide anything from me. Just so long as you're straight with me, I'll be straight with you, and everything will be just fine." He downed his drink in several swallows, and poured himself another.

Harvey lifted his cup into the air, and grinned affably. "You're number one with me, pal," he said, and downed his drink like it was water. Behind the grin, he trying to decide which desk drawer he was going to keep *his* stash in.

Eventually, Harvey moved in with Jenny, and she became pregnant. Three months before the birth of their daughter, they laid her mother to rest in Oak Junction Cemetery, right next to her father. The house became theirs, free and clear, and promptly Harvey became master of his own domain.

It would take several weeks before they would move into the master bedroom, though; every time Jenny entered the room she would envision all ninety-five pounds her mother lying on the bed in a fetal position, bald and incontinent, looking up at her with eyes that were hazy with the acceptance of her approaching death. It was like watching a child die, and Jenny always thought it an odd twist of nature that people came into this world in the fetal position, only to come full circle in their lives to leave the world in the same position.

Not until they had moved all the furniture out of the bedroom and cleaned it from top to bottom did she feel comfortable enough to occupy the room. They had thrown away the old double bed her mother had died on and bought a new bed of their own. But even after they had scrubbed the old oak dresser inside and out, sometimes she could faintly smell the perfume her mother always wore in better days, the perfume she had always kept on the dresser, along with the other items that Jenny used to play with as a child.

Gradually, things moved on, as they always do, and Jenny Duncan became Jenny White in the little church over on West

Church Street, the good Reverend Earl Mott performing the ceremony in front of a few friends and neighbors, while Evelyn Mott cradled little two month old Ashley in the front pew. All in all, things looked pretty good for the newlyweds, but then again, they always do.

Harvey sat behind the desk in his office, already drunk at just five minutes after one in the afternoon, absorbed in the bleakness of the old paneling on the walls, the cracks in the ceiling, cobwebs in the corners. It seemed a reflection of his life, a road that led to nowhere but this room, this old room with its Playboy calendar on the wall and bottle of booze hidden in the desk drawer. His thoughts drifted back to the night before.
Cain...
His power and influence seemed endless, and he offered things to those who were willing to accept his way of life.
My life is shit, he thought. *What has God ever done for me?*
He went to the front of the store, and informed the head checker that he would be leaving for the day, and she would have to lock up at closing time. She readily agreed, anxious to get the boss and his pungent whiskey breath out of her face for the day.
Harvey grabbed a six-pack of tall boys out of the cooler, locked up the office (he had no doubts that certain employees would love to ransack his office to drink his booze, and maybe lift a few bucks out of the petty cash box), and left by the rear entrance. He climbed into the Ford Taurus station wagon he and Jenny had bought used a few years earlier (a car he so lovingly referred to as the Brady mobile), popped open a beer, and drove off into the hot afternoon sun.

Twenty minutes later, Harvey pulled up to the curb in front of the church. Even though he had to take a piss, he opened another tallboy and chugged down half of it to try to calm his heart, which was now beating furiously in his chest.
What am I afraid of? He thought. *He won't hurt me.*
I think.
He finished off the beer, and tossed the bottle on the floor, where it clanked against another empty. He lit a cigarette and climbed out of the car. The sun was scorching hot, and as soon as he left the air-conditioned environment of the car, beads of sweat began

to form on his forehead. His sunglasses glinted as he headed up the walk.

The church looked different, as if it was no longer a church, but someone's residence, which he supposed was now the case. The sign on the grass was gone, the grass itself browning with dehydration. The marigolds along the walk were drying up and wilting over in sorrow. The cross that once stood atop the short bell tower was gone, and now a large crow roosted there, watching Harvey as he approached the front stoop. There was a loud flurry of wings, and the crow *cawed!* before taking flight, promptly smacking onto the sidewalk at Harvey's feet. It fluttered around like it had a broken wing, and after a moment lay still.

It was almost enough to make him piss his pants again, and he was suddenly reminded of his straining bladder. He glanced around cautiously, and went around to the side of the church. His cigarette hung from one side of his mouth as he drained himself, chuckling as he purposely sprayed onto the wall.

"Ahh, better," he said, tossing his cigarette into the puddle.

He returned to the front entrance and pulled open one of the doors. Cool air washed over him as he stepped inside and let the door swing closed behind him. The interior of the church was dim, the only light bleeding through the two small stained glass windows that flanked the front entrance. He folded his sunglasses and tucked them into his shirt pocket, and walked slowly up the aisle toward the pulpit.

"Hello?" he called out. His voice sounded alien in the hushed silence. He moved closer to the doorway that led to the back hall. "Mr. Cain? Are you here? Shit, I guess not," he said into the silence, and turned to leave.

And was face to face with Cain.

Harvey, in fact, almost walked right *into* Cain before drunkenly stopping himself short. Momentarily startled, he stammered to find words. "Oh, I...I'm sorry. Didn't see you there."

"Who are you?" Cain asked.

"Um, my name's Harvey. Harvey White. Nice to meet you, sir." He timidly stuck his hand out, and when Cain only looked at it, he withdrew it.

"What do you want, Harvey White?" Cain seemed to study Harvey up and down, tilting his head left and right as if trying to get a better view of him.

Harvey searched for words that wouldn't quite come; he had had a pretty good idea of what he wanted to say on the way over, but now that he was face to face with the man, this man with overwhelming fortitude, his mind went blank. "Well, I...I just wanted to talk to you."

Cain looked Harvey in the eyes. "Are you afraid of me, Harvey?"

"Yes, I am," Harvey said, swaying on his feet. He found that he could not break eye contact with Cain, was trapped in a hypnotic embrace.

"You're drunk, Harvey."

"Yes, I guess I am," Harvey said.

"Would you like something to drink?"

"That would be great. I'm very nervous." The ice broken, Harvey relaxed somewhat, and let out a large breath tainted with beer.

"Come with me, my friend, we'll talk," Cain said, and headed down the hallway toward the church office. Harvey followed him down the hall, and through a doorway on the right.

Here was the former office of the late Reverend Mott, the office where he had conducted all of his church business, had spent hours creating sermons that he had hoped would reach into the hearts of his friends and neighbors, and had even counseled a few couples on the importance of communication and patience in the great institution of marriage.

It was also the office where he had breathed his last breath while being consumed by the tortuous internal fire created by Cain.

Cain sat down behind the desk that was still cluttered with various papers and forms, and motioned to one of the folding chairs that sat in front of the desk.

"Have a seat, Harvey." He pulled open one of the desk drawers and produced a bottle of whiskey and two Styrofoam cups. "A man's got to have his hair of the dog handy, just in case of an occasion such as this, isn't that right, Harv?" He poured them both a drink, and held one out for Harvey. "A lot of people just don't understand, but I do. I think we both do."

Harvey gazed at the amber liquid in the cup, swirled it and soaked it up with his eyes; the more he looked at it, the less resistance he had, and he found himself downing it in huge gulps, and boldly holding out the cup for more. Cain smiled and poured another dose into Harvey's cup. He drank his own, and then poured himself another, as well.

"You may not realize it, Harvey, but I understand you. I understand you all too well, and I want to help you."

" Sometimes I wonder if anyone understands me, Mr. Cain," Harvey said, still gazing into his cup.

"I know the feeling, Harv. You're sick and tired of society dictating the rules by which you live, telling you what's right and wrong, forcing you to conform to someone else's idea of a good life. You spend your life slaving away just to make ends meet, and in the end it's all for nothing. You still have your same life, your same boring existence, your same routine, and it seems to have no end. Death is all you have to look forward to, Harv, death is all that awaits at the end of that long road."

Cain was digging deep into Harvey's emotions, poking at the sore spots, and Harvey suddenly had tears welling up in his eyes. He tried to wipe them away with his hands, embarrassed that he, a grown man, was letting his feelings get the best of him.

"I'm sick and tired of my job, and I'm sick and tired of my wife nagging me all the time. I just wish things could be better, you know?" He downed his drink, and held the cup out for more, and Cain graciously obliged.

"I do know, Harv, and it doesn't have to be that way. Things can change. You can be a man again, feel powerful. You can quit that worthless job, and never want for money. You can do whatever you want with your life, and no one can stop you. Let me show you, Harvey White. Take my hand."

Cain stood up and offered his hand. Harvey finished his drink and set the cup down on the desk. He stood up, swaying slightly from dizziness. He had done it. He had gone to Cain, and bared his soul, and now there was no turning back.

"Show me," he said, and he grasped Cain's hand.

9

When Lucas returned to the library, he had the pages he had copied from the book, and a couple dollars in change; he would make sure that this was no wasted trip. He saw the same librarian at the checkout desk, and anxiously approached her.

"Hi, remember me?" *he asked, grinning sheepishly.*

"Of course I do. You wanted help with the Internet, right?"

"Yep, that was me."

She made a note of the time, and marked it on the small tab of paper before handing it to him. "Ok, let's go over to number five, and get you going." *She lead him over to the computer stations, and in no time had him logged on to the Internet, and doing different searches.*

"This is easier than I thought," *he said.* "Thanks a lot for helping me."

"It was no problem at all. What is it that you're working on, if I may ask?"

Lucas produced two folded up sheets of notebook paper from his back pocket. "I'm doing a project for school," *he lied,* "but I'm having trouble with it." *He unfolded one of the papers and handed it to her.*

"This looks like some kind of old English. This is for history, right?" *She asked, glancing up from the paper.*

"Yeah, it's for history," *he lied again.* "But, I don't really understand. How can this be English? I don't even understand what it says."

"That's because it's an old form of English. It wasn't always like what we use today. Centuries ago, English was like a different language altogether. Over time, it evolved into what we use now."

"Centuries ago?" *Lucas asked, his heart racing.*

"Yes. Back in the days of the knights and castles, and that sort of thing. Of course, I'm no expert, but I have heard it referred to as Old English and Middle English."

"Wow, I never knew," *Lucas said, and thought:* That's why some of the words looked familiar!

Someone nearby cleared their throat, and the librarian looked up to see several people waiting impatiently at the checkout desk.

"Oops, gotta go. If you need anything else, just ask. Good luck on your assignment," she said, and hurried over to checkout. He heard her softly apologizing to the people in line for keeping them waiting so long. He typed in keyword Old English, and clicked on search. When the search results came up, he just stared unbelievingly. He knew it was only a matter of time. Just a matter of time.

He found a web site that offered a guide that translated Old English to Modern English, but discovered that at eighty-four pages in length, he had seriously underestimated what it would cost to print out the information he needed.

He returned a week later, with a ten-dollar bill he had stolen from his mother's purse, and printed out what he needed. The librarian was a little taken aback by the size of the job, but nonetheless printed out all eighty-four pages and handed them over.

"Eight dollars and forty cents," she said. "Did you get everything you needed for your assignment?"

Lucas grinned slyly. "Oh yes, everything I needed."

He climbed into his father's truck, and sat looking over some of the pages. He immediately recognized a word from the book, and was not surprised when he saw the translation: Demon.

"First things first, my friend. First, you have to show me that you really mean business," Cain said, shaking Harvey's hand. His grip grew tighter, and Harvey felt the knuckles of his right hand popping and twisting together. He clamped his teeth, and tried to maintain a straight face.

Cain squeezed tighter.

"There are those among us who would see me hurt, or even dead, and in the end, I will give their souls away. But, there is one who at this very moment is plotting against me, one who will not accept what I have to offer. Prove to me your allegiance, Harvey. Do me this one task, and I'll give you what you want."

He released Harvey's hand, which he had squeezed so hard it had gone white from lack of blood. Harvey shook the life back into his hand.

"What do you want me to do?

When Harvey arrived home, his eyes were half shut, and his face was flushed. He stumbled over the stoop and reeled, almost falling on his face. Jenny appeared from the kitchen, took one look at him, and said, "My God, Harvey, you're wasted. What are you doing home so early? And how the hell did you get home?"

"How do you fink I got home?" He jerked his thumb toward the front door. Jenny went past him and opened the door; the station wagon was parked askew on the front curb.

"Jesus, Harv, you could have gotten yourself killed. Or worse yet, you could have killed someone else. What were you thinking?" She stood with her hands on her hips, glaring at him with all the ferocity of a mother scolding a child. Without a word, Harvey stumbled past her, down the short hall, and into the master bedroom, where he promptly collapsed onto the bed and passed out.

Jenny sat down on the couch and buried her face in her hands. She listened in disgust to the sound of his snores coming from down the hall. A sudden thought popped into her head, and she walked down the hall to Ashley's bedroom, which was right across the hall from where Harvey lay unconscious.

The door was slightly ajar, and peeking through the crack she saw her daughter still in the midst of her afternoon nap. She was so small and fragile, a picture of naiveté, of pure innocence.

Harvey's sudden appearance sparked something in Jenny, brought up a red flag, and she had a sinking feeling that Harvey was involved in something horrible, something that could only mean trouble for her and Ashley.

That night, Jenny slept on the couch; she could not stand to be around Harvey when he was drunk, especially *this* drunk; when he drank heavily his breath turned rancid, and even his sweat smelled of alcohol.

Sometime in the night, a noise awoke her, and she turned over to see a dark figure moving through the shadowy living room toward the kitchen. Her heart took a frightful jump, but then she realized by the way the figure was swaying that it must have been Harvey. He disappeared into the gloominess of the kitchen, and a minute later, she heard a cigarette being lit. Then, the patio door slid open, and she heard him shuffle outside.

She lay in the dark, listening, unable to move for fear of being discovered and caught in another confrontation with a man who was almost surely still under the influence of his beloved alcohol.

A few minutes later, she heard low murmurs coming from the patio. At first, she thought that perhaps Harvey was outside talking to someone, involved in some kind of midnight conspiracy.

He's alone. My God, he's alone, and he's talking to himself.

She listened intently, trying to understand what he was saying, but it was useless; her heart thumped in her ears, making it difficult to hear anything but the sound of her own fear.

The murmurs stopped, and she heard his bare feet shuffling across the kitchen floor. Sometime during the night, he had managed to get his shoes off. She lay as quietly as possible, and pretended to be asleep as he came into the living room. But, instead of going down the hall, the shuffling grew closer, until she could hear his breathing, could actually *feel* him standing over her.

Her heart raced uncontrollably, and she had to hold her breath to keep still, to keep up a semblance of sleeping. She dared not open her eyes, even the slightest, for fear that his face might be looming within inches of her own, glaring at her with bloodshot eyes, and breathing on her with that familiar fetid breath he always had after one of his binges.

The moment seemed to stretch on forever, but he finally shuffled away. She heard the creaking of the bedsprings from the master bedroom. She opened her eyes, and took several deep breaths. Soon, his rhythmic snoring penetrated the silence.

She laid in the dark, biting nervously at her nails, listening to the voice inside her head tell her that something was definitely wrong with Harvey. Something other than the booze, or bad temper, something she couldn't put her finger on. Whatever it was, she was afraid.

When Harvey arrived home from work the next day, he had a large paper sack under one arm, and without a word to Jenny, he went into the kitchen and set the sack down on the kitchen table. Jenny was sitting on the couch looking at a photo album with Ashley. She heard the distinct *clink* of bottles hitting together, and rolling her eyes, thought: *Here we go again.*

"Just a minute, honey, I'll be right back," Jenny said, and went into the kitchen. Harvey was just grabbing a beer from the refrigerator. "Well, you're looking better today," she said sarcastically. "But I can see that won't last long." She looked at the sack on the table.

"I'm having a couple of friends over tonight," he said. He popped open his beer and drank half of it down. "You and Ashley will have to stay in the bedroom and watch TV, or something."

"What are you talking about, Harv? A party? You're having a party?"

"Will you calm down? No, it's not a party. Two friends are coming over for...a kind of meeting. And like I said, you and Ashley need to disappear."

"Why? Why do we have to disappear? Does this have something to do with Cain?"

"What if it does, so what?" he said, finishing his beer. He crumpled the can and tossed it into the garbage, immediately grabbing another from the refrigerator.

Jenny's heart sank. "Please tell me you didn't go to see that man, Harv."

"He has a lot to offer, Jen. I think we should listen to him."

"Oh my God," she said. "Harvey, that man is a murderer. He's taken over this town, and threatened to kill us all. He's something...I don't know...evil. I won't be a part of it, Harv, no way."

Harvey's demeanor changed, and he stared at her with cold, emotionless eyes. "You already *are* a part of it. We all are. Things are going to be different around here from now on, whether you like it or not. Now get lost!"

Jenny backed out of the kitchen without a word, her eyes wide with disbelief. She now knew what it was before she had not been able to quite pin down - it was Cain. Her husband had gone to see Cain, had probably *joined* him, and now her world was changing before her very eyes.

The whole town, even her husband, was tainted by this evil, and she felt a desperate fear growing inside her. She had to get out, get away somehow, to take Ashley as far away from Oak Junction as she could get before the evil could destroy their lives.

She sat down on the couch next to Ashley, who was still leafing through the photo album. "Mommy, is daddy mad?" she asked. Tears sprang to Jenny's eyes, and she hugged her daughter close.

"No honey, don't worry. Daddy's not mad," she said.

But he is mad, she thought. *Mad as a hatter. And if we don't get out of here, something very bad is going to happen.*

Jonathon Mott was locking up the library for the evening at right about the same time Harvey White was herding his wife and daughter into the bedroom for the night so he could entertain a couple of friends. He had sat inside all day, brooding over the death of his parents. Not one person had entered the library the entire day, and it seemed to amplify the loneliness he felt at their absence. He seemed blanketed in a shroud of grief. And yet, something kept him going, kept him ticking, and it burned in him like a red-hot poker.

Revenge...?

It was only six o'clock, and the sun still glared, fierce and merciless, in the cloudless blue sky. He walked east on Broadway, turned right onto 3rd Avenue, and headed down toward Main. The trees that lined the avenue swayed gently in the summer breeze, and Jonathon noticed that the town seemed strangely quiet for such a beautiful day. There were no cars on the streets, no people; even in a town as small as Oak Junction, there were still the occasional pedestrian and traffic as people went about their daily routines.

He passed a sparrow lying dead in the gutter.

Father, where are you? Mother, he thought. *Mother...*

Something was else missing, too.

Birds. Where are all the birds?

During the summer months, Oak Junction's bird population usually exploded, the trees along the streets alive with the clamoring and chirping of birds. Jonathon had even done a story in the town newspaper the previous summer about the problem the town was having with the excess amount of bird droppings on the sidewalks and gutters.

Now the trees were empty, void of any activity. There were no birds on the power lines, no birds on the roofs of any of the buildings, no birds twisting and spinning around in small flocks, following each other in liquid motion.

He turned left onto Main, and was immediately in front of the tiny newspaper office. Next door, Jaspar Hendricks sat on the bench in front of the hardware store, looking up and down the street as if he were waiting for someone.

"Hello, Jaspar," Jonathon called out, as he pulled his key ring from his pocket.

"Come on over here, Jonathon," Jaspar said, waving one bony hand in the air.

Jonathon sat down on the bench and asked, "How are you, Jaspar?"

"Well, I don't know, really. I'm looking for my friend, Hank Tooley. Have you seen him?" Jaspar's voice sounded hoarse, and he had an empty look in his red-rimmed, watery eyes.

"No, Jaspar, I haven't seen him around. Have you tried calling him?"

"Yep. Family doesn't know where he is, either. Say they called the sheriff. He's looking, too. I think he went and ran off because of that fella that came to town. Bad man, that one is. I heard tell of animals dyin' out at some of the farms, you know. They been dyin' ever since *he* showed up and loosed his devil in this town. Took your parents, you know. Killed 'em. Yep, he's a bad one, all right. Whole town's gonna to die. Whole town."

Jaspar got shakily to his feet and shuffled away, shaking his head and mumbling to himself. Jonathon watched him until he disappeared around the corner. The old man's words echoed in his head, and filled his heart with sadness.

Took your parents, you know. Killed 'em.

Jonathon thought about that night in the field, how his mother had collapsed, empty and lifeless, after being sacrificed to whatever that thing was Cain called his *god*, and he had to fight back the tears. Jaspar was right; the whole town was going to die.

Unless someone figures out a way to stop this guy, he thought. And then, another thought: *Best to keep ideas like that to yourself, Jon, or else you could end up joining the rest of the family.*

Jonathon noticed the closed sign hanging in the front window of the hardware store.

Whole town's gonna die....

He decided to stop in at the diner for some coffee before going to the newspaper office. *What am I going to write about, anyway? The devil that came to town?*

"Well, hello there, Jonathon," Betty said from behind the counter. "Long time, no see."

"Hi, Betty. How about some coffee?"

"Sure, hon. Comin' right up."

Jonathon sat down at the counter next to Hal Winder, who had a half-eaten doughnut and a cup of coffee sitting on the counter in front of him. The only other people in the diner were two locals sitting in a booth at the front window. Hal looked over and nodded to Jonathon, and then went back to watching Betty.

"Here ya' go, hon," she said, setting the cup down in front of him.

She stood there quietly while he poured sugar and cream into his coffee, and stirred the mix together. She bent over the counter, and spoke in a low voice. "Say, I'm real sorry about your parents. Real angels, both of 'em. Are you holdin' up ok?"

"Yeah, I guess you could say I'm holding up," Jonathon said, nodding.

"Me too, son. Real sorry," Hal said.

"If you need anything at all, you just let me know, ok?" Betty said.

"Sure thing."

Jonathon sat in silence for a moment, and then turned to Hal. "I hear some of the farmers are having problems with their animals."

Betty and Hal looked at each other, then at Jonathon.

"Where'd you hear that?" Hal asked, sending Betty another knowing look.

"Oh, I don't remember. Someone just happened to mention it to me." Jonathon tried to stay nonchalant about the whole thing, cool as a cucumber. But inside he was itching to get all the information he could, anything at all to help him in his cause.

The two men in the booth had stopped talking altogether. They just sat and sipped their coffee. He leaned over closer to Jonathon, and whispered, "I don't think we should be talkin' about this here," and motioned his eyes toward the booth.

"You're not planning on puttin' that in your paper, are ya'?" Betty asked.

"Well, no…" Jonathon started to say.

"Chickens," Hal whispered.

"What?"

"Chickens. Lost some chickens. Like they had a disease, or somethin'. The rest just ran off. It's that man. He's the disease."

"Hal!" Betty said.

"Let me tell him, Betty. Someone's got to say something. You heard right son. I got neighbors with sick livestock, even a dead dog."

Nate came around from the kitchen, where he had apparently overheard some of the conversation. "You stop that talk right now, Hal. I don't need any trouble in my diner. And you," he said, looking at Jonathon, "you just get right on outta here. Coffee's on the house."

"Hey, I'm really sorry," Jonathon said, and got up to leave.

"That's ok, hon," Betty said, glancing over at the booth. One of the men was on the pay phone by the restrooms, talking and looking right at them. "You better go now."

On his way out of the diner, Jonathon noticed the man on the phone was still staring at him. He stepped out into the late afternoon sun, and crossed over 3rd Avenue to the newspaper office. He pulled out his keys, plugged one into the deadbolt, and twisted. It clicked free, and he pushed open the door and stepped into the dim interior. It smelled of ink and paper and dust. The old printing press near the back of the shop had collected a fine layer of dust, seemed to gather a layer of dust in as little as one day, but then again, the entire place seemed to collect dust like a vacuum.

The front area was the heart of the tiny operation, the work area itself, littered with boxes and stacks of paper, old newspapers, and cartons filled with bottles of ink. At the rear was a small office, and Jonathon walked back and switched on the light. The desk was piled high with papers and forms, and more dust, and somewhere a telephone that didn't work. He shook his head and switched off the light, and went back to the front. He crossed his arms over his chest and looked around the room at the clutter.

It's hopeless, he thought. *The way things are now; it's hopeless to continue. I think it's time to clean this place out and...*

A flash of sunlight off metal caught his eye, and he saw a police cruiser pulling up to the curb in front of the office. Sheriff Craven climbed out of the car and swaggered toward the entrance. Jonathon already knew what the sheriff wanted, knew what this conversation would be about, but one thing was still a mystery to him.

Why is everyone giving in so easily? No one is the same anymore.

But I am. Why?

Craven stepped inside, and took off his sunglasses.

"How are you, Jonathon?" he asked. The grim look on his face only confirmed Jonathon's suspicions. This was no social call.

"About as well as can be expected, Sheriff. And yourself?" Jonathon was still gazing around the room, avoiding eye contact with the sheriff, scratching his head as if stuck in the middle of some major decision.

"I'm doing great, son. I just wanted to have a heart to heart with you real quick, make sure we're on the same page."

"You know, I'm thinking of just emptying this place out and selling it. I mean, the newspaper business just isn't what it used to be, you know." He looked at the sheriff and nodded, as if to say: *Yep, I think that's just what I'm going to do, yes sir!*

Craven stood patiently and waited for Jonathon to finish his little act.

"What do you want, Sheriff?"

"Look, son, I like you, always have, and I liked your parents. I'm real sorry that things turned out this way for you. But now it's time for you to move on. You can't be asking questions around town about things that don't concern you. You'll just ruffle people's feathers, and the next thing you know, well, let's not go there. Are you getting what I'm saying, Jonathon?" The look on his face softened, and it was the face that Jonathon had always remembered on the man.

"I think I am, yes."

"Now, let me ask you something else. You're not planning on putting anything in your paper about this talk going around town, are you?"

Jonathon saw beyond the soft expression, beyond the mild mannerisms of the man standing before him, and saw beneath the facade a changed man, and he would have to indulge him with lies if he wanted to survive the day.

"No, Sheriff. Like I said, I'm thinking of getting rid of everything. Either way, I'm out of the newspaper business for good. I think I'll just concentrate on the library. In fact, I'm thinking of making a run up to Arlidge to see if I can scrounge up some extras from their library."

"That sounds like a real good idea, son. Real good. Sounds like you're on the right track. And if you stay that way, everything will be fine. If not - well, I can't guarantee anything. Just don't end up like your parents, Jonathon. I don't want to see that happen to you, too."

Jonathon dropped the bullshit for a moment. "Where are my parents, Sheriff?"

The softness in Craven's face gave way to the grim hardness again, and he said, "Let it go, son. It's over. They were well taken care of…after. You need to forget about it."

"Ok, Sheriff. No more questions, I promise. Time to move on."

"Do I have your word?"

"Sure, you have my word." Jonathon held out his hand and Craven shook it.

"Good luck with the library, Jonathon," he said, and a few moments later Jonathon watched him pull away from the curb and disappear from view.

"Sure, Sheriff. You have my word that I'm going to do everything in my power to get that son of a bitch that killed my parents," Jonathon said aloud.

He left the office, locked the deadbolt behind him, and started down the street toward home. He noticed another dead sparrow lying on the sidewalk under the shadow of the tree it apparently fell from, and he stopped to ponder it for a moment.

He stared at the bird for a long time before going home.

10

The evening wore on, cooling off somewhat as the sun began to drop into the western horizon, stretching shadows to impossible lengths, and promising relief from the burning rays of the summer sun. 2nd Avenue was unusually quiet, except at one house, which was located about halfway between Broadway and Church Streets. And things were just getting underway at the White residence.

Jenny and Ashley lay on the bed in the master bedroom watching sitcoms, and listening to the annoying racket her husband and the two men who had shown up earlier were making out in the kitchen.

"What are they *doing*, mommy?" Ashley asked, scrunching her face together.

"They're just having fun, honey. They're noisy, huh?" She laughed, and torture-tickled Ashley until the little girl almost had tears in her eyes. She finally let up, and let Ashley lay there, gaining control of her breathing again, and wondered: *What would I do without her? God, thank you for giving me the most wonderful gift of my life.*

A huge burst of boisterous, drunken laughter erupted from the kitchen, and although on the outside Jenny was able to joke about it for Ashley's sake, on the inside a more serious side of her was perplexed, fearful. The purpose of this little party was not clear, and that intensified the feeling even more. And, of course, there was one other thing to consider.

Cain. Where does Cain fit in to this? Has he brainwashed the entire town?

Jenny put her ear to the bedroom door and listened. One of the men was talking about Cain. *"...told me the same thing...he would give me money...can you believe it?"* She could hear only bits and pieces of their conversation, but it was enough to ascertain that Cain seemed to be at the center of everything. *"...all the pussy I want, and I...making me hungry..."* This brought another wild burst of laughter. *Men,* Jenny thought.

A short while later, the voices calmed down somewhat, seemed to be discussing something of a more serious nature. She returned to her place at the door, listening intently to the muffled voices from the kitchen. *"...make the call...Craven...."* What could they possibly want with Sheriff Craven?

The voices went quiet, and then she heard Harvey's voice: *"Hello? Sheriff Craven? Hi, this is Harvey White, over on 402 North 2nd Avenue. Hey, listen, Mr. Cain wanted me to -"* Jenny heard the patio door slide open, and Harvey's words became indiscernible as the men stepped out onto the back patio. She went to the window and peeked out through the blinds. Night had fallen, and several houses down a streetlight cast a faint yellow glow onto the street.

She bit her lip nervously, and waited.

"What happened to you, Sheriff?" Paul Mayfield asked, as he watched Sheriff Craven pin notices up on the bulletin board. Craven didn't bother turning around. "What do you mean?" he asked.

"You know what I mean, Frank. You've changed. You're...different. You were the perfect example of everything good in this town. If anyone had good morals, it was you. Now that Cain's here, all that's gone out the window. You're not the same man."

"Look who's talking," Craven said, turning around. "The man who keeps *fuck* magazines in his desk drawer."

Mayfield was bewildered by what he was hearing; in the five years he had worked with the sheriff, the harshest language he had heard him use was *damn*. "It's not the same thing, Frank, and you know it. You and most of this town have become accessories to murder. This man, Cain, he's brought something to this town that just isn't right. It's evil, and if you believed in God, you would do something about it. It's just not right, Frank."

"Maybe I haven't changed at all, Deputy," Craven said, visibly growing angry. "Maybe I just went along with this stupid life because it's all I had. I need something more, and now I have it. What about you, what do you have?"

"I have God, Frank."

"What has God ever done for you, or me, for that matter?"

"I don't know. I just don't know. But I *do* know that this is all wrong. It can't go on."

"What are you trying to say, Deputy?" Craven asked.

"I'm saying that I'm thinking of calling the state police in on this, and stopping this madness once and for all."

"I wouldn't recommend doing that."

"Are you going to stop me, Sheriff? Are you going to tie me up, and feed me to that fucking thing, whatever it is? Is that what it's going to come to?"

"No, Paul, I don't want to kill you. But I'll warn you right now, if you do anything rash, I can't guarantee your safety. Cain will not allow any interference."

The telephone on Craven's desk rang, and he picked it up quickly as if welcoming the interruption. "Sheriff's office," he said, and listened. "Yeah...is that right?" He glanced over at Mayfield. "Sure, I'll get someone over there right away." He hung up the phone and sighed deeply. "I need you to go over to 402 North 2nd Avenue, and check out a disturbance. Man's name is Harvey White. I'm sure you know him"

"What's the use, Sheriff? There's no law in this town anymore," Mayfield said.

"Just do your job, Deputy, and there won't be any problems."

"Sure thing, Sheriff," he said cynically, "and when I get back, I gonna call the state police. I don't know exactly what's gotten into you and this town, but once we get rid of Cain, I'm sure we can work things out." He donned his hat, and left, his keys jangling against his hip.

The party had moved back into the kitchen, and now the three men were louder than ever, charged with excitement, and Jenny considered going out there and telling them to keep it down, but decided against it. She was no match for three drunken men, men who probably had the same dangerous mentality as Harvey, or maybe worse.

The doorbell rang, and she heard, and felt the heavy footfalls across the living room floor, and the squeal of a hinge as the front door opened. She rushed to the window and peeked outside. A police cruiser was parked in front of the house.

The sheriff?

She went back to the door and listened. Ashley climbed off the bed and headed for the door as well, but Jenny whispered, "Shhhh, go back to the bed, honey, ok?" The little girl climbed back onto the bed and laid on her stomach, her face propped up in her hands, studying her mother's every move.

"Hey, Deputy, how are you?" She heard Harvey's voice boom. *Deputy. What was his name? Mayford? Mayfield?*

All the men exchanged greetings, and then Deputy Mayfield was saying something, and she pressed her ear harder against the door. *"...some kind of disturbance..."* Then she heard Harvey's voice: *"...just an excuse...talk to you...something has to be done about Cain..."* She heard the last part of what Harvey was saying plain as day, and her muscles and nerves relaxed. She gave a sigh of relief. That was it - this was all a cover to have a meeting about what to *do* about Cain.

She heard all of them go out on the back patio and slide the door shut. Although she couldn't hear them at all now, some of the mystery had been lifted, and she sat on the bed and hugged Ashley tightly, mentally crossing her fingers in hopes that things would return to normal.

Ten minutes later, Ashley said, "Mommy, I'm thirsty."

Jenny bit her lip, and looked at the bedroom door. "Maybe mommy can get you something." She opened the door a crack, and heard muffled voices from outside. "Honey, you stay here, mommy will be right back," she said, and crept out into the hall. She padded down the hall and peeked around the corner into the kitchen. Several glasses half filled with liquor sat on the table, and the air was thick with smoke. The men were still outside, and the vertical blinds over the patio door were closed. She could hear murmurs from the other side of the glass. "Just in and out," she whispered to herself, and snuck over to the refrigerator.

She pulled it open, and scanned the shelves. Beer. More beer. *Jesus, Harv,* she thought, *if I had all the money you spent -*

Ashley screamed from behind her. Startled, she turned and saw Ashley clutching at one of the vertical blinds, holding it askew, her eyes wide and body trembling as she stared out through the glass. Jenny felt goose bumps rise on her skin, not just from the scream, and the site of her daughter filled with terror, but also because as a mother she could *feel* Ashley's terror emanating off of her in waves.

She rushed over to snatch up her daughter, to snatch her away from whatever was causing this strange reaction in her, and then she caught site of it herself, and for a moment she, too, was frozen on the spot, mesmerized by the bizarre scene on the back patio.

Deputy Mayfield was laying flat on his back on the cement patio, one man kneeling on his chest while the other stood by watching. Harvey was kneeling down on the patio, grasping a handful of the deputy's hair in one hand, while moving something back and forth in the other hand, something shiny, something that reflected the light from the bare light bulb that illuminated the patio.

She saw the pool of blood growing under the deputy's head, and then she realized what Harvey was doing. The thing Harvey was moving back and forth was the bow saw he used to trim the trees when the limbs were overgrown.

Harvey was cutting off Deputy Paul Mayfield's head with a bow saw.

Jenny shrieked, and Harvey looked up, caught a quick glimpse of his wife before she grabbed Ashley away, leaving the vertical blinds swinging against the glass. She ran sobbing through the living room, clutching Ashley to her bosom, yanked the front door open, and rushed out into the night air. She went across the lawn, and was immediately cut off by Harvey, who had bolted around the side of the house like a man on fire.

He jumped right in front of her, and spread out his arms. "Where ya' goin', honey?" he asked through his teeth. She smelled the whiskey on his breath, saw the glazy eyes, and her skin crawled in revulsion.

"N-nowhere, Harv." Jenny hitched and sobbed, while Ashley clung tightly around her neck, tears streaming down her face. "We-we just g-got scared, that's all."

"Ashley, go in the house," Harvey ordered.

"No, mommy, no!" she cried, clinging even tighter to Jenny's neck.

"Put her down, Jenny. Now!" Harvey yelled. She felt spit and hot whiskey breath hit her in the face. She looked around desperately for some chance of escape, any help at all, and saw only a couple across the street sitting on lawn chairs and quietly watching the events unfold.

"Help me," she said, but they only stared. She looked back at Harvey, who looked ready to explode, and gently set Ashley on the grass.

"Mommy, no," she cried, reaching up for the safety of her mother's arms. Jenny bent down and stroked her hair. "Go inside, honey, I'll be in a minute, I promise."

"Yeah, go inside, Ashley. Mommy will be right in. You just saw daddy playing a game, that's all. Just a game. Now go on inside."

"Go on, honey," Jenny said, and her daughter ran across the lawn and into the house, crying out as she stumbled over the threshold. This whole scenario taking place under the blanket of night was too surreal, to nightmarish, and Jenny thought that she might lose her mind if it went on any further.

As soon as Ashley disappeared through the doorway Harvey slapped Jenny hard enough to knock her down onto the grass. She let out a little cry of shocked surprise, looked up at Harvey, and asked, "Harvey, what's going on?" She put her finger to her lips and felt warmness flowing from one side of her mouth. The people across the street, people with whom they had never really associated with, suddenly laughed out loud, echoing across the barren street.

"I told you, Jenny. Things are different, now. I'm going to live my life the way *I* want to live my life, and Cain's going to help me do it." He swayed on his feet as he spoke. "You have two choices: you either be my wife, and do what I say, and everything will be just dandy. Or, you can take the hard way out, and end up like Mayfield. Is that what you want, Jenny? Do you want me to cut your fucking head off? Because I will." More laughter from across the street. Harvey smiled, and waved at the people in the lawn chairs. He bent down and picked her up by the armpits, and she stood there with her arms dangling at her sides in total capitulation.

"If you ever, *ever* try to run away from me again, I will find you, and I will kill you. Do you understand that?" He raised a clenched fist as if to hit her again.

Jenny held up her hands, palms out. "Yes, I understand. Please, Harvey, I understand."

"Now go take care of our daughter," he said, shoving her against the shoulder. She tripped and again fell on the grass (more rollicking laughter from the neighbors). She picked herself up and managed to get herself back inside, and back to the bedroom, where Ashley lay with her face buried in a pillow. When she saw her mother come through the door, a red hand print emblazoned across her face, blood trickling from the corner of her mouth, grass stains on her hands and knees, she erupted into tears.

"Mommy, mommy," she cried, and Jenny rushed over and held her daughter close to her, savoring the only source of warmth and goodness and love that she had left in the world.

11

The night was clear, the darkness overhead twinkling with stars. Trees swayed gently, and the corn in the fields whispered in the warm summer breeze. Harvey drove over to the church with a parcel in a bloodstained plastic shopping bag sitting next to him on the seat. Harvey's two accomplices were taking the rest of the parcel out to Oak Junction cemetery to dispose of it in a more traditional manner.

He lit a cigarette with the car lighter, and thought about the package: *I've got a man's head right here in this bag, and it doesn't bother me a bit.* The other two guys were grossed out at first by the whole thing, but they served their purpose well. Cain had given Harvey their names and the numbers to call, and now he couldn't even remember their names. Yet, he could recall quite well the feeling of power and freedom he had as the two men followed his every order as he cut off the deputy's head.

One of the men had smashed a brick over the deputy's head to knock him out, and they weren't even sure at that point if he had been alive or dead, but when Harvey started to cut across the throat, blood had jetted out onto the cement, and they knew he was still alive.

He cut off his head while he was still alive!

That was when his bitch of a wife had peeked in on him, and that pissed him off. So after he had taken care of *that* situation, he went back and finished the job. The bow saw did great work, even on the bone, but it wasn't a clean job; the jagged edges of the blade chewed through everything, leaving the flesh and gristle hanging ragged on the edges of the cut. Still, it had served its purpose, like the two men whose names he could not for the life of him recall. And yet, oddly, he could recall other things....

The ragged ends of skin waving back and forth as he sawed, the last wet intake of air as he cut into the windpipe, the grim determination as he cut through the bone, the smile on his face as the head tore free...

It was all he could think about the entire day, all he could do to smother the anticipation long enough until the moment of truth came. And he did it without hesitation, without a moment of human regret or conscious, and he accepted this new facet of himself all too easily. And he didn't even stop to consider how this could be. He just knew that it felt *good*, felt like he could do anything, as if Cain had given him a whole new lease on life.

Harvey parked the station wagon in front of the church, grabbed the plastic bag, and got out of the car. The cool night air felt good on his skin and face, and he stood and savored the feeling for a moment. Then he headed up the sidewalk, bag swinging at his side.

The church was dark, foreboding, a shape against the night that no longer resembled a church, but a haunted house that kids might sneak into in the middle of the night on a dare.

He pulled on the brass handle, and the door swung open effortlessly. The interior was almost pitch black, save for the dim light emanating from the back hall, and it was toward this light that he walked, wondering if he should call out to announce his presence.

Cain saved him the trouble. "Come on back, Harvey, and show me what you have."

Harvey walked into the church office and lifted the bag in the air like a prize kill. "I have what you wanted, Mr. Cain." Although Harvey had drunk more than enough of the sauce, he was surprised at how much control he had over his actions; Harvey was all too well acquainted with the effects of too much alcohol, had lived much of his life under the influence, and at that moment he felt remarkably sober.

There seemed to be heat coming from somewhere in the room, a warm glow as if from a fire, but he was more involved with the matter at hand to worry about it.

Cain sat behind the desk, the corner of his mouth lifted up in a sinister half-grin. "Take it out of the bag, Harvey."

He placed the bag on the desk, and lifted Mayfield's head out by the hair. Paul Mayfield's eyes were still half opened, his mouth agape, tongue protruding out as if waiting for a doctor to put a tongue depressor on it. Ragged strands of flesh hung down from the neck, and shook and jiggled as Harvey displayed the head.

"Very good, very good, indeed. Let me see it," Cain said, reaching out with both hands. Harvey handed him the head, and Cain took it and held it in front of his own face. "Well, well, Deputy Mayfield. You're not looking too well today, are you?" Harvey chuckled, and then shut up when he noticed Cain was not laughing. "This is the face of failure, Harvey White, the face of someone who cannot accept what is, and what will be. Someone who decided to take the gamble, and lost. Take a good long look, because it won't be the last time you see this expression." He looked closer at Mayfield's face. "It's a shame you chose death over me, Deputy. We could have been friends."

He tossed the head back to Harvey, who flinched, but managed to catch it in his arms like a football. "Put it in the bag, and leave it there," Cain said. He reached down behind the desk and produced a brown satchel, which he set on the desk in front of Harvey.

"I reward those in my favor. You've done well, Harvey, quite well. Open it," he said, nodding his head toward the satchel. Harvey pulled the strap from its buckle, and split open the top of the satchel. His eyes went wide and his mouth fell open in astonishment. He reached inside and pulled out a handful of cold, hard cash. He had never before seen so much money in one place, even as manager of the Greenview Market, taking deposits to the bank on even the best of days.

"Quit your job, Harvey, and live your life. Do as you wish. Of course, with this comes new responsibility. Do you understand?"

"Yes sir, Mr. Cain," Harvey said, and stuck out his hand, which Cain took firmly and shook. But, instead of releasing his grip, he squeezed harder, and the smile on Harvey's face faltered, became crossed with fear.

"You *will* let me know of any situations that need to be…taken care of, won't you? After all, we don't want anything to stand in the way of our prosperity and good fortune, now do we?" He released Harvey's hand, and smiled. "Go on your way, Harvey. Till we meet again."

Harvey hesitantly picked up the satchel, as if at any moment Cain might rescind the offer, but Cain only smiled. "Thank you, Mr. Cain. I'll be sure to let you know if anything comes up," he said, and turned to leave.

"I'm sure you will, Harvey. I'm sure you will."

After Harvey left, Cain pulled open a drawer that had already been partially open, and pulled out the book. He ran his fingers over the cover, which had become habit over time, and felt the electric impulses shoot into his fingertips. *Another soul for you, soon,* he thought.

12

Clay was dead.

Only one week had passed since Lucas had last seen him.

Lucas had been asleep in his room on a Tuesday morning (he had dropped out of school, much to his parent's dismay, but he had made it quite clear to them that is was a decision he would not regret), when his mother tapped on the door, and opened it a crack.

"Lucas? Are you awake?" she whispered.

"I am now," he said groggily. "What do you want, mom?"

"I need to talk to you about something really important. Can I come in?"

Lucas sat up in bed, his jet-black hair sticking up in licks and curls. "Like I said, what do you want?" he asked, glaring at her with a face that seemed older than his years.

"Well, it's about Clay. He's...he's gone."

"What do you mean, gone? Who cares, mom? Can I go back to sleep now?" He fell back and pulled the covers over his head.

"What I mean is, he's dead, Lucas."

Lucas sat up, and looked at her suspiciously as if she might be pulling a fast one on him, and asked, "What did you say?"

"I said, he's dead, son. They found him this morning, in their barn. He...hung himself." She looked down at the floor, hands clasped together in front of her. "His father just called. He thought you should know, even though you two haven't been, you know, hanging around together too much lately."

"Why would he go and do something like that?" Lucas asked, even though he already knew the answer.

"They don't know, Lucas. They just don't know. Sometimes people keep things locked inside for a long time, and it can become too much. You just never know."

"I need to be alone, mom," Lucas said, and she left the room, closing the door behind her.

His bedroom was dimly lit from the thin white curtains over his window, curtains that glowed with the late morning sun. He watched dust motes circulate throughout the room.

Clay had killed himself. He didn't feel remorse or pity, just a certain curiosity as to why Clay had taken his own life. Clay never seemed unhappy, never seemed depressed, and yet…

Lucas found himself thinking about the dead mice scattered around the book. They were just tiny skeletons now, but every now and then a fresh one would appear, decomposing right next to the book. Death no longer frightened him; in fact, he was intrigued by the whole idea of death.

Lucas went to the funeral ostensibly to see his long time friend off to whatever awaited him, but he really just wanted to see his friend lying there dead, wanted to see the reality of it; he had been to only one other funeral in his life, that of his grandfather, when he was ten years old.

At first he had been afraid, not knowing what to expect, as death was a new concept for him. But after they had arrived at the funeral home and he saw how peaceful his grandfather looked, the fear had been replaced by curiosity.

He had seen his mother approach the coffin and softly stroke one of the withered hands, while she dabbed her eyes with a handkerchief. When it came time for him to approach the coffin, he stood for a long time scrutinizing the body. His grandfather looked like he was sleeping, and at peace, but there was something unnatural to the whole thing that Lucas couldn't quite put his finger on.

But then he reached out as his mother had done, and touched one of the withered hands, felt its leathery stiffness, and he realized that it was the attempt to make him look lifelike that made it seem strange. He was no longer alive, no longer thinking, breathing, no longer a man. It was like looking at a department store mannequin, one who had been living only days earlier.

Finally, he was hauled away by his father, but he never forgot the experience, never forgot the leathery feel of his grandfather's hand, the bulges of veins that no longer pumped blood, but were filled with something else that seemed to freeze him in time.

He wanted to relive that experience now, to see and touch the face of death, to realize its reality. He had to suppress his excitement while inside the church, but his heart raced with anticipation.

When they entered the church, the Pedersons were standing by the coffin, which was flanked on both sides by large flower *arrangements on stands, and they were gazing reflectively down at Clay. Lucas approached with his parents, and they all exchanged handshakes, Mr. And Mrs. Cain offering their condolences. Mr. Pederson shook Lucas' hand, and patted him on the shoulder. "Thanks for coming, Lucas. Clay would have been happy." Mrs. Pederson hugged him very lightly, as if he were made of glass, and said, "Yes, thanks for coming, Lucas." Her eyes were bloodshot and weary, rimmed with tears.*

"I'm sorry. Very sorry for you both. He was a great guy," Lucas said with false remorse. "I didn't know he had any...you know, problems."

"He didn't, as far as we knew. One day he was fine, and then..." She burst into fresh tears, and Clay's father put his arm around her and led her away. Lucas looked into the coffin, at his old friend who now lay in state, and tilted his head to one side as he studied the features. Clay's blonde hair was combed down neatly, and his face was covered in makeup, but Lucas could still see the underlying bluish tint of the skin.

He saw something else under the makeup, as well, something down on Clay's neck, and he bent over to get a closer look. The mortician had applied the makeup thickly here, trying to hide the telltale ring of purple and black bruises around the neck. Lucas closed his eyes, and tried to imagine what Clay had looked like hanging in the barn. When he opened his eyes, his mother was standing next to him.

"Are you alright, Lucas?" she asked.

"Yes, mom, I'm ok. Just thinking."

His mother wandered off, and he turned his attention back to Clay. He reached out and touched one of Clay's hands; unlike his grandfather's hands, these were smooth, but they still had the same leathery feel to them. He laid his hand over the cool flesh, and thought: You won't say anything now, will you?

After the funeral, Lucas went out to the barn to work on his translation of the book. He had learned some interesting things over the last couple of weeks, but progress was slow. As it turned out, the translation guide that he had gotten from the library didn't provide him all he needed to unlock the book's secrets. He found himself returning to the library again and again, browsing an Internet that seemed infinite. But his spiral notebook had begun to fill up, and offered a vague idea of what the book was all about.

Lucas was going to be very powerful, indeed.

13

Rusty Withers had been the only mailman in Oak Junction for as long as anyone could remember. He was very thin, and at fifty-eight years old, had a complete head of gray. He often told folks that he stayed so thin from all the walking he did. Fact was, he didn't do *that* much walking, he was just naturally thin. He *did*, however, spend a lot of time motoring around in his white postal Jeep, especially to the outlying farms in the area.

The sun was just rising on the eastern horizon, and Rusty was busy sorting mail in the back room of the tiny post office. True to the postal tradition, he arrived without fail every day at sunrise, getting ready for the day's deliveries. And he had always been a trusted part of Oak Junction.

He noticed a magazine in a black plastic sleeve. Without bothering to see who it was addressed to, he ripped it open and pulled out the skin magazine. "Hello, ladies," he said, browsing through the pages. He tossed it aside, and picked through the rest of the day's mail before loading up the Jeep.

A short while later, he pulled onto the dirt lane that lead to the Winder farm, and headed toward the farmhouse, the Jeep bouncing along over potholes and ruts. He stopped in front of the house and turned off the engine. A short distance away was a barn badly in need of paint, and some makeshift pigpens, now empty save for the decaying corpses of Hal Winder's stock. Several dead chickens lay scattered around the barnyard. On the other side of the house a field of tall, healthy corn was soaking up the morning sunshine.

Ignoring the dead livestock, he got out of the Jeep, and whistled a tune as he ascended the front porch, Hal Winder's mail in one hand.

"Got your mail, Hal," he called, rapping on the screen door. No response came from within the house. "Hal, you in there?"

He heard a slight humming in the air, like an electrical current flowing through a transformer. He turned his head back and forth, trying to figure out where the sound originated. Finally, he determined it was coming from the direction of the corn.

When he moved closer to the corn, the humming grew louder, only now it was more of a buzzing.

"Hal, are you out there?" Rusty yelled into the corn. He pushed into the corn and the insane buzzing grew louder. He would stop, listen for the sound, and then move on, hopefully toward the source of the sound. Not too far in he saw the obscured shape of a scarecrow, turned toward it, and the buzzing grew louder still.

He pushed into a small clearing, and here was a scarecrow mounted high on thick posts, and here also was the source of the buzzing. Flies were buzzing ecstatically around the scarecrow, crawling on its face and body.

Hal Winder was the scarecrow.

"Well, I'll be damned," Rusty said, gazing up at Hal Winder's corpse. Thick leather straps held it in place, around the wrists of the outstretched arms, at the feet, which were crossed over one another, around the chest, and around the neck. Hal's eyes were still open, hazy and lifeless, and two large ears of corn had been jammed into his mouth, splitting it open on one side. Someone had taken the time to stuff hay into the shirtsleeves and pant legs to add authenticity to this bizarre caricature. The flies were everywhere, and would be laying eggs, and maggots would soon be feasting on the remains.

Rusty looked curiously up at Hal Winder the scarecrow, Hal Winder with the flies and the corn jutting out of his mouth. "You know, you always did have a big mouth, Hal," Rusty said to the corpse, and he laughed all the way back to the Jeep.

Later, he would pull up in front of Paul Mayfield's modest home, and fall into a laughing jag that would last five minutes at the site of Mayfield's head mounted on a pole in the front yard. He took one look at the tongue that was wagging out between blue lips, and laughed until he was red in the face.

That same morning Jonathon got up early, showered, gulped down some coffee, and went out the door, walking east on Tower Street. Soon, he came to where the road ended, intersecting with 3rd Avenue North. But instead of turning north or south, he went straight across 3rd Avenue and into the field beyond.

He trudged through the weeds and lumps of parched soil, past the rusted hulk of a long forgotten car (he couldn't tell what kind of car it was, but then again, he was never any good with cars), and soon arrived at his destination.

He saw the black wrought iron fence that was infested with rust, the old headstones thrusting up crookedly like old teeth, some fallen over; Oak Junction lacked any real funds for a regular maintenance plan for the cemetery, so it slowly fell into ruin.

Most folks went off to some of the nicer cemeteries in Arlidge or Greenview to put their loved ones at rest. Of course, their were still a few hardcore residents who insisted on being buried in town, and their relatives would come and clean up the area to make things nice for the burials. And you had civic-minded groups who would volunteer from time to time to clean up the place. They would pull weeds, rake the soil, and fix headstones, anything to brighten it's appearance. But inevitably, Oak Junction Cemetery fell back into ruin, a victim of Mother Nature, and the local kids who came out at night to be spooked, and to vandalize.

Jonathon walked around to the main entrance, and looked up at the words that arched across the gates: Oak Junction Cemetery. The gates used to be locked with a thick chain and padlock, but now they were ajar, open to anyone who wished to visit.

He pushed open one of the gates, and it moaned and complained with age as he stepped past. He walked through the middle of the cemetery, gazing around at the headstones, some of which were so old that the engravings were no longer legible. As he approached the rear of the cemetery, he saw what he had been looking for, and his heart dropped.

There were fresh mounds of dirt here, at least thirty of them, and he knew his parents had to be among them. Among those poor souls who had fallen victim to the disease which infected the town.

What kind of deaths did they suffer?

Jonathon fell to his knees, and tears began to fill his eyes.

"Parting is such sweet sorrow."

He turned and saw Cain standing directly behind him; his Cadillac was parked a short ways down the access road. He stood up, wiping his face with the sleeves of his shirt.

"What do you want?" he asked.

"Oh, I come here often to visit, or meditate, or just ponder over death itself. It's such a mysterious thing, death."

"Where are my parents?" Jonathon demanded, and he could feel his cheeks flushing with anger.

"Oh, they're here somewhere, mixed in with the rest of the wasted lives."

"I'm going to kill you someday, you bastard," Jonathon hissed.

"Let me tell you a little secret," Cain said. "The sheriff seems to like you. Seems to think that you'll eventually come around, and being the intellect that you are, I was actually hoping you would become a valuable part of our union. This is why you are still alive, Jonathon. But tread lightly, because I could change my mind at any time, and then I would have to kill you, just like I killed your father. He died miserably, Jonathon, don't end up like him. Put the past behind you, and move forward. Be strong, not weak. He was weak, and in the end, he paid for it. Don't end up like your father, Jonathon, I'll leave it up to you." Cain quickly turned and strode away, a figure in black that seemed to represent everything evil Jonathon had ever known.

He stood and watched him walk away, fresh tears streaming down his face. He wanted to run up behind Cain and strangle the life out of him, but he knew it would mean certain death. No, there had to be another way to face up to Cain, and he had to find it. He took one last look at the fresh mounds of dirt, and started walking home.

Jenny woke up early, and immediately felt the dull throbbing in the side of her face. She put a finger to her lips, the left side swollen. She lifted her head and looked around the room, had a moment of disorientation, then realized that she was in Ashley's room. The night before, she and Ashley had come in here and fallen asleep together in the little girl's twin bed. Ashley was still asleep next to her, her face a picture of pure innocence.

The bedroom door was ajar, and she got up and padded over to it, and peeked through the crack at the closed bedroom door across the hall. She could hear Harvey's muffled snores coming from the other side of the door. He would probably sleep for hours, until last night's booze had lost its magical affect, and then he would have to get up and start the whole process over again. It almost made Jenny sick just thinking about it. And after last night, she was so repulsed by Harvey, that even now she was scheming, the wheels of her mind spinning furiously, conjuring up a plan of action.

She went into the bathroom, quietly closing the door behind her, and checked out her face in the mirror. The handprint on the side of her face had turned into a nasty bruise, and there was still some dried blood on her swollen lips. She stared at her countenance for a long time, almost as if she were seeing another person, a person from another place, another time.

She started to brush her straight, dirty blonde hair, and without realizing it started crying; the normal act of brushing her hair around her bruised face made her see just how *abnormal* the situation was, how wrong and hopeless things seemed. She blew her nose and dried her tears, and peed, staring blankly at the wall in front of her. She flushed the toilet and waited until it finished filling up and all was quiet again.

She cracked open the door, heard the monotonous snores, and crept into the hall and down to the kitchen. She passed the living room on the way, and the morning sun was streaming thinly through the closed blinds, illuminating the room with fresh light. The kitchen was lit with fresh light flowing through the small window above the sink.

Jenny walked slowly across the old kitchen linoleum, the floor creaking slightly under her weight. She separated the vertical blinds across the sliding glass door, squinting at the fresh light, and what she saw confirmed that last night had indeed been real, and not some nightmare or figment of her imagination. Paul Mayfield's corpse was gone (was now, in fact, under one of the fresh mounds of earth in the cemetery), but a thick pool of congealed blood was still drying on the cement, and there were thin streams that spiked out from the main pool. With sickening surety she thought: *Oh my God, that's where his blood shot out of his veins. He was alive when they did it! My God, he was alive...*

She felt her gorge rising, and put her hand over mouth, shutting her eyes and letting the blinds swing loosely back into position. She heard a *creak!* behind her, turned, and almost walked right into Harvey. She let out a tiny shriek, and jumped back.

"Harvey, y-you scared me," she said, visibly trembling.

"Is something wrong?" His hair stuck out in all directions, and he had a thick growth of stubble on his cheeks. His eyes were bloodshot, more bloodshot than she had ever seen them. She could smell sweat mixed with alcohol all over him, and it was all she could do to stand near him. All he was wearing was boxer shorts, and the site of him almost naked, which at one time used to turn her on, now turned her off in a big way. "Not making any plans, are you?" His breath was fetid, like something had crawled down his throat and died.

"No, Harv, no plans. I just got up."

Harvey merely turned, went into the bathroom, and she heard him urinate heavily into the toilet and flush. A moment later he went back into the bedroom and closed the door behind him.

She leaned against the counter next to the sink, and took a deep breath. If she was going to get away, she would have to be very careful, indeed. There was just no telling what Harvey would do.

14

Ninth disappearance in nine months, police baffled

Sioux City - Police are still looking for clues in the recent disappearances of eight young women from the Sioux City area, and now a ninth has been added to the list as of yesterday, police say. Denise Miller, 18, of Sioux City, went out with friends Saturday night to a local dance club, and several hours later disappeared without a trace. Police are advising that all women curb any nighttime activities until the perpetrator or perpetrators have been apprehended. Photographs are being published daily in all the local papers, and flyers have been posted all over town. Police urge anyone who may have any information at all regarding these missing individuals to contact them immediately.

The article was dated in April, three months earlier. Jonathon had driven his father's Ford Ranger into Arlidge, and now sat in the Arlidge County Library, staring at the microfilm scanner, poring over all the state's larger papers, searching for anything even remotely similar to what was happening in Oak Junction.

He had heard about the disappearances, everyone had, it was on the TV news and in all the papers. But, he wasn't sure if there was any connection or not; he would need more evidence than this to connect it with Cain, but it was a start.

He kept scanning, and suddenly saw an article in the same paper, dated the very next day, and knew he had his connection:

Mysterious deaths of livestock leave local farmers searching for answers

Sioux City - Area farmers say that for the past several months their livestock have been mysteriously falling ill and dying, and now the farmers are demanding answers, sources say. Local veterinarians have inspected the animals and taken blood samples, but have yet to find the cause of the illnesses. The livestock consists of mostly cows, but chickens have also died, and even disappeared, and in one case, a family dog fell ill and died virtually overnight. One farmer, who stood watch over his stock during the night, reported seeing one of his cows just 'teeter over' to the ground, and die within several hours.

Jonathon stared at the article for a long time. He thought: *Now I know what you've been up to, you bastard. But why did you leave? Were the police getting too close, or did you just need a change of scenery?* Jonathon thought that it was probably the former, that Cain had been close to being exposed, and skipped town to let things cool down.

But why here? Why Oak Junction?

Jonathon kept searching for any activities in and around Sioux City, which seemed to be at the center of everything. He soon found another article in the Sioux City Herald, dated only a month before:

'Shriveled' corpse found, police searching for leads

Sioux City - Two hikers, whose names are being withheld, discovered the body of a woman in a wooded area about ten miles outside Sioux City. The two made the gruesome discovery early yesterday morning, and immediately notified authorities. Police say they have not identified the body, and in fact are having a hard time pinpointing the women's age because of the unusual condition of the body. Police were willing to speculate that this might be connected to the recent disappearances of eleven young women, but that was as far as they would go on the issue.

Jonathon kept scanning, dizzy with excitement. Then he found an article dated several days after this last one:

Suspect held in connection with disappearances, murder

Sioux City - A suspect was detained and questioned yesterday in connection with the recent disappearances of eleven young women and the bizarre discovery of the shriveled corpse of a woman, sources say. Lucas Cain, 20, of Sioux City, was detained after being apprehended at the site of the most recent discovery, where hikers discovered the shriveled body of a woman early Tuesday morning. Police have not yet been able to identify the body as of yet, but are following up several leads. Cain claimed that he was out walking, and stumbled onto the site mistakenly. He was held for three hours while police searched his apartment and his car, and then later released when no evidence was found to link Cain to the crimes. The Chief of Police pleaded 'no comment' when asked if he still considered Cain a suspect, or was in any way related to the tragedy that occurred shortly after Cain was released, when one of the detectives that questioned Cain suddenly turned his gun on his coworkers, killing three and wounding another before being brought down by detectives.

How can that be? Jonathon thought. *Cain looks like he's at least thirty-five years old, yet according to the date on this paper, a month ago he was twenty. Whatever it is he's doing, it can't be good for him, either. What is his game?*

Jonathon made copies of all the articles, and sat at a secluded spot in the library to consider his options: *Do I risk calling the police? Would they believe me? And what if they did, what then? Send someone into town to investigate? They'd probably be killed, and Cain would figure out a way to brush it under the rug. And then I would die, and so would the hopes of anyone else in town that wasn't a part of Cain's plan. Or was there anyone left? And if I run now, he'll never be stopped, and they'd probably find me anyway, and kill me.*

He killed my parents...

At that last thought, Jonathon realized that he already knew what his only *real* option would be; he would have to find a way to stop Cain, to kill him if he had to, and he would have to act alone, or run the risk of exposing his intentions to the wrong people. He sat in the library for a long time, wondering if he would come out of this whole thing alive.

There *were* people left, ones who for some reason hadn't fallen victim to Cain's spell. Most of them, however, had fallen victim to intimidation and fear, and with quiet compliance had gotten on with their lives, always wondering if they would be the next one chosen for Cain's ritual.

Of course, a small group of town's people had decided that getting live bodies for Cain from outside sources might be the best solution, and Cain himself readily agreed, as long as he had final approval of the methods used to obtain these live bodies.

Cain was just as pleased as pudding to see everyone following his plan, and he rewarded folks one way or the other, even to the point of rewarding some of the farmers with fabulous crops, extra large and healthy; they were the ones who fell in step with Cain. There were a few others who remained reserved about the whole thing, and many who were dead, but all in all, Cain had the town in the palm of his hand.

But while there were those who were too afraid to do anything but give in, there were also those who were too afraid *not* to do anything.

Gil and Louise Garret were among those not influenced by Cain. They had, in fact, been planning a simple escape ever since being forced to watch Evelyn Mott's soul being literally sucked from her by that ungodly apparition that Cain had summoned up from Hell, or wherever it was from.

They were both still in shock over the whole affair, and because they weren't tainted with Cain's evil, it played over and over in their minds, a living nightmare that drove them closer and closer to escape, to getting away from the core of the madness.

It seemed to Gil that escaping sometime in the middle of the night was best, the cover of darkness providing an easy means of slipping out of town unnoticed. Their children had grown and moved away, so it was just the two of them, and Gil thanked God over and over again in his prayers for sparing them this insanity.

Their plan was very simple, and perfectly feasible, at least to them, so they gathered some things together (mostly clothing, money, some food, and of course, pictures of their children), and packed it all into a couple of suitcases and several small bags. Then they simply waited for the right time, even though they knew that *no* time would be exactly right, but there at least had to be a time that *felt* right. A time when they could both summon up enough courage to flee and never look back.

That time came a little more than a week after Jonathon's visit to the Arlidge County Library. It was a Thursday evening when Gil announced the time had come.

"Are you sure?" Louise asked, suddenly frightened at the prospect of really going through with it.

"Sure I'm sure," Gil said. "If we wait any longer we'll never do it. Tonight's a work night, and everyone will be sleeping. We'll just drive right on out of here, and no one will even know we're gone. I've got to protect you somehow."

Louise said, "Oh Gil," and put her arms around him, hugging him for a long time before letting go. "I love you, dear," she said, and went into the kitchen. As soon as she disappeared through the doorway his smile faded, replaced by worry and fear. What he had said had been very gallant, but if the truth were known, Gil was more worried about his own hide than anything else. He had an acute fear of pain and death, and each time he thought of the ritual he pictured *himself* up there, and how he would go crazy, absolutely *mad* if ever faced with that situation. His heart raced just thinking about it.

A few minutes before midnight, they grabbed what belongings they had chosen to take with them, and stacked everything by the kitchen door, which led out onto the driveway. They turned off every light in the house except the kitchen, where they sat at the kitchen table drinking coffee, and waiting. They said nothing for the next hour, both lost in their own worlds of possible outcomes, and they both knew without saying what was going on in the other's mind.

Finally, Gil cleared his throat, and said, "We better go." Louise merely nodded her head, her eyes filling with tears. Gil held her for a while, then said, "I'll go check the windows," and went into the living room. Louise stood and cried, mostly from the sadness that filled her heart at the prospect of leaving their home of so many years. They had many wonderful memories here, in this house they had shared since they were first married, this house where they raised two wonderful boys, both now in college. They were leaving the only life they knew behind, and running blindly out into the world.

Gil peeked through the blinds on the living room window, scanning the street for any signs of life. Luckily, there were no streetlights nearby, the closest one being two houses down. None of the houses seemed to have any lights on, as if everyone was tucked in and fast asleep, and Gil felt a ray of hope glowing inside him. He went back into the kitchen, not knowing that he had missed one crucial thing while checking outside.

Louise was visibly trembling now, fresh tears streaming down her face. "Are you sure we should do this, Gil? What if they catch us?" Gil noticed just how frightened she was, and he held her in his arms again, comforting her, calming her, until he felt the trembling stop. He stepped back, his hands on her shoulders, and said, "I just checked - it's like the whole town is asleep. I'll just bet that no one will even notice anything. Look, you just hang tight, and I'll put everything in the car, and then all you'll have to do is climb in, and we're off." He smiled widely, and she smiled, wiping the tears from her face.

He slowly opened the kitchen door, and night air burst in as he stole out into the darkness and opened the trunk of his old Ford Galaxy sedan. The stars shone overhead, and the air was alive with a symphony of crickets.

What he had missed earlier when peeking out the window was so small that anyone would have missed it - the glow of a cigarette. Across the street and one house down, a man was sitting on the steps of his front porch smoking a cigarette and taking in the cool night air. If Gil had watched for another few seconds, he might have seen the glow of the cherry as the man took a drag and blew it out into the night air.

Gil brought out two suitcases and tucked them neatly into the trunk, and went back inside the house. The man across the street waited until Gil returned inside, then flicked his smoke away and went into his house. A minute later, he was back on his porch, watching as Gil loaded more bags into the trunk of his car.

Louise, no longer crying, was sitting at the kitchen table with a worried look on her face. Gil came in, closing the door behind him, and sat down across from her. "Well, this is it. Are you ready?" he asked.

She merely nodded, and they both stood. Gil held the door open for her, then followed her outside. He opened the passenger side door for her, and the old hinges creaked, causing them both to flinch. That was when Louise looked up, and her heart sank as she simultaneously saw the sheriff's cruiser pulling to the curb in front of their house, and the tiny orange glow of a cigarette being smoked across the street in the darkness of someone's porch.

"Gil, look," she whispered.

Gil saw Sheriff Craven's car stopping at the curb, and said, "Get in the car, Louise."

"But Gil...."

"Get in the goddamned car!" She sat down on the seat, and Gil slammed the door shut before heading around the back of the car to the driver side.

Craven's voice cut through the air like a knife, echoing up and down the empty street. "Gil, you just hold up there. I need to talk to you." He started across the lawn toward them.

Gil climbed in the car, locked his door, and said, " Lock your door, hurry!" He pulled out his keys, stuck one in the ignition, and started the engine.

"Gil, maybe we should wait," Louise said, looking over her shoulder at the oncoming figure.

Gil jammed the car in reverse and punched the gas. Tires squealed as they lurched backwards into the street. They could hear Craven shouting something, and then they were already shooting forward into the darkness, the dash lights splashing dim green light on their faces. Gil thought: *This old beauty's still got some balls.* Then he glanced sideways at Louise, and had another thought: *I can't let them get me, no way, no way...*

Gil's house was on Church Street, between 3rd and 4th Avenues, and even though he *needed* to go west over to 3rd, he purposely went east and swung a quick right on 4th, heading south toward Fairview Street.

Gil checked the rearview mirror, and saw only blackness behind him. "See, Louise? No one's following us. It's gonna be ok." But he gritted his teeth nervously. Just when he thought he would be able to take 4th all the way down to Main, flashing red and blues appeared in the rearview, spinning colors lighting up the street like some bizarre disco ball. "Oh, shit," Gil said.

Gil swung another right on Fairview, jumping the curb and almost knocking down a street sign. Louise's head hit the roof of the car (the Ford no longer had seatbelts, hadn't had them in years - they were so frayed and worn that Gil had torn them out), and she cried out, holding the top of her head.

"Gil, that hurt! Please stop, you're going to get us killed!" Tears were rolling down her cheeks now.

"If we stop now, we'll be killed for sure! Don't you get it, Louise? We have to keep going!" Gil yelled, as his eyes kept glancing up at the rearview mirror.

He gunned the engine, and it responded with the deep moan of a four-barrel carb. Craven wheeled onto Fairview just as Gil was turning left onto 3rd. Gil shot down 3rd, and a few seconds later, Craven appeared behind him, and started gaining on him. Four barrel or no, the Ford was no match for Craven's cruiser. Craven quickly caught up, and bumped into the back of the Ford.

"GIL, STOP!" Louise screamed, clutching at the seat.

"SHUT UP! DO YOU HEAR ME? JUST SHUT UP!" Gil screamed so loud that he literally choked on his own words.

Craven again bumped into the Ford, this time whip lashing their heads back, and Gil was momentarily disoriented as he finally reached Main and pulled a right, swinging in a wide arc to the other side of the street, where he hit the curb in another head jarring bounce. Louise screamed and clutched the sides of her head, a woman on the verge of a nervous breakdown.

They managed to make it to the point where 1st Avenue intersected with Main and headed south toward Zeb's station, and the frontage road that led to the highway. Craven didn't just smack them this time - he *smashed* into the rear of the Ford just as Gil was twisting left onto 1st. The Ford's rear end fishtailed, and Gil came very close to losing control. The blacktop abruptly ended and the dirt road began, and rocks flew up and bounced off the underside of the car.

Gil looked in the rearview and saw the red and blue lights cutting through the dust cloud behind him, and flashing off the trees scattered on both sides of the road. The Ford's headlights pierced the dark before them, and Gil had a clear view of the road ahead.

"Gil, please! I'm begging you!"

Gil looked at her and shouted, "For once in your life, will you shut the fuck up?" Louise looked at him like he had just slapped her in the face. Then Gil turned his attention back to the road, and his heart leaped in his throat as he saw a figure standing there.

Cain!

Cain, dressed all in black, stood dead center in the middle of the road, and Gil had just enough time to see him illuminated in the glare of the headlights, sneering face and eyes glowing like silver coins, before he swerved to the left; it was more out of instinct than anything, a snap decision.

The Ford slid sideways on the gravel before straightening out again, which greatly reduced their momentum. Otherwise, Louise would surely have gone through the windshield when they hit the tree. Instead, her head bounced off the windshield, leaving a spider web of cracks expanding outward from the point of impact, and she immediately fell unconscious.

Gil had seen the tree rushing up toward them in the headlights, and a second later his head and chest slammed into the steering wheel. The world swirled around him, and he was vaguely aware of steam escaping from under the hood of the car, and an eerie silence surrounded him, then darkness.

When Gil woke up, the world was rushing past him. He tried to move, but for some reason couldn't move his arms or his body. Then he dimly realized that he was handcuffed in the back of Sheriff Craven's police cruiser, with a seat belt and shoulder strap holding him in place. He turned his head to the left, and a bolt of pain shot into his skull. He closed his eyes, then opened them and saw Louise strapped onto the seat next to him, still unconscious. Tiny rivers of blood ran down her face and dripped onto her blouse. He felt something sticky on his face as well, and when he tried to move, another bolt of pain hit him, this time in his chest.

Gil groaned and tried to sit back, but only found his handcuffed hands were unwelcome obstacles.

"You should've stopped, Gil. Things would have been a lot easier. But now, I don't know," Craven's deep voice said from the front seat. "You're lucky to be alive."

"Where are we going?" Gil croaked.

"To jail, of course. Fleeing from a police officer is a crime, don't you know?" Craven chuckled at this last comment, and Gil felt sheer dread creeping up on him. "Now you'll have to answer to Mr.

Cain, and I don't think you're going to like what he has to say. But don't worry, we'll get someone in to take care of those wounds for you."

The world was swirling again, swimming in circles, and Craven's last words seemed to come from very far away.

Then, darkness again.

When they pulled into the parking lot behind the small brick building that served as headquarters for Sheriff Craven, both the Garrets were conscious. The only light in the parking lot was a small glass globe mounted on the wall above the rear entrance, and its dim yellow glow barely stretched beyond the doorway.

Craven parked next to the door and shut off the engine. Gil turned to Louise; she was conscious and staring blankly at the back of the driver's seat, several trickles of blood drying on her face. He was about to say something, but changed his mind. He was more worried about what was going to happen to them now - to *him*.

The car seemed to lift up as Craven hefted his heavy frame out and went around to the other side to where Gil sat. He opened the door and said, "Alright Gil, you first." He reached across and unbuckled the seat belt, then helped Gil get out of the car. As soon as he straightened up pain flared in his chest, and he doubled over, and would have lost his balance and fallen, had Craven not been holding on to him.

"God, it hurts," Gil said. Craven said nothing. Instead, he led Gil over to the metal door, pulled a set of keys out of one pocket, and unlocked the deadbolt. Craven reached inside and switched the overhead fluorescents on, revealing the small booking room. To the right was a huge metal desk piled high with forms, with a small room behind that, and to the left several folding metal chairs were lined up against the opposite wall. Straight ahead was a door that led to the front office area, and to the right of that, a small hallway in which were two holding cells.

Craven guided Gil down the hall to the holding cells, Gil crouched over the whole time. Craven took out his keys again and unlocked one of the cells. He removed Gil's handcuffs. "Get in," he said.

Gil struggled over to the bunk attached to the back wall, and sat down very slowly, trying to keep the pain to a minimum. The bunk consisted of a blanket, pillow, and a mattress that was only two or three inches thick. Along the wall next to the bunk were a stainless steel sink and toilet. Gil noticed that the adjoining cell was identical.

Craven shut the cell door and turned the lock. On the other side of the bars, Gil sat bent over on the bunk, arms crossed over his chest, his face a grimace of pain.

"I'm in a lot of pain, Sheriff. I need help. Look, I'm sorry, I just got scared, you know? I never meant to cause any trouble. I swear, we'll never do it again," Gil pleaded.

"It's out of my hands, Gil. You should have stayed put while you had the chance." He disappeared down the hall before Gil could say anything else. He went outside, and opened the door on Louise's side of the car. He unbuckled her seat belt and helped her stand up. He saw the dried blood on her face, and said, "Don't you worry, ok? I'll get some help over here as soon as possible."

She looked into Craven's face and said, "I didn't want to go, Sheriff, I swear." Tears spilled down her cheeks. "Gil was so hell bent on running, I didn't know what to do. We didn't mean any harm, honest."

"I'm sorry, Louise, it's just the way things have to be. Let's go inside now." He took her inside and down the hall, unlocking the door to the other cell. He removed her cuffs, and she went inside and sat on the bunk.

"Why are you putting her in there?" Gil asked.

"I think she wants to be alone right now, what do you think?" Craven said, glaring through the bars at him. Craven went down the hall, leaving them alone in their cells.

"Louise? Louise, are you alright?" Gil got nothing but silence in return.

A short while later, Gil heard someone enter the back office, and then Craven appeared with Betty Atwood, the waitress from Nate's diner. She was carrying a large paper sack, and she plopped it down on one of the two folding chairs that sat directly across from the cells. She was wearing light blue sweats, and her red hair was in disarray, as if she had just woken up (Sheriff Craven had, in fact, banged on her screen door until she answered, half asleep and clad in a robe).

Louise seemed to be asleep, so Craven addressed Gil.

"Betty here used to do some volunteer work over at the hospital in Arlidge. Now, she was good enough to come over at this hour and help you two out, so I expect you to show her some respect."

Betty smiled at Craven, and then pulled a large plastic bowl out of the sack, along with a couple of washcloths. "Where can I fill this up?"

Craven pointed to the sink inside the cell. "Right over there, my dear." He unlocked the cell door and stepped inside with her. She went over to the sink and looked around for a moment, trying to figure out how to turn on the water.

"Just push the button on the wall," Craven said. She pushed it, and cold water spilled noisily into the basin. After a few moments, it stopped. "You have to keep pushing it," the sheriff said.

Betty pushed the button several times until the water warmed up a bit, and then she filled the bowl. The noise had awakened Louise, who was now sitting on the bunk with her back to the wall, knees pulled up to her chest. The dried blood on her face had turned a dark rusty color, and she made no effort to clean it off. It seemed to enhance the angry vibes that were obviously coming from her side of the room.

Betty dabbed the wash cloth into the water, and began to clean Gil's face and the top of his forehead, where a nasty goose egg had swelled up; it reminded Betty of the cartoons she used to watch as a kid, the ones where someone would get banged over the head with a hammer, and a huge goose egg would instantly pop up.

"Raise your head a little more," she said.

"It's hard to straighten up. My chest hit the steering wheel. God, it hurts," he said, his face contorting as he attempted to lift his head up more.

"You may have cracked a couple of ribs. I've got some sample packs of pain medicine - Frank, will you go get me some water?"

Frank? Gil thought, *Frank?*

Craven returned with a paper cup filled with water from the cooler in the front office. Betty handed Gil two large white pills, took the water from the sheriff and handed it to Gil. "Give him two every six to eight hours if he needs it," she said. "Do you need something, too, honey?" she asked Louise through the bars. Louise absently nodded her head.

They left Gil's cell, and Craven locked it up tight. They went into Louise's cell, where Betty dumped out the pinkish water from the bowl, rinsed it, and filled it with fresh water. She gently cleaned Louise's face; found a bump on the top of her head encrusted with dried blood. She cleaned it, Louise wincing every time Betty touched the bloody split in the middle of the bump.

"You're lucky," Betty said. "It's not bleeding that bad, but you'll have to keep holding a bandage to it." She went and pulled some gauze out of the paper sack and gave it to Louise. Craven brought in another cup of water, and Betty gave two of the pills to Louise. Her hands shook as she took the cup of water and swallowed the pills.

Betty stroked her hair. "You gonna be alright, hon?" Louise offered a weak smile and nodded.

They left the cell, and Craven locked the door. The loud click as the bolt hit home had a strange finality to it.

"You two get some rest," the sheriff said. "You'll probably have a visitor in the morning, so be prepared for that." The two left, and a moment later, the door to the rear parking lot opened, and then closed, the deadbolt locking into place. The cells were blanketed with silence.

"I'm sorry, Louise. I didn't think anything would happen. I'm so sorry."

"You should be, Gil. To tell you the truth, I don't think you were thinking at all."

"Well, maybe they'll -"

"Shut up, Gil. Just shut up, and leave me alone." She laid down on the bunk facing the wall, pulling the green army blanket over herself.

Gil sat in silence, fear beginning to gnaw at his insides. All kinds of terrible scenarios raced through his mind, and he wondered what it would be like to die.

It was still very early in the morning when Gil woke up to find Cain sitting on one of the folding chairs across from the cells. There were no windows in that section of the jail, the only light being that of the fluorescents, which seemed to leave the cells in a neutral zone between night and day.

"Good morning, Gil," Cain said. He wore jeans and a sweatshirt, which he would have to change later as the temperature rose, baking the earth in its midday heat.

Gil had only slept a couple of hours, and that was only because of the pain pills Betty had given him earlier. Now the pain was back, and as he tried to sit up, it shot into his chest as if a stake had been driven into his ribs. He groaned and doubled over, again clutching his chest as if it would somehow relieved the pain.

"Hurts pretty bad, huh?" Cain asked, regarding Gil with sadistic curiosity.

"Yeah, I think something's broken," Gil said.

"You made the wrong decision, Gil, took the wrong path. I'm very disappointed. But yet again, I'm very happy about the whole thing. Do you know why, Gil?"

Gil shook his head.

"Because in a few weeks, we're going to have another town meeting, and you're going to be the guest of honor. How does that make you feel?"

Louise sat up on her bunk, rubbing her eyes and yawning.

Cain said, "Ah, and you, the innocent victim. Dragged into this whole mess by this idiot. And yet, you were willing enough, weren't you? All you had to do was say no."

With some effort, Gil stood and shuffled over to the bars. He grasped them and put his face between them. "We were just scared, Mr. Cain. We didn't know what to do. I swear we'll never do it again. Never."

"I told you we would get into trouble," Louise said. "Please, Mr. Cain, we'll be good, I promise. My *husband* just got a little jumpy." She put a lot of emphasis the word husband, glaring momentarily over at Gil.

"Oh, I understand," Cain said. "We all get a little jumpy from time to time."

"So you'll let us go?" Gil asked.

Cain stood, stepped over to Gil, and offered his hand. "Take my hand, Gil." Gil stepped back and hesitated. "Take it." He reached out and grabbed Cain's hand, and Cain's grip got unbearably tight.

The sky was red, filled with black clouds that drifted slowly from one horizon to the next. The landscape was a barren, sandy wasteland, littered with bloody corpses as far as the eye could see. It was scorching hot here, but the pain in his chest was gone.

He walked among the dead, and watched in horror as some moved and twitched, even though most had at least one limb missing. The blood ran from their stumps, absorbing into the sand, being *sucked* into the sand. A man with no arms or legs gawked up at him, his lips moving in soundless expression, eyes rolling around in their sockets.

Then he heard Cain's voice.

"Look at them, Gil. The weak, the frightened. They chose the wrong path. Like you, they just could not accept the inevitable. Now, they feed *him* with their life's blood. *You* will feed him, Gil!"

A short distance away, the ground burst open with a spray of sand, and then *he* rose up, the beast Gil had seen during the ritual in the old cornfield. His wormlike body oozed out of the sand as he advanced on Gil. He thought his heart was going to explode from his chest. He tried to move, but was no longer in control of himself.

The beast reared back and roared into the crimson sky....

Gil was still screaming when he realized he was back in the jail cell. He stopped, but it seemed like a residue of the scream was still present in the room, overlapping the silence. He was soaked in sweat, and the pain in his chest again flared up. He worked his way over to his bunk and sat down, bending over with his arms crossed over his chest in another attempt to ease the pain.

Louise sat on her bunk, trembling in the aftermath of what she thought was going to be her husband's death. He had gone stiff as a board, and his eyes had looked as if they were going to pop right out of his idiot head. But when he had started to scream (that was the point at which she thought he would crumple dead to the floor), Cain released his grip, and Gil came back to reality.

"Make yourselves comfortable," Cain said. "You're going to be here a while." He walked down the hall toward the back office, his new tennis shoes squeaking on the floor.

15

Before witnessing the ritual in the woods that night several years before, Lucas never realized, never really stopped to think, that behind the façade of the world as he had known it was another, darker world, one filled with unimaginable beings. But as he translated more of the book, he soon discovered where the darkness in his heart had come from, why he was so fascinated with death.

The book was filled with incantations for performing impossible tasks and summoning demons to the mortal world to perform specific functions. It described the worlds where they were kings; rulers of places filled with torture, death, and trapped souls. These demon kings could bestow upon humans supernatural powers not meant for the sunlit world of people.

Lucas was intrigued by one demon in particular, the writer of the book, and one of the most powerful of all demons: Morgoroth. But, intrigued as he was, he still had enough fear left in him to prevent him from using the book. He knew the time would come, though, and he also knew that there would be no turning back.

He needed a place of his own that would afford him more privacy, some place where he could experiment with the book without interruption or fear of discovery.

Although his parents were still disappointed over his decision to quit school, they were hopeful at the prospect of Lucas finding a job, so they allowed him to drive the truck into Sioux City to search for employment.

After a week of searching, of endless applications and interviews, Lucas Cain landed his first job in a small bakery in downtown Sioux City. It was full time, and the pay was decent enough, and he could ride into town with his father every day. In fact, he had to be there earlier than his father, but it didn't seem to bother Mr. Cain at all; Lucas realized that getting up outrageously early every day and going to work pleased his father, who would go to a nearby diner to drink coffee and read the newspaper until his own shift started.

In his mind, riding to work every day with his son was almost like a bonding experience, and he always had plenty of small talk to go along with the ride. But Lucas only heard half of what his father said because he was always so distant and distracted, and the words sounded foreign to his ears.

One morning, as they bounced and rumbled in the pick-up down the dirt access road that led to their property, Lucas made an announcement.

"Hey dad, after work today, would you mind stopping at a bank so I can start a savings account?"

His father was tickled pink at the prospect of his son starting his own bank account. It was one step closer to independence, to manhood.

"Sure, Lucas," he said, smiling. "I'll help you if you want."

Lucas smiled sheepishly. "Well, I kinda wanted to do it on my own, you know?"

"Oh, you bet. At least let me recommend a bank for you, ok?"

"Thanks, dad. I didn't know which one to use anyway."

This is too easy, Lucas thought.

His father went right on smiling and driving, and Lucas again let his thoughts drift ahead, to the time when he would leave home for good, leave his old life behind for a new life that was still shrouded in mystery, yet waited patiently for him to become a part of its timeless cycle.

A year later Lucas had his own apartment, a studio on the fifth floor of a dilapidated five story building in downtown Sioux City. It wasn't much, but it suited him perfectly. The rent was cheap, and he could take a bus or even walk to work every day. Sometimes, he liked to sit by the open window and watch the activity down on the street. The city was noisy, filled with people, and he loved being a part of it.

At night, as he lie in bed (a sofa sleeper he bought used at a thrift store - he and his father had a hell of a time getting it on the elevator, but they managed to barely escape having to tackle five flights of stairs with it), he oftentimes heard the downstairs neighbors arguing at the tops of their lungs, which would more times than not be followed by a brisk pounding on their door by the building superintendent or the cops.

Lucas always thought it hilarious how it could go from nuclear war to dead silence in a split second with just a knock on the door.

And then there was the book. He had pretty much translated the whole thing, and every day he took it out, touching it, feeling its static current flow into him, calling to him. As time went on, his fear subsided, and his longing to use the book grew stronger. He had insane dreams of worlds beyond comprehension, worlds that thrived on death and destruction, on blood and greed. At first the dreams were rather disturbing, even for him, but he eventually accepted them, even enjoyed them.

And his heart grew darker.

He had heard somewhere that the name Lucas meant 'bringer of light'. That disturbed him to no end. He rather enjoyed his last name, though, and its implications, so he started to refer to himself as Cain. He even told his coworkers to call him 'Cain', and at first they laughed, but it eventually caught on because it seemed to match his new demeanor.

It was just one more step of his journey into darkness, one more step toward the total corruption of his very soul. And then one day, he could stand it no more. He was going to use the book.

He chose a Friday night because it would allow all weekend for him to experiment with the book. But actually, he was only concerned with one part of the book: an incantation that would bestow upon him powers over the physical world, and with his touch, over the mind of man. The possibilities were endless, and he trembled at the thought of taking his first step into this strange and wondrous land.

And so it was on that summer night, a good year before he had ever heard of Oak Junction, when he opened the book and stepped into his new life.

An hour later, he was still sitting on the couch, bathed in sweat, delirious and incoherent, eyes darting frantically around the room. He had taken the first step, and it was a much larger step than he ever dreamt it would be. The room started to spin, faster and faster, until it was just a blur, and then it stopped as he fell over unconscious.

He awoke later with a start, sitting up and grabbing himself to see if he was all there. His clothes were still damp, but the delirium was gone, and now there was an odd calmness to the room, like the calm before a storm; only this was the calm after the storm.

The book still lay open on the coffee table, open to the very page he had used, so he reached over and closed the book. It seemed to have a new feeling to it, a new energy, subtle yet more powerful than anything he'd ever known. He thought about what had happened when he had recited the words, and shivered. He put the book away, and pulled out the hide-a-bed. *He stripped out of his clothes and crawled under the covers. He stared at the ceiling for a while, listening to the late night downtown traffic drift up through his open window. Finally, sleep found him.*

When Cain woke up, the sun had already risen, and judging by the noise, the world outside his window was busy with its normal Saturday routine. Soon, the apartment would be bathed in heat. He climbed out of bed, and without making it, folded it up and shoved it into its frame. He threw the cushions onto the couch, then went into the bathroom and urinated.

When he returned, he sat on the couch, the events of the night before replaying in his head. He had indeed stepped into a new life, for now he was required to perform certain tasks in return for his new powers. He had to give souls to his new god, which meant committing murder; however, he *didn't have to commit murder, the beast would take care of that.*

But little did he know how much he would come to enjoy the act of murder. For now, it was mysterious territory, this thing called death, but oh, how he desired to learn more about it.

He noticed the coffee table was still on the other side of the room, where he'd pushed it the night before in order to open the hide-a-bed. He went to stand up, but changed his mind. He stared at the table, willing it to return to its place on its own. He concentrated, focusing on nothing but the table, but to no avail. He felt anger rising inside, and he thought: Why won't the fucking thing move?

Just as he turned his head he heard a slight movement from the other side of the room, and again he focused his attention on the table. It seemed different, as if he were looking at it from a different angle. He tried again to move it, straining so hard he thought his head would explode.

The table seemed to be denying him, and he fell back against the couch, frustrated and dizzy. When the dizziness subsided, he sat up straight and yelled, "Move, you bastard, move!" His eyes went wide as the table whispered across the carpet a few feet, then stopped in the middle of the room. Cain laughed out loud.

"It worked, it really worked!" he said, and suddenly the prospect of participating in the act of murder, or whatever it was, didn't seem so bad after all.

He pulled on a pair of jeans and a tank top, a pair of worn out high tops, dragged a comb through his hair, and went out the door, heading for the elevator. It shivered as it descended, and Cain wondered how long it would be before it finally gave up and slammed to the bottom of the shaft.

It came to a rough stop, and the doors opened to release its only passenger. He walked across the threadbare carpet to the front entrance, and found himself standing outside on the sidewalk in the noonday sun. He donned a pair of reflector sunglasses, and headed west on 10th Street, wind blowing through his long black hair.

The traffic was heavy, and downtown was resonant with its constant drone, along with the strong odors of gasoline and exhaust fumes. There were a lot of bodies out on this fine summer day as well, and Cain watched as the stream of people flowed by him, seemingly oblivious of his existence.

He stopped and leaned against the red brick façade of a department store, contemplating his next move.

A couple of women stopped in front of one of the store's windows, pointing at the merchandise and nodding their heads in approval. One of them had her hair tied back in a ponytail, and was wearing a white sun visor. Cain focused on the visor, and it suddenly flew off of her head as if a strong wind had taken hold of it, and fell to the ground.

"Oh, hell," he heard her exclaim, as she bent down to pick up the visor. It slid down the sidewalk a few feet, and she followed along, still bent over. Just as she was about to grab it, it slid a few more feet along, right into the path of oncoming pedestrians. She snatched it up just before it got trampled, and returned to where her friend stood laughing in front of the display window. She had a puzzled look in her eyes, and shook her head before pulling the visor back on. The two moved on, passing right in front of Cain as they strolled down the sidewalk.

Cain felt his confidence growing, yet it seemed to be growing in a negative *direction instead of positive. Nonetheless, it was getting stronger, and he could feel its warmth rising in him like anger.*

An old man approached, leading a small terrier on a leash. Even though the day grew hotter by the minute, the man wore a tattered gray sweater that looked about fifty years old. He wore glasses with the flip-up shades in front, standard issue for the retirement crowd. He was almost entirely bald, save for a few strands of white hair fluttering around the sides of his head.

Cain noticed with amusement how the sun glinted off the top of his head as he stood by while the terrier sniffed at a signpost. It lifted its leg and pissed on the post, sniffed at it again, and waited for its master to lead him on.

The old man seemed to be preoccupied with something across the street, and he lifted his dark lenses and craned his head to the left, squinting for better focus. The terrier sat at his feet panting, tongue hanging out of its mouth, dripping drool onto the sidewalk. The leash was slack; in fact, the old fart barely had a hold of it.

Cain's mind filled with dark thoughts, and the urge was irresistible. He focused on the dog, and let the hatred rise in him again.

Then, he pushed with his mind.

The terrier yelped as it skidded out into the street between two parked cars, yanking the leash right out of the old man's withered hand.

"Buster!" he called in a gruff voice. The terrier yelped one more time, perhaps from the force of the push, or from terror, or from both, but its last plea for help was cut off as a car thumped over its midsection, squirting its entrails out onto the road. "Oh my God!" the old man exclaimed as he stumbled out into the road.

The car stopped in the middle of the lane, and a man jumped out and ran over to where the dog lay in a pool of blood. The old man was there, saying, "Oh my Buster, my poor buster..."

"Mister, I'm so sorry, he just ran out in front of me. I'm sorry. Is there anything I can do?"

"You killed my dog, isn't that enough?" he asked, looking down at the splattered remains.

"Look, I didn't mean to, he ran out in front of me."

The old man wasn't listening. He just stared at the remains of his dead pet.

"Fine, have it your way," the man said. He looked around him, then went back to his car and drove off as if leaving the scene of a crime. A few passersby had gathered around the old man, attempting to help. The traffic in the lane behind them had stopped, and now some of the vehicles were pulling into the other lane and going around them, some cruising by slowly to get an eyeful of the crushed dog in the street.

Cain left his post in front of the building, leaving the chaos in his wake. His feeling of power was extreme, pulsing and throbbing in his veins. He was anxious for more, hungry for more, and he had *other experiments in mind. And he had all day. He strode down 10th Street, a man with a mission.*

A few blocks down, he came to the bank where his father had taken him to open his first savings account, the same bank he had used ever since then to cash his paychecks. He had his most recent paycheck in the back pocket of his jeans, and he had made sure to endorse it on the back before leaving his apartment.

The bank closed early on Saturdays, but he still had just enough time to cash his check. He went inside the air-conditioned environment of the bank, nodding absently at the security guard standing inside the doorway. There were only two other customers in the bank, and the atmosphere was subdued, grinding down for the day.

"Next? Can I help you?" a teller asked. A girl with blonde frizzy hair smiled at him over the counter. He recognized her from his frequent visits to the bank. She looked young enough to be his little sister.

"How are you, today?" she asked.

"I'm just great," Cain said, smiling broadly. "How are you doing?"

"Pretty good. Just getting ready to go home," she laughed.

"Well, before you go, would you cash my check for me?" he asked, putting the check face up on the counter.

"Oh, I think I can do that," she teased. She reached for the check.

What had the book said? The mind of man with just a touch?

Just as she picked up the check, he reached out and touched her hand.

One hundred dollars more!

"I'm sorry," he said, "but I can't remember if I endorsed that or not." He pulled his hand back, and she flipped the check over and saw his signature.

"You sure did," she said. She opened her cash drawer and counted out the bills, grabbed some coins out of their slots, and began to count out the money on the counter.

"Ok, there's one hundred, one hundred fifty, two hundred, twenty, forty, sixty, eighty, three hundred, twenty, forty, fifty, five and six, and forty two cents."

But there was one more bill in her hand, and she laid it on the pile of cash, which she slid across the counter to Cain. She winked at him, and said, "You have a great day now."

"Thank you very much, you too," he said, grabbing the pile of bills and pocketing them. He scooped the change up, smiled one more time at her, and left, nodding again at the guard by the door.

He walked down the street a few blocks, and stopped in front of a deli. He wasn't hungry, though - what he really wanted was to count the money the teller had given him. He remembered exactly how much his check had been, even had the stub to prove it. Three hundred fifty six dollars and forty-two cents.

He pulled the wad of bills out of his pocket and counted. A smile crossed his face. Four hundred fifty six dollars and forty-two cents. She had given him an extra hundred. He had told her to, and she had come through with a wink. Just one touch.

He stood outside the deli for a little while, watching foot traffic go by, and tried to put suggestions into people without a touch. There was no response. That was it, then, just like the book said: The mind of man with just a touch. Cain could not remember when he had felt so good, so high.

He went into the deli and ordered a sandwich to celebrate.

Cain's first ritual really wasn't a ritual at all; it was more like plain old, cold-blooded murder. It was an experience he would remember the rest of his days, to watch a life slipping away with his own eyes, to see the frightened stare of someone in the throes of death. It stoked the fire within, fed the blackness in his heart, and washed away any goodness that remained. He had truly turned to the other side, and he didn't bother looking back.

A week after he had greased the dog on 10th Street, he walked onto a used car lot on Grandview Boulevard to find himself a ride. He was getting very tired of hoofing it everywhere he went, and he simply detested buses. It was time for some wheels.

When he came upon the car lot, he recognized it from the commercials he saw while watching late night TV. Grady's Used Cars, owned and operated by the one, the only, Smilin' Jim Grady. He was one slick talker, all right, and he had a lot of slick deals, right here in the heart of Sioux City, so come on down and pay us a visit.

The lot was festooned with strands of multi-colored pennants, stretching out from the small white building in the center of the lot that served as the office, to all corners of the lot. There were also strings of flashing gold lights that ran from pole to pole around the *perimeter of the lot, and when night fell, Smilin' Jim would flick the switch in order to grab folk's attentions. And that kept him smilin'.*

Most of the cars were older models, shined and primed to look in tip top shape, when actually, most of them had left their better days far behind them. But, they glittered and gleamed in the hot afternoon sun, and Smilin' Jim would tell you that these babies had lots of mileage left on them, oh yes, they just didn't make cars like that anymore.

To Cain, they still looked like shit, but there was one vehicle on the lot that really caught his attention, really pushed his button.

*He browsed between the cars, waiting for Smilin' Jim to make his appearance. He knew it was only a matter of time, like flies on shit. A man with slicked back hair (*slick hair for the slick talker, Cain thought*) and a plaid sport coat that was louder than the shine on the cars came out of the office and made a bee-line for Cain. He wore sunglasses that he could have stolen off Elvis himself.*

"Afternoon, son! Afternoon! Jim Grady, smilin' that is," he said, smiling and revealing a set of choppers that would be more at home in a moose's mouth. He clutched Cain's hand in a hearty handshake. Cain could see the sun reflected on the Elvis glasses. "You look like a young man that's ready for a good deal!"

"You bet I am," Cain said. "I see your commercials all the time, so this is the first place I thought of."

Two can play at this game, *Cain thought.*

"Well, I'm really glad to hear that, son, really glad you decided to pay us a visit."

Cain went dead serious and got right up in Smilin' Jims face and asked, "The problem is, can I trust you?" Smilin' Jim's animal smile faltered, and then Cain burst out laughing, patting Jim on the back. And then Smilin' Jim was laughing, pointing at Cain with one thick finger.

The mind of man with a touch...

"Oh, you're a funny one, alright," Jim said. "Can't get enough of that *around here."*

"Anything to keep you Smilin', Jim," Cain said.

Jim laughed out loud. "Say, aren't you one? I'd say you picked the right place to come to today. Bet you're gonna sweet talk me right out of one of these fine automobiles, am I right?"

"You got me pegged," Cain admitted.

"That's ok, son, that's what I'm here for, to pass the good deals on to good folks like yourself. Now, tell me, is this your first car?"

"Yeah, my very first, so I was hoping to get something reliable, you know, low maintenance."

"Well, like I said before, you've come to the right place. Let me show you a few of our models over-"

"Oh, I've already picked out the one I want," Cain said.

"Oh? And what model did you have in mind on this fine day?"

"That one over there," Cain said, pointing to a car that was parked next to the office. "I want that one right there." He pointed at a black Cadillac with tinted windows. It was by far the sweetest ride on the lot.

"Sorry to disappoint you, son, but that one's not for sale. Oh no, that baby's mine. Nineteen seventy-seven mint condition Cadillac. Runs like a dream. Yes sir, the only car for me. What else can I interest you in today?" Smilin' Jim asked.

"I really, really like the Caddy," Cain said.

"Yeah, she's a beauty, ain't she? Too bad she's not for sale. But we have a lot of other cars for you to choose from, so why don't we take a look?" He waved his arm away from the Caddy that stood like a black jewel in the hot summer sun.

"Well, I guess I'll be going, then," Cain said, and turned to leave.

"Just like that? I'm sure we can come up with something for you, and probably right in your price range, too."

Cain said, "Look, you're a nice man, and everything, but I just need to think about it for a while, I guess. Thanks, anyway." He stuck his hand out, and Smilin' Jim grasped it firmly and shook it. And Cain held tight while he did some heavy thinking.

Just a touch...

"You just take your sweet time, son, and come back to see us when you're ready. We'll help you get the car you need."

Cain released his grip and walked toward the street, and when Smilin' Jim called out to him, his face cracked wide with a grin.

"Wait a minute, son. Come on back here, now," Jim said, a confused look in his eyes. Cain dropped the silly grin and went back to where Smilin' Jim was standing, which happened to be right next to the Cadillac.

"You have something for me?" Cain said, dropping the act.

"Well, I was thinking. How about if I just give you this here car, just for being a nice guy." He patted the hood, leaving a sweaty handprint that evaporated in seconds.

"That's mighty nice of you, Jim." He shook Jim's hand again.

"You know, it just so happens, I've got the title to this here baby right inside. Don't want to leave too much laying around the house for the wife to get her mitts on, if you know what I mean," he said, and he stood confused for a moment, then said, "Come right on in."

Cain followed him into the coolness of the office, and over to a desk against one wall. Jim took out a key ring from his slacks and unlocked a filing cabinet next to the desk. He pulled open the top drawer, and flipped through the files, finally lifting out a manila folder and placing it on his desk.

"And, it just so happens, I'm a notary public," he said, and again he seemed to dwell on what he had just said for a moment before moving on. "Ok, I'll just sign here where it says 'lien release', and you just have to sign there, where it says 'new lien holder'." He produced a notary seal from a desk drawer and stamped the title.

"There, she's all yours. Signed, sealed, and delivered. Take good care of her, son."

"Oh, I will," Cain said, and shook Smilin' Jim Grady's hand one last time. Jim handed him the keys to car, and sat down behind his desk, lost in confusion.

Cain climbed into the Caddy, which was rather hot from the midday sun, and started the engine. It came to life with ease, and Cain switched on the air conditioning before pulling out into the street.

Meanwhile, Smilin' Jim Grady sat behind his desk, watching the clock on the wall tick the minutes away. He had to wait exactly fifteen minutes. He didn't know how he knew that, but fifteen minutes was how long he had to wait before carrying out his last act as the sweet talkin', car lot walkin', Smilin' Jim Grady.

At exactly fifteen minutes, Jim opened a desk drawer, the same one he had produced the notary stamp from, only now he produced a .38 caliber pistol he kept for emergencies. It was the same gun Cain had caught site of when Jim had opened the drawer the first time. Right before Cain shook his hand for the last time.

He put the gun in the pocket of his sport coat, grabbed a set of keys off the board mounted on the wall behind the desk, went outside and climbed into a 1989 Chevy Celebrity.

He drove out to the suburbs, out to his five-bedroom home with the two-car garage and swimming pool, where he promptly shot his wife through the head as she sat on the sofa watching a soap opera. He then sat down at the kitchen table and wrote a short suicide note before putting the gun to his own head.

The full moon was still several weeks away, but Cain didn't want to wait until then to perform his first ritual; either way, he had to perform the ritual during the full moon in order to keep his powers. But, he'd had a taste of things to come, and he was hungry for more. He would perform one now, just to quench his growing thirst for death, and perform one later, to quench his new god's thirst. He was like a child who couldn't wait until Christmas to open his gifts.

And so it was on a sunny Friday afternoon when Cain, still smelling of fresh bread and doughnuts, stopped off after work at a hardware store, purchased several items, and threw them into the trunk of his new car. He wasn't quite sure how the night would turn out, so he wanted to play it safe, just in case.

He parked the Caddy in the parking lot behind his apartment building (he couldn't see the back of the building from his apartment, so he found himself going outside at regular intervals, just to check up on it), and rode the cranky elevator up to the fifth floor. Once inside, he yanked the hide-a-bed out of its frame so he could catch a few winks.

He tossed and turned for the first hour, unable to get his mind off of his task. He thought about all the remote places outside of Sioux City he had visited; there were many that would afford him the privacy he needed, nice wooded areas that were void of people. They reminded him of the night he and Clay had chanced upon the ritual in the woods, the night he had stolen the book. He fell asleep and dreamt of cornfields under a full moon, and of figures in black robes with no faces searching, searching for the book.

He awoke at dusk, the burning summer sun already below the western horizon, at that calm time when the city was caught between day and night. Soon would be the time of the ritual, when darkness finally conquers light, and those of the seedy underworld crawled out of their hiding places to walk the streets.

He poked his head out of the window, and found the air was blessedly cool now (he had only a small fan to cool the apartment, and all it seemed to do was circulate the hot air).

Cain took a long, cool shower, savoring the cold water. It awakened his senses, and by the time he stepped dripping out of the tub, he was ready to step out into the night. He willed the towel hanging over the small bar on the wall to fly into his hand, as if someone standing there had tossed it to him. He held it out in front of him momentarily, still in awe over his newfound abilities.

He dried off and combed his hair in the mirror, suddenly aware of just how long his hair had grown. "Wow, you're starting to look like a hippie, Cain, old boy," he said to his reflection. He went out to the living room, to the small closet where he kept his clothes and shoes, odds and ends, and dug around on the top shelf until he found what he wanted. If someone had been peeking in his window at that moment, they would have seen a strange site indeed - a man standing naked in his living room, holding and caressing a large black book of sorts, and talking to himself all the while. Any closer, and they would have seen the tiny blue sparks crackling at his fingertips as he stroked the cover of the book.

Most of his clothes hung from wire hangers (except underwear and socks, which were stacked in neat little piles on the top shelf, right next to a tattered comforter that was also folded as neat as could be. It was in the middle fold of this latter that he had been hiding the book, for lack of a better place), and he pulled out a fresh pair of jeans and a black tee shirt he had bought just for the occasion. He also pulled out a fresh pair of socks, and something else as well - a new pair of black square- toed boots. The moment he had seen the boots, he knew he had to have them. Wearing them, he felt tough, unstoppable.

Once dressed, he took a look at himself, and said, "The man in black. I like it." He sat down on the sofa and opened the book on the coffee table in front of him. With a pencil and piece of notebook paper, he copied down the words he would need, from a page that had a drawing of the beast holding a body in his arms, the soul rising out of it like smoke.

The couple in the apartment below began to argue, their voices muffled yet still discernible, and Cain stamped a boot heel onto the floor several times, silencing the voices. Something pounded on the floor, and a muffled voice proclaimed, "Fuck you!" Cain smiled and went into the bathroom to finish combing his hair.

He left his apartment, rode the elevator down to the lobby, and strolled out to the parking lot. He unlocked the Caddy and climbed in, relishing how the car seemed to lock the silence inside. The interior smelled of leather and pine (he had one of those scented trees hanging from the rearview mirror). The car easily started, and ran whisper quiet, and Cain was always amazed at how something so quiet could have so much power behind it. He would think of himself: I am just a man, yet, so much power....

He hit one of the buttons on the door panel next to him, and his window hummed down, allowing the cool night air to circulate around him. He pulled out onto 10th Street and headed east, toward a section of town that was a known haven for prostitutes, pushers, and the unfortunate homeless that had nowhere else to turn.

Cain had considered different options before arriving at this one: the cute girl at the bank had caught his eye, but he was in the bank constantly, and that meant exposure. He considered going to a bar, but once again he would be risking exposure. The supermarket meant daylight activity, and that was out altogether. One way or another, it had to be a female. Attempting this for the first time on a man might prove disastrous, as he really didn't know what to expect. No, it had to be a female, one he would be able to approach without distraction.

He pulled down a dark side street that seemed to be lined with ancient buildings, once a part of a thriving industrial district, now neglected and impoverished, home to a different class of citizens.

He got out of the car and locked it, looking around to see if there were any other people on the street. Satisfied he was alone, he strode down the sidewalk, boots echoing off the cement and into the void.

Two blocks down, he stopped and peered around the corner of a building. There, the streetlights were lit, and the occasional car cruised by, stirring up old newspapers that littered the street.

There, too, was life. Standing a short ways away, under the dim glow of one of the streetlights, was a women dressed in a halter-top and mini-skirt. She paced back and forth, shaking her blonde curls (which Cain guessed was a wig), and sticking her ass out at the passing motorists. Farther down were two more women who were sharing a joint and talking amongst themselves.

Cain walked around the corner and said, "Hey beautiful, where have you been all my life?" She swiveled around on a pair of bright red platforms, and regarded Cain curiously with her hands planted on her hips, a tiny purse slung over one shoulder.

"Well, right here, sugar, waitin' on you," she said. "Are you looking for some friendly company?"

"That I am," Cain said, eyeing the breasts that were cradled in the halter.

"Well, you came to the right place. Course, you could be vice. Are you a cop, honey?"

"Hell, no. I'm just looking for a good time." Cain smiled.

She said, "Pull out your wallet, hon, I just wanna make sure there ain't no badge."

Cain pulled out his wallet from a back pocket and flipped it open. "See? No badge. But I do have lots of money." He started to pull a few bills out of the wallet.

"Oh, don't do that here, hon, you'll get us both arrested for sure. You got a car?"

"You bet I do, ready and waiting. By the way, nice to meet you, uh...."

"Connie. Name's Connie, hon. But I don't know your name," she said, shaking his hand.

Just a touch...

"Well, you can call me anything you like, beautiful," he said, holding her hand.

"Ooh, I like you. C'mon, baby, let's go somewhere private so Connie can take care of you."

They walked the two blocks to the car with not a complaint from the hooker. She looped her arm through Cain's, and strolled along with him like it was the most natural thing in the world to be doing. The cold routine she had acquired from her many associations with men was replaced with something akin to love. She kept kissing Cain on the cheek and running her hand through the back of his hair.

When they reached the car, Cain again scanned the desolate street for any signs of life. He let Connie in on the passenger side, then went around and let himself in.

"Wow," she said, looking around the interior of the car. "You got a nice ride, sugar. And a big back seat, too." She reached over and grabbed his crotch, and licked his ear. "Want me to do a little polishin', hon?"

Cain felt his erection grow under her grasp. His heart was pounding wildly; he had been with girls before, but none with the experience or willingness as this one. He found himself giving in to desire, and it somehow made him feel weak.

He thought about the book, what it meant to his future. He felt angry with himself for even harboring such frivolous thoughts when there were more pressing issues at hand. He reached down and gently removed her hand, feeding her mind with ideas that would make his job easier.

"I'll tell you what," he said, "let's go somewhere more private so we can really *have some fun.*"

Confusion crossed over her features, and then she smiled and nodded. "Yeah, ok. Yeah, that's a great idea, baby. More private."

The Cadillac pulled away from the curb, slicing into the night air, carrying two people to a destination from which only one would return.

Cain drove west out of town, his passenger quietly watching the headlights sweep across their path.

"You ok?" Cain asked.

"I'm better than ok, hon," Connie said, her voice filled with seduction.

"Good, we'll be there soon," he said.

They went another ten miles or so, traveling along open fields and woods, until coming to an area with more woods on the left and a small lake on the right. The water was black and motionless, forbidding in the darkness.

Cain turned left onto a dirt road that curled off into the woods; it was here that he had discovered that the road led to several small campgrounds that looked as if they hadn't been used in a while, except maybe by beer guzzling teenagers (Cain was by rights still a teenager, but he no longer considered himself part of that particular faction).

They came to a point where a thick chain was strung across the road, the headlights illuminating a small white sign with red letters hanging from its center proclaiming 'No Entry'. Dust settled in the glare of the headlights before Cain switched off the lights and engine. He turned to his passenger, touched her hand and smiled.

"Well, here it is," he said. "What do you think?"

Something crossed her mind, and she said, "Let's get kinky, baby. What do you say? Ooh, I can't help myself, there's just something about you!" Something else crossed her mind. "Hey, you got any rope? We could have some real *fun.*"

"Wow, you must be reading my mind. It just so happens that I *do* have some rope."

Then Connie did something that caught Cain by surprise. He was about to open his door when she grabbed him by the arm and said, " Hold up a minute, sugar. We need to talk money." She rubbed her thumb and fingers together in front of his face. Even though he had pounded her mind with notions and ideas, that *part of her, the part that says no money, no fuck, held precedence over everything else at that moment. The money was a much too important part of her life, her driving force, and her very livelihood.*

He took out his wallet and pulled out of it two one hundred dollar bills, which he promptly handed over to her. "That enough?" he asked, already knowing the answer. He could tell by the gleam in her eyes that it was, indeed, enough. It was more than enough. Connie was a twenty-dollar whore, if anything, and two hundred was probably more than she made in a few days' time.

"You and me are gonna get along just fine, hon, just fine." She folded the bills and tucked them into her purse, and got out of the car. Cain purposely led her away from the car a ways, then said, "Oh, wait here a minute, I forgot a few things. Silly me." His boots crunched on the gravel as he walked to the back of the car and opened the trunk. The last thing he wanted was for her to see the contents of the trunk; it could trigger another reaction in her, possibly ruin his scheme.

He grabbed the coil of rope and slung it over his shoulder, then grabbed a plastic shopping bag with several items inside and shut the trunk.

When Connie saw the rope, she said, "Oh, we're gonna have some fun, now. I'm gonna have fun tyin' you up, hon." Another surprise. He was supposed to tie her up. Cain realized he was going to have to work on his abilities in order to weed out the flaws. He took hold of her hand and said, "Actually, I was thinking of tying you up first."

It took her a moment to respond, but even in the dark he could tell the thoughts he sent her had taken hold. "Oh, I knew it! You are the kinky one!"

A sliver of moon hung in the sky as they followed the dirt path into the woods. They passed several small camping spots until Cain finally turned onto another path that led a short ways off into a clearing. A weathered picnic table with peeling green paint sat next to a blackened barbeque. Nearby was a metal drum overflowing with trash. Cain set the bag and coil of rope on the picnic table and put his hands on his hips, surveying the site. The night was calm, quiet, save for the crickets chirruping from their hidden lairs.

"That looks like a good spot over there," Cain said, pointing to the gnarled trunk of a nearby tree. He took the bag over to the tree and began lifting out the six thick white candles he had bought at a gift shop around the corner from his apartment. He placed them in a way so that it formed a circle with the tree, brushing away the spots under the candles with his hand to keep them sturdy, and then

stood and brushed his hands off on his jeans. He produced a book of matches from his pocket and began working his way around the circle, crouching and lighting the candles one by one.

Connie leaned against the end of the picnic table and watched all this with idle curiosity. The candles formed a glowing ring of light, at the center of which stood Cain. He motioned to Connie.

"Come here, beautiful." She dropped her purse on the table, and stepped cautiously between the candles.

"Ooh, I love it!" she said, giggling. Cain grabbed her and pushed her up against the rough bark of the tree. He pushed himself against her and began kissing her neck. He could smell sweat underlying her cheap perfume, but it was better than kissing her on the lips. He could only imagine where her mouth had been. "Baby, I'm gettin' hot. Go get that rope."

"You wait right here," he said, cupping her breast through her halter. He retrieved the rope, and then walked behind the tree, uncoiling it as he went. He reached around and gently pulled one of her arms around behind the trunk. He circled the rope around her wrist and began forming a knot.

"Not too tight, ok hon? I ain't goin' nowhere."

He finished the first knot, making sure it was tight enough to hold her, even if she did *want to go somewhere. He pulled her other arm around; there would be a gap of about two feet between her hands. He knotted her remaining hand to the free end of the rope, and returned to the ring of glowing light. It cast an eerie glow on the woman tied to the tree.*

He stood staring at her, his smile now just a thin straight line.

"What ya' lookin' at?" she asked. "Let's get to it."

He could see candlelight reflected in her eyes. It intrigued him, this light in her eyes, for soon it would be extinguished, the flame would burn no more. He studied her a moment longer, then stepped outside the circle. He reached into a pocket of his jeans and brought out a piece of notebook paper, which he unfolded and held out before him, trying to read the words that were scrawled across its surface.

"What are *you doing?" Connie asked. From her position on the tree it looked as if she had no arms.*

"Shut up, bitch," he said. "Damn it!" He turned and headed for the Caddy, and from behind, he heard Connie mutter something and then she called out, "Hey, where you goin' man? You get back here right now!"

Cain ignored her while he opened the trunk of the car. There were two more items in the trunk, one of which was a flashlight, and this he grabbed before returning to the now angry women who was tied to a tree in the middle of nowhere.

"Hey, asshole, untie me right now! Game over, you hear?"

Cain looked at her pensively, like a scientist studying a specimen in a cage. It was clear that she was no longer under his influence. Had the impressions he fed her mind simply worn off over time, or had her anger helped to shed off the confusion, as if awakening from a dream state. Cain thought it was the latter, although the former couldn't be discounted just yet.

Cain switched on the flashlight and aimed at the paper.

"Get me the fuck off this tree, do you hear me asshole?" She struggled with her bonds, but to no avail. "Fuck this," she said, and started to scream. "HELP! SOMEBODY HELP ME!"

"I told you to shut up," he hissed at her, but she screamed even louder.

"HEEELLLLPPP!" Her screams pierced the calm with an alarming intensity, and it only served to feed his growing anger.

"I said, SHUT UP!" He focused with his mind, focused on the big mouth that was causing all the alarm, and her mouth clamped shut, biting off the very tip of her tongue. Cain saw the tip fall to the ground. No blood could escape from the lips that were tightly pressed together. She continued to scream into her closed mouth, short, irritating bursts of muffled madness. She stamped her feet as Cain read from the paper.

"Ic clypian eow Morgoroth, hlaford sceadu, ge-etan sawols, becuman don min offrung."

Connie fell silent as he spoke, except for her low moans of pain, and her eyes were wide with terror as he repeated the words, watching the circle of light as if waiting for something. He crumpled up the paper and shoved it back into his pocket.

"I don't understand. What am I doing wrong?"

Connie resumed her muffled cries, tears streaming down her cheeks. Cain paced back and forth, boots crunching through dried leaves and twigs, and when he could take no more he turned and focused on her mind, the gray matter inside her head, and squeezed. Her eyes rolled and her head bounced against the rough bark of the trunk as blood began to pour from her nose and ears. It seeped from the corners of her eyes, mingling with the tears. Cain released all of his influence, and saw her mouth fall open, spilling blood over her halter and skirt. Her head lolled around, eyes still rolling aimlessly around in their bloody sockets. He had literally squeezed the life from her brain. Her legs buckled and bent, but her arms held fast; she twitched and made gurgling sounds, a puppet tangled in its strings.

Cain stomped to the rear of the car, angry at his own failure, angry that he had a mess to dispose of anyway, which heightened the disappointment and uncertainty he now felt. He opened the trunk, and pulled out the remaining item, a brand new shovel he had purchased along with the rope.

He started off into the woods with the flashlight and shovel, then changed his mind and came back to the ring of light. He blew out all of the candles, gathered them up and put them into the plastic sack, which he left on the picnic table before picking up shovel and flashlight and again heading into the woods. He passed Connie without so much as a glimpse in her direction. He heard her sickening gurgles fade as he went deeper into the trees.

He found a spot that suited his needs, and he set the flashlight on the ground next to his chosen spot, and began to dig. He stopped and thought: Wait a minute, why am *I* doing the work? He dropped the shovel and stepped back a few feet, and focused all his attention on it. It went upright on its own, and Cain pushed as hard as he could. The shovel sank in only an inch or two, and clattered to the ground as he let go. His heart was beating fast, his breathing heavy, as if he had just worked out at the gym. This particular ability would have to be worked on more than the mind control, as it seemed to drain him physically.

He sat against a tree and rested a few minutes to catch his breath, then stood and picked up the shovel and again began to dig. He had heard on different occasions how police had found bodies in shallow graves here and there, and he had always thought it quite stupid of someone to just leave a corpse barely covered with earth, only to be uncovered with the first heavy rainstorm, or perhaps some camper digging a hole in which to take a dump. Little as he liked it, he would have to make his grave as deep as he could, to guarantee the evidence would never be found.

An hour later, he sat on the edge of the grave, legs dangling inside, bathed in sweat and still not satisfied with the depth of the yawning hole

. He decided to walk back to the campsite and check on the hooker, who was now just a vegetable tied to a tree. He stood right in front of her, yet she was unaware of his presence. She no longer had an intelligent awareness of anything. Cain considered his *handy-work, and felt a feeling of power rise in him like flames in a furnace.*

It felt good.

He returned to his work, digging and chopping through thick roots, hitting the occasional rock, and finally called it quits after another hour of labor. He was surprised when he stood up straight, and was chest deep in a fresh grave. Enough was enough.

He picked up the flashlight and walked back to the campsite, the night air cooling his sweat soaked skin, blowing through his damp hair. He was weak, and he was quite sure that by morning his muscles would scream with soreness.

He untied Connie's hands, and she collapsed to the ground, head twitching in the dirt and leaves. Cain coiled the rope and threw it on the picnic table next to the bag of candles. He grabbed Connie by the armpits, and jerked her to her feet. He let go, and she went down like a sack of potatoes, one of the bones in her leg snapping in the process. She registered no pain, though, only went on glaring at the world with those empty eyes.

Cain rolled her onto her back, pushed his arms under her back and legs (one of which was surely broken, he could feel the nub of bone trying to penetrate her skin), and lifted her up into his arms. She wasn't a very large person, but she certainly felt heavy now, after all his back-straining labor. He grunted and bore the weight, hurrying as fast as he could to the gravesite.

The grave was a black hole under the blanket of night. Cain had to drop Connie on the ground and hurry back for his flashlight. When he returned, she was laying in a fetal position, now barely moving. She had lost a lot of blood, and her brain had suffered serious trauma, and the life was slowly draining from her, rendering her too weak to do anything but look around with those incomprehensive eyes.

Cain shined the light in her face, watching her eyes move around, trying to decide what came next. He kneeled next to her and rolled her over until she rolled right into the hole. She fell to the bottom with a heavy thud! *He aimed the light into the hole. She was on her back, limbs twisted like a rag doll. Cain laid the flashlight on the ground next to the grave, and picked up the shovel. He stood solemnly over the grave, listening to the crickets, and the sound of his own heart thumping in his chest.*

And then he buried her alive.

Cain returned home exhausted, yet exhilarated. Although his plans had gone awry, he had still managed to perform the rest of his functions, to witness first-hand what it was going to take to carry out his ritual once a month. And he was pleased with his work. The gravesite looked like it had never existed. He left no trace, no track, had even gone so far as to park his car on the main access road, then walk back and sweep away the tire tracks using his power over the physical world; weak as it may have been at this point, it wasn't too weak to stir up a little dust.

Then he thought about the hooker. Connie.

It was strange to think about, indeed, but didn't she actually struggle *a little as the dirt was being flung onto her broken body? Maybe she had had a grain of coherent thought left in what used to be her brain after all, or maybe it was mere animal instinct, but as the dirt hit her face, went into her mouth, she* had *struggled a bit, only to fall motionless under a heavy layer of soil. Cain had shoveled faster and faster, his mind racing, teeth grinding together. It was absolutely invigorating!*

The blackness in his heart had grown that night, sinking its teeth deeper into his very soul, clouding his mind with its dark glory. Now, there truly was no turning back.

The first thing he did upon entering his apartment was open the closet door in hopes that the book would tell him exactly what he did wrong. When he opened it, and the light from the living room fell on the closet floor, there lay the book, open to the very page of the ritual. Cain picked up the book and immediately felt its energy flow into his hands. He thought: I was supposed to use the book! The book will call him!

He leaned back on the sofa and smiled. The powers he had acquired were his own, but that's where the powers stopped. The book was the real *power, the only thing that could summon the beast into this world, and it would take a combined effort to perform his ritual.*

He thought about how he had found the book, moved out of its hiding place of its own accord. He would have to make a new hiding place, just to be sure the book stayed put. It would not be very beneficial to have someone just walk in one day to find the book lying around somewhere. He used to keep the book under the floorboards of the barn, so maybe he could do something similar here. And eventually, he did just that.

Several weeks later Cain found himself back at the same campsite, a full moon glowing above in the evening sky. One thing was different, though - the woman tied to the tree. This one's name was Amber, a brunette he had picked up on the same street where he had picked up Connie, who now lay curled up in the bottom of a makeshift grave not far from where the both of them stood.

Giving Amber suggestions had been much easier than Connie; Cain had been practicing his abilities, at home and on the street. It seemed that the stronger his mind became at moving solid objects, the stronger it became at feeding thoughts and ideas and images into a person's mind. But a person could overcome those thoughts and ideas, but only with a strong enough emotion like anger or fear. Of course, it was virtually impossible as long as Cain kept touching the person.

With Amber, it was almost too easy. It wasn't only the money that counted with her, it was also the sex. She loved it as much as the money, and was very excited at the idea of doing something kinky like sex tied to a tree.

When Cain returned from the trunk of his car with the book in his hand, she merely smiled and asked, "And what are you up to?" Cain's touch had almost given her a high.

"Oh, I can't tell you just yet, it's a surprise."

"Goody, I love surprises," the girl said, and Cain thought that if she had been untied, she would now be jumping up and down, clapping her hands together.

Cain opened the book, took a deep breath, and read the incantation: "Ic clypian eow Morgoroth, hlaford sceadu, ge-etan sawols, becuman don min offrung."

"I can't understand what you're saying. What language is it?" she asked, a silly grin on her face.

Instead of answering her question, Cain read the words aloud again, and waited. Just when he thought he may have failed again, he saw something, just a hint of something, and he closed the book, peering closer at the space in front of Amber where he had seen a slight wavering, a displacement of the very air.

"It's getting hot, don't you think, baby?" Amber the hooker asked, dropping the smile for a look that was closer to concern, maybe even fear. "Don't you feel it?"

He put his finger to his lips, and said, "Shhhhh." She just stared at him with wide, child-like eyes.

The air inside the ring of lights was wavering, and turning into a green haze that crept around her feet and legs like smoke. Cain's heart pounded excitedly as he felt the ground rumbling like a small earthquake. A shadow flowed over them like liquid, and Amber went to say something, but was cut off by the explosion that burst the ground in front of her wide open. She screamed as clods of earth flew everywhere, some hitting her hard enough to disintegrate and fall into her top (her jeans were too tight for anything larger than a hair to fall into them).

Cain took a couple steps back from the ring, and the newly formed hole in the ground at Amber's feet. The hair on the back of Cain's neck rose and prickled as the beast, author of the book, rose out of the ground. It spoke to him without moving its lips, which were curled over rows of needle-sharp teeth. The language was not comprehensible, yet he did understand the meanings behind it.

A soul to feed my hunger, blood to quench my thirst.

Then the voice was gone, and all he could hear was Amber screaming as the beast dug his fingernails (and didn't he hear the crunch of bone?) into the sides of her head. His worm's body slithered out more as he bent forward, his twisted features curiously taking in her screaming countenance. Cain somehow got the idea that the beast actually *savored this, like a good meal.*

Cain's eyes went wide as Morgoroth sucked the very life and soul from the girl. It poured from her like smoke, from her eyes, nose, mouth, and went straight into the beast's hungry maw. Her face and body shriveled and caved in on itself. Then, he released her, and howled into the night sky. Then he was gone, disappearing into the ground, with everything, every bit of dirt, every leaf and twig, returning to its previous spot, a film moving in reverse.

Silence prevailed. Even the crickets had gone quiet. Cain realized he must look like an idiot, standing there with his head tilted back, eyes popping out, chest rising and falling. He shook his head and blinked his eyes. The ring of candles still burned, flames waving in the slight breeze. And then there was the girl.

Only it wasn't the girl anymore, it was shriveled thing *tied to that tree,* a thing that no longer had eyes. A smile crossed his face. He had done it! It had happened so fast, and yet, he could see every detail in the back of his mind. That vision would forever be planted in his memory. And it had actually *spoken to him!*

He hesitantly approached the candles, and stepped into the circle. He walked over the very spot where it had happened, but it was exactly the same as it had been before. Good old solid Mother Earth.

He blew out all the candles and returned them to the bag, and went behind the tree to untie the hooker's hands. To his surprise, as soon as he lifted the rope, her hands slipped out of the knotted loops that were once tight around her wrists. He almost laughed as he untied the knots anyway, and took the rope and candles to the trunk of the Caddy. It was the same routine all over again, and yet, this one smacked of success.

He left the corpse by the tree, and, sporting the flashlight and shovel, walked to the same spot where he had buried Connie. He started to dig only a few feet away from the other grave; actually, the shovel *began to dig, though he still wasn't strong enough to push it down more than a few inches at a time with his mind. But it was still a wondrous thing, to watch a shovel working on its own, digging and throwing, digging and throwing.*

The progress with the shovel was slow, so he took over, and he found the going much easier if he focused with his mind, and pushed with his hands at the same time. He dug out the grave in half the time it took him the first time. He stood in the grave with the shovel propped under one elbow, and pondered over the success of the evening. He felt like some psychotic caretaker in an old cemetery, perhaps from the old black and white films he used to be fascinated with as a kid.

This produced a laugh from him; a sick, unstable laugh that did not sound like it came from his own lips. He climbed out of the grave, and returned to his ritual tree for Amber. He found her corpse surprisingly light, nothing compared to the weight of Connie's still intact body.

She felt strangely empty as he carried her to the grave, a rubbery sack with bones slithering and sloshing around in the remaining liquid. He tossed her empty body into the grave, and covered it up quickly, the vision of the beast still planted in his mind.

He hid the grave with leaves and twigs, just as he had the first time, until he was satisfied it looked untouched. With his mind, he destroyed any evidence that anyone had walked through this part of the woods, swishing the leaves on the ground around like tiny whirlwinds. Again, he parked the car out on the access road, and mind-swept the dirt road leading to the campground. Then, with spirits high, he drove off, Cadillac slicing easily into the night.

16

Gil and Louise Garret had been sitting in jail for the better part of two weeks when Cain paid a visit to Jonathon at the old newspaper office on Main Street.

Jonathon had loaded his father's Ranger with cleaning supplies: several buckets, a mop and broom, a bottle of pine cleaner he found under the kitchen sink, a box of rags; it was all too familiar to him as he had gathered everything together, knowing exactly where his mother had kept all the cleaning supplies, just as he knew where his father kept all the various tools he had collected over the years, some probably older than Jonathon himself.

It was up too him to take care of things now, and that would take a little doing, because up until now he had let everything go unhampered by blade or cloth. The lawns were grossly overgrown, and a layer of dust had collected throughout the house, something his mother had always kept to a minimum with her ceaseless housework. Dirty dishes were piled up on the kitchen counter, food dried and unrecognizable on their surfaces.

When he decided to stay, that meant bringing things back to normal, at least to some *semblance* of normality. And he had two good reasons for this: One, he wanted the town to think that he'd given in, and was moving on with his life. He wanted to draw as little attention as possible to himself while he figured out what to do about his parent's murderer. And two, it was just downright impossible for him to live like a slob. The whole atmosphere of the house seemed to drown him in depression, and he was beginning to feel like part of the disease that was infecting the town.

Therefore, for several days following work at the library, he went straight home and cleaned house. The lawns were nicely mown, the smell of freshly cut grass a blessing to his senses, and the inside of the house looking and smelling better everyday.

He also thought it was time to clean up the newspaper office, perhaps empty it out and sell the printing press, and give someone else a chance to start a business in the small office.

And so it was on a simmering August day that Cain's black Cadillac pulled up to the curb behind the Ranger as Jonathon was busy unloading things and taking them inside. The office door was propped open with a brick to air the place out, the same red brick he always used on days like this to keep the door open so that the fine summer breeze could circulate inside and cool things off a bit.

Cain got out of the car and walked up to the sidewalk. He was wearing boots, jeans and a red tee shirt that was almost painful to look at. Jonathon, on the other hand was ready for work, donned in shorts and a tank top, sandals flopping against his heels as he walked.

"Hello, Jonathon," Cain said, following along as Jonathon carried a mop and bucket into the office. He dropped the items on the floor, turned and faced Cain, arms crossed across his chest.

"And what are we up to today?" asked Cain.

It was difficult for Jonathon to control his anger and hatred for this man, but if he were to accomplish anything, he would have to learn. "I'm just cleaning up the place a bit. I'm thinking of selling it."

"Oh? That's too bad. I actually had some business to throw your way. Just some flyers, you know."

"Well, as you can see," Jonathon said, looking around at the clutter, "I'm pretty much out of business."

"I'm willing to pay a lot for this job, Jonathon. I'm sure you could use the money."

Jonathon's anger was rising to the surface; he couldn't help it, and it showed when he spoke.

"Look, I don't want your money, or anything else. I'm sure you can find someone else to do the work. Go down to Arlidge, I sure there are a lot of fine printers there," he said, and walked around Cain toward the front door, but before he reached it, the door slammed shut, shaking the glass and sliding the brick halfway across the sidewalk toward the street.

"You know that would be impossible," Cain said, turning around. "Not for this job, anyway. I need *you*, Jonathon."

"And if I refuse?"

Cain walked toward him, hand outstretched. Jonathon quickly jumped back and said, "Please, don't touch me. Don't ever touch me."

"Ah, still angry, are we? I understand. Well, to answer your question, quite simply put, if you refuse, you die. You simply become part of the growing population out at the cemetery. We wouldn't want *that,* now would we?" He produced a sheet of paper from his back pocket, unfolded it, and handed it to Jonathon. "You need to have this done within the next day or two. I'd do it myself, but I no longer worry myself with such menial tasks. The sheriff will be by to pick them up before Friday. Five hundred pages. That's all I ask. Don't disappoint me, Jonathon."

The front door clicked and swung open, and the brick, which was sitting in the middle of the sidewalk, scraped across the cement back to its place against the door. Cain strode out into the sunlight, climbed into his car, and drove away without another look at Jonathon.

Jonathon unfolded the plain white paper and read the words written across the top: Attention: *There will be a town meeting Saturday Night, 10:30, in the field just north of the old Willard farm. Everyone is required to attend! Special circumstances contact Sheriff Craven. By order of Mr. Cain!*

Jonathon knew exactly what it meant; Cain was going to perform his sacrifice or ritual or whatever it was, subjecting some innocent soul to his demon god. Jonathon wondered who it might be this time. And then another thought occurred to him, and he said out loud, "Don't worry, Cain, I'll be there, too." He set about cleaning his press, readying it for its next job.

17

The days were long and edgy for Jenny, even longer for Ashley, who really did not know what was happening in this fair town, or what was happening to her father. What she *did* know was that she and her mother spent long hours watching TV in her bedroom, on the same TV Jenny had taken from the master bedroom.

As soon as Harvey had noticed the TV missing, he confronted Jenny, who said quietly, "I'm just trying to spend more time with Ashley, that's all Harv." And Harvey, who was undoubtedly drunk, dismissed it with a wave of his hand.

Of course, that was when Harvey was at home sleeping, eating, or drinking, which was all he seemed to do anymore. Fortunately for Jenny, Harvey was gone most of the time, out doing God knew what, but the lack of knowledge about his time away from home scared her even more, especially after the incident with the deputy. And it was obvious that he wasn't working anymore, and yet he had money. He gave her just enough to pay the bills, go grocery shopping, and he always had cash.

And Harvey always made it clear to her, in his own subtle ways, that there would always be money, and everything would be fine, as long as she stayed put, and didn't try anymore of her *stunts,* as he had put it. And she always made it clear to him that she was over that now, and just wanted to get on with things. And she would go so far as to let Harvey *kiss* her, even though it sickened her, just to cool his jets. At least she had managed to keep him out of her pants.

There was one small part of her that missed her husband, the one she used to have, that is, the one she had during the happier times. But she knew that man was gone forever, lost in a world ruled by evil, a man that had become very dangerous, indeed, and if she wasn't careful, she might not last long enough to escape.

Escape....

The thought crossed her mind again, as if waiting for an answer, but as of yet, she had none. She thought about escaping during the night when Harvey was out and about, but realized that by now, the eyes and ears of the town were on folks just like her, the ones who hadn't quite fallen in with the program. She couldn't take the car because Harvey always had the keys, and he wasn't about to let her drive it anywhere.

Everyday, she toiled over this puzzle, looking for even the tiniest hole she could slip through and disappear with her daughter. And then one day the answer came to her, delivered right to her mailbox. It was a bright yellow flyer folded in half and neatly tucked with the rest of the mail. She unfolded it and read it, then read it again. It was the key to the puzzle, and there would be only one chance.

Part 2
The Gathering

1

Where the hell am I?

This thought had entered Amanda Townsend's mind more than once over the past forty-five minutes or so, each time sounding more urgent than the last. She ejected the CD she'd been listening to, and tossed it on the passenger seat, where the rest of her CD's lay scattered.

She pondered over the sound of her Honda Civic coursing down this lonely stretch of highway, tires humming on pavement, wind howling through the window, which was rolled down a crack. She rolled it down all the way, and let the night air hit her full on the face. The digital clock in the dashboard said: 12:10am.

She hadn't seen a familiar sign in miles; this scratch of highway seemed void of any life whatsoever. She watched the fading yellow stripes zip by her in the glow of the headlights, and it seemed to her that the beams didn't go very far before succumbing to the night.

She could still hear Drew's voice echoing in her head.

"You shouldn't be driving alone at night, you know. There are a lot of crazies out there." To which she had replied, *"Hey, I'm a big girl now, Drew, I can take care of myself."*

"Can't a guy look out for his kid sister?"

She smiled as she remembered the conversation. It was just like Drew to be thinking of his sister instead of worrying about himself. After all, *he* was the one whose life was in disarray. And how ironic was that? He was a lawyer who handled mostly DUI's, bankruptcies, divorces, and he was now suffering of a broken heart from his *own* divorce.

Go figure.

But he didn't fool anyone; well, not *her*, anyway. She saw through the false happiness he wore on his face everyday. She knew her brother all too well. Even at dinner at her parent's house earlier that evening, he'd been sporting a five o'clock shadow, something that was not typical of him. He was twenty-six, clean cut and good looking, and although he wasn't vain, he liked to look his best.

Her parents were quick to agree with Drew, though, and she felt the familiar irritation trying to dig its way under her skin, the way it used to when she was a kid. Drew was the older brother, hence, always right.

Her mother had followed Drew's remark with one of her own: *"He's right, you know. You really shouldn't be driving by yourself. I hear about young girls getting abducted and killed all the time. Don't you ever watch America's Most Wanted?"*

"I don't have time for a lot of TV, mom. Dad, help me?"

"They're just looking out for you, that's all. Don't want the boogey man to get you!"

He tried to put on a scary face, but his wrinkled, worn out face was already scary enough, and it only succeeded in a burst of laughter around the dinner table. But her father knew that, and he laughed right along with them. When the laughter had died down, she was still defending herself.

"Look, I like driving at night - it's cooler that way."

"At least call us when you're halfway there," her mother had said.

"C'mon, mom. You'll be in bed."

"I won't be," Drew interjected. Amanda had smiled and tilted one hand toward her brother.

"See, case closed."

She looked at the cell phone on the dashboard. She had called Drew after passing through Cedar Rapids, and true to his word, he had still been awake. He reminded her that Cedar Rapids was *not* halfway between Iowa City and Cedar Falls, and that she would have to call again, to let him know that she was getting close to home, which in this case, was a student housing complex just off the University of Northern Iowa campus.

"Whatever. You're the one losing sleep over it," she had said, but she had an idea that her brother was losing a *lot* of sleep these days anyway, was up late at night nurturing his broken heart.

They had been married only a year, a frigging *year,* for God's sake, when she had suddenly decided to back out of the marriage. How's that for dedication? That had been four months earlier; the mandatory ninety-day waiting period for divorces had come and gone (a colleague of Drew's did the divorce for him), but the residue of the whole thing still lingered, still had its ugly claws sunk deep into his shattered heart. Most days, it was a battle between pain and hatred, and although hatred wasn't one of his strong suits, it was still there, reminding him everyday that he had been just too trusting. He had *loved* her. What more did she want?

Amanda thought about calling him, actually reached for the phone, but pulled her hand back. She *wanted* to call him, just to let him know that she loved him, and things were going to be all right. But she was lost, and that was *really* why she wanted to call, wasn't it? And to make that call would be to admit that she was still a little girl who needed watching over, needed help, and she just could not let that happen. She was almost twenty years old, a business major at college, and her family still treated her like a child. No, she would take care of this one on her own.

She had been about twenty-five minutes out of Cedar Rapids when she had called Drew, approaching the intersection that would send her down the lonely highway. It wasn't really an intersection though, it was more of a slim fork in the road, and she had almost taken the wrong way the last time she made this trip, and it had been daylight then. It had also been the first time she had driven home from college.

The split in the road boasted two small highway markers in the middle of it, Highway 6 to the left, 151 to the right. Highway 6 led northwest to Cedar Falls, 151 took a northeasterly route. And it was just before this split in the road that she had decided to make the call. And it was just about the time when he was telling her that she would have to call again, and she had tilted her head back and laughed, that she had unknowingly passed the fork in the road and just kept going straight, which was actually the right fork. To take the left fork, she would have had to switch into the far left lane, which took a wide swing over and merged with Highway 6.

She had already been headed into a part of the state she had never been in before when she said, *"Whatever. You're the one losing sleep over it,"* hit *end* on her cell phone, and placed it on the dash.

A while later, she had passed a green highway marker: Arlidge 5.

Arlidge?

She couldn't remember passing a town called Arlidge before, but she *had* only made this trip once before, and therefore very likely there would be unfamiliar towns or landmarks. She had shrugged it off, kept pushing ahead, CD player jamming with the wind whistling through her window, which was cracked about an inch.

She had seen the sign marking the turn-off for Arlidge, and had seen the lights of the city nestled in the distance like jewels glittering on black cloth. She had patiently pushed on, just *knowing* that a familiar sign was going to appear at any moment, reassuring her that she was not, Lord forbid, lost or anything like *that*. She could hear her mother's voice now: *"I told you not to drive alone at night."*

Then she had passed another turn-off that was simply marked: Exit 265.

That was about the time she had started to bite her lower lip as she stared out at the darkness in front of her. And she had glanced more than once at the cell phone vibrating slightly on the dash.

Two miles later, she had passed a sign announcing: Greenview 15.

Ok, you've never heard of these places before. Admit it, Amanda. You're lost. You're going to have to swallow your pride and pick up that phone and call big brother. Wait, on second thought, why don't you just turn around and go back? Yeah, that's it, just go back until you know exactly where you're at, and try again. That way, you won't have to listen to Drew rubbing it in.

But maybe it wouldn't hurt to call...

She drove in silence, the wind whipping her hair out behind her.

She reached for the cell phone, and at the same time headlights flashed in her rearview mirror. She put her hand back on the steering wheel, watching the lights as they grew closer.

I'll just let whoever this is pass, and then I'll turn around and get the hell out of Dodge, she thought.

She eased off on the gas, and the Honda slowed its pace. The headlights quickly grew, lighting the interior of her car, making it impossible to look at the bright glare in her mirrors.

"C'mon, pass already," she said, squinting at the rearview. The vehicle shifted to one side, as if to pass, then shifted back and slammed into the Civic's rear end. Amanda's head snapped back against the headrest, and she cried out in surprise. Something smacked into her stomach, and she looked down to see her cell phone sitting in her lap.

She instinctively hit the gas and pulled away from the other vehicle. Blood rushed through her veins and her arms stiffened on the wheel, hands grasping like clamps. "Oh my God," she said, her voice wavering. "Please, leave me alone!"

The words were barely out of her mouth when the vehicle slammed into her again, metal crashing against metal. Pain ran up her stiffened arms as she tried to hold herself steady. Her cell phone clattered to the floor at her feet, and she heard CD's scattering around the other side of the car.

She thought fleetingly: *Ok, Why the hell did I do this? If I had just stayed home, I wouldn't be here!* Then, as the headlights approached again: *Please God, help me!*

But at the last second, the other vehicle swerved over and flew past her like she was standing still, and according to her speedometer she was doing a little over eighty. She got a quick look as it passed; a pick-up, perhaps an older model, she wasn't sure. And then its taillights shrunk to tiny red spots, then disappeared altogether as it rounded a bend.

It took a moment for her to break the shock. She hadn't even noticed, but the wind at this speed had been whipping her hair against her face, and into her eyes and mouth. Tears were streaming out of her left eye and running toward her ear.

She gathered her wits and slowed the car down, pumping lightly on the brakes. She thought about stopping for a minute or two, and then bagged the idea as she pulled a u-turn and sped off in the other direction. She pushed harder on the gas, her eyes flicking to the rearview mirror every couple of seconds. She saw nothing but darkness falling away behind her. And darkness gaining on her. And then…

No!

Headlights suddenly lit the night like flares, and the crash to the rear end of her car came unexpectedly. The Civic lunged forward, and she slammed her foot on the brake pedal. She heard the roar of the other engine as the truck slammed into her again, and the Civic fishtailed, the passenger side swinging out in front of her until she was facing the other direction.

Tires squealed as she slid forward and over toward the other side of the road. A cloud of dust plumed up as the car shot across the gravel shoulder, tilting sideways as it slid to the bottom of the ditch, still garnering enough momentum to tip the Civic straight up on its side. Amanda heard everything loose in the car fall to the passenger side, which was now the bottom. The engine stalled.

The seat belt was biting into her hip, and as she struggled to find the clasp, she heard the sound of the truck diminishing. She managed to twist around in time to see the tail lights disappear from view.

She tried to push the seat belt's release, but the pressure from her own weight was too much. With her left hand, she grasped the window frame and pulled up as hard as she could, and stabbed the release with her thumb. It unlatched, and she immediately fell downward, her right thigh digging into the gear lever.

"Shit!" she screamed as she fell against the passenger door. Her first thought was: *Gotta get out! Gotta get out, now! Oh, God!* And as an afterthought: *The phone! My phone!* She cracked her head on the dash when she bent to search for the cell phone, groping around frantically among CD's and pop cans until she felt the familiar shape in her hand. She latched onto it, and began to literally claw her way out of the car.

Pushing against the seat with her feet, she pulled herself out and onto the driver's side of the Civic (which was now the *top* of the car), and crouched there, huffing and puffing, a knob of pain throbbing in her thigh.

She looked around and realized the ditch she was in wasn't all that deep. In fact, the car was taller than the ditch. She looked in the direction the truck had gone; the road was dark, and oddly quiet. The stars twinkled mysteriously overhead, and as she looked skyward, she heard a distant drone. It became louder, and headlights appeared. *Those* headlights.

"Oh my God, Leave me alone!" she cried. She bent at the knees and jumped, swinging her arms forward. She hit the far side of the ditch on the incline, her knees almost popping her in the jaw. Regaining her balance, she crawled the rest of the way up, spared one look at the oncoming vehicle, and ran toward an open field, fighting a limp from her bruised thigh.

As she fled, she turned and saw the truck stopped next to her car. Its lights went dark, and she was barely able to discern two figures climbing out of the truck and crossing the ditch. One switched on a flashlight and was waving it to and fro as they followed her.

And ahead she saw the corn.

Tall and green, a lush wall of healthy corn loomed up, and she plunged headlong into it, desperate for someplace, anyplace to hide. She couldn't hear her pursuers for all the noise she was making, but she had to stop to catch her breath. She had a terrible stitch in her side, and strands of sweaty hair were plastered to the side of her face. All she could hear was her own harsh breathing.

The phone....

She hit *menu* and the display splashed green light on her fingers. She arrowed through the directory until Drew's number appeared, and she hit *send.*

One ring. Two. "C'mon, answer!" she pleaded with the phone. She heard her brother's voice, and relief washed over her like cool rain.

"Drew, help me. You gotta help me…some people are trying to kill me…I'm not joking, damn it…I don't know, they ran me off the road, and they're chasing me…By some town, Green-something, I don't remember, I'm in the middle of a corn field, for Christ's sake…I…wait…I hear them! They're coming! Help me, please help me!"

She could hear them thrashing into the corn, and voices, as well. As she started to run, she dropped the cell phone into the dirt, and she came to a halt, looking around for it. The voices were close, *too* close, and she realized her time had run out. As she ran off, leaving the phone behind, she felt as if she had left her only hope behind. And she began to get a sinking feeling, like the final curtain after a show.

2

He saw his bride standing over by the table that the caterers had meticulously designed with food, talking with her father and a few other people, some from both sides of the family. Almost everyone had showed, and the reception hall was packed.

She was beautiful. As he watched her hug her father and wipe a tear from his eye, everything around him seemed to fade away, and his heart swelled with happiness. She seemed to glow, like a goddess walking among mere mortals. Of course, it really didn't matter where they were, the supermarket, the mall; she always had that effect on him. She was so perfect that she was almost intimidating. But, he didn't care, as long as he had her.

Rose turned and saw him watching her, and she tilted her head slightly and smiled, her eyes filled with wonder and amazement at this man who loved her so much, and was willing to commit his very life to her.

Someone was talking to him, nudging his shoulder, but he didn't care. He walked toward his new bride, and the little group surrounding her turned and saw him coming, and raised their champagne glasses in a toast. Rose's loving smile suddenly faded, and she fled into the crowd, a streaming flash of white.

Drew stood in the middle of the group, looking desperately around the room and calling her name. The others were laughing and drinking champagne as if nothing was wrong. He saw a streak of white on the other side of the room and he ran after it, pushing through the crowd, who didn't seem to notice his rudeness.

But she wasn't there.

Then he saw her running through the front doors of the reception hall, out into the bright afternoon sunlight. He called her name and followed her. As soon as he ran outside, barely catching site of his car, which had been decorated by mischievous friends, his environment changed. Now he was standing in the middle of his living room, watching the swinging door to the kitchen flap back and forth.

He ran into the kitchen, and saw Rose with her hands on a counter, leaning forward with her head hung down. As soon as she heard him enter the room, she straightened and turned. "Why are you following me?" she asked. Tears streamed down her face.

"We need to talk about this!" Drew said. He was very scared and confused.

"I already told you, Drew. Can't you accept it? It was a mistake! I should never have gotten married! I just need to go back to my life!"

"But why can't you have your life with me?" Drew pleaded.

"Christ, Drew! Do I need to say it? Ok, I will! I don't love you! Get it through your head, ok? I don't love you! Just get on with your life!"

She ran into the living room, and again he watched the door as it flapped to a halt. The telephone rang, a high bleating that seemed to come from outside the room. It rang again, and Drew saw alternating currents of blue and white light against the walls, the murmur of voices and a crowd of people laughing.

Drew opened his eyes and gazed sleepily around the cluttered room. An empty potato chip bag and some pop cans littered the coffee table. The TV was still on, splashing light throughout the dark room. The movie he'd been watching had ended, replaced by a re-run of *Three's Company.*

He was wearing only socks and underwear, complimented by his blue terry cloth robe (actually, it was *her* robe, but now it was *his*, and he'd been wearing it ever since she left), and a five o'clock shadow that had grown darker over the past few hours.

Another burst from his cell phone brought him fully aware, and he snatched it up from the coffee table.

"It's about time you called...hold up, hold up, what's wrong? ...Ok, you can quit joking around, I'm not in the mood...ok, ok, who are you talking about...tell me where you are, I'll call the police...Amanda...Amanda?"

He heard a dull *thump*, and then silence for a moment. He almost hit *end,* but paused when he heard someone on the other end.

"Hello? Amanda?" Someone was breathing heavily into the phone, like an obscene caller.

"Who is this?" Drew demanded. The line went dead. He set the phone on the cushion next to him, got up and turned on the living room light, squinting as his eyes adjusted to the brightness emanating from the ceiling fixture. He began pacing the carpet, thoughtfully stroking his stubbly face. "What the hell was *that* all about?" he asked out loud. He picked up his phone and tried her number.

The wireless customer you are trying to reach is not answering or -

He hit *end* and dropped the phone back onto the sofa. He stood quietly in the middle of the room, momentarily overwhelmed, as he had been a thousand times before, by just how large and empty the house seemed now that he lived alone. The feeling passed as fleetingly as it had come, and he said, "Ok, Amanda, this had better not be a joke or something, or you're going to be in big trouble!"

He walked into the kitchen, robe now untied and flowing out behind him, and turned on the light, heading straight for the refrigerator. But instead of opening it, he pulled a small piece of paper out from under a magnet stuck to the door. It had various important numbers written on it, including the fire department and police. Drew took the paper over to the wall phone by the swinging doorway and dialed the number for the police.

After several rings, a woman answered, *"Police dispatch, may I help you?"*

"Well, yes. The problem is, well my sister just called, and -"

"Sir, what is the nature of your call?"

"I guess I need to file a missing person's report." Drew already knew it was too soon to file that type of report, and he also knew the next question before it was out of the dispatcher's mouth.

"How long has the person been missing?"

"She's only been gone a few hours, but -"

"Sir, the person or persons involved must be missing at least forty-eight hours before a report can be filed."

Drew sighed heavily. "Yes, I know that, but I think there's foul play involved. She called and said someone was trying to hurt her. She's driving back to college tonight, and I think she's in trouble."

"Hold one moment, sir." The line went thankfully quiet for a minute or two; the last thing he wanted right now was elevator music. The line clicked, and a man's voiced boomed in his ear.

"Sir? My name's Roberts, I'm the shift supervisor. The dispatcher said you had a problem with a missing person?"

"Yes sir," Drew said, *"my sister."*

"Ok, I'm sure that she already explained to you that we can't file a report until she's missing for forty-eight hours, unless, of course, there's been true evidence of foul play. The dispatcher mentioned a very distressing call you got from your sister?"

Drew gave him all the details of the call, what little there was, the whole time listening to Roberts tapping the keyboard of a computer. He felt a kind of dread coming over him, and his mind drifted, wondering where Amanda was, and what was happening to her.

What if she's dead?

Robert's deep voice broke his reverie. *"Ok, hang on just one moment, Mr. Townsend."* The line went still again, but Drew could hear papers being shuffled in the background, and Roberts talking to somebody as he returned to the phone. *"Ok, I've got a state map here. You say she was headed for Cedar Falls, correct?"*

"Yes sir. University of Northern Iowa, Cedar Falls."

"That means she would have taken Highway 6 all the way. But you mentioned she said something about being by a town called Green-something or other, and the only town in that area is Greenview, and in order to get there, she would have to leave Highway 6 for 151. Where did you say she was when she called?"

"She said she had just passed Cedar Rapids. Do you think it's possible she took the wrong way and got lost?" Drew felt the dread inside him deepen.

"It's hard to say, Mr. Townsend. Does she know anybody in Greenview?"

"Not that I know of," Drew said, and then, "No, she wouldn't know anybody there. I don't think we've ever heard of the place."

"Well, the only thing I can think of at this point is that she took the wrong cutoff a ways after Cedar Rapids, and probably got lost. But from the information you've given me, she may have gotten more than just lost, so what I'm going to do is contact the police in Greenview and tell them the situation. Hopefully, they'll be able to spare some manpower to go out and take a look around. In the meantime, I suggest you sit tight, and wait by the phone in case she calls again."

"What about the report?" Drew asked.

"I've got it filled out and ready to go, Mr. Townsend, and I'm going to waive the forty-eight hours so we can get the ball rolling on this. So hang in there, and we'll do everything we can, ok?"

"Ok, thank you very much Mr. Roberts. I hope to hear from you soon."

Drew hung up the phone and sat down at the kitchen table. He again thought of his sister out there somewhere, alone, helpless. He had always watched out for his kid sister when they were growing up, and the protective bond he had for her seemed to never fade away.

He opened one of the kitchen drawers, and pulled out a phone book. He laid it on the table and began thumbing through all of the public information pages at the front of the book. He stopped and put his finger down on a page. "There you are," he said softly. His finger was resting on a map of the state, directly on the city of Greenview.

He thought about calling his parents, then thought the better of it. *No use worrying them right now,* he thought, *at least until I find out what's going on.* He went into the bedroom (which seemed equally as large and empty as the rest of the house) and threw on some clothes. They were the same clothes he had worn earlier in the evening, and still smelled of cologne.

Out of the bedroom closet he pulled a light jacket, and a shoebox from the overhead shelf. He set the box on the bed and tipped off the lid. Inside were a small .38 caliber revolver, and a box of bullets. He loaded the gun, making sure the safety was on, and put it in his jacket pocket. He returned to the kitchen, where he tore the map out of the phone book and neatly folded it before shoving it into a back pocket of his jeans.

Drew picked up the kitchen phone and dialed Amanda's number, and got the same recording. He sighed, looked around the kitchen, then turned off all the lights and left.

3

Two things happened when Amanda reached the other side of the cornfield: First, she spied some buildings nearby in the darkness, one with several windows glowing with light, and second, when she made for the lights, she went sprawling over something she'd been too flustered to see, and hit the ground face first. She stood, spitting dirt and gravel out of her mouth, and quickly turned to see what she had tripped over.

Oh my God, she thought. *It's a horse. It's a dead fucking horse!*

She took off for the lights, which were now clearly coming from a house. She felt the wind blowing against something wet and warm on her face. Her breaths came in harsh gasps as she reached the porch. Amanda banged on the screen door, looking behind her to see if her pursuers had caught up with her. She could barely make out the dark hulk of the horse lying at the fringes of the cornfield.

She banged on the door again, and she was suddenly bathed in yellow light as the porch light came on, and the inside door swung open. A man's voice said, "Can I help you?"

"Help me, please," she said to the figure on the other side of the screen. "Someone's trying to kill me! I need to call the police!"

"Oh my God, you're hurt," the figure said, propping open the screen door. "Come in, quick!" He held the door open while she rushed past him, then closed and locked the door. He was an older man, graying at the temples, wearing faded jeans and flannel shirt that was hanging loose and unbuttoned, exposing the tee shirt underneath. "You're bleeding. We better get you cleaned up," he said, moving toward a dimly lit hallway.

"Wait," she said, her breathing still coming in hitches. "We need to call the police!"

"Ok, young lady, you go into the bathroom right down that hall, and clean yourself off, and I'll call the sheriff right now. Go on, you're bleedin'," he said. Amanda went down the hall to find the bathroom, taking comfort in his soothing demeanor.

Amanda heard the man pick up the phone as she worked her way down the hall, peering into rooms as she passed by them. She reached into a doorway and felt for a light switch. This was a bedroom. The bed was unmade, and dirty clothes were scattered everywhere. The room stank of sweat. She suddenly felt embarrassed, as if she had intruded on something private, and she quickly switched off the light.

Across the hall was another room, and she fumbled for the switch. A single bulb glowed above a medicine cabinet, which was mounted on the wall above a small sink. There were dirty clothes in the bathroom as well, mainly tattered pairs of underwear that she was almost certain would reveal ugly brown stains if examined more closely. She raised a lip in disgust, and looked in the mirror. Her eyes widened with shock. On her right cheek, just below her eye, was a large red scrape. Blood was oozing in several places, and there were tiny pebbles planted here and there in the wound. She touched a finger to it and felt a stab of pain in the tender flesh. There was a smaller scrape along her jaw line, not as serious as the one on her cheek, but just as tender.

Amanda heard the man's voice from the living room, and she listened, head cocked.

"*Hello? Sheriff Craven? This is Angus Swapp, sorry to bother you late like this, but it seems we have an emergency. Well, this young lady just came to my door...no, I don't know her name...anyway, she came to my door claimin' that someone was tryin' to kill her or somethin'. She's pretty beat up...well, I don't...*"

His voice faded as he walked into the kitchen, and she could no longer understand what he was saying. But, she had heard enough to almost feel ashamed over the disgust she had felt over this man's dirty house. Dirty house or no, this man was helping her, probably saved her *life,* and for that she was eternally grateful.

She rinsed her face off in the sink, wincing as the hot water stung the raw flesh. She dabbed at her face with a towel (this didn't smell too hot, either), and walked into the living room.

"Hey, I'm sorry, but I think I got a little blood on your towel here-" She stopped talking as soon as she saw the gun. Angus Swapp was standing in the living room, among furniture that looked old, yet cozy, and he was holding a shotgun in his hands. Her face must have revealed the fear that rose in her, because he raised a hand to her, palm out, and said, "Now don't you worry a bit. I'm just going outside to look around. The sheriff is on his way, and everything's gonna be ok. You just hang tight right here. And don't you worry about that towel, young lady. The most important thing is you're safe." He smiled and confidently nodded once, and she felt at ease again.

"Please, be careful," she said.

"Don't worry about me. I'll be right back."

He unlocked the door and went outside, shutting the door behind him. She looked around the living room, lightly touching the towel to her wounds. Two lamps lighted the room, one next to a tattered green sofa, and another next to a recliner in one corner. Deer antlers were mounted on a paneled wall, right above a portrait of John Wayne. An old console TV sat under the picture window (the window was currently covered with thick drapes decorated with stains of an unknown origin) that overlooked the front of the house. Various photos were arranged on top of the television, and Amanda started to walk toward the TV to have a look, but the sound of the screen door creaking open stopped her in her tracks.

The front door opened, and in walked Angus Swapp, shotgun cradled under one arm. She felt relieved to see him, and began to smile, but her smile faded as another man walked into the house behind Angus. He carried a long flashlight. The truth began to dawn in Amanda's mind, a sad and sick truth that before this moment was unthinkable. She had walked right into their hands. Somehow, some way, she had inadvertently fallen into some conspiracy that was taking place here, one from which she could not escape.

Angus spoke first. "Now, you just sit tight young lady, until the sheriff comes, and everything will be easier for all of us."

"You gave us quite a run," the other man said, and then to Angus he said, "I think Cain's gonna like her." They both laughed, and at that moment a desperate thought flashed through Amanda's mind: *Back door. There has to be a back door.*

She spun around and ran for the kitchen doorway, and collided with another man, one who had apparently been standing there the whole time. He wrapped his arms around her, squeezing so tight she thought she might suffocate. He reeked of whiskey and sweat, and when he spoke, a fresh cloud of alcohol breath puffed against her face, into her nostrils.

"Just where the *fuck* do you think you're going?" he asked.

"Ok, Harv, don't kill her yet. We need her alive," the other man said.

"I know, I know," Harvey White said, and she cried out as he pushed her to the floor.

Angus waved the shotgun toward the recliner in the corner. "You just go and sit over there, and no more trouble!"

Amanda stood and walked over to the recliner, fearful that at any moment he might decide to kill her anyway by putting his shotgun to her head and blowing it into mush. She sat down, and air went whooshed out of the cushion as her weight collapsed it. The site of these three men was just too much for her; she began trembling uncontrollably, slowly shedding tears.

"W-what do y-you want?" she asked, looking directly at Angus. She couldn't bring herself to look at the other two, especially the one who stank so badly. There was just no telling what *he* might do.

"You just stay quiet until the sheriff gets here. He'll take care of you," Angus said.

Amanda's mind was spinning: *What do they want with me? They're gonna kill me, I know it. But the sheriff? He can't be a part of this, too, can he? I want to go home!*

4

Drew drove his Escort west on I-80, taking the northbound exit for Highway 6. An hour later, he was passing through Cedar Rapids. He stopped at a convenience store and bought a large coffee, and a state map. He sat in his car, sipping coffee to fend off the fatigue of long nights awake, fighting the pain in his heart. But, in his heart he also had a great love for his kid sister, and it was that love that was now spurring him on, the pain numbed by a greater purpose.

He studied the map under the dome light, looking for anything else that might have helped in his search, but it offered nothing more than the torn out page of the phone book had offered.

The coffee started to work its magic on him, if only temporarily, but it was enough to keep him moving, enough to keep him focused. Rose's face fleetingly crossed his mind, as if it were showing him random images just to torture him, and he felt the old pang of pain in the center of his chest.

But this time, instead of wallowing in it, he dealt with it in a different way. He pushed the thought out of his mind, gritted his teeth, and said, "Fuck you, Rose!" It felt good. No, it felt *great.* When he turned onto the onramp for Highway 6, he couldn't help but smile. *That's one hell of a therapy,* he thought.

About thirty minutes later, Drew came to the split in the road; he could see now how easy it could have been to miss it, to go to the right, which led to 151, and points northeast. It was as if going either way was a continuation of the same route. He swung to the right, almost sure he was now following his sister's path.

He passed a marker that said: Arlidge 5. He would not stop in Arlidge, not just yet, anyway. Greenview was his first destination, but he nonetheless drove slowly down the dark, two-lane highway, watching both sides of the road for any signs of his sister's car.

The highway took a northwesterly turn, and Arlidge came and went, after which he passed a spot in the road that he would have been very interested in, indeed. In fact, if Drew had been there about thirty minutes sooner, he would have seen two men, one rather old and walking with a limp, extracting Amanda's car from the ditch with an aged wrecker with the word *Zeb's* painted on the driver's side door in crude white letters.

He did, however, see the marker for Exit 265, and made a mental note of it. And it would be here that he eventually would learn of an evil he never knew existed.

Gil and Louise Garret both sat up on their respected bunks as Sheriff Craven came down the hall, keys jangling at his hip, escorting a young girl in handcuffs toward the cell. He unlocked Louise's cell, the door groaning as it swung open. He unlocked Amanda's handcuffs and gave her a little push into the cell. She stood rubbing her wrists, looking around the small space.

Craven was staring at her in a way that made her self-conscious, as if he were undressing her with his eyes. He was, in fact, undressing her with his mind.

"You *are* a pretty young thing, aren't you?" he said, licking his lips.

"Why can't you tell me why you're doing this to me?" she pleaded, brushing her hair away from her face.

"I told you," Craven said, "you'll find out soon enough. In the meantime, we could have us a little fun, know what I mean?"

She backed away from him, until the backs of her legs bumped against the bunk where Louise sat watching the whole exchange with disgust. "Sit down, sweetheart," she said to Amanda, who did just that, never taking her eyes off the sheriff.

"Have it your way," he said, and slammed the cell door shut. He locked it up and strolled off, whistling some off-hand tune.

Amanda dropped her face into her hands and cried. "There, there," Louise said, patting her gently on the back. Amanda raised her teary face, and looked questioningly into Louise's eyes.

"What is going on here?" she asked. "Why am I here?"

"Cain is what's going on," Gil said from the other cell.

"Hush up, Gil," Louise said.

"What is he talking about?" Amanda asked. "Who is Cain?"

"We really don't know *who* he is," Louise said, sighing. "All we *do* know is that he's some kind of devil. He has...powers. Like black magic, or something."

"He's not a devil, Louise, he's just a man with a terrible power," Gil said.

"Who's he?" Amanda asked.

"Oh, that's my *stupid*, and I do mean *stupid*, husband. He's the reason we're here. Have been for a couple of weeks." Gil remained mute at this last remark. "Gil over there thought that we could just waltz right out of town without saying anything. It turned out to be the worst thing we could've done. Now, we're probably going to end up food for that *thing* Cain calls his god." Now Louise's eyes were tearing up. "If we had just stayed put, Gil, we wouldn't be in this mess!"

"How the hell was I supposed to know this would happen?" Gil asked. He stood and walked over to the bars separating the cells, clutching them with both hands. Amanda noticed that his clothes were wrinkled, and he was sporting a beard. He lowered his voice. "This guy has some kind of evil magic he uses to call this...this *thing* right out of the ground. He *sacrifices* people to it. He does this kind of ritual, and out it comes, and you don't *even* want to know what it does to people. The whole town is brainwashed, I tell you. People just aren't who they used to be. That's why I wanted to run. Before we ended up dead, or worse, tied to a pole for Cain's ritual. I guess Louise doesn't understand that."

"Don't lay that guilt trip on me, Gil. Remember, it was *your* idea." Louise turned to Amanda. "He is right about Cain, though. He's not... natural. And I've never seen anything so horrible in my life. I almost fainted. That thing, it just sucked the life out of poor Mrs. Mott."

She stopped speaking for a minute and stared off into space, and Amanda knew that at that moment she must have been reliving some terrifying memory. She snapped out of her trance and said, "The town is crazy, you know. We're never gonna get out of here." She burst out crying, and Amanda put her arms around her and held her close. Gil returned to his bunk and lay down.

Fear surrounded Amanda and closed in on her relentlessly, and as she held Louise she found herself shedding more tears of her own.

5

When Drew pulled into the Greenview Police station, it was still dark, and he was again feeling the fatigue taking its toll on him. He got out of the car and stretched his legs. He walked up to the entrance, and pulled on the door, but found it locked. Zipping up his jacket against the cool early morning air, he peered through the glass door. The building was brightly lit on the inside, but he saw no one.

Next to the door was a metal speaker grill with two black buttons underneath. Above one button were the words Press for Officer on Duty. Above the other was one word: Speak. Drew pressed the first button and heard a harsh buzzing from somewhere inside the station. Just when he was about to push it again, a voice crackled over the speaker. *"Can I help you?"*

He pushed the speak button. "Yes, My name is Drew Townsend, I'm from Iowa City. I'm here to talk to someone about my missing sister."

"One moment, sir."

He saw a man in a dark blue uniform appear from a back hallway and walk through the inner office toward the door, sorting through a key ring as he went. He jammed a key into the deadbolt and unlocked it. He held the door open for Drew and said, "Come on in."

He led Drew over to a desk, and beckoned for him to sit in one of the chairs in front of it. The policeman sat behind the desk, and began sorting through some papers. "I just got the call a little while ago, and I passed that info on to everyone on duty. As far as I'm concerned, this no longer just a simple case of a missing person. It's much more serious than that now."

Even through the strain, Drew felt something akin to relief wash over him. "Thank you so much, Mr., uh, Mr.-"

The policeman stood and offered his hand. " I'm officer Davis." He sat down again. "I know it must be very frustrating, Mr. Townsend. Um, why don't you tell me what happened, and we'll see if we can make any sense of this."

"She was driving back to school alone. We told her she shouldn't be driving alone at night, but she wanted to spend more time with us before she left. We had dinner over at my parents' house. When she left, I made her promise to call me on her cell phone when she was halfway."

"Ok, according to my notes, she was on her way to Cedar Falls, is that right?"

"Yes, that's right. University of Northern Iowa. Only I don't think she made it. I think she took the wrong turn-off after Cedar Rapids and got lost."

"I think I know what you're talking about. It's more like a split in the road. Confusing if you're not watching what you're doing. What makes you think she went the wrong way?" Davis asked.

"Well, she called me right after she went through Cedar Rapids. I remember telling her that Cedar Rapids was not halfway, and she was going to have to call me again. I've always been, you know, a little protective of her."

"I understand."

"Anyway, it wasn't long after that when she called again, only this time she was telling me that someone was trying to kill her. I thought she was joking at first, but she insisted she wasn't. I know my sister pretty well, and she wasn't joking. She said that they ran her off the road. When I asked her where she was, she said by some town called 'Green-something', but she wasn't sure. Oh, and she also said she was in a cornfield. Then she got real panicky, said she could hear them coming. It sounded like she dropped the phone, and then she was gone. Then I heard someone else breathing into the phone, then the line went dead."

"Could it have been her breathing into the phone?"

"I don't think so. I kept saying her name, but there was no answer. Just that heavy breathing. Then nothing. When you look at the map, there *is* no town with 'Green' in it on the route to her college. But, if she had accidentally taken the wrong highway and gone this direction, well, here we are. Greenview."

"You say she claimed she was run off the road?"

"That's what she said," Drew said, nodding his head.

"Did you see anything out of the ordinary on your way up here? Anything at all?"

"No, just that crazy intersection. But it is pretty dark."

"Ok, to be honest with you, I think you're right. She may be around this area. But at this point, there's really not much we can do besides keep a close eye on things. And after we file the report, a detective will be assigned to the case. In the meantime, I can call over to Arlidge and let them know the situation. Maybe they've heard something. I suggest you go on home and wait for us to call. There's really nothing else you can do here. I'm sorry."

"I think I'm gonna look around the area for a while," Drew said, "and see if I can come up with anything." He stood and shook Davis' hand again.

Davis said, "You're more than welcome to do that, Mr. Townsend. But I do caution you - if you see or find out anything at all, you need to call us first. Don't try to take matters into your own hands, ok?"

"I promise, I'll call you first," Drew said. "Thanks for your help." Davis escorted him to the door.

"Good luck to you. We'll keep in touch," Davis said, and he pulled the door shut and locked the deadbolt in place. He offered a little nod to Drew and then walked off to wherever he had been hiding in the first place.

Drew shoved his hands in his pockets and looked up at the stars. They seemed so distant, mysterious. He thought: *Where are you, Amanda?*

He cruised through the dark, silent streets of Greenview, and for a while he thought the entire town might be asleep; he did discover, however, that there *was* activity going on in some parts of the town, a town that he could actually refer to as more of a city.

He didn't spend much time there, though, it just felt wrong. If she had been run off the road, it was very doubtful that it had happened in the city. That would attract too much attention. It had to have happened somewhere on the highway. It just made more sense.

But he couldn't give up; something was very wrong here, and he would just have to keep at it if he was to make any progress. He got back on the highway; yawning and gazing bleary eyed at the headlight beams, he made the drive to Arlidge.

All the way he tried to focus on the road, looking for any sign of Amanda, but his tired eyesight was so poor, it was all he could do to make it into Arlidge. He pulled into an all night market and turned off the engine. He tilted the rearview mirror down and looked with disgust at his reflection. His hair was askew, and the stubbly growth was now thickening into the beginnings of a beard. "You look like shit, Drew," he said to himself. He combed his hair back as well as he could, and went inside the store.

He bought a large danish and a bottle of orange juice, and returned to his car. He consumed most of the danish and downed the juice while staring at the empty interior of the market. The clerk was reading a magazine, and Drew thought, *Must be lonely to work this time of night. What the hell, though. Sometimes it's better to be lonely, huh Drew?* He tilted the seat back a little, and closed his eyes. *Just going to rest my eyes,* he thought.

He awoke to the sound of the clerk tapping on his window. He rolled down his window, and fresh air filled his lungs.

"Are you ok?" the clerk asked. He was a tall thin man who looked more like a bible-toting preacher than a store clerk.

"Um, yeah, I'm ok. Just fell asleep. I'm fine. Hey, listen. Where's the nearest hotel?"

"Right over there," the clerk said, pointing across the street. Drew twisted around and saw a hotel directly across from the market. In his weariness he had missed it altogether.

He went back inside the store and bought some disposable razors and shaving cream, then headed over to the hotel. After checking into a single room, he pulled off his shoes and crawled onto the neatly made bed. His body felt like it was sinking into a cloud, and he drifted off almost immediately.

When he woke up, the sun was slipping through a crack in the drapes.

Amanda...

He went into the bathroom and looked at himself in the mirror. He looked like he was in the throes of a monster hangover, only without the alcohol. He stripped out of his clothes, splashed water from the sink onto his face, and then spread a thick layer of shaving cream over his stubble. The cream had a clean, fresh scent to it, and as he scraped off the stubble, he began to feel more like his old self. When he finally wiped his face clean with one of the white hotel towels, he looked in the mirror and said, "Now that's more like it."

He got into the shower and let the hot water run over his head and back for a long time before he picked up hotel soap and unwrapped it, throwing the wrapper out onto the bathroom floor. It was only hotel soap, but today, it was the best soap in the world. The only down part to the whole thing was that he would have to get into his old clothes, but he nonetheless felt worlds better.

He dressed and combed his hair, marveling at how good his face looked without the stubble. His jacket was hung up in the little nook just outside the bathroom, and from one of its pockets he produced his cell phone. He punched in Amanda's number, but wasn't surprised to again hear the recording.

Drew walked over to the hotel lobby, and approached the man behind the counter.

"Can I help you, sir?" the man asked.

"I'm looking for my sister," he said, producing the 5x7 of Amanda he taken out of the frame on his mantle. The man looked closely at the photograph, and shook his head.

"I haven't seen her, I'm very sorry. Have you been to the police?"

"Yes, but I'm doing a little looking on my own." He folded the picture and tucked it into his back pocket.

"Well, good luck, sir."

"Thank you very much, I appreciate it."

"Have you been to Greenview?" he asked Drew.

"Yes, in fact, I just came from there, thanks." Drew started to walk away, but stopped with the desk clerk's next question.

"How about Oak Junction? Have you tried there?"

"Oak Junction?"

"Yeah, it's about halfway between here and Greenview. It's not a city, or anything like that, just a tiny little town. I don't even think there's a sign on the highway for it. Just an exit."

"Oak Junction?"

"Oak Junction," the man confirmed.

"Thank you very much, you've been a big help," Drew said, hurrying toward the door. He left the hotel lobby, climbed into his Escort, grabbed his sunglasses from the glove box, and started the car. *I'm still looking, kid,* he thought.

As Drew drove north along Highway 151, the new sun was glaring like a fiery furnace above the eastern landscape. He moved slowly along, pulling over every now and then to let the faster traffic pass by. But even in the daytime, traffic was minimal, and he found himself pulling over anyway, just to get out and look around.

He noticed the cornfields were creeping up closer on both sides of him, especially to his right, on the east side of the road. And just when he was turning this over in his mind, he saw something on the road that made him pull over to the side and just stare.

I'm in the middle of a cornfield, for Christ's sake....

It was pretty easy to see in the daylight, and if he had been watching a little closer earlier that morning, when it was still dark, he would have seen it then, too. But he had been just too tired.

Running down the middle of the southbound lane were two black stripes, which ran for about twenty yards before curling over into his lane and ending at the gravel shoulder. In several spots, the intense early morning sun twinkled off bits of tail light lens, glittering red and white on the flat blacktop.

He thought: *Oh my God, how could I have missed this?*

Drew got out of the car and walk up to the point where the skid marks connected with the gravel. His heart beat faster as he saw the tell-tale signs; the long swipes in the gravel the tires had made before digging into the soft soil at the top of the ditch, and the two shallow trenches down the side of the ditch where the tires had dug in before the vehicle came to a rest at the bottom, where the weeds and mud had been crushed flat by the weight of something very heavy.

He walked farther along and saw tracks in the gravel, and even footprints. There were two sets of impressions running diagonally out of the ditch. *This is where they pulled her car out,* he thought. *But then what?*

He went down into the ditch and walked toward the depression in the bottom. That was when he saw the marks, about halfway up the other side of the ditch, the marks of someone digging their way to the top. Scrambling up the embankment, he saw tracks leading off toward a cornfield. But something else caused an uneasy feeling to creep up on him: There was more than one set of tracks.

6

Around the same time Drew was inspecting the scene of the accident, Cain was waking up, his tired body throbbing with pain. But this was not a pain associated with an injury, nor that of a first time workout. This was the pain of *age*. Even back in Sioux City he had been feeling the effects, and seeing the effects; now, as he gazed at his reflection, he saw an entirely different person from the one that had stolen the book. Not one that had aged six years, but one that had aged *twenty* or *thirty* years.

He had long ago scoured the book looking for a way to reverse the process, but to no avail. So, he accepted this as part of the price he had to pay for his powers, but it was a price that oftentimes made him feel *weak*, and *weakness* was no longer a part of his vocabulary.

And although he would be the last to admit it, his mind, his very thinking, had changed so drastically that the Lucas Cain that had found and stolen the book had not only ceased to exist on the outside, but on the inside, as well. He was wholly consumed by the book, and mad with the darkness and the power that he lived with daily.

He was in a particularly dark mood, and it was on these occasions that his fixation with death was at its apex. The mystery behind it, and what it felt like when the very life drained from your body, and your heart stopped beating.

Cain got dressed and went into the tiny office where he kept the book. He pulled it from a desk drawer, lightly ran his fingers over the cover, the static sparks dancing on his fingertips, and then held it close to his chest and closed his eyes.

When he opened them, he was outside, standing near the fresh graves at the rear of Oak Junction Cemetery. He squinted in the sunlight, then began to walk around the graves as his eyes adjusted. A mild breeze stirred his raven black hair, and finally he stood with the sun to his back. He tried to picture what the corpses now looked like, decomposing in simple dirt graves, food for the worms.

He noticed his shadow stretching out before him, over the grave nearest him and onto the next.

"You were all weak, and now you are dead. You lay rotting in my shadow, the shadow of Cain." There was no emotion in the statement, no anger, no sadness, only detachment.

The grave in front of him began to bulge outward, slowly at first, then all at once as the corpse that was buried there rose out of the ground and stood at the foot of its own grave. It had been a man, a man who had a bullet hole in his forehead, and skin that was dark with decay, shriveled and sucked in so that this man was now a skeleton sporting a layer of putrid flesh and clothing that hung loosely on its frame. A man who no longer had eyes. Cain was disappointed not to see worms oozing out of every orifice. Still, he was transfixed by this vision, this thing of beauty, and he tilted his head one way, then the other, as he looked into the face of death.

Tonight, he would witness death again, would feed the growing hunger for evil that most of the town's people were feeling. And he would do it again in several days time, for this night's ritual would not be the only ritual, no, it would be merely one of several he would perform. Just the mere thought that he could exercise his power, his *privilege* to do so, made his skin crawl with anticipation. A cold shudder ran up his spine, and he smiled, again clutching the book to his chest. And then he was gone.

The corpse, no longer blessed with Cain's company, collapsed in on itself, into a twisted pile of flesh and bone. But there would be no crows to peck and scratch at this corpse. Not today. Not in Oak Junction.

When he appeared back in his church, his body screamed with exhaustion; that little trick always took its toll on him, drained him of his energy, just as on the night of the Garret's foiled escape. That time had been difficult on him as well, which is why he so quickly vanished as soon as he saw the Garret's car smash into the tree. He didn't trust letting even the sheriff see him in that exhausted state. He had yet to perfect his powers, and until he did, it would remain one of Cain's dirty little secrets.

7

Not far from where Cain had just awakened, Jenny and Ashley White were just waking up in Ashley's room, rubbing their eyes at the rays of warm light streaming through the bedroom window. Jenny turned on the TV for Ashley, and then went to the kitchen to make breakfast, passing the master bedroom and Harvey's incessant snoring along the way.

He had come home around three in the morning, and had gone straight to bed. She didn't have to see him to know he was drunk; he was drunk twenty-four hours a day, sure as the sun rose everyday. He hadn't made a big deal of her absence from the bedroom, but *had* mentioned it a few times, as if waiting for her to give in, and start sleeping with him again. But as always, she would casually remark how he was gone most of the time, and she just didn't like to leave Ashley alone, and she just couldn't help it if she always fell asleep watching TV in Ashley's room. So far, she had gotten away with it; Harvey had other things on his mind, and that probably saved her from being forced into sex with this raging drunk that used to be her husband. The problem was, she didn't know how long that would last. And she had an idea that when the time came, Harvey would take what he wanted no matter what.

She took a frying pan out of the cupboard, set it on the stove, and grabbed a carton of eggs from the refrigerator. She cracked four eggs into the pan and tossed the shells in the garbage, which was already filled with beer cans. She winced at the loud clanking of the eggshells hitting empty aluminum cans.

She used a wooden spoon to stir the eggs together into scrambled eggs, Ashley's favorite. As she watched the yellow goo slowly harden, she was already thinking about what was going to happen later that night.

The ritual....

Cain was going to sacrifice another poor soul tonight, out at the old Willard place. Harvey wouldn't miss it for the world. And he would almost certainly want her to tag along, as well. And that was the last thing she needed.

She would have to be very convincing tonight, very convincing, indeed.

8

Drew followed the tracks across an empty field, finally stopping in front of the cornfield.

This is where she called me from, he thought. He began to feel the first stirrings of fear, as if he were walking into a danger zone, one from which he might not return. But to walk away would mean turning his back on Amanda, and this was something he just could not bring himself to do. He entered the cornfield.

The soft furrows revealed a flurry of tracks, and a short ways in he noticed that two sets of tracks broke off, one to each side of a center set. He kneeled and touched his hand in one of what were obviously sneaker tracks. *Amanda's* tracks. He continued on, the other sets of tracks flanking him on either side.

He came to an area where the tracks seemed to stop, pointing in a different direction. The two outside sets seemed to converge on this spot before splitting up again. He tried to picture what had happened that night: *Amanda running through this cornfield pursued by two people, presumably men. Stopping at this very spot to call her brother for help. Hearing the pursuers approaching, she runs, either throwing or dropping her phone, most likely the latter. This much was pretty clear, but the rest, that was a different matter. And that's what scared him the most.*

He resumed following the tracks at a slower pace, afraid that at any moment he might chance upon his sister's body beneath these stalks of corn, nude and curled up, already in the throes of rigor mortis. Instead, he only saw more prints.

As he neared to edge of the field, he saw the shapes of buildings forming between the stalks, and as he drew even closer still, the rotting hulk of a dead horse. The buzzing of flies was almost as intense as the smell, and he thought it quite odd that someone would just leave a dead horse lying around like that.

He stayed just inside the corn, peeking out at the nearest of the buildings, a farmhouse with an exterior that looked like it had weathered a thousand grueling summers, and just as many harsh winters. There was also a barn, also in rather poor shape, and a small stables in front of which was a corral made of crude wooden posts.

The rising sun cast long shadows away from the buildings, and Drew thought: *Aren't most farmers up before the sun?* The whole scene seemed serene, empty. Unnatural. He gathered his courage and stepped out of the corn, and walked over the packed dirt toward the house, skirting around the dead horse on his way.

Boards creaked as he stepped up onto the porch and knocked on the screen door. He heard nothing from within the house. He opened the screen door, its rusty hinges complaining, and knocked on the inside door. Still nothing. He stood quietly and listened for any movement within the house.

As Drew stepped off the porch and walked toward the corral and stables, and the view of more corn with the small town beyond, Angus Swapp was on the telephone waking up Frank Craven.

The ringing of the telephone broke the silence of the bedroom, but did nothing to influence the two figures asleep in the bed. But after the second ring, one of the figures turned over and reached out with one hairy arm, grasping blindly for the phone. He managed to find it halfway through the third ring.

"Hello?" he answered, voice groggy with sleep.

"Hello, Sheriff?"

"Yeah...and this better be good."

"I thought I better call you. I think it's important."

"Who is this?" Craven asked, sitting up in the bed.

"This is Angus Swapp, Sheriff, and like I said, I thought I better call you about this. There's some stranger pokin' around my place out here, was even bangin' on my door. I'm thinkin' he might have somethin' to do with that girl."

Now he had Craven's attention.

"What's he look like?"

"Well, he's pretty young, and he ain't dressed like one of the locals."

"What's he doing now?" Craven asked.

"He's over by my corral. Looks like he's tryin' to get a good look at the town. Ok, now he's headin' on over to the cornfield. Yep, he's gone. Looks like he came in the same way she did. You want me to do anything, Sheriff?"

"No, don't do anything, Angus. But thanks for calling me. You did good. I'll mention it to Cain."

"Thanks, Sheriff. Anything to help. Bye, now."

Sheriff Craven hung up the phone, and shoved the covers off of his naked body. Betty turned over and asked, "Are you going somewhere, Frank?"

"Yeah, gotta go take care of business."

Betty pulled the blanket down, exposing both of her breasts. "Are you *sure* you need to go right now?" she asked, one side of her mouth turned upward in a sly grin.

"Oh man," he said, gawking at her. His hair stuck up comically on one side of his head. "Yeah, I'm sure. But don't you worry. I'll be back before you know it." He leaned over and gave her a peck on the lips, copping a quick feel. "You can count on it."

Drew took Exit 265, which was really just a turn lane, and found himself on a gravel road that went north and south, and he turned right, driving north up the dusty lane. To the west were mostly woods, and to the east, several farms flanked by cornfields, one through which he had just followed his sister's tracks. Ahead, he spied a gas station, one that by it appearance had apparently been there a long time.

He parked next to the old building and got out of the car. He saw an old man in greasy blue overalls limping toward him. The man looked like he had just woken up, and indeed he had - all it took was one little phone call a few minutes before to get him up and around.

Zeb, this is Sheriff Craven. There's a stranger coming into town, and he might just stop at your place. I want you to get your ass up, and make yourself be seen, so maybe he'll stop for sure. And then I want you to keep *him there as long as you can. Do you here me? You keep him there as long as you can.*

And Zeb, being as old as he was, and as hung over as he was, struggled to get up as fast as he could, to get those old joints in gear, but it just wasn't fast enough. The stranger's car could have driven right by while Zeb was still in the bathroom, fighting off the dizziness while he took his morning piss.

Fortunately for him, the stranger *had* stopped, and now all he had to do was detain him for a while. He lumbered toward Drew in the bright, early morning sun (which was like a spike through his head today) and waved one hand.

"Good mornin' to you, young man." His voice was broken by a throat-full of phlegm, and he spat a large glob onto the ground. "What can I do for ya' today?"

"Hello, sir," Drew said, offering a hand. "My name's Drew Townsend. How are you?"

"Well, I'm just fine, just fine. Zebediah Brown," he said, shaking Drew's hand. His fetid breath hit Drew right in the face. "But you can call me Zeb. Everyone else around these parts does."

"Ok, Zeb. Hey listen, I wonder if you could do me a favor, and take a look at this photograph." He pulled the folded 5x7 out of his back pocket and handed it to Zeb, who looked at it with watery, bloodshot eyes.

"Pretty girl, who is she?"

"She's my sister, and she's missing. Have you seen her, or anyone that looks like her around town?"

"I'm real sorry to hear that."

"But have you seen her around town?" Drew asked again. Zeb studied the picture again, and then said, "This sun is killing me. Can't take it much anymore. C'mon inside the office, and I'll have another look."

Drew followed him into the office, where Zeb laid the picture on the counter, flattening it out with his gnarled hands. "You know, there's been so many people comin' and goin', I can't be sure. How about I get us somethin' to drink?" He limped toward the cooler.

Drew was growing impatient, and furthermore, was getting the idea that this old man was playing some kind of game with him. "Look, I don't want anything to drink, I just want to know if you've seen my sister."

"Just hold on, young man, and I'll look again. I said I would. And don't you worry about the drink, it's on me." He handed Drew a can of Coke, and Drew immediately set it down on the counter.

"Thanks, I'll drink it later."

Zeb popped open a can of beer, guzzled half the can down, and wiped his hairy face with the sleeve of his overalls. "I know, I know, it's kinda early for this, but they say it's the best cure for a hangover, and right now I'm really needin' it. Now, let's take a look at that picture."

He leaned over the picture, and a drop of beer ran down his beard and dripped onto Amanda's face. Drew picked it up and wiped it off on his jeans, then held it out in front of Zeb. Zeb tried to grab it, but Drew pulled it back. "Can you please just look at it?" He asked, his voice straining with irritation.

"I'm tryin' to, but ya keep movin' it around," Zeb said. He opened his mouth and released a loud, fragrant burp. That was it.

Drew folded the picture and slid it into his back pocket, shaking his head.

"Thanks, anyway," he said on his way out, leaving the can of pop on Zeb's counter.

"Look, I said I'd -" But the rest was lost as the door swung shut behind him. He was glad to be out in the fresh air again, able to breath without the smell of farts or burps or rotten morning breath.

He almost made it to his car when he heard tires crunching on gravel, and he looked up to see Craven's cruiser flying down the road toward the station, creating a long dust cloud behind him. Drew thought: *Why is he driving so damn fast? Did he know I was here?* Drew knew he should be glad to see the sheriff, but that feeling was dampened by his growing suspicion. Something here just didn't feel *right*.

Sheriff Craven pulled up in front of the station, and got out of the car. His tan uniform was wrinkled, and his hair still stuck up in places after the quick comb and water job he performed on himself before he left Betty's place. Drew couldn't help but notice the huge revolver bouncing on Craven's hip as he walked over to him.

"Good morning, officer," Drew said, walking out to meet him.

"And good morning to you, son." He shook Drew's hand amiably enough, but there seemed to be sternness in his manner, and Drew could see it in the lines of his face. "I'm Sheriff Craven. What can I help you with today?" He stared at Drew with wire-rimmed reflector shades that brought back a scene in a movie he had once seen.

You gonna be settin' here a spell.

"Drew Townsend. I'm looking for my sister, here's a picture of her." He pulled out the photograph of Amanda and handed it to Craven. He could see the reflection of the picture in Craven's sunglasses. "She came up missing yesterday, and I think she's around here."

"Now, what would make you think *that*, Mr. Townsend," Craven said thickly, handing the picture back to Drew. Instead of putting it away, he tried to hand it back.

"Don't you need to make a copy of that, or something?"

"Don't need to. Let me ask you again - What makes you think she would be around here?"

"Because she called me last night from the middle of a cornfield saying that someone had run her off the road, and -"

"Whoa, hold on there," Craven interjected. "Do you know how many cornfields there are in this part of the state?"

"Well, yes, but...." Drew was almost afraid to go on.

"But what?"

"But I found skid marks out on the highway I think were from her car. I even saw footprints in a field."

"What you saw was the scene of an accident we had last night with one of the local drunks. Had a little too much of the sauce and ended up in that ditch. Some folks from a nearby farm heard the crash, and came to help. There are probably the footprints everywhere. Look, I know you want to find your sister, but she's not here. Have you gone to the police anywhere else?"

"Yes, I went to Arlidge and Greenview," Drew lied. He *had* gone to Greenview, but not to the Arlidge police, but at this point, he thought it best that he plant the idea in Craven's head that a lot of people knew he was here. He added one more little white lie. "I filed missing person reports at both towns, and they're out looking now."

Sheriff Craven looked visibly agitated. "Well, I can tell you right now, she's not here."

"Would it be any trouble if I looked around town a bit, maybe show her picture around?" Drew asked, but he somehow already knew the answer. Later, he would regret pushing any farther than that, but sometimes people do dumb things in the name of love.

"Actually, what you need to do is climb in your car, and go on home. She's not here." Craven put his hands on his hips to punctuate his command.

"Sheriff, if I could just -" Drew was cut off in mid-sentence when Craven planted his meaty fist in his stomach. He dropped to dirt on his hands and knees, gasping for air.

"This is the last time I'm going to tell you, son, she's not here. Get in your car, and get the fuck out of here. And if you're thinking of telling the police, think twice. Who are they going to believe? A sheriff with an impeccable record, or a total stranger, one who just *could* be wanted for robbery in this town. Get the picture? Go away, son. Go away, and don't come back."

Drew finally managed to get to his feet, but was still doubled over and holding his stomach as he stumbled over to his car. As he grabbed the door handle, Craven spoke again.

"Do we have an understanding, Mr. Townsend?" Craven asked, hands again on his hips.

Drew couldn't speak; he was still hitching for air, but he did manage to nod in reply before getting into his car. He winced in pain as he sat down and started the engine. As difficult as it was, he still managed to drive out of town, rolling down the window to let the fresh air into the car. He thought about stopping for a minute, just to get his composure, but changed his mind. Craven would surely check to see if he had *really* left town. He got on the highway and drove straight for his hotel room in Arlidge.

He now knew that Amanda was somewhere in Oak Junction. He also knew that calling the police would probably do no good. He might, in fact, end up in trouble himself. Or something worse.

You gonna' to be settin' here a spell.

The sheriff had said something that had stuck in Drew's mind: *He had a little too much of the sauce and ended up in that ditch.* Drew never mentioned the ditch, but the sheriff spoke as if he *had* mentioned it. Of course, it could be coincidence, but he didn't think that very likely. This town had something to hide, and he would have to find out what it was if he ever wanted to see his sister again.

9

Dusk was just blanketing the town as Jenny was cooking dinner (meatloaf, mash potatoes and gravy, biscuits - Harvey's favorite), while Ashley sat at the kitchen table, a small pile of crayons and a coloring book set out before her. She quietly and intently scribbled, occasionally looking up to make sure mommy was still in the kitchen.

Jenny was in front of the stove when Harvey walked into the room.

"Something smells good in here," he said, walking up behind her and putting his arms around her. He tried to kiss her neck, and the odor of whiskey filled her nostrils.

Hang in there, she thought.

She gently removed his arms and turned around, flicking her eyes toward Ashley. Then she smiled and winked at him. He smiled and winked back. *So far, so good.*

"Listen," he said, "after the ritual tonight, I was thinking, well, you know."

Careful, careful...

"Oh, about that. I'm just going to stay home with Ashley, ok? I mean, I just don't want her to see that right now, you know."

The smile began to fade from Harvey's face, and for a moment Jenny thought she was going to be on the receiving end of his hand again. Instead, he pointed out what she already knew.

"But Cain said *everyone* had to come," Harvey said. Jenny held out the flyer for Harvey to read.

"I know, Harv," she said as good-naturedly as she could. "But it also says special circumstances contact Sheriff Craven. So I did. He said it was quite all right, he understood completely. He's really a nice man. We should have him for dinner sometime."

She thought that last was a nice touch.

"And after the ritual, we can, well, you know." She flicked her eyes toward Ashley, then tilted her head and winked. Harvey's smile returned.

Bingo!

Asshole, Drew thought. He touched the tender round patch in the middle of his stomach; let his shirt drop over it. He had returned to his hotel room and slept most of the day before getting up to shave and shower. It was now nine-fifteen, and darkness was taking over where daylight had left off. He knew he was taking a big chance, but it was one he had to take. He just could not leave his sister behind.

A partially full moon was rising into the growing darkness as Drew sped down Highway 151 toward Oak Junction. By the time he reached the spot where he discovered the skid marks, the eastern horizon was filling with stars, the west bruising with purple and blue.

He pulled over and thought about his next move, then decided it would be better not to park here; no doubt that sheriff would be on the lookout for him. He quickly spun around and took off in the other direction, traveling about a mile before turning around and parking. He tried to park as far off the road as possible, but judging by the way the car was already leaning, if he moved any farther over, he would himself end up in the ditch.

He sat in silence thinking: *Is this all going to be worth it? What if she's dead? Maybe I should have called the cops after all. Yet again, if I did, she would probably be dead for sure.* It all seemed confusing, as if there *was* no right answer. But, what bothered him the most was the indecision, and he found himself taking the .38 from the glove box, putting it in his jacket pocket with his cell phone. He got out of the car, and set the alarm with the key chain remote. *Beep! Beep! Beep!*

He went to the front of the car and surveyed the area. Although he couldn't see the spot where he believed Amanda's car left the road, he could see the very cornfields through which he had followed her footprints. In front of him was a large open area, followed by thick woods. He slid down the embankment and climbed up the other side, then broke into a run until he had crossed the open field and reached the woods. Here he stopped to catch his breath (which took several minutes, and he thought: *Man, I need to take up jogging*), and check to see if anyone had seen him.

He peeked out from behind the cover of trees, but everything had turned into dark shapes. At this distance, the cornfield to the north was a large black mass under the starry sky. The cool summer wind blew back his hair, and whispered through the trees. It was a lonely, ominous sound that reminded him of Halloween when he was a kid. The sound the October wind made through the trees late at night, when all the kids had gone home, the houses had grown dark, and the dead leaves danced and scraped along the sidewalks and empty streets. He would lie in bed at night and listen to that wind, and the voices of the long dead it carried with it.

He crept north in the shadowy realm of the woods, oblivious of what awaited him ahead.

10

The prisoners in the Oak Junction jail heard the thick metal door to the booking room open, then slam shut, which caused them all to start, especially Gil and Louise, because the moment they both dreaded had finally arrived. For Gil, it was especially bad, and his hands started to sweat, his heart pumping like mad.

Amanda looked up and saw Sheriff Craven appear in the hall, then another man, dressed all in black. Black jeans, black tee shirt, black boots, over which he wore a black overcoat. His long, jet-black hair had thick streaks of gray running through it. Perhaps on any other occasion she would have laughed at the way this person was dressed, maybe walking down the street, or in a grocery store, but she knew as soon as she saw him that this man was not to be laughed at.

Cain walked past Gil's cell, offering him a cursory glance, and stopped in front of the women's cell. Amanda gaped at him, almost shivering in his presence.

"You look frightened, girl. What's your name?" Cain asked.

"Amanda," she replied. "Why am I here? What have I done?"

"You're here because I want you to be here," Cain said. "And you have nothing to be frightened of…yet. But you," he said, looking at Gil with his dark, emotionless eyes, "you have something to be frightened of, to be sure. Take him first, Sheriff."

Craven opened the cell door and walked over to Gil, who was still sitting on his bunk with his hands clamped so tightly to the edge that Craven had to force them off before he could handcuff him. He escorted Gil out of the cell, and as they passed, Cain said, "Don't give us any trouble, Gil, you'll only make it worse."

Cain stood staring blankly at Amanda until Craven returned for Louise. As Craven handcuffed her, tears filled her eyes.

"Where are you taking me?" she asked, her voice little more than a squeak.

"You're going to have front row seats for the show, my dear," Cain said. Then to Amanda, he said, "I'm sorry, but you'll have to sit this one out, but I assure you, you'll have your turn." He turned and followed the sheriff out the door. Amanda heard the deadbolt click into place, and then she was alone with the silence.

Leaving the body had been a big mistake, and it almost exposed Cain, but he had always been careful, and the police walked away empty handed. But it had been too close for comfort, and when he saw his name in the papers, he knew it was time to go. Powers or no, he could not afford any attention.

For almost a year, Cain performed his rituals, leaving the residents of Sioux City wondering just what was happening to all those girls. He took great joy in reading accounts of the missing girls in the newspaper, and how police had no clues as to the whereabouts of the missing persons. It strengthened his ego, being the only person alive who knew the truth.

And as he grew more powerful, his intellect grew as well, and eluding the police all this time became child's play.

And yet, he had slipped.

It wasn't a matter of stupidity, or forgetfulness, it was a matter of just plain over-confidence.

The beast was gone, but Cain stood wide-eyed and delirious, totally exalted by the sheer power of it all. Candlelight flickered across the shrunken countenance of the corpse tied to the tree. In the silence, the crickets resumed their nighttime chorus.

Dizziness overtook him, and he felt a shiver run down his spine. He was floating on clouds of glory, and the feeling swept him away. He capered around the corpse, laughing like a small child in a playground, putting his face right up to its face, and laughing even harder. He spun around and around until he thought he was going to fall over.

He concentrated on the corpse, and it started to dance and jiggle against the thick tree trunk. Cain laughed until he thought he would burst, and screamed out in glee, his cries piercing the night like the cries of a banshee.

He even made the corpse smile. *A sickening grin that lifted loose, wrinkled folds of skin around it.*

He untied the corpse, and sat just outside the ring of candles while he made it dance like a grotesque puppet. Finally, he let it drop to the ground, and gathered up the candles and rope, and of course, the book. At that moment he felt so powerful, so unstoppable, that he left the corpse right where it had dropped. It stared up at him with empty eye sockets, and Cain decided that one more act was needed to confirm his supremacy.

He urinated on the corpse.

He walked back to his car thinking that it just didn't matter; if someone found the body, it would send a shockwave through the city, and the police would crawl like ants over the area, searching for precious clues. But it wouldn't matter. He was untouchable. He drove home with his teeth clenched and his blood pounding in his ears. But the elation would not last forever. In fact, it would barely last the night.

When he awoke the next morning (around 11 o'clock - he no longer needed the job at the bakery, as he had a steady flow of money coming in from sources that really didn't know they were giving it to him), feeling hung over, and his muscles complained when he tried to get out of bed. He lit a cigarette (something he had just started to enjoy occasionally, although it would never prove to be a habit with him) and sat on the edge of the bed, yawning and stretching his arms, and feeling much older than his years. If he could have seen a before and after photo set of himself at that moment, the before photo from perhaps six months before, he would have been shocked. He did indeed notice the changes that were taking place physically, but seeing himself in the mirror every day gave it a gradual descent to his own eyes, a minor change, lessening what to another would have been obvious changes.

As he sat trying to fend off the effects of his slumber, the events of the night before came rushing back, and he found himself both surprised and shocked at what he had done. He felt an urge to return to the campground, and bury the evidence next to where the others lie decomposing in their makeshift graves, but it was an urge he had to fight off if he wanted to stay anonymous. He decided instead to keep a very close eye on the papers for any news regarding the campsite. It was the only safe thing to do.

He considered that they may never find it, or perhaps some animal might have dragged it off somewhere to devour it, in which case there wouldn't be much of anything left to worry about anyway. As it turned out, he was not that fortunate.

The story appeared the very next day, in the morning edition of the Sioux City Herald, and although Cain was not happy with his decision to leave the corpse exposed, he was also disappointed that the article didn't make the front page. It was, in fact, so small that he thought: They're holding something back. Assholes are waiting for someone to tip his hand. *It read:*

'Shriveled' corpse found, police searching for leads

Sioux City - Two hikers, whose names are being withheld, discovered the body of a woman in a wooded area about ten miles outside Sioux City. The two made the gruesome discovery early yesterday morning, and immediately notified authorities. Police say they have not identified the body, and in fact are having a hard time pinpointing the women's age because of the unusual condition of the body. Police were willing to speculate that this might be connected to the recent disappearances of eleven young women, but that was as far as they would go on the issue.

Although he was quite sure that the police could make no connection between the corpse and him, he was bothered by the sloppiness of it, and he brooded for two days before finally giving in to his urge. He now understood why criminals sometimes returned to the scene of a crime. The trouble with that was, the cops knew it, too.

But, he had to go.

He felt weak, stupid, for letting himself fall into a situation such as this, especially since he had mastered his powers, and sharpened his intelligence to a level he had never experienced before. He knew he had not left anything incriminating at the campsite, and yet....

Two days later Cain forced himself out of bed around eight a.m. (an outrageously early time for him to be getting up), showered, dressed, and hit the road in his Caddy, which was shining like a black diamond in the sun. The day he had read the article, he had taken the car to a detail shop, where they cleaned the car spotless inside and out. Afterwards, he searched the car himself for anything incriminating, anything at all. He ditched everything from the trunk in the dumpster behind the apartment building, knowing fully well that the truck from the refuse company would be there early the next morning to empty it.

Now satisfied that he was clean, he made the trip out to the campsite in the early morning sun, the same campsite where he had performed many rituals, hiding the bodies in the woods a short distance away - the same site where he had even performed his ritual in the snow. *But by then, his powers were strong enough so that even the frozen ground offered no resistance to his shovel.*

When he arrived at the chain across the dirt road, he immediately saw the yellow police tape surrounding a large area of the woods. That they had included such a large area in their crime scene had Cain wondering just how close they had come to his burial grounds.

He got out of the car, and looked around. He had even dressed differently, as if out hiking or walking, and that would prove to be a blessing. In the meantime, he felt absolutely idiotic in his shorts (he had ruined a perfectly good pair of black jeans to make them) and tank top. He even had his hair neatly pulled into a ponytail.

He ducked under the police tape, and walked straight for the camp site, feigning the bizarre curiosity of a motorist passing by the scene of an accident, searching for the mangled remains of the victims, or the paramedics wheeling away someone covered with a sheet on a gurney, red blossoming on white.

Not only had the police gone through a lot of trouble to surround the area with tape, they had also surrounded the campsite itself, but he could tell by the scattered footprints that there had been a lot of activity here. There was the aged picnic table, and the barbeque, and the tree that had been agent to so many deaths.

He walked around the tape this time, going into the woods, where he stopped and looked around again, taking no notice of the dead robin on the ground near his feet. He was alone. He didn't walk all the way to the burial ground, just far enough to know that although it was within the boundaries of the tape it had not been found. A smile crossed his face at the thought of policeman and detectives swarming through the area for clues, tromping over the graves of the eleven missing girls whose disappearances had perplexed them so.

His edginess abated, he walked back to his car, only to find he had visitors. An unmarked Ford sedan was parked directly behind the Cadillac, and two men in suits had his car doors open, and were leaning inside as if looking for something.

Cain strolled confidently toward them and asked, "Can I help you?"

Both men stood up, not bothering to shut his car doors, and the one closest to him, the one with the bald head and goatee said casually, "Why, yes you can, sir. You can begin by telling us who you are, and why you are entering a crime scene?"

"My name's Lucas Cain, and I come here all the time to walk, or think, or whatever. Have I done something wrong?"

The younger of the two walked around from the other side of Cain's car, and opened a back door to the sedan.

"We're going to have to ask you to come with us, Mr. Cain," he said, standing by the open door.

"Whoa, wait a minute," Cain said, waving both hands out in front of him. "I don't even know who you guys are. I'd like to see some ID first, if you don't mind."

"Oh, certainly, Mr. Cain," the bald one said. They both held out their ID's for him. "I'm Detective Carlyle, and this is Detective Noble," he said, motioning to the young one, who nodded inertly, keeping his eyes glued on Cain.

"Do you know what happened here, Mr. Cain?" Carlyle asked.

"No, I have no idea. So why do I have to go with you?"

"Because you have violated a crime scene, and we are obligated to interview you, whether we think you are guilty of anything or not." Carlyle stared right into his eyes when he spoke, and Cain supposed he was trying to be intimidating, and it was all Cain could do to keep himself from staring this man down. No, this was not the time to show them what was what. But, he did not look away from the stare; instead, he offered his hand to Carlyle. "Nice to meet you, Detective."

Just one touch…

Instead of shaking his hand, Carlyle said, "I need to check for weapons. Are you carrying any weapons?"

"Of course not," Cain said, allowing Carlyle to pat him down.

"Please, get in, Mr. Cain."

"What about my car?" Cain asked. "You're not going to leave it like that are you?"

Carlyle motioned Noble over to Cain's car, and the younger detective closed the Caddy's doors. "Don't worry about your car, we'll take care of it."

"What do you mean by that?"

"Mr. Cain, get in the car," Carlyle demanded.

Cain slid onto the back seat, and Noble slid in next him. Cain's little play at connecting with Carlyle's mind had not worked, but here was another opportunity sitting right next to him, an opportunity to at least turn the tide in his favor.

"Am I under arrest, Detective Carlyle?" Cain asked from the back seat.

"You are not under arrest, Mr. Cain. This is merely a routine procedure, and should not be construed as an accusation."

"That's fine with me, Detective, I'm just worried about my car."

"Like I said, we'll take care of it." Cain knew they were going to search his car, looking for the tiniest speck of evidence linking him to this crime. He also knew that if they damaged his car in any way with their tow truck, he was going to be one pissed off man.

On the way into town, Cain glanced down and saw Noble's hand resting near his on the seat. As Carlyle made his way down the dirt road, swerving occasionally to miss several of the more threatening potholes (Cain knew where the bad ones were by heart), Cain managed to let his body shift closer to Noble, and he was able to let his hand touch Noble's several times, just long enough for his purpose.

Cain is an innocent man. He has done nothing wrong. There is no evidence against him.

Cain pushed these thoughts as hard as he could, hoping they would catch and hold for a while.

Noble turned to Cain. "Why would you want go into a crime scene anyway, Mr. Cain? You know it could be dangerous."

Carlyle looked at them in the rearview mirror.

"I know it was stupid of me, I'm really sorry." Cain said.

"That's ok," Noble said, smiling widely, "it happens all the time. We'll get you in and out in no time."

Cain smiled inwardly, and watched the passing landscape as they drove toward town.

At the station, the detectives ushered Cain into a small room with a small plate above the door that read: Interrogation Room 1. He expected a room with a large two-way mirror along one wall, but that was not the case here. It was just a small windowless room with tan cinderblock walls, furnished with a table and four metal folding chairs.

"Just hang tight, Mr. Cain," Carlyle said, and they left him alone in the room, locking the door behind them on the way out.

After a few minutes, they both returned, jacketless, ties loosened from the summer heat. Carlyle sat straight across from Cain, Noble to his right. Carlyle placed a mini tape recorder in the middle of the desk, and said, "This will save us a lot of time, Mr. Cain, as opposed to paperwork."

Bullshit, Cain thought, that's just in case I say something incriminating, so you can throw it back in my face, asshole.

Then the questions began, and at first they seemed fairly routine, but after about forty-five minutes of beating around the bush, Carlyle started in with what Cain supposed were the "tricky" questions, the logic being that if Cain knew any information that only the police knew, he had obtained that information first hand, and was therefore the one responsible for the crimes. Police had been doing this for years, but Cain would still prove to be a stone too hard to crack.

"How long have you been going to prostitutes, Lucas?" Carlyle asked. *This was one time when Cain would have to put up with being called Lucas.*

"I've never been with a prostitute. It's illegal, and spreads diseases."

"Really? Well, what if I told you that we have a witness who saw your car in an area of town near 10th Street, an area known for pushers and prostitutes?" *Carlyle was doing his best to apply the pressure, and Cain had to force himself to remain serious.*

"I'd say that your witness is either lying, or needs glasses," Cain said calmly. *He noticed Carlyle was gritting his teeth now.*

"Mr. Cain, you have to admit, the average person knows better than to violate a crime scene, unless there's reason," Noble said. *At first Cain thought that his suggestions had lost hold, but as the interview went on, he would discover that it was just his routine running on autopilot, like when the whore had asked for her money even after he had planted her head with ideas.*

"Yes, I understand what you're saying, Detective Noble, but you have to admit, people* are *curious about things, and -"

"What things, Lucas?" Carlyle asked.

"A yellow tape that says crime scene, Detective," Cain said, looking into Carlyle's eyes. *He could almost see them redden with anger.*

"Were you expecting to find something?"

"No, not really. Just curious."

"Maybe something you left behind?" *Carlyle was pushing now, trying to break him down.*

"You mean from one of my walks? No, I don't think I lost anything," Cain said, *rubbing his chin and looking up at the ceiling as if considering the idea.*

"Don't play fucking games with me, Lucas. It'll just make it harder on yourself." *Carlyle's face was turning red with anger.*

"I think you're the one playing games, Detective," Lucas said, smiling.

"Detective Noble, will you question the suspect for a moment? I'll be right back." Carlyle left the tiny room, slamming the door.

Then Noble reached over and pressed pause on the recorder (they had already gone through a entire tape), and started to talk, and Cain knew that his suggestions had held.

"You know, Mr. Cain, he's right. You really shouldn't play games. It won't serve any purpose. You and I both know that you had nothing to do with this crime, but in the meantime, we need to favor Detective Carlyle, ok?"

"Ok, I'm just a little upset over this whole thing, but you have a deal." Cain shook his hand amiably and smiled. Noble smiled and released the pause button on the recorder, and asked Cain a few obligatory questions.

Carlyle entered the room again, and he now seemed more composed, at ease.

"Well, Lucas, you'll be happy to know that they didn't find a thing in your car. In fact, that's gotta be the cleanest car I've ever laid eyes on." Cain knew exactly where Carlyle was going with this one, but he'd promised Noble no more games, so he played it cool.

"Wouldn't you, Detective Carlyle? It's a mint condition 1977 Cadillac, worth a lot on the open market, and it's my pride and joy. It really is a fabulous car."

"Yes, it is a nice car, Lucas. By the way, where did you get such a fine automobile?"

"A friend of mine was getting divorced, and he didn't want his wife getting it, so he gave it to me, and let me make payments. I'm still paying on it."

"Ok, ok, well let's get back to the crime scene," Carlyle said.

"By the way, just what crime are we talking about?" Cain asked. Not once during the entire interview had either of the detectives mentioned the nature of the crime. Cain saw fresh sweat forming on Carlyle's shiny dome.

"Why don't you tell us," he said.

"I can't tell you, because I don't know what you're talking about." Cain played it sincere, not wanting to stoke the anger he knew was rising again in Carlyle.

"What do you think happened there, Lucas?"

"Look, I really don't know, I swear. I'm sorry to make you mad, but I just don't know."

After three hours of questioning, they finally released Cain, and he actually thought that Carlyle believed him now, because his behavior changed outside the little room.

"Look, I'm sorry if I got a little rough in there, but we have to be rough sometimes. We're just doing our jobs." He shook Cain's hand, and Cain smiled. This was one instance when the cards were just naturally in his favor.

"It's ok, Detective, I know you have a job to do. And I also know that this world would be a scary place without people like you."

"Thanks, Lucas."

Carlyle led Cain down to the basement of the station, to a garage lit by bright fluorescent overheads. He saw the Cadillac, and two men in white coveralls storing several spotlights on tall stands in a utility closet. Cain could picture the scene: The two men scouring his car for evidence, a spotlight on each side pouring intense light into the car, revealing anything and everything inside.

"Have a good day," Carlyle said, and walked back toward the elevator. One of the men in coveralls punched a button on the wall next to the garage door, and it rose up with a metal clatter, spilling sunlight into the bay. Cain drove out and watched in his rearview mirror as the door trundled down behind him.

He pulled out into traffic and drove home, where he would begin packing for his trip to Oak Junction.

Carlyle silently rode the elevator up to the main floor. He saw Noble sitting at his desk, sorting through paperwork. The office area was alive with its usual hubbub of typewriters, low murmurs, and shuffling papers, not to mention the occasional slamming down of the telephone, followed by the usual profanities. He walked up and stood in front of the desk, a blank look in his eyes.

Noble looked up and said, "So, what next, partner?"

Carlyle pulled his gun from his shoulder holster, and put a bullet into Noble's head. Carlyle then turned around and began firing at the other detectives before Noble, eyes wide and mouth gaping, fell over sideways to the floor. Turmoil followed; bodies were flying everywhere as people ran, jumped, and ducked for cover. Carlyle managed to kill two more detectives, and seriously wound one before a volley of bullets from three different directions brought him down.

The next day, on his way out of town, Cain stopped and picked up a newspaper. The story had made front-page news.

"Now, that's more like it," he said, and drove away.

11

Drew saw lights flashing between the slender dark shapes of the tree trunks, and he heard people talking and laughing. He came close to the tree line, and saw people parking their cars along a road, and walking in small groups. This was the eastern most section of Old Farm Road, just before it bent northwards, running toward the old Willard farm, beyond the edge of town.

Most of the people were drinking beer, and some were even carrying coolers. It was as if they were on their way to some event, like a fireworks show or a barbeque. The 4th of July had long passed. It would not have mattered, anyway; the 4th came and went in Oak Junction with really no celebration to speak of, save for the yelps and howls of a car load of drunks that had traversed the streets for a few hours that night.

Drew sank back into the trees and moved east, until he was past the point where the road turned, where the woods continued northward as well. There were vehicles parked along both sides of Old Farm Road, and as Drew crept through the trees, they blocked much of his view as he searched the crowd for a familiar face.

He soon came to the point where this section of the trees ended, and beyond he could make out the derelict buildings that used to be the Willard Farm. Once the most prosperous farm in town, it was now slowly eroding away. No one in town knew exactly what happened to the Willards; no one, that is, except Jaspar Hendricks, the only one left in town who was actually around when old man Willard died, leaving the farm in the hands of his incompetent son Jacob Willard, who squandered the family money and led the farm into bankruptcy, losing ownership to the bank. And the bank was never able to sell the property, as it was no longer a viable risk, what with most of the stock and machinery already sold. Inevitably, it fell into ruin.

The town's people were walking north up Old Farm Road, past the farm itself, and Drew was forced to travel farther east into the woods before he could move north again. As soon as he was behind the old buildings, he saw flickering yellow lights ahead and to the left, on the other side of the old barn, and he slowed his pace as he drew closer to the tree line.

He then saw the sources of the lights: torches. A large ring of them planted in the ground around what looked like a thick post. He was instantly reminded of drawings he had seen somewhere of witches being burned at the stake during the witch trials of Salem. His mouth fell open.

The field was filling with people; men, women, even some children, and he noticed that some of those in the crowd were holding torches. A bad feeling overtook him as he stood there in the shadows, his hands against the rough bark of a tree, the wind breathing through the leaves above. He was misplaced, suddenly out of touch with reality, thrown into something that only happened in dreams. Only this was one dream he would not be able to escape from by waking up.

The din of the crowd became like the drone of insects, and fear caused him to fall to his hands and knees. His left hand sank into a cool wetness, and when he lifted it to look, he saw the tiny white shapes of maggots curling and twisting in the dark fluid stuck to his fingers. A small cry escaped his lips before he was able to subdue it, and he frantically shook his hand until he was sure all of the larvae were gone. He peered down into the overgrown ivy and saw the carcass of a dog, a hole in its mid-section were his hand had penetrated the putrefied flesh, into the feeding den of the maggots. *Holy shit*, he thought, *this gets better all the time!*

He retreated into the woods so he could move farther north to a different position, mouth still turned down in revulsion as he crept through the ivy. Something caught his eye, and he stopped, standing as still as a statue.

About twenty yards north of him he saw a figure crouched against a tree, but it was impossible to tell who it was, or what he or she was doing at that distance. He went farther back into the woods, and leaned against a tree. He pulled out his gun and clicked off the safety. He had never used the gun for anything but target practice, and creeping around in a dark woods with a gun drawn just intensified the surreal feeling he was experiencing at this point.

He took a deep breath and slowly began to work his way toward the field, the distant voices again growing louder. It became clearer to him that the figure was watching the goings-on as well, but that still did not dampen the fear he felt as he worked his way closer.

The ivy that covered much of the ground rustled softly around his feet as he crept up behind the figure.

He saw long hair tied a ponytail. And the figure was holding something in front of his face.

Binoculars?

The din was louder now as he approached the figure, who he was almost sure was a woman. She seemed to be absorbed by all the activity, people milling around, drinking beer and laughing it up in front of the ring of torches.

He was almost on top of her now, and he was trembling, sweat running down his forehead even in the cool night air. He held the gun out in front of him. He wasn't quite sure of what to say or do, but the twig that snapped under his foot as he took his next step saved him the trouble of having to figure that one out.

The figure spun around, and Drew realized now that it was no woman. This was a young man with small wire-rimmed glasses and a ponytail.

The man lost his balance and fell back onto his butt, and dropped the binoculars to his chest, where they dangled on a thin leather strap. His hands scrambled for purchase on the ground to regain his balance, and when he was sitting upright again he saw the gun, and immediately squeezed his eyes shut.

"What are you doing?" Drew whispered to the stranger.

The man opened his eyes. "I - I thought you were going to kill me," he said.

They spoke in hushed tones.

Drew lowered his gun and said, "I'm not going to kill you, I just want to know what the hell's going on in this town. Who are you?"

"My name's Jonathon Mott. You're not from around here?"

"No, I've never been here before," Drew said, crouching lower.

Jonathon got up onto his knees and moved closer to Drew. "I thought you were one of Cain's men."

"Who's Cain?"

"You don't want to know. But I'll tell you right now; it's not a good idea for you to be here. If I were you, I'd leave now, and never look back."

"I can't do that. Not until I find my sister, anyway," Drew said.

Jonathon seemed alarmed. "Your sister? What about your sister?"

"She disappeared in this area last night, and I have good reason to believe that she's in this town. Your sheriff in his all too kind manner drove me right out of town at the mention of it."

"That would be Sheriff Craven," Jonathon said. "And if your sister's here, there's a good chance she's sitting in the jail with the Garrets. And -"

"And what?"

"And it might be too late. I'm sorry, but like I said, this is not a place you want to be right now."

"I can't just leave her behind," Drew said. They both fell silent for a moment, listening to the ruckus in the field.

"So, what are *you* doing here, anyway?" Drew asked.

"I'm trying to get a look at the book," Jonathon said.

"What book?" Drew was falling farther into confusion, and Jonathon knew all too well the desperation the other was feeling.

"Look, I don't have time to explain...." He realized he didn't know the other's name.

"Drew, Drew Townsend." They shook hands in the darkness, and Jonathon continued.

"If I can get a real good look at the book, maybe we can both get what we want."

"And just what is it *you* want?" Drew asked.

"I want that son of a bitch Cain dead."

Jenny and Ashley were finally alone in the house. Harvey had left a short while earlier, and Jenny had actually kissed him goodbye.

She had *kissed* him. And as soon as he had left, she rushed into the bathroom and washed her face and mouth, brushed her teeth, to get rid of the smell and bitter taste of cheap whiskey.

She made sure Ashley was dressed in pants and a warm shirt, along with a jacket, and had her sit down on the sofa.

"You wait right here while mommy gets ready, ok?"

"Where are we going, mommy?" Jenny looked into her daughter's innocent face, and did what any other mother would have done to protect their child from the harsh truth.

"We're just going for a little walk, sweetheart," she lied, and she had to fight back tears as she walked away, wondering how anyone could ever want to harm a child; children lived in their own world, filled with innocent vulnerability, unable to defend themselves against those who prey upon that innocence.

Jenny went into the master bedroom and turned on the light. At first, all she could do was stand there shaking her head, her hands planted firmly on her hips. The room was a shambles; Harvey's dirty clothes were everywhere, and along the side of the bed where he usually slept empty potato chip bags and beer cans littered the carpet. The nightstand was also littered with cans, some blackened around the rims with wet ashes from being used as ashtrays. The room stank of cigarettes and sweat and stale beer.

Normally, she would have gone through the room like a whirlwind, leaving it clean and smelling like fresh laundry (this she would do often, if only for her own sake), but these were not normal circumstances, and she no longer cared about the condition of the room, or the rest of the house, for that matter. After tonight, Harvey could shit in the kitchen sink if he wanted to, which is probably what he was going to do when he got home.

Suddenly, the urgency of the situation spurred her on, and she yanked open one of her dresser drawers, and pulled out several bras and panties. Then a thought occurred to her: *What am I going to carry everything in?* She had not considered this little fact before, could not *believe* she didn't think of it sooner.

She rushed over to the closet, and slid open the door on her side, the guide wheels squealing in their tracks. From among the blouses and dresses that hung there she chose an old leather jacket she'd had ever since she met Harvey. She shrugged it on, and began looking for something to carry their things in. On the shelf above were old shoeboxes filled with photographs and letters. The floor was cluttered with the many pairs of shoes she owned, most of which were dress shoes, growing old and dusty with misuse.

She slid the door shut, almost cringing at the noise (how many times had she asked Harvey to please, please spray some lubricant or *something* up there, that sound drove her crazy), then slid open his side, trying to ignore the horrid squeals it made.

His shelf was piled high with the various caps he'd collected over time, but never seemed to wear unless his hair was out of whack, but these days he didn't seem to care much about personal hygiene.

A lot of the clothes that had been hanging on his side of the closet were gone, most likely part of the population of clothes scattered across the room, and now there were mostly empty wire hangers and a few flannel shirts that were too warm for the season.

On the floor was an unusually large pile of clothes, and it struck her as a little unusual, the way the mound of clothes was stacked, almost *sculpted*, into the corner. She kicked at the pile, and instead of giving way she felt resistance. She crouched down and quickly tore away the clothes, revealing an old satchel. She grabbed it by its old wooden handle and lifted it out of the closet. She sat on the edge of the bed with the bag at her feet, regarding it with suspicion and disgust. Whatever Harvey was hiding in this bag, it could not be good. She unbuckled the strap and opened the satchel, and her heart leaped in her chest.

She had never seen so much money in her life. There were bills of all denominations in the satchel, and when she sank her hand into the loose mass she felt stacks of money still banded together at the bottom. She closed the bag and began pacing the room, weighing her options: She could leave the money, and just disappear as she had originally planned, taking her chances on eventually finding help for her and her daughter, or....

Take the money! He's going to be pissed off either way, he'll just be a little more *pissed off, that's all.*

There was one more thing that she wanted to take, something she hadn't actually thought of until seeing the cluttered nightstand. She pulled open the little drawer, and among the general clutter was Harvey's pride and joy - a 9mm Glock he had purchased long ago under the pretense that they needed protection. He liked to take it out for target practice once in a while, and Jenny always followed her golden rule: Never go target shooting with a drunk.

She checked to make sure the safety was on, noticing that it was loaded.

You stupid ass, Harvey. Only an idiot would leave a loaded gun lying around where a child could get it.

She put the gun inside the satchel, and stood staring at the bedroom door.

Jenny never felt so frightened in her life as during that moment when she snatched up the satchel and ran into the living room. She was violating something very important to Harvey, and having possession of the satchel left her feeling exposed, guilty of a crime for which punishment would surely be severe. Nevertheless, it was her ticket to freedom, and it was now or never.

"Come on, sweetheart, let's go," she said to Ashley, who climbed off the sofa and grabbed her mommy's hand before the two of them left the house for the last in their lives.

12

Sheriff Craven leaned against his cruiser, which was parked in front of the old Willard barn, next to one of the fields that had been abundant with corn when the farm had still been active. The Garrets sat handcuffed in the back seat, both leaning forward to avoid the pain of sitting against the cuffs. On the drive over, Louise remained silent, but Gil had whimpered like a whipped dog.

"What's wrong with you, Gil?" the sheriff had asked.

"These handcuffs hurt, Sheriff. They're way too tight," Gil had replied. But the sheriff knew better, and so did Louise, because she had looked at him incredulously, as if he had shit pouring from his mouth, which was basically what it was.

Craven, although his demeanor was usually serious, watched the crowd with mild amusement. He normally would have been pulling his hair out by now, but these days he rather enjoyed this kind of thing. In fact, he couldn't wait for Cain to show up so they could put that whimpering fool Gil Garret out on the post and shut him up for good.

Craven's former life, former temperament and personality were fading away, to the point where he could not remember having any real decency or goodness.

His walkie-talkie crackled, and he heard a tinny voice.

"Sheriff, you got a copy?"

He grabbed it from his belt and held it to his mouth, pressing the send button.

"This is Craven, go ahead."

"Sheriff, this is Verl Hunter. We got a car out here on route 151. Come on back." Verl had recently become the new owner of Frandsen's Hardware, and was still waiting for the new sign that proclaimed "Hunter's Hardware" to arrive from Arlidge. He and Mike Frandsen were never the best of friends, especially since Frandsen had outbid him for ownership of the store years before. It was something Verl never forgot, and it was just lately that this little incident had resurfaced in his mind, gnawing and picking at his every thought until one day he couldn't take any more. He simply walked into Frandsen's Hardware one day and blew Mike Frandsen's head off with a 12-gauge shotgun. "This store should've

been mine anyway, asshole," he had said to the headless corpse behind the counter.

Now Verl was part of several teams that Sheriff Craven had on 24-hour patrol in and around Oak Junction, especially during the rituals.

Craven stood up straight, still staring at the crowd. "What's your twenty, Verl?"

"About two, maybe three miles east of the exit. What do you want us to do?"

"What's the make and model?"

"Just a minute...uh, yeah, it's a Ford Escort."

"Did you check the registration?"

"Uh, no. The car's locked up tight."

"Well break a fucking window, dimwit," Craven snarled into the walkie-talkie.

"Hold on."

After a minute, the radio crackled again, and Craven could hear the car alarm in the background.

"Says it belongs to Drew Townsend of Iowa City. Hey listen, Sheriff, we gotta shut this damn alarm off -"

"Verl, listen to me," Craven said.

"Right here, Sheriff."

"After you take care of that alarm, go and fetch Zeb, and help him tow that fucker over here to the Willard barn. Then, you contact the other two teams and start looking for Mr. Townsend. I'll hook up with you after we're done here, understand?"

"Loud and clear, Sheriff."

Sheriff Craven's blood boiled as he thought: *Mother fucker came back! Well, you just made the biggest mistake of your life, because when I get my hands on you, you're going to regret ever being born.*

He walked to the edge of the field and scanned the surrounding woods and fields, now shrouded in the cover of night.

You're out there, somewhere, and I'm gonna find you....

13

The town's folk had moved in closer to the ring of torches, and Drew and Jonathon had to change to a position much farther north in order to get a decent view, which left them viewing everything somewhat from the side. It was unnerving seeing the sea of faces, some looking in their direction, but they were well hidden under the shadowy canopy of trees.

A cheer rose up from the crowd as Cain walked between torches to the ring's center, carrying the book in one hand as a student might carry a book to school. He raised one arm to the crowd like a politician waving to his supporters, except he lacked the smile and charm of the average politician; instead, he gazed upon them expressionless and silent.

"Who's that?" Drew asked.

"That, my friend, is Cain," Jonathon said. "And that is the book."

"What is this, some kind of cult or sacrifice?"

Jonathon turned to Drew, his face solemn, and Drew could read in his face a seriousness that was unsettling. "Both. But I have to warn you right now, you're going to see something...something *unnatural*. Disturbing, to say the least. Are you up to it?"

"I don't have any choice," Drew said. Jonathon nodded and put the binoculars to his eyes.

When Cain spoke, he commanded everyone's attention, and all eyes followed as he paced back and forth inside the torches, gesturing with his free hand. He was dressed in black, long black overcoat billowing out behind him as he walked.

"My friends, my brothers," he said to the hushed crowd, "we are here tonight to bear witness to, let us say, a *cleansing* of our quaint little town, to rid ourselves of an undesirable element."

The crowd cheered, some stabbing their torches into the air.

Drew looked over at Jonathon as if to say: *What the hell?*

"Sheriff Craven, bring forth the defectors," Cain called out loudly. From the direction of the barn, Craven appeared, leading two people toward the flickering ring. Their faces were filled with terror in the glow of the torches, and as soon as they appeared, the crowd began to call out.

"Kill the traitors! Take their souls, take their souls!"

One man yelled, "Let's skin'em alive!" This last brought on a quiet contemplation from more than a few among the crowd, and for a moment Drew thought with horror that they actually *were* going to skin them alive.

Craven led Gil Garret over to the post and handcuffed him to it. Louise stood on wobbly legs, tears streaming down her dirty cheeks. Craven then led Louise to the front of the crowd, just outside the ring of torches, and forced her to her knees. A few moved in closer, and Craven said, "Stay away from her."

"You're gonna die, bitch," one man said, and spat on the back of her head.

Cain watched this little act of fidelity, and smiled.

"Here, we have the Garrets, two who have chosen to not only defy me, but to deceive me, possibly to even try to *hurt* me. But it is not only me they choose to reject, it is all of you, as well. Our way of life. We have become a close-knit family, if you will, and I have extended my hand to all. But when someone *slaps* that hand, well, that is…unacceptable."

This brought a roar from the crowd, along with more catcalls. The crowd calmed down again, once more focusing on the man in black in the center of the ring. Sparks floated delicately upward from the torches, winking out against the backdrop of the sky.

"So, let these two stand as martyrs, examples for one and all. Do not turn from me, lest you plan on giving your life."

This time there were no cheers, no catcalls. Cain's words sank in with deadly conclusiveness, striking fear in the hearts of even the most loyal.

In the darkness of the woods, Jonathon tracked Cain's every move with the binoculars. He still had the book at his side, his arm covering the emblem on the front. "Damn!" Jonathon said.

"What is this guy? The Devil?" Drew asked.

"Something like that," Jonathon said. "But I have an idea that under all the talk and flash is a normal human being, and if I could just figure out what that book is, we could put an end to this once and for all."

"You're taking on a lot. In case you haven't noticed, he has the entire town in his hand."

"He killed my parents," Jonathon said. "I owe them that much."

"I'm sorry, I didn't know…."

"It's ok. It's not your fault." He put his hand on Drew's shoulder. "Just be prepared, this isn't going to be pretty.

Jenny's house was pretty much in the center of town, so that left her with only one direction to take in order to get out of Oak Junction, and that was west, right past the church. *His* church, or whatever it was now. If she went north, they would only be moving away from civilization, and that did them no good. If she went east, that would take her toward Old Farm Road and the Willard Farm, where the entire town was now gathered. South was no good, either; it was the busiest part of town, and there was a greater chance of running into someone there, someone who perchance was *not* at the ritual. East was her best hope. Once she got passed 1st Avenue N., she could hurry through the field between the church, which lay at the dead end of North Church Street, and Randolph Street, which was farther south enough to allow her safe passage. After that, farmland and woods.

As they stood in the front yard, Jenny scanned the street for any sign of life. All was dark, even the houses, except for the dim yellow pools of light the streetlights cast onto the street at irregular intervals.

Jenny led her daughter across the street and between two houses, clutching the satchel with one trembling hand. Her heart was pounding, and her breathing was heavier; it was the realization that there would be no returning here, and that they were basically running blindly out into the world, the money their only savior.

The money. When he finds out, he's going to blow his top. And after that, he's going to try to find me, and kill me. My girl, my little girl...

They were standing next to the house where her neighbors had sat on lawn chairs on their front lawn, laughing at the way Harvey had slapped her down to the ground, and when she remembered the humiliation she suffered that night, it stoked her determination.

Looking both directions, she led Ashley into the backyard, and up to the chain link fence that ran behind most of the houses along this section of 2nd Avenue. On the other side of the fence was a strip of no man's land, a thin field separating these back yards from those over on 1st Avenue North.

She lifted Ashley over the fence and eased her down on the other side.

"You're either getting bigger, or mommy's getting lazy," Jenny said, dropping the satchel on the other side.

"Mommy, where *are* we going? Are we running away?"

The fence rattled noisily as Jenny climbed up and dropped to the other side. She dropped to one knee next to Ashley.

"Look, honey, we're just going away for a while. Everything here is…is just crazy."

"Is daddy gonna come?"

She grabbed Ashley by the shoulders. "Not right now, sweetheart. Daddy's going to stay here a while."

"Mommy?"

"What, hon?"

"Is daddy crazy, too?"

Tears sprang to Jenny's eyes.

Yes, dear, your father is *crazy, and he's also a murderer. And the rest of the town is crazy right along with him, and if we don't get out now, we'll probably end up dead. And by the way, we're no longer a family, and you'll probably never see your father again.*

"Daddy just has…problems, honey. He'll be ok." She hugged her daughter close and said, "We have to go, now."

She grabbed Ashley's hand, picked up the bag, and they made their way across the weedy field to another chain link fence that marked the boundaries of the back yards on 1st Avenue North. The huddled down, listening for anything out of the ordinary. She thought for a moment that she heard the sound of people cheering, very faint as if carried on the wind like spirits. She shuddered to think what might be happening out at the old Willard place.

Again, she lifted Ashley over the fence, tossed over the bag, and then climbed herself over, the clatter of the fence unnerving in the nighttime quiet. She only saw over to the side of a house, and from here they could see 1st Avenue.

"Wait right here," Jenny said, and went to the corner of the house to check the area. To her left, she saw nothing but an empty street, void of any life, or even any cars for that matter. Just the streetlights, populated by moths and mosquitoes. She peeked around the corner of the house to her right; it was as quiet and desolate as Main Street in a ghost town.

They hurried across the street to the homes lining the west side of 1st, but instead of stopping, Jenny kept them moving between two houses, and into a back yard that thankfully had no fence.

They were in yet another field, this one littered with large chunks of cement and wood, the remnants of buildings long since demolished. To the north was Church Street, and to the south, Randolph Street. The field narrowed as they approached the old church, and she felt her nerves wind up like rubber bands as it came into view.

The moonlight put the church in odd relief against the black sky, and lent it an eerie semblance akin to something that belonged in the middle of an ancient cemetery - it reminded her of death, of evil and violence, this building that had once been the symbol of everything wholesome and good in this town. They moved quickly past Cain's lair, and even Ashley seemed to notice the *wrongness* of the place, for she stared at the now unholy building until they had gone far past it, and into the woods on the west side of town.

The woods were dark, ominous, and it took all the courage she could muster in order for her to run headlong into the trees, into a shadowy world where the moonlight could not penetrate the canopy above them. She set down the satchel, and plopped down into the ivy, leaning against a tree. She pulled Ashley onto her lap and held her tight.

"Mommy, are you ok?" she asked.

Jenny kissed the back of her head. She could still smell the baby shampoo she had used on her earlier that day. "Mommy's ok, sweetheart. Just a little scared. Are you ok?"

"Yes, mommy. I'm scared, too."

"I know, sweetheart, I know," Jenny said, rocking Ashley in her lap. "We have to keep going," she said, lifting Ashley off of her lap and standing. She picked her up and carried her into the woods. Ashley had her arms wrapped around Jenny's neck so tight that she thought she would strangle. "Ashley, please, you're choking mommy. Don't worry, I won't let anything happen to you."

The little girl loosened her grip somewhat, but she still had a strong hold on Jenny's neck, and by the time they would break out on the other side of the woods, her neck would be cramped from the constant pressure.

They began their trek through the woods, trying to follow the tree line, but staying far enough inside so as not to be seen. The trees were everywhere, dark vertical shapes shooting upward into the mass of branches and foliage above them. There were no sounds, only the slight breeze sighing through the leaves, and the ground ivy rustling around their feet as they made their way south.

As they emerged from the trees and into the open field, the first thing they saw were the headlights and tiny red stars of the tail lights of Zeb's old wrecker as it sat idling at the side of the station. They were quite a distance away, but she still saw the shadow of someone as it passed in front of the headlights.

Jenny carried Ashley back into the trees and set her down, crouching down herself as she watched the activity at the station. As each minute passed, she grew more desperate. Southeast of her position was the dirt road that curved downward from 1st Avenue South as it left town on its way toward Zeb's, and the highway beyond. On the other side of that, more woods. That seemed like the next logical step, so she picked up Ashley and hurried to the dirt road, filled with frightful visions of a car, perhaps *Harvey's* car, barreling down the road at them like some hungry mechanical predator.

Her skin crawled as they crossed the road, and she barely made it to the other side before she could no longer carry her daughter. Jenny held her hand as they ran into the swatch of woods that she knew lay on the fringes of more cornfields. She stopped to gather her wits, and looked down at Ashley, who was staring straight ahead at nothing. She remained silent, and Jenny was sure that the little girl was beginning to understand the seriousness of their plight. Her face was a small, pale circle of confusion in the darkness.

They left the protection of the trees for a field of tall, green corn, the very same field where only the night before a young college student had run for her life from two total strangers, only to be taken in and betrayed by a local farmer.

The going was difficult, as they were traveling against the direction of the furrows, and they kept tripping over mounds of dirt, leaves from the stalks brushing and scraping against their faces and hands.

"Mommy!" Ashley said, tugging at her arm.

"Alright, alright, let's go this way," Jenny said, and they turned south, walking in a furrow between two tall rows of corn. She had the satchel clutched tightly in her left hand, and Ashley's hand in her right, which was awkward, since Ashley was walking behind her, so she finally let go and said, "Stay close to mommy, hon." She kept looking over her shoulder to make sure the little girl was there, following right along in her tracks. Their shoes sank into the soft soil, leaving a set of tracks that ran parallel to another set of tracks that they had already crossed over at one point without even noticing.

When they reached the place where the corn ended and the open field began, Jenny knew they were close to the highway. And she also knew that if they followed the highway, it would eventually go south into Arlidge.

And freedom.

The sky was dotted with stars and a moon that was almost full, and it was a sight that always filled Ashley with wonder, curiosity, and all those questions to which she just knew her parents had all the answers.

But tonight was not a night for discussing the wonders of the universe, or what the moon is made of, or how the sun shines; tonight was a night for fearful and confusing flight, rushing headlong into an uncertain future. And as Jenny was about to find out, it was a night for disappointments.

Right about the time when Jenny and Ashley were somewhere in the middle of one of Angus Swapp's cornfields, Zeb's wrecker had rolled by out on 151, in the same direction that they were headed. And when they neared the ditch at the edge of the road, Jenny's heart sank. She could clearly see the wrecker down the road a ways, a large spotlight on the roof of its cab shining backwards onto the car that Zeb was in the process of hooking up. There were two men standing next to the car watching Zeb work, and as soon as Jenny saw the rifles in their hands, she grabbed Ashley's hand and pulled her back toward the cover of the corn.

Once inside the rows, she fell to her knees and pulled Ashley close to her, tears springing to her eyes.

"What's wrong, mommy? Are you scared of those men?"

"Yes, honey, I'm scared of those men," she said, sniffling.

"Are they bad men like the ones that came home with daddy?"

Jenny hesitated, unsure of just what would be the right thing to say to a little girl.

Yes, honey, they are bad men, and I'm very afraid because if they catch us, they'll probably take us back to daddy, and if they do, daddy will kill us. Or maybe, just maybe, the bad men will not waste any time, and just shoot us where we stand. And I have a feeling that those aren't the only bad men walking around with guns and bad attitudes, honey, so if these guys don't get us, somebody else will.

"I don't know, honey, but we won't let them see us, will we?" she said optimistically.

"No, mommy, we won't let them see us," Ashley said. She put one small finger against her lips and said, "Shhhh."

Jenny almost laughed, even though on the inside she felt hopeless, almost regretful with what she had done. At that moment all she could do was watch and wait, and wonder if they were really going to make it out of this horrid place alive.

14

Gil strained at his bonds as he pleaded with Cain, tears glistening on his cheeks. He tottered on legs that looked as if they might at any second collapse under his weight.

"Please, Mr. Cain, pleeeaaasee. I'll never do it again, I promise. I was just scared, but now I know I shouldn't have been afraid."

The audience of town's folk laughed at his pleas, at this grown man who had once been a respected member of their community, laughed and tittered as he whined and begged for his very life. Gil lashed out at the derision, screaming like a child, "Stop it! All of you!"

He turned his attention back to Cain, who had opened the book and was paging through it lackadaisically, as if Gil's begging was going in one ear and out the other.

"Please, Mr. Cain, I'll do anything, anything at all. I want to join you. I won't be afraid, I promise. Pleeaaase."

"Oh, you'll be afraid, all right," Cain said, and this brought more laughter, especially from those who were celebrating by guzzling as much beer as they could get their hands on. Cain stood absorbing the reaction, the ring of torches blazing around him.

Cain closed the book, oblivious that he was allowing the person hiding in the woods with a pair of binoculars a *very* good view of the front cover, a very good view indeed. Jonathon quickly handed the binoculars to Drew, and said, "Hurry, take a look. Tell me what you think that is on the cover of that book."

Drew looked though the binoculars, and said, "I'm not sure. It looks like…like a face. It looks gold. Shit, I can't see it now." He gave the binoculars back to Jonathon. "What do you think it is?"

"I'm not sure, either, but I *think* it was a skull."

Drew considered that for a moment. "You know, you could be right. Keep looking."

Out on the field, Cain was speaking again.

"I'll tell you what, Gil Garret, I'll make you a deal. I'll let you live and join me, but only under one condition."

"Yes, Mr. Cain, yyeeess! I'll do anything you say, I promise!" He nodded his head ceaselessly as he spoke. "Just name it, Mr. Cain, I'll do it! I promise!"

"Well, then," Cain said with a dramatic wave of his arm, "all you have to do is trade places with her." He pointed at the other half of the Garret family, who was on her knees gaping up at Cain as if it was the most ridiculous thing she had ever heard in her life. The crowd fell silent with this new development, and all eyes were glued to Gil.

Gil blinked, and shook his head. "What? What are you talking about?"

"Let me spell it out for you, Gil. You give the word, we set you free, and your wife gets to step up to the plate."

In the trees on the edge of the field, Drew's eyes were wide with disbelief at the scene unfolding before him. "Is this guy fucking crazy, or what," he whispered.

Jonathon gripped Drew's arm and pulled him closer. "Drew, you're going to have to stay in control of yourself if you want to see the rest. Can you do that? Can you see someone get murdered, and not make a sound? Because if you can't, you need to go now. I'm just trying to give you fair warning. If we get caught, he'll kill us, plain and simple."

Drew nodded slowly, and Jonathon released his grip.

"My w-wife?" Gil said, looking into Louise's eyes. Her expression was forlorn, discerning, her mind filled with the sudden certainty that maybe she had never really known her husband, had never known the inner workings of the man she married. And her life hung in the balance of what she *didn't* know.

"Yes, Gil, your wife. She takes the fall, and you go on living your miserable little life."

"Can't you l-let us both go?" Gil asked.

"And disappoint all these people?" Cain waved his arm at the crowd, and they cheered in response. "No, Gil. These folks came all the way out here to see someone die, and someone is going to die!" This last he yelled in Gil's face, and the town's folk went wild, screaming and cheering, waving torches against the black night sky. Their faces were filled with hateful expressions of anger and lust for death. When the noise died down, Cain asked, "So, what's it going to be, Gil?"

Gil looked back at Louise, and she saw the sad truth in his eyes.

"No, Gil. Please," she said, shaking her head, "you can't do this."

"I'm sorry, Louise." Fresh tears poured down his face. "I'm so sorry."

Cain motioned Sheriff Craven over to release Gil. Craven unlocked the cuffs, and led Gil to the edge of the ring, where he promptly threw him down into the dirt. The people nearest to him were glaring at him with disdain. Craven went over and helped Louise to her feet.

"Gil, what are you doing?" she screamed. "You can't *do* this!" She struggled against Craven, who held fast to her arms. Gil lowered his eyes, unable to look shame in the face. His face was flushed with a mixture of embarrassment and relief. Craven unlocked her cuffs, and she broke away from him and ran toward Gil. Louise tripped over her own feet and went sprawling to the ground in front of Gil.

"Gil...you said you loved me!" she cried. Gil took one glimpse at her and quickly looked away.

Craven snatched her by the armpits and yanked her to her feet. With one hand clamped on her bicep, and the other clamped on the back of her neck, he led her over to the post. As he pulled her arms around the post and locked them together, she stared at Gil with eyes that were not only alive with the flames that burned in the circle around her, but alive with an inner fire as well.

"I hope you burn in Hell, you son of a bitch!" she screamed at him.

"Hey, Louise," a man's voice called, and she saw a scruffy looking man walk up and send Gil rolling on the ground with a good swift kick to the ribs.

"Enough!" Cain said. He walked over to Louise, and spoke very quietly. "Love hurts in more ways than one, my dear. It is what makes us weak. Life and death is all one can count on in this world, as you are about to find out."

Cain went over to Gil, and, grasping the hair on the back of his head, forced him up on his knees. "You will watch her die, my friend, you will watch every last moment. And when you do, you will remember my name!"

Cain walked to the edge of the torches, held his book high over his head, and said the words.

When Drew saw the beast appear and draw out Louise Garret's essence, her very core from her body, his heart leaped in his throat, and he found himself gasping for air. He felt as if his hair had just turned white from shock. It was over quickly; the beast vanished into the ground, and what was left of Louise Garret crumpled to the ground.

Drew turned away, trying to force air back into his lungs. "W-what in the…name of God," was all he could muster.

"I don't know, Drew. I don't think anyone does. He says it's his god, but I don't know what it is. Maybe it's the Devil, I don't know. Now you know why I'm trying to stop him. It's insane, the way this town has changed."

"My sister…Amanda," Drew said.

"He'll kill her, too. But I'm almost sure she's still alive somewhere. Maybe the jail. I have a feeling he *needs* her for his ritual."

"I've got to find her," Drew said, and stood up. His legs were shaky, and he had to lean against a tree until he regained his balance.

"The first thing we need to do is go somewhere, anywhere, where we can figure this whole thing out," Jonathon said.

"My car, it's out on the highway. I have a hotel room in Arlidge. We can go there."

"Are you ok to walk?"

"Yeah, I'll make it. I've just never seen…I don't know," Drew said.

"Believe me, I know. It's a shock to the system. We better get out of here while everyone is still occupied."

They ran deeper into the woods, going south toward the highway.

A green mist was dissipating around Cain's feet as he approached Gil Garret. Behind him, Sheriff Craven was removing Louise Garret's empty corpse from the post. Tonight, however, there would be not one, but two fresh mounds in Oak Junction cemetery. Cain looked down at Gil, and said, "You know, I really hate cowards."

He pushed with his mind, just like on the night with the whore, when he had scrambled her brains to shut her up.

Get me the fuck off this tree, do you hear me asshole?

Gil Garret grabbed the sides of his head and screamed, rolling around on the ground, his face contorted with pain. Then the screaming stopped, and his face went lax as he laid flat on his back, arms and legs twitching, eyes rolling around aimlessly.

"I do not tolerate weakness," Cain said loudly. He then turned to the quiet crowd of people. "In two days the moon will rise full in the sky, and it is on that night that each of you will return here to witness again what you have seen here tonight. Now go home, celebrate your new lives."

The crowd began to disperse, and Craven pointed down at Gil and asked, "What do you want me to do with him?"

"We're going to take him to the cemetery with the other one, and we're going to bury him properly," Cain said (Cain, in fact, would watch as Craven buried Gil alive, with his wife's corpse on top of him), and Craven immediately picked Gil up in his arms, and carried him to his cruiser, where he deposited him in the trunk on top of the pile of flesh that was once Louise Garret.

"I'll meet you over there," Cain said. "I want to help you with that one."

"Yes sir, but I think I need to let you know, we might have a little problem in town."

"My car's this way," Drew said, as they were crossing the field to the highway. When they reached the ditch, Drew stopped dead in his tracks.

"What's wrong?" Jonathon asked.

"My car, it was right over there! Now it's gone!"

"Are you sure? You said you parked down the road a ways."

"Yes, I'm sure. It was right there," Drew said, gritting his teeth.

"Take it easy, you could be wrong. Let's go farther down. Maybe it's there."

They walked in silence for about five minutes, and finally Drew stopped.

"Look, we would have seen it by now. We need to go back," he said, and started walking the other way. The fact of the matter was, they had been hunkered down too low to see on the other side of the ritual field, where an aged wrecker driven by an old man in coveralls deposited his car in a decrepit old barn, right next to his sister's Honda.

"First we need to talk about this," Jonathon said. "If they have your car, obviously they know you're here, and that means Cain will have people out looking for you. I don't think I have to tell you what they'll do to you if they find you."

"And you don't have to tell me what they're going to do to my sister, either. Jonathon, you said you were looking for a way to stop him. Maybe kill him. And the way I look at it, it's my only hope of seeing my sister alive again. I'm scared to death, I don't mind telling you, but I just can't leave her."

"So what do we do now?" Jonathon asked, keeping stride with Drew.

"Well, you said if you got a good look at that book, you might be able to figure out a way to end all this."

"Yes, I did say that...wait." Jonathon threw his arm across Drew's chest and brought him to a halt.

"Look over there."

Ahead of them in the distance two tiny flashlight beams swayed back and forth in the darkness.

"What do you think they're doing," Drew asked.

"Need I say? Let's get out of here." Jonathon looked around, and pointed at the dark mass to the north of them. "There!"

The dark mass was actually a cornfield, stalks tall and strong, rustling softly in the breeze. They went in about ten yards and huddled between rows, watching for any signs of Cain's men.

A few minutes later, the lights came into view again, out by the highway. They could barely make out the two figures crossing the field, but Drew thought he saw one of them carrying a rifle. He tapped Jonathon on the shoulder and pointed, and Jonathon nodded in silent response. Bits and pieces of conversation drifted over to them, but nothing perceptible.

The men with the flashlights disappeared from view, walking in the direction of the spot where Drew had left his car. Drew went to say something, but Jonathon put his forefinger to his lips. He tilted his head, as if listening for something, and then Drew heard it, too. It came from behind them, deeper into the corn, a tiny voice that said, "Mommy, I'm scared."

15

After Jenny saw the wrecker go past, with what she would later find out to be Drew's car in tow, she decided to chance another peek down the highway to see if the coast was clear. "Stay right here, and don't move. Mommy will be right back," she said, and ran bent over out into the open toward the highway. Again, her hopes were shattered as she saw the two figures with flashlights walking back from the spot where the wrecker had been.

She had barely enough time to make it back to the corn and her waiting daughter before the men were actually crossing through the field in front of them. Although the men were still out by the highway, Jenny suddenly felt that she had lost all control over the situation, and her feelings of fright and hopelessness were stronger than ever; she felt panic taking over. She started to shake all over, felt sweat running down her forehead. For the time being, she was lost, her thoughts racing frantically around in her head.

Maybe I should go back. If I hurry now, I could make it home before Harvey gets home. He'll never know. But what if he is home? What then? Maybe he wouldn't be so mad, maybe...oh, who am I kidding? He'll kill me. And what about Ashley? Oh my God, what about Ashley? He might hurt her, he might....

Somebody came into the cornfield. One, maybe two people, and by the sound of it, they were headed straight for them. Then the sound stopped, replaced by the soft breathing of the wind on their faces. "Get behind me," Jenny whispered into her daughter's ear.

"Mommy, I'm scared," Ashley said, and the sound of her voice made Jenny start. She put several fingers over Ashley's lips and whispered in her ear again. "Don't talk, honey, don't say a word. They'll hear us, you don't want *that,* do you?" The little girl shook her head. "Good. Get behind me, and be really, really quiet. Everything will be ok."

Ashley sat cross-legged behind her mother, her head ducked down, too afraid to even peek. Jenny delicately unbuckled the satchel, felt inside for the Glock, and pulled it out. She closed the satchel, and set it behind her next to Ashley. Then Jenny made sure the safety was off, and held the gun out in front of her with two hands.

Her heart was pounding as if she'd just stepped off a treadmill at a gym. Somewhere, a cricket began to *chirrup* in the corn.

And then *they* were moving again. Whoever had come into the corn was moving toward them, slowly and stealthily, but she nonetheless heard them, could almost pinpoint their direction by the quiet rustling of the corn.

She saw two dark figures working their way closer, and soon they were almost right on top of her. She held up the gun with two sweaty, shaky hands, and whispered harshly at the two figures.

"Don't come any closer, or I'll shoot! I swear to God, I will!" Her mouth had gone dry, and she found it hard to swallow, and her words came out sounding foolish, even to her own ears.

They stopped moving, and Jenny could see that they had their hands raised in front of them, palms out.

And then a voice whispered back: "Don't do that, you'll get us *all* caught."

"Who are you?" she asked.

"My name's Jonathon Mott, I work over at the library. You've probably seen me there. I'm the librarian."

Jenny stood up, and peered at them. Ashley stood up as well, but Jenny said, "Stay right there, honey." She looked closer at Jonathon.

"You're Reverend Mott's son, aren't you?" she asked, and she then she remembered that horrible night, the first night Cain had introduced his vile ritual to the town by giving away Evelyn Mott's soul to his...his *god*, he had called it. She had cried with sorrow that night, sorrow at the death of Mrs. Mott, and at the certain downfall of the beautiful little town in which she had been raised. But, the one who had suffered the most was the young man with the ponytail, the one Cain had forced to watch as his mother was mercilessly taken from him.

"I-I'm sorry. Your parents, he..."

"He killed my parents," Jonathon said, "and he's going to kill more, including this man's sister if we don't stop him. Please, put the gun down, we're on your side."

"Who is that?" she asked, pointing the gun at Drew.

"Drew Townsend. And he's right. My sister disappeared last night, and I'm almost positive he's got her somewhere in town. Please, I've got to help her."

Maybe it was the sincerity in Drew's voice, or the hopeless despair she felt, but what ever it was, she lowered the gun, and walked right up to them.

"I guess if you were going to hurt us, you would've done it by now," she said, clicking on the safety and putting the gun in her jacket pocket.

"You don't have to worry," Drew said, and then, "Who do we have here?"

They all turned to see Ashley standing idly by, as children are often forced to do while *grown-up* talk is exchanged, and Jenny went over and swept Ashley up in her arms.

"I'm sorry, honey. I almost forgot about you."

And sometimes a habit with children is to stare curiously at the grown-ups they don't know, and Ashley was no exception to this rule; she had seen Jonathon at the library many times, but Drew was someone new, someone *different*, and Ashley couldn't help but to stare at the mysterious face in the darkness while the grown-ups conversed.

"What are you doing out here, anyway?" Jonathon asked.

Jenny was reluctant to answer, afraid that she might be saying the wrong thing to the wrong people.

"We're going away," she said. " Away from this horrible place."

She started to cry, and Drew put his hand on her shoulder, but she instinctively pulled back.

"You'll have to trust us if you want to get out. We'll help you, I promise," he said.

"I'm sorry," she started to say, but Drew spoke again.

"Don't be. We're all a little jumpy. I just saw something that doesn't quite jive with the world I grew up in, and to tell you the truth, I'm still a little freaked out."

"He saw Cain's ritual?" she asked Jonathon.

"Yes, he saw," Jonathon said, looking down at his feet.

"Who was it? Who did he kill this time?" she asked, looking longingly into his eyes. Moonlight glimmered off the wet lines on her face.

"The Garrets," was all he said, and the three of them fell silent, as if letting this unbelievable yet undeniable bit of information sink into their collective thoughts.

"So what now?" she asked.

"Well, I don't think it's safe to try walking out of here, Cain's probably got patrols everywhere. Especially since they found Drew's car," Jonathon said.

"I saw them tow it away," Jenny said. "That old man from the gas station. Zeb."

"Yeah, I met him this morning at his gas station. And I also met the sheriff, who was quite anxious to get me out of town, to say the least," Drew said, wincing as he touched the sore spot on his stomach.

"Well, we can't stay *here* all night," Jonathon said. "It's only a matter of time before they find us. And for all we know, he could have to whole *town* out looking for us by now."

Jenny said, "My husband will be with them. When he gets home, he's going to blow his top when he sees that I'm not there."

"Is your husband like *them*?" Jonathon asked.

"He's worse. I saw him…hurt someone. And he threatened me. He made it real clear what would happen if I tried to run away."

"He hurt that policeman's head!" Ashley exclaimed, still staring at Drew.

"Yes, honey, he did," Jenny said, and then to the other two she said, "He's changed. He's really dangerous, and I don't think he'll stop until he finds us."

"Then we need to find a place to hide out quick, until we can figure out a way to get you and your daughter out of here," Jonathon said.

Drew said, "If I remember right, this is the same field I followed my sister's tracks through just this morning. There's a farm on the other side. I went there looking for Amanda, but nobody was there. At least I *think* nobody was there. It *was* kind of convenient how the sheriff showed up at the gas station right after I did."

"That's Angus Swapp's place," Jenny said. "He lives by himself, runs the place pretty much by himself ever since his wife died. He has two sons that come out sometimes to help him out with the heavy stuff, but other than that, I pretty sure he's alone."

"How do you know all this?" Drew asked.

"It's a small town. Everybody knows everybody else. Well, almost, anyway."

Drew nodded, and then a thought occurred to him. "I have an idea. It's crazy, but I don't think we have any choice."

They listened intently, whispering back and forth, this tiny gathering of fugitives that stood in the middle of a cornfield on a warm summer evening, and when they were done, they struck out across the field, three grown-ups and one child, each of the adults determined, and yet uncertain if they were doing the right thing. They walked in the shadow of doubt, that dark and ugly thing that was always there at the backs of their minds, always there to remind them that things could go wrong, very wrong, and that they may never walk away again.

Part 3
The Book

1

Harvey White drove home with a smile on his face, and an erection in his pants. He was totally exhilarated from watching Cain perform his ritual, his deed, and now he was focusing all that energy toward one thing: Jenny. All he could think about in his drunken state was that sly smile on her face, the wink of her eye; he had never been more ready.

But all that changed as he pulled up in the driveway and turned off the engine. The smile faded from his face, and the bulge in his pants softened.

Every light in the house was off.

He got out of the car and strode to the back patio, hoping to see the light from the kitchen spilling out onto the cement where he had once killed a man with a bow saw. The back patio was dark.

"Fuck!" he said, and tried the sliding door. Locked. He ran down the driveway to the front of the house, and tried the front door. It was locked as well, and he fumbled with his key ring to find the house key (Jenny knew it would take him longer to get inside if he had to deal with something as small and simple as a key while he was drunk, and she figured it would buy her a little more time). "Fuckin' BITCH!" he yelled, not caring who heard.

He burst through the door and into the living room, his keys still dangling from the lock, and fumbled for the light switch. He rushed into the kitchen, then down the hall to Ashley's room, where he kicked open the door so hard, the knob slammed into the wall and left a perfectly round hole in the sheetrock. Harvey switched on the light. Ashley's bed was empty and unmade.

My money. My fucking money...

When Harvey went into the master bedroom, he immediately knew she had been in there; one of her dresser drawers was still open, but the worst of it was, *his* side of the closet was open.

The closet!

He took one look at the pile of clothes in the corner, and flew into a rage. He tore out the clothes, throwing them helter skelter across the room. The satchel was gone.

"I'LL KILL YOU!!" he screamed, and tore the closet doors from their tracks. He threw one over the bed, where one corner of it bit into the wall by the dresser. He punched the wall by the closet, missing a stud by about an inch, leaving yet one more hole for the growing collection.

He went into the kitchen, lungs bellowing in and out, blood pumping with adrenaline, and grabbed a half empty bottle of whiskey from a cupboard. He unscrewed the cap and hurled it across the room. Tipping the bottle to his mouth, he gulped down as much of the liquid fire as he could before having to stop for air. A small trickle of blood ran down the side of his hand from a cut on his first knuckle, and that took him far enough over the edge to do something entirely out of character - he threw the bottle as hard as he could, and suddenly the world seemed to slow down, came crawling to a stop as he watched the bottle spin through the air in slow motion, trailing out thin tendrils of amber fluid as it went. He could even make out some of the words on the label as it made one of its turns, before smashing into the refrigerator. It exploded in all directions, and the sound of glass shattering seemed to pierce into his brain like a thousand tiny nails, and he covered his ears and screamed incoherently.

Then he was at the wall phone punching in the number to the sheriff's office, throwing tiny specks of blood onto the numbers. Glass crunched under his shoes as he listened to the ringing at the other end. He finally gave up and slammed the receiver down into its cradle.

He opened the refrigerator (which now had a huge splat of glass shards and whiskey on the front of it), and pulled out a cold beer. He had more of the hard stuff somewhere, but he figured now was not a good time to drink himself asleep. He found some caffeine pills in the bathroom medicine cabinet, and he swallowed two down with beer. He shoved two more into the front pocket of his jeans and, grabbing another beer from the refrigerator, went out to his car.

He hesitated before getting into the car as something crossed his mind, and he ran back into the house.

"You bitch," he said, as he gazed into the nightstand drawer. "That gun ain't gonna save you now."

2

It's difficult for the average person to try to imagine what goes on inside the gloomy corridors of a criminal's mind as he or she commits their acts against humanity. Even with all the confessions, interviews, and books released about the subject, only the perpetrators themselves know for sure what *really* happens in the mind, what thoughts and images provoke their actions.

These very thoughts and questions ran through the minds of the three people who stood in the total darkness of Angus Swapp's house, considering just what it would take to perform a criminal act such as the one they were planning. All were hesitant, but in the end, as time ran out, necessity and sheer desperation would be their motivation.

The darkness was so thick here that it had been all but impossible to find their way around, to find suitable spots until their quarry walked into their trap.

"I can't do this," Jenny said from somewhere in the inky blackness.

"Look, it isn't easy for us, either, but we don't have a choice," Drew said. "After all, we're not really going to *hurt* anybody." His voice echoed in from another room.

"I know, but it just feels so wrong," she said.

"What this town is doing is wrong, and I think we all know what's going to happen to us if we don't do *something*," Jonathon said from his place near Jenny and Ashley. "And I'll tell you what, we need to make it look good, I mean, *really* good, so we can have total control over this guy. He might be dangerous, maybe tricky. We can't take any chances."

"Try to think like a criminal, or better yet, one of Cain's people. They seem to be experts on it," Drew said.

"Think about something that really makes you mad," Jonathon said.

"You're right," Jenny said. "All I have to do is think about Harvey, the way he treated us, and my blood boils."

"He makes me boil, too, mommy," Ashley said, and they all laughed.

"And my parents," Jonathon said, and fell silent for a moment. "My parents. What about you, Drew?"

"My sister is all the motivation I need, angry or not. I -" Drew stopped mid-sentence. "Quiet, I hear something." Silence enveloped the room, and they all could hear tires crunching on gravel as a vehicle pulled up in front of the house. "Here we go," Drew said.

They heard loud, boisterous voices, and laughter.

What if there's more than one, Drew thought. Jonathon and Jenny were both shaking slightly with fear as the moment of truth came.

They heard a car door slam shut, and the vehicle pulling away, motor fading in the distance. Drew's heart jumped as somebody yanked open the screen door, and turned the doorknob on the front door, not three feet away from where he stood.

For an instant the silhouette of a thin man stood in the open door way, then blended with the darkness as the man shut the door. There came the soft *flick!* of a light switch, and the two living room lamps came on, bathing the room in warm light, and giving Angus Swapp a bird's eye view of the .38 revolver pointed at his head.

"Whoa, Whoa!" Swapp cried, and jumped backwards against a wall, almost knocking an old black and white photo in a frame from its nail. It bounced dangerously close to falling on his head.

"Don't fucking move," Drew said, gritting his teeth menacingly. "I will not hesitate to blow your brains all over that wall!" The photograph (an ancient shot of a farmer on an old steam tractor) was still swaying slightly over Swapp's head.

"What do you want?" he asked, holding his hands in the air.

"I want to know where my sister is," he said, "and I think you know."

"Please, don't shoot me. I don't know anything about your sister."

"Then why did you call the sheriff on me this morning?"

"Sheriff? I didn't call the sheriff -"

Drew put the gun right in his face. "Don't fuck with me!"

"Ok, ok," Swapp said, turning his face away from the muzzle of the .38. "I saw you on my property, so I called the sheriff."

"And?"

"He told us to call if we saw any strangers around town."

Jonathon walked into the room from the kitchen, followed by Jenny and Ashley. They all gathered in the middle of the living room, Ashley sitting down on the recliner, mouth stretching in a huge yawn.

"Hey, I know you folks," Swapp said. He pointed at Jonathon. "I was friends with your father, young man."

"How about my mother, were you friends with my mother?" Jonathon asked.

"What's that supposed to mean?"

"I'm just wondering how it felt, being friends and all, to watch my mother die the way she did. You were there, just like everyone else. You were there tonight, too. What is it with you people?"

Swapp stood scowling at them, and then finally said to Jonathon, "I enjoyed watchin' your mother die."

Jonathon rushed at him, clamping his hands around the older man's neck, and slamming him against the wall, where the old photograph lost its hold and fell, glancing off Swapp's shoulder on its way to the floor.

"I'm going to enjoy watching *you* die, too," Jonathon said, digging his fingers deeper into the sides of the old man's neck. Swapp gagged and clawed at Jonathon's hands, but Jonathon held fast, and red was beginning to rise in the old man's face.

"Ok, Jonathon, that's enough. If he gives us any more trouble, we'll let you take care of him," Drew said. He looked over at Jenny, who was watching him with mild curiosity. It was the first time they had seen each other in the light (they had been too afraid to use any lights when they entered Angus Swapp's house through the unlocked front door - they had, in fact, felt and bumped their way through the dark rooms to find suitable places to hide), and Drew unconsciously took a double take at the pretty young woman standing in the living room. She had long, straight dishwater blonde hair, and a perfectly proportioned face that he knew must have had men looking over their shoulders. She had a figure that certainly did not reflect a pregnancy, and yet a little girl who looked just like her was slumbering on the chair behind her. She seemed to sense the awkwardness of the moment, and she looked away, jamming her hands into the pockets of her black leather jacket.

Drew had only seconds to register all this before focusing his attention back to Swapp, who was frowning at him, rubbing the reddening marks on his neck. Drew thought it odd that he could almost *feel* Jenny watching him from behind.

Or was it just wishful thinking?

In fact, how was it he could even be harboring such thoughts, given their current situation? He felt a momentary wave of confusion, and thought: *Amanda, I've got to think of Amanda!*

"Into the kitchen," Drew said, waving the gun toward the kitchen doorway. Jonathon went first, followed by Swapp, and then Drew. "Have a seat," he said to Swapp.

Swapp sat down at his kitchen table, which was covered with all kinds of mail, mostly piles of old junk mail that he apparently never got around to tossing out. The kitchen sink was filled with dirty dishes, and some looked as if the food encrusted on them had indeed been there for a long time. Jonathon noticed a mound of blue mold growing on the bottom of an old saucepan, and shook his head in disgust.

"God, don't you ever clean?" he asked, but Swapp only glared at them.

"What do you want with me?" Swapp asked. "Do you think you can get away with this?"

Drew walked over to Swapp, grabbed a handful of his greasy hair, and yanked his head back. He shoved the barrel of the gun into his cheek, and he knew it must have hurt, but he had to make this look good, or else risk loosing their edge.

"I won't hesitate to fucking kill you, asshole. You're going to do exactly as I say, or I put a bullet in your brain. And wipe that fucking look off your face before I blow it off."

He noticed Jenny watching from the doorway, and she had a mixed look of fear and concern on her face that said she almost believed this herself. Swapp was buying into it, because he lost the expression of disdain.

"Look, I'll do anything you want, just don't shoot me," he said.

Drew released his hold and wiped the greasy residue from his hand onto Swapp's shirt. "As long as you're a good boy, you'll come out of this with your brain still tucked neatly in your head. But keep in mind; it only takes a split second to remedy *that*. Got it?"

Swapp nodded.

"Now, where do you keep rope?" Drew asked.

"In the barn," Swapp said, "but you don't need it, I ain't goin' anywhere."

"Just a little insurance, my friend, just a little insurance. Jonathon, think you could run out to the barn and find the rope? I'll keep an eye on our friend, here."

"Sure. You got a flashlight, old man?" Jonathon asked, stretching his fingers to remind Swapp of his recent necktie fitting.

"Bottom drawer," Swapp said, tilting his chin toward the grungy drawers by the sink. Jonathon dug through the general clutter and produced a silver flashlight with greasy fingerprints planted all over it. He found an old dishtowel in another drawer, and used it to wipe the flashlight clean. He tried the switch to make sure it worked.

"Hope you don't mind," Jonathon said, tossing the smeared dishtowel onto a counter crowded with dishes. "Hell, you weren't using it, anyway." He headed toward the doorway, and Drew said, "Watch yourself out there."

"You can count on it." He went into the living room, and pulled a thick curtain aside for a quick peek outside. Satisfied no one was around, he opened the front door and went out onto the porch, closing it behind him. He took one more look around, and ran in the direction of the barn, which stood tall against the night sky.

The moon glowed softly above as he reached the barn doors. He pulled one open, and it shook as if dangerously close to falling apart, rusted hinges screeching loudly as he went inside and pulled it closed behind him.

The darkness enveloped him, filled with the scents of moldy wood and machine oil, and he felt butterflies in his stomach at the thought that he might not be alone. He pointed the flashlight straight ahead and flicked it on. He jumped slightly as an old John Deere tractor confronted him, its headlights staring back at him like large round eyes. "Shit, give me a heart attack," he said. He shined the light around the interior of the barn, saw empty stalls along one side, and a loft above that he had absolutely *no* intention of exploring. Along the other side, against the aging wood that made up the barn's north wall, was a clutter of assorted tools and greasy machine parts. He shuddered as he saw a pitchfork leaning against the wall. He'd seen too many horror flicks, and knew that it was one of the weapons of choice for the assorted serial killers and maniacs that ran rampant in America's movie theaters. So much for good clean fun.

Sweeping the beam across the expanse of the barn, he saw a coil of rope hanging from a large hook that had been mounted on the side of a square post. As he walked over the creaky boards, he heard something go scuttling away, and he shined the light in the direction of the noise, but saw nothing. His nerves were beginning to tighten, and he quickly grabbed the coil of rope from its hook, and made for the rickety doors.

He pushed the door open a crack, and saw that he was still alone. Another shudder ran through him as he thought about the pitchfork. The darkness of the barn held too many secrets, and he quickly stepped outside, pushing the door tight against its frame. He ran for the house like a child afraid of the dark, or better yet, what was *in* the dark chasing him, always just one step away from latching onto a leg or an arm.

Once inside the house, Jonathon locked the door and went into the kitchen, the rope slung over his shoulder. Drew and Jenny were leaning against a counter, watching Swapp as he nervously played with his fingers on the kitchen table.

As soon as he saw the rope, he said, "At least let me go to the bathroom."

"Let's go." Drew waved the gun toward the hallway, and followed Swapp as he went down the hall and into a room on the left. He hit the switch, and the single bulb above the sink bathed the room in a dim dingy glow. Swapp tried to close the door, and Drew stopped it with his foot. "Leave it open."

"You're gonna watch me piss?" Swapp asked, frowning at the thought of another man seeing what he considered a below average piece of manhood.

"Damn straight," Drew said. In the kitchen, Jenny looked at Jonathon and rolled her eyes at the sound of Swapp urinating. When he was done, he zipped up and flushed. "Alright, let's go," Drew said, and as he turned something in a pile of dirty clothes caught his eye. He escorted his prisoner back into the kitchen, and handed the gun to Jonathon.

"Keep an eye on him," he said, and went back to the bathroom.

"Where you goin'?" Swapp called after him.

Drew switched on the light and picked up the item that had caught his attention. It was a white towel, no longer the bright white it had once been, now more of a graying rag than anything. He looked closely at the rusty smudges on one end, sniffed at it, and under the moldy smell of damp cloth he picked up another smell, one that was so faint, yet familiar.

"What did you find?" He hadn't even noticed Jenny standing in the doorway.

"What does that look like to you?" He held the towel out for her inspection.

"It's blood," she said. "I've seen it on my own towels, believe me."

"Ok, what do you smell?"

She sniffed at the bloody end of the towel, and grimaced. "It smells like it hasn't been washed in a year."

"I know, but try again."

This time recognition dawned in her eyes, and she suddenly knew what Drew was getting at. "I think I smell perfume," she said.

"My *sister's* perfume," he said. "Let's go talk to our friend."

Back in the kitchen, Drew tossed the towel onto the table in front of Swapp.

"What the fuck is this?" he asked, planting both hands on the table and putting his face close to Swapp's.

"I don't know what you're talkin' about," Swapp said.

Drew caught both Jenny and Jonathon by surprise as the palm of his hand connected with the side of Swapp's face with a fleshy *slap!* that echoed off the kitchen walls.

"Does *that* jog your memory? Tell me now, or it will get worse, I guarantee it!" Drew's eyes were wide with anger, and the others knew that this was no act. This was the real McCoy, and if Swapp didn't say something soon, Drew was going to blow his top.

"If I were you, I'd come clean now, before he really gets pissed," Jonathon said, still holding the gun on the old man.

Swapp looked up at Drew, his cheek turning red from the impact with Drew's hand.

"Ok, ok, don't hurt me. There was a girl, came to my door last night lookin' for help. She was in some kind of accident. Not hurt real bad, just cut up a little."

"What did she look like?" Drew asked.

"Well, I don't know. She was real young, had long dark hair. Looked about eighteen, nineteen."

"Did she say what her name was?"

"No, I swear, I don't think I ever got her name."

Drew looked up at Jonathon and Jenny, and said, "It was my sister. Amanda was here." He looked back down at Swapp, and Swapp could hardly stand to look Drew in the eye, so intense was his glare. "Where is she?"

"The sheriff's got her now. It's the truth. I didn't lay a hand on her. Neither did the two that were chasin' her. I wouldn't let 'em touch her, I swear. Sheriff Craven came out and took her away. She's probably in the jail."

Drew stood up straight and took a deep breath. "You're very lucky you told me the truth. You might make it out of this alive yet. Let's tie this asshole up."

They took Swapp, along with one of his kitchen chairs, into his musty smelling bedroom. They used a steak knife to cut the rope into sections (much to the dismay of Swapp, who now claimed it was ruined), and bound his hands around the back of the chair, using a section to fasten him to the chair itself. They then bound his ankles together, and likewise fastened a section to hold his legs tight between the two front legs of the chair.

Drew stood in front of him, hands on hips. "Do we need a gag, or are you going to be a good boy?"

"Please, no gag. I won't say a word."

Leaving the bedroom door open a crack, they went into the living room and sat down, all three visibly relieved that they had pulled it off. Ashley was fast asleep on the recliner, head on the armrest, her mouth wide open with a tiny runner of spit hanging from her lower lip.

"Do you think you can find out anything about that book?" Drew asked.

"I'll try my computer at the library, but I promise you, that'll be my only hope. I doubt very much that Cain will allow anyone in or out of town right now," Jonathon said.

"Just who the hell *is* this guy, anyway?"

"Well, all I've been able to find out so far is that he came from Sioux City," Jonathon said, "and that his real name is Lucas Cain, and get this - he's only twenty years old."

"That's impossible," Jenny said. "He's got to be at least forty."

"It's true. And it just so happens that Sioux City has had a string of disappearances over the last year or so."

Drew said, "I remember that. So you think Cain is responsible?"

"I'm sure he is. It seems he got sloppy and left a body lying around, a *shriveled* body, according to the police. Sound familiar? And to top it off, he was caught hanging around the crime scene, and they actually took him in for questioning, but they had no evidence against him and had to let him go. He told them some story about being out for a walk, or something. The way I figure it, he made a beeline for Oak Junction."

"But why Oak Junction?" Drew asked.

"I don't know. Maybe he's been here before. Or maybe it's just a nice little place to hide out in."

"I still don't get it," Jenny said. "He looks so *old*."

"I think I have a theory about that, but I'm not sure -"

Jonathon stopped speaking, and they all looked at each other as Drew's cell phone began to ring from his jacket pocket. He pulled it out, hit *talk*, and put it to his ear.

"Hello?"

An unfamiliar voice spoke on the other end, a cold, calculated voice that sent shivers down Drew's spine.

"Hello, Drew Townsend."

"Who is this?" he asked, looking back and forth between Jonathon and Jenny. He saw the fright in Jenny's eyes, and knew this was not the first time she had tasted this kind of fear.

"Oh, come, come, Drew, you're really not that stupid, are you?"

"Where's my sister?"

"She's alive and doing well, my friend. In fact, she's very anxious to see you. Why don't you come into town and pay her a visit? We can all have a nice chat."

"You better not lay a hand on her, or I swear, I'll -" The muscles in Drew's jaw were tightening, and his fingers were squeezed tightly around the cell phone.

"You'll what? You can't beat me, Drew. You can't beat this town. You'll never make it out of here alive. Why don't you give up now? I'll make it real easy on you. Quick and painless. Otherwise, I can make the pain last forever."

"You're right, I'm not that stupid."

"Ok, Drew, have it your way. But keep this in mind - in two days time, your sister is going to be the guest of honor at a little party I'm throwing. A going away party. I hope you can join us."

The line went dead, and Drew hit *end* before shoving the phone back into his pocket.

"He say's he's going to kill her in two days," Drew said.

"How did he get your number?" Jenny asked.

"He must have Amanda's cell phone. She would have my number programmed into it. But the way he sounded, he thinks it's just me, so maybe that'll give us an edge."

"That may be true, but when Harvey finds out I'm gone, all hell is going to break loose."

"Your husband?"

"The one and only," she said.

Jonathon said, "The best thing to do now is just wait here. I'll sneak back into town, and find out what I can about that book. If I don't open the library at least for a while, he might put two and two together. I'll call back here at exactly ten o'clock, so you'll know it's me."

Jenny asked, "Can you make it?"

"Piece of cake," he said. "His goons won't know a thing. I'm just one of the local crazies walking home." Jonathon wrote down Angus Swapp's number on a piece of scrap paper, and said, "Just keep an eye on *him,* he might be tricky."

"Be careful," Drew said. He turned off the living room lights, and once again they were bathed in a thick darkness.

"Ten a.m.," Jonathon said, and slipped out the door and into the night.

3

Cain placed Amanda's blue cell phone down on Sheriff Craven's desk. His long black hair hung around his shoulders, framing a ruddy face that was now thick with stubble. Craven tried to avoid looking directly at Cain, as he had visibly changed in the short time he had known him from a sturdier looking individual to someone who sported gray streaks at his temples, and crystal blue eyes that had become darker, hazy, like frosted glass.

"Get some extra men together and do a door to door search. No one's home will be excluded. No one."

"Right away, Mr. Cain," Craven said, and the sound of his own voice, slightly changed of its own accord, a little deeper, a little rougher, reminded him that perhaps they *all* had changed in their own ways, had become *better* in their new lives.

Craven picked up the phone, then it dropped in back into its cradle as Harvey White burst through the front entrance of the station, his wind-blown hair sticking up at odd angles as if he had been driving around town with his head hanging out of the car window - which was almost the case, because he'd spent the last hour cruising the streets of Oak Junction in search of Jenny and Ashley, and more importantly, his money.

"We've got a problem," Harvey said, nearly out of breath.

Cain and Sheriff Craven listened impatiently as Harvey conveyed to them what had happened, and when he was done, he stood staring wide-eyed at Cain as if awaiting orders. Cain's expression became colder as he listened, and Craven was sure that Cain was going to kill Harvey on the spot. Instead, he walked over to him and put a hand on his shoulder.

"Here's how I look at it, Harvey. *We* don't have the problem, *you* do. I don't care how you do it, but take care of the problem, or else *you* will have a very *big* problem, indeed."

"She can't get out of town, Harvey, we've got men everywhere. Just find her, and take care of it," Craven said.

Harvey gaped stupidly at Cain; the last thing he had expected was to be put on the spot like this, and it now seemed as if the ice beneath his feet was cracking more every second.

"Do you have another problem, Harvey, or has the alcohol finally turned your brain to mush?" Cain asked.

"Um...no, sir," was all Harvey could mange.

"Then get the fuck out of here," Craven said, and Harvey turned and disappeared out the door without another word. They heard his car door slam shut, and his car squealing out of the parking lot.

"Think he'll find her?" Craven asked.

"In the end, it won't matter, Sheriff," Cain said. "It just won't matter."

Drew emerged from the bedroom down the hall after checking on Swapp, where he found him dozing off with his head tilted down, his chin pressed into his chest.

"He's sleeping," Drew said softly. Jenny had laid Ashley down on the battered loveseat and covered her with a blanket she found in a linen closet at the end of the hall. All the lights in the house were now dark, except for the faint glow of the lamp in the corner, next to Swapp's recliner. Drew sat next to Jenny on the sofa.

"Are you alright?"

"Yeah, I think so," she said. "How about you?"

"I'm ok. I just wonder if Amanda's ok," he said sullenly.

"Hey, I'm sure she is," Jenny said, taking Drew's hand in hers and patting it. "Well find her."

Drew glimpsed down at his hand, and Jenny realized that she was still holding it, and she felt embarrassment rising in her cheeks. The funny thing was, she was almost sure she had seen a little color in Drew's cheeks as well. She gently let go of his hand, searching for the words to break the overwhelming silence. It was Drew who spoke first.

"So, what *is* wrong with all the people in town? Are they brainwashed, or what?"

"I don't know. It seemed like a day or two after he showed up, everyone started to change. They got...mean."

"So Cain just waltzed into town, and virtually overnight, he has the whole town in the palm of his hand?"

"Yeah, that's pretty much it," Jenny said, nodding.

"What about people like you and Jonathon? How come you're not like everybody else?"

"I don't know that either. But I think they been getting rid of the ones who don't, you know..."

"Conform?"

"Yeah, that's the right word, I guess. Conform."

"And Harvey, he's like them?"

"Worse. He used to drink pretty heavily before, but now," she paused. "I saw him kill the deputy sheriff, right on our back patio." Drew saw tears spring to her eyes. "And the worst of it is, *Ashley* saw, too. She saw him hit me, and threaten me. I just don't know how all this is going to affect her." Tears rolled down Jenny's cheeks, and Drew felt no trepidation as he put his arm around her shoulders and held her against him. Eventually, he felt the tenseness drain from her, and she relaxed in his arms. This embrace was different from what she had always known; it was tender and soothing, and she found herself giving in to its warmth, as a child might give in to the healing embrace of its mother.

Finally, she sat up straight, dabbing at her eyes with the sleeve of her shirt.

"You ok?" Drew asked.

"Yes, I think so. Thank you." She looked into his eyes, and saw mirrored there a fear, an uneasiness that was impossible to hide. "This has been hard on you, hasn't it? You must love your sister very much."

"I do. We were always very close. She probably won't admit it, but she depends on me. I've always looked out for her, and I always will. If I could just let her know that I was here, close by. I feel like I haven't been around for her much lately." He looked Jenny squarely in the eye. "I just went through a pretty bad divorce. And I'm a divorce lawyer myself. Is that a kick in the pants, or what?" He managed a wan smile.

"Was is hard for you?" Jenny asked.

"It was very hard for me. I put my heart into that marriage, and she tossed it aside like yesterday's news. I felt like she not only broke my heart, but my self worth, as well. I guess for the last year, I've pretty much been hiding out at home doing the self-pity thing. And my family has kind of been tippy-toeing around me, wondering when I'll come around. Pretty sad, huh?"

"No, it's not *your* fault. I can tell you're a wonderful person. She just doesn't know what she's missing. You deserve to be happy."

"The funny thing is, until this happened, every time I thought about her was painful. But when I thought about her yesterday, and I felt that old pain come back, I actually got *mad*. I mean, here I am trying to find my sister, someone who is so important to me, so special to me, that those other feelings seemed suddenly worthless.

And I said something that made me feel so much better. I don't know why I didn't think of it before."

"Oh? What was that?"

"Well, you'll have to excuse my English, but I said, 'Fuck you, Rose!' and I really *meant* it. I felt better than I had in a long time." Drew was actually smiling now.

"You said it out loud?" Jenny asked, smiling at the very thought of it.

"Yep. Out loud. I'll tell you what, it's great therapy. You should try it."

They both broke out laughing, and Jenny said, "You may have something there."

"Thanks," Drew said, then, "You know, we should probably try to get some sleep. You can sleep here, and I'll keep watch."

Jenny's smile softened. "I don't know if I can sleep right now. Will you just stay with me for a while?"

"Of course," Drew said, and he again put his arm around her shoulders, and let her lean against him. A short while later, he heard her slow, rhythmic breaths as she succumbed to her weariness. He fell asleep with his head propped against hers, the light scent of her hair in the air, and the light of the sun still hours away.

Harvey drove slowly through the darkened streets, passing an occasional car on its way home from the night's festivities, squinting as headlights glared across the smeared windshield of the station wagon. He passed small groups laughing and staggering along the sidewalks, and he frantically looked for any sign, just a glimpse of her face, all the while knowing she would not be there.

But rational thought was gone, the faces floating by like the faces in a carnival to a little boy who is hopelessly lost, and crying for his mother to appear out of the surreal sea of strangers. Harvey ran his fingers through his greasy dark hair, and heard Cain's voice repeat itself with sickening clarity.

...take care of the problem, or else you will have a very big problem, indeed.

He turned onto Main Street and drove past Nate's Diner, watching his reflection in the darkened windows, and saw only a hint of the man behind the wheel, a ghostly face that he did not recognize staring back at him. He saw the same face in the window as he passed Frandsen's Hardware (now Hunter's Hardware), and a very real and cogent thought seemed to pass at the front of his mind: *That is the face of a dead man.*

Harvey turned north on 4th Avenue, and drove up to Broadway, where he turned east. The blinds were drawn over the windows of Sheriff Craven's office, but the interior lights were still on, shining through the cracks in the blinds, casting long stripes of light across the sidewalk. A dark shape passed in front of the window, and Harvey felt anger welling up like a shot of hot whiskey in his stomach.

I helped that fucker, even killed that asshole Mayfield for him. Now he treats me like some child.

Harvey passed the dark windows of the Grove Market, not looking at the glass, not wanting to see that stranger looking back at him, the one that looked like he was already dead.

He turned up 2nd Avenue, and here the town seemed quiet and empty, like all the people had suddenly vanished into thin air like ghosts. All that was left was the drone of the engine, valves clicking, pistons pumping louder and louder into his quiet reverie, until it was almost *pounding* at his skull, a mechanical pulse that seemed to bore into his brain.

Just when he thought he would go insane, his own driveway loomed up on the right, and he swerved into it and slammed on the brakes, squealing to a stop. He turned off the key, and the drone went quiet, replaced by the subtle clicking of the engine as it cooled.

He got out of the car and leaned against it, running his hand over his face and hair. He could hear the giant oaks in the neighborhood rustling softly in the midnight breeze.

Harvey went into the house and turned on the living room lights. The silence seemed to have a sound all its own, an overwhelming emptiness filled with frustration and resonant of those who had lived there.

He went from room to room, switching on every light in the house. Taking special notice of the master bedroom. He went into the kitchen, crunching on broken glass, and pulled a beer from the refrigerator. He took a long, satisfying pull from it, wiped the runoff from the side of his face with his sleeve, noticing the cut on his knuckle. He looked up and saw the specks of blood on the phone, and screamed as loud as he could, the sound reverberating throughout the empty house. He yanked open a kitchen drawer, the contents spilling to the floor in a loud metallic clatter. From the scattered utensils he chose a large steak knife, and he took this and his beer into the master bedroom. He took a swig from the beer and set it on the dresser, then went to the closet, and slid open the door reveal Jenny's side. He pulled a blue blouse from a hanger, and laid it out as nice as you can be on the bed.

"YOU BITCH, I'LL KILL YOU!" He screamed, as he sank the knife into the blouse, and deep into the mattress. He kept screaming his insane murder cries, until it seemed to come from every corner of the room, repeatedly plunging the knife into a simple blue blouse that at that moment represented what he hated most in the world: Jenny White.

4

Thick bars of bright morning sunlight cascaded through the east windows of the library, dust motes swimming in its warm yellow glow. Jonathon sat behind the checkout counter, staring at the image on the computer monitor in front of him.

There it was. *The book. Cain's* book.

It had taken Jonathon well over an hour to find it; the Internet was inundated with sites dedicated to everything from simple books on casting spells and healing, to the more complicated volumes containing satanic rites, and the complex rituals used to summon various demons. He knew that such a world had existed for centuries, but had never imagined a world this extensive, this *boundless*.

On the screen before him was a photograph of a rough sketch done on parchment that was obviously faded and delicate with age. It depicted a large, thick book, bound in leather or something similar, with a crude skull that had no lower jaw pressed into the front.

This book had to have been hundreds of years old, and yet, had he not seen Cain holding this very book only the night before?

Below the photograph was the following text:

Photograph of drawing done in 1455 of the Grimoire of Shadows, or Demon Grimoire, better known as The Lost Grimoire, from the journal of John Holland.

In 1454 England, self-proclaimed alchemist John Holland claimed he had summoned an actual demon using "black magic and earthly elements". Holland also claimed that while under possession of this demon, known only as "Morgoroth", he penned the now famous Grimoire, word for word, straight from the mouth of the beast.

He insisted that Morgoroth was a demon king from Hell, and instilled into the book great powers which Holland himself could summon by reciting incantations from the book.

Holland's odd behavior and obsessions gained him a bad reputation among his peers, and he was subsequently dubbed a heretic by the leaders of the Township of Lancashire, and forced into permanent exile.

He settled in Essex, England, and lived the life of a recluse until the disappearances of two small children again brought him unwanted attention. He was never accused of any crimes, but shortly thereafter, in 1455, John Holland himself disappeared, never to be seen again.

The tiny cottage he lived in burned to the ground, leaving no sign of Holland. The only remaining evidence that John Holland had ever lived there was his charred journal.

The surviving pieces of text, along with the drawing, are now kept in a vault in the Institute for Ancient Studies in London, England, and are only available for licensed research.

Holland's book, however, was never found. But in 1532, a man by the name of Albert Pennygood claimed that he had possession of the book. Pennygood was the founder of a secret order of witches, whose purpose was so secret they had no name. They claimed that their prophesy put forth a specific year and time when the Dark One himself would send forth one of his minions to appear among them to give them the book, so that they may break a hundred year silence and become all powerful, and bring forth such a time of wickedness and darkness that mere men would crumble at their feet.

But Pennygood claimed their rightful time had been lost when John Holland used his reckless methods to conjure Lucifer's messenger, and obtained the book through misguided hands. Pennygood further claimed that Lucifer appeared to him in a dream and told that hidden among the text in the book were the secrets of the time and year of when he who could claim the book would bring about the Armageddon.

He died days later, never discovering the secrets of the book. But Pennygood told his witches that Lucifer had charged a demon king with forever protecting the book as punishment for allowing a mortal to steal the book. According to the stories and texts that have been handed down over the centuries, this demon, called Morgoroth, was better known as Behemoth, the demon ruler of an invisible desert known as Dundayin, which reputedly lay somewhere east of the Garden of Eden.

Behemoth could take the form of large beasts, but his true form was that of a large human, with the horns of a ram and the body of a worm. Behemoth was a demon of gluttony, feeding on the bodies and souls of humans.

After the death of Pennygood, the book again disappeared, and without Pennygood to guide them, many of the witches were hung as punishment for their sins, but most vanished into obscurity.

The book resurfaced again in the early 1700's, but that claim was never substantiated. Since then, there have been accounts of the book appearing in parts of Europe, Germany, and more recently, the United States.

It is now the most revered and sought after Grimoire among those in the dark practices, referred to as The Lost Grimoire, because of its elusive and mysterious nature.

On the other hand, some scholars claim that there has never been any real evidence to support its existence, and that the book never existed at all. The only known rendition of the book, the drawing from John Holland's journal, along with the few remaining sections of text, are considered by many to be the nonsensical ravings of a madman.

Below are the last remaining excerpts from the badly damaged journal of John Holland. They have been translated from Old English into Modern English:

...and when I summoned the demon I lost all account of where I had been, and I was taken to Hell, or perhaps his Hell, I would think the latter, for I do not think that even Lucifer himself would lay claim to this place.

It is a place of living death, as I saw the bodies of the unfortunate ones, and they should have been dead, yet they lived in their own suffering.

The sky was of as blood, with clouds as black as the soul of this beast, and...

...the very ground they lay upon was likened to a sandy shore, but this was not any grain of God, for it fed from the bodies, taking the blood of life, and yet they lived...

...and the rumbling became great, and in the distance the beast appeared, moving through the soil as a fish might swim through water, and he burst from the unholy ground before me, and rose to the height of two men....

...he must surely be the spawn of Lucifer, unholy and unnatural even in his world. His upper body is that of a devil-man, with Lucifer's horns and eyes red as the coals in a fire. His lower half is that of a giant worm, or leach, and I believe it is this that he has been cursed with from some unholy union with Lucifer.

And I swear by my own sanity the beast's mouth was filled with a hundred thin fangs that I have not seen the likes of as my life on Earth as a man, for they gleamed like no fang I have seen. His hands are long and gnarled, and cursed with long fingernails old and twisted, likened to the tips of daggers. He opened his devil's mouth and vomited out the very soul and blood of a man, and that man was reanimated before me, and the beast tore from him his arms and his tongue from his mouth.

...as I feared that I may go mad at the vision of the beast before me, and become as the unfortunate ones around me. They gazed upon me with eyes that long for the sweet taste of true death, so horrible is their suffering.

He spoke to me, and yet his mouth did not move. His words were as my own thoughts, and the words were not of the Earth, for it was the language of only the vilest of things, and I was not my own self. Yet, I began to understand the beast's words, somewhere deep in my mind, and it told me of what I was to do. This is the last I have known of his realm, for I had feared my mind was gone, and I was to be locked in the bottom of a dungeon with the likes of which I would formerly despise.

I am not dead, nor have I gone insane, for I awakened this night at my table with a book fashioned from rough hide resting before me. The pages are filled with script and drawings, but I have no recollection of this, or how long I may have been possessed by the demon. I am weak and ravenous, yet I must discover what I have done with my own hands. I do not know how I could have fashioned such an image, and yet my eyes see the death's head pressed into the book, and of gold, no less.

...touch reveals a life energy within the book, as if it may be alive unto itself. I find myself more consumed with each passing day, and it is my life, I fear, that it draws from, for many are the times when I feel weakened, and can do no more.

I took to wrapping the book tightly in cloth, and I traveled by horse to the country, to the grazing fields of sheep and cattle. It was here that I unwrapped the unholy book and held it out in the sun for a period of time. By my word, the book grew more powerful, almost unbearable to touch.

...could not return to the grazing fields, for in a day's time my horse had died in the stable, and had to be dragged out to prevent any harm to the other animals. I paid in gold coin to have another horse, and I rode to the fields. It is that day that I began to see the works of the book.

Most of the cattle were dead, or had fallen ill, and lay bloated in the fields, as were the sheep. The shepherds were in the fields, and I rode to them. They told me blight had taken most of the beasts, and would surely take more. I made haste away from the stricken place, but not before I saw the dead and rotting jays that lay everywhere. There was not a bird in the trees or sky, and not a call or singing.

I have since kept the book inside, and bound with the cloth, but I find I cannot resist the strange power it now has over me. I feel I have been at my leave at times, for as I have gazed openly at the pages, the influence has most surely drifted beyond the confines of my cottage. It is the truth that in the court nearby a man of nobility took the head of a peasant for not stepping around his lord. In the

square, I did witness....

...two nights at my table, with the book open in front of me, yet I have no recollection of this. I dare say I have become part in some secret text, but I know not what I write. I search the pages, and they are all the same. When I held...

I find that I need the magic from the book. Oh, the wondrous things I could do. The incantation...

...vile thing, but I took great pleasure in it. I know now I am truly bound.

...a thing as this. My very heart and soul...

...not by fire or water or blade. It is too strong, now. I have become certain that the book preys upon those with blackness in their hearts, strengthens their blackness ten fold. I know this for I have walked through the township with the book wrapped in its cloth. I allowed some part to lay open, for I will gather men unto me to perform the ritual of the demon Morgoroth. I have seen acts of murder and rape in the very streets, and yet there are those whose hearts are truly with their God, for the book cannot spoil them. They surely will die. I am weary.

Jonathon read over the text one more time.

The birds, the livestock, all dying as if disease or plague had spread rampant through the area. And how many times have all of us been exposed to the book? It's draining the very life from Cain, so what's it doing to the rest of us?

Jonathon looked up at the clock on the wall; the time was right on the screen in front of him, but the plain round clock had been his time keeper ever since the library had opened a few years back. It was nine-fifty a.m. In ten minutes he would pick up the phone and call Angus Swapp's farmhouse.

5

Amanda was standing in the field by the old Willard farm, and she was calling out to Drew, but he couldn't hear what she was saying. Every time he moved closer to her, she moved away the same distance. She kept cupping her hands around her mouth, calling out, straining to be heard, but there was only silence, and the fuzziness of her features.

The sky turned gray, and a huge, dark shadow began to flow across the field toward her. Drew panicked, and screamed her name, and her mouth soundlessly kept asking, "What? What?" He ran toward her, but she was always the same distance away, always in the path of the dark shadow.

Thunder boomed like drums across the heavens.

Drew awoke to the sound of heavy pounding on the screen door. The sun was up, had been up for a while, and with the thick stained curtains drawn over the living room window, it cast the room in a soft, dim green.

Jenny was still fast asleep, as was Ashley, and he realized he still had his arm around Jenny's shoulders. He gently shook her awake as more pounding came on the screen door, and he put a finger up to his lips, and whispered into her ear.

"Quick, take Ashley into a back room, anywhere. Stay there. Don't make a sound."

Still in the throes of sleep, Jenny stood and pushed her arms under her daughter's sleeping form, and the little girl stirred. She picked up Ashley, blanket and all, and padded down the hallway. A second later, Drew heard a door close softly at the end of the hall. The pounding came again, this time with voices.

"Angus, you in there? Get outta bed, we need to talk to ya'."

Drew moved one edge of the curtain, not more than a hair's width, but it was enough to see the two men standing impatiently on Swapp's porch. They both had shotguns. Drew went into the kitchen and grabbed the knife they had used to cut up Swapp's rope, then went into the bedroom.

Swapp was still asleep, head hanging limply at an angle. *He's going to have one hell of a neck cramp*, Drew thought. He shook Swapp by the shoulders, and the old man raised his head and opened his mouth to say something, but Drew covered his mouth with one hand. In his other hand he had the .38 pointed directly at Swapp's face. Drew got close to him, could smell sweat and stale beer, and whispered into his face.

"You make a sound, just one little noise, and I will blow your fucking balls off. You're going to answer the door, and tell them you're sick or something, and you haven't seen a thing. Then get rid of them. I'll be watching you, and if you even blink fucking wrong, I'll kill you and them, you got it?"

Swapp nodded, and Drew removed his hand from the man's mouth, wiping the clamminess off on Swapp's jeans. Then he was moving quickly, cutting through the ropes around his legs and feet.

The screen door was pulled open, and one of the men pounded on the door.

"Come on, Swapp, open the fuck up! We don't have all day!" Drew heard someone jiggling the doorknob, and made short work of the rest. He pulled Swapp from the chair, and his skinny legs almost buckled under him, but Drew held tight, almost dragging him into the living room.

"All right, all right! Just hold on, would ya?" Swapp called out, throat rattling with phlegm. Drew stood behind the door, glaring at the old man, aiming the .38 at his head. Swapp shot him a sideways glance and opened the door a few inches.

"What the hell do ya' want this early in the mornin'? You boys woke me up!"

"Hell's bells, man, what took ya so fuckin' long?" one man croaked. "Are you fuckin' deaf, or what?"

"I told ya', I was sleepin'. I ain't feelin' too well. What's this shit about?"

The other man spoke up. "We're looking for that guy that was on your property yesterday, the one you called the sheriff about. He's hiding out around town somewhere, looking for the girl that was here the other night. His sister, or something. Have you seen anybody around?"

Drew could see a small wedge of shadow from the shotgun moving back and forth on the warped porch boards. If he had leaned over just a fraction of an inch, he could have made out the blue postal uniform Rusty Withers was wearing that morning.

"I ain't seen or heard anybody. Now can I get back to sleep?"

"Aren't you gonna' let us in?" the other man asked, and Drew felt the muscles in the hand holding the gun tense up, his forefinger twitching and wet against the trigger. He noticed the clock on the living room wall; it was inching close to ten o'clock. He looked at the old black telephone on the end table, and suddenly it was no longer an ordinary phone, and not just because it was a model no one ever used anymore, but because it was a living, breathing thing with a life of its own. And at any time, it might decide to scream bloody murder, and blow the whole thing.

"Look, I told you guys," Swapp said, with true conviction, "I ain't seen anybody, and I don't feel too well, so will you go away and let me get the fuck back to sleep?"

Good boy, Drew thought. He looked at the phone again, and although he knew he had plenty of time, for a second he was sure it was going to ring.

"All right, don't bite our heads off, we're just doing what we're told. Just be on the look out. They can't get out of town, so they've got to be somewhere," Withers said.

"I'll keep an eye out, don't you worry none," Swapp said.

Drew heard the porch boards creak and moan under the weight of the men as they descended the porch and walked across the trampled dirt away from the house. Swapp shut the door, and Drew motioned for him to lock it tight. He heard an old suspension groan, two doors slam shut as they climbed into an old Ford pickup. The engine roared to life, and there was the destructive grinding of gears before the truck wound its way down the dirt road. Drew ran to the curtain and chanced a peek. He saw two forms in the cab of a rusted pickup just as it rounded a bend.

"You just saved yourself a cheap facelift," Drew said. "Ok, back to the chair."

"Before ya' do that, at least let me piss. I'm about to blow a gasket here," Swapp said, dancing around like a boy in school.

Drew again watched Angus Swapp relieve himself in the bathroom, and he could smell the thick stench of the urine as it wafted up from the toilet. Swapp released a particularly rancid fart to finish the whole thing off, then walked into his bedroom and sat down on the kitchen chair.

"Jenny, it's ok now," Drew said, and the door to the spare room popped open, and Jenny walked down the hall, followed by Ashley.

"It's right there, honey," Jenny said, and Ashley immediately scurried into the bathroom and closed the door.

"Ooh, it stinks, mommy," a tiny voice said on the other side of the door. The toilet flushed, and Ashley quickly exited the bathroom, holding her nose. She stood in the hall watching as Jenny held the gun on Swapp while Drew tied him up. She stared at the old man as if she had never seen such a horrible countenance before, and through the curious and faultless eyes of a child, he could have passed for whatever it was that lived under every child's bed, waiting for an arm or a leg to hang over the side so it could pull them under and eat them alive with its horrible, crooked teeth.

They left the bedroom door open a crack, and returned to the living room. Drew opened his mouth to say something, and the old black phone on the end table next to the sofa let off a shrill ring. Jenny snatched a handful of Drew's shirt, and closed her eyes.

"Oh shit," she said, and put a hand on Drew's chest. His heart was pumping like a piston. "You too, huh?"

Drew nodded. The phone was still ringing, and he suddenly remembered what Jonathon had said: *Ten o'clock*. And that's exactly what the battered clock hanging on the wall said. Drew picked up the phone.

"Jonathon?"

"Yes, it's me. You sound like you just saw a ghost."

"We just had a couple of locals out here with shotguns looking for yours truly. We had Swapp send them away. I'm pretty sure they bought it. What did you find out?"

"Plenty. It seems that Cain's book has quite a history, none of it good," Jonathon said. *"Supposedly this book dates back to the 14th century."*

"That's impossible," Drew said.

"Believe it. A man named John Holland claimed a demon used him to write the book back in 14th century England. And get this - this demon is in charge of protecting the book - it eats people's souls for lunch. And this guy Holland claimed the book gave him magic, but was drawing energy from him and leaving him physically drained. But, it turns out that the book was intended for a secret sect of witches, who claimed they were supposed to bring forth Lucifer to rule over the earth. The problem is, no one knows where the book is, because it has a nasty habit of disappearing, along with whoever touches it."

"And you think somehow he got hold of this book?"

"I'm positive. I don't know how, but he managed to get his hands on a book that people have been searching for for years. It's how he's able to summon this demon, Morgoroth, for his rituals. And it's how he's been able to control people - the book is like a disease. As far as I can tell, birds and animals are the most affected

by it. That's why all the livestock in town are dead. And there are no birds to speak of, except all the dead ones laying around town."

"But why animals?" Drew asked.

"It's been known for years that animals are more tuned in to this kind of thing. You know, hiding in the basement when a storm is coming, or barking at ghosts. I think we have a version of that here."

"But why aren't all the *people* dying. Why aren't *we* dying?"

"According to John Holland's journal, this book literally sucked the life from him, and corrupted everyone it was exposed to. It exploits the dark side of humans, sort of spoils any goodness they may have. But he also went on to explain that the book affected not everyone. His theory was, if a person had a strong belief in God, their soul couldn't be corrupted."

"Is it possible that the book is doing the same thing to Cain that it did to this Holland fellow?"

"I'm sure it is, which would mean that he was never meant to have the book. But that doesn't mean that he couldn't figure out how to use it."

Drew looked over at Jenny, who was now sitting on the couch with Ashley. He had forgotten all about the old brown satchel she had refused to let him carry the night before. It now sat at her feet.

He asked, "So what's Oak Junction got to do with all this?"

"I think he had an agenda. Even if he didn't know about John Holland's journal, he surely knows the book has some kind of purpose. He was more or less on his own in the city, and it was too hard to keep his activities quiet. So, he picked out a small town where he could walk right in and take everyone by surprise. Power in numbers. Those who don't follow him end up dead, or sacrificed in his ritual. With the whole town corrupted, he could pretty much do what he pleased.

"So what do we do now?"

"We have to get the book away from him, it's the only way. We just have to figure out a way to do it without getting ourselves killed. And we have to do it before tomorrow, or you may never see your sister again."

"That's not much time...why can't we just shoot this guy? " Drew asked, locking eyes with Jenny.

"After what I've seen, I doubt it would have any affect. He probably has some way of protecting himself, and even then, we'd have the sheriff and the rest of the town to contend with. Anyway,

think it over, see what you can come up with. It's best I don't go back out there. I might be seen. I'll call you back every two hours."

Drew hung up the phone and sat down next to Jenny. "What *is* in that bag, anyway?"

"This is what Harvey's *really* worried about," she said, and unbuckled the satchel. She spread the top open and showed Drew the contents.

"Holy crap, what did he do, rob a bank?"

"It's blood money. I think Cain gave it to him to kill the deputy. Anyway, I didn't even know about it until last night. I figured I could start a new life with it. But you can bet when he got home last night he blew a fuse. And the way he is now, he won't stop until he finds me. And then…" She looked down at her feet, as if saying the words would make it reality. "I'm afraid for us, Drew. You don't know Harvey."

Drew kneeled down in front of her, and took one of her hands. "I won't let anything happen to you, I promise."

She looked into Drew's face, and saw the promise in his eyes, the sternness and hope there, and she *did* believe.

6

    Lucas had never seen John Holland's journal, had never really thought about looking any more into the book. By the time he had finished his translations, he was so consumed by the book that his mind was too muddled by confusion and conflict. It had diseased his old way of thinking, and pointed him on a whole new path.
    But Lucas knew that the book had some kind of affect, especially on animals. Every day he saw the bones of all the unfortunate barn mice that had ventured too close to the thing hidden under the floorboards of the barn. What he failed to consider, though, were the scores of dead mice scattered unseen everywhere beneath the barn, side by side with the larger, collapsed forms of the many rats that had burrowed beneath the barn to raid nests. There were also several gophers that had surfaced under the barn, and had died in the darkness of their tunnels.
    And above, in some of the darker corners of the loft, were the nests the barn swallows and sparrows had constructed against the thick beams that supported the sagging roof. During the spring and summer months, birds were always flying in and out of the various holes in the walls of the barn. Lucas grew up hearing the hungry chirps of the baby birds that populated the many nests at the top of the barn, as they waited impatiently for the adults to bring back their life giving sustenance.
    But Lucas had been much too involved with the book to notice that the barn had grown quiet. If he had climbed up into the loft, he would have seen the dried skeletal remains of the numerous birds that had once made it their home. Eventually, they just stopped coming altogether, and the little ones left alone in the nests quickly withered away.
    In fact, the entire barn had become a no-man's land, a resting place of the dead, and while the occasional mouse or rat still fell victim to the unseen forces within the confines of the barn, birds seemed to sense something was amiss there, seemed to sense the death of the place, and never ventured within its walls.
    It wasn't until Clay's funeral that Lucas Cain, gazing down at his old friend's lifeless form, thought about the dead mice and made a connection between to two. Later that day, after Clay was put into

ground (a scene which Lucas had simply detested, all the tears, all the sadness), and everyone went to the gathering afterward to console Clay's family, Lucas excused himself and went home alone.

He found what he was looking for in his parent's closet - a pile of his mother's old material, neatly stacked on top of her sewing basket, which was filled with small bits and scraps of material, buried among spools of thread and various pin cushions. About midway down the pile, he spied some black material, and pulled it out from the middle of the stack. It was a large square of black velvet, the remnant of some old project from his elementary school days, or perhaps a dress his mother had made for a neighbor. No matter, because it had a new purpose now.

Lucas took the material out to the barn, and with it he tightly wrapped his precious parcel. And it was this very material that Lucas Cain would keep wrapped around the book (whenever he didn't purposely have it out in the open, that is) until the end of his days.

So far, the book had affected none of his family, and while his attitudes and ideals had changed, he had no intention of allowing them to be touched by his secret. Even his twerp of a little brother. He had no real reason to hurt them; he just wanted to be left alone.

Living in the city, however, he could never be certain who would be exposed to the book as he sat up nights staring at the pages, his apartment window wide open, nor did he really care. It could have been an invisible caress on the cheek, or a subtle whisper in one's ear, to make someone arrive home a different person than what he or she had been as they sat eating breakfast earlier that morning. He just didn't care.

The downstairs neighbors had proved to be a nuisance, though, and Cain actually starting leaving the book near his open window in hopes it would all come to a head, and he had been right. And hadn't he sat quietly upstairs, listening and smiling, as his neighbors erupted into the worse brawl yet? Yes, he had. And he had nodded in satisfaction as he heard her screams, and the tremendous thumps as her husband smashed her again and again against the thin apartment walls. Oh, there must have been some serious damage to those walls, yes sir, and oh yeah, she must have been pretty damaged herself.

Just about the time when her screams had become brainless gibberish, the police busted down the door, and wrestled the raving husband to the floor. His bellowing seemed to shake the entire building.

In the newspaper the next day, Cain read about the whole thing, reveling in how quiet it was downstairs. The husband had been taken to jail, with charges still pending, but it looked like he would be going up the river for a while. She was in the hospital, banged up but alive, with a fractured skull, two broken arms, a broken nose, and numerous hairline fractures.

The whole thing made him realize the potential of the book, but the city was just too damned big to do anything with any reasonable amount of control. So, it was off to the library again, this time to find a new home. Something down to earth, something small and quaint. Home, sweet home.

He poured over every book he could find about Iowa, and found that there were so many small towns, he didn't know where to begin. A small, leather-bound volume squeezed between several much larger books caught his eye. He pulled it out and looked at the title on the cover: Iowa: A Small Town History.

While leafing through the weathered pages, he made a startling discovery - an entire chapter dedicated to a tiny farm town called Oak Junction. Cain immediately liked it.

It seemed that during the 1940's, a family by the name of Willard purchased some land just outside of Oak Junction, and built what would be one of the most prosperous farms in the area. But when the patriarch of the family, Abner Willard, died of a stroke in 1945, the farm went bankrupt. It now stood abandoned, an aging testament to a once thriving family business.

And so Cain, aging but still strong with his unbending determination, drove into Oak Junction one day to sweep everyone off their feet, so to speak. And while he physically took control of the town, he gave them a dose of the book, and in no time, they were coming around mentally, as well. He exposed everyone to the book time and time again, and soon most of the town was corrupted.

But what Cain didn't count on were the few who weren't *changed by the book, in fact seemed to fight it off. These folks had too much of a belief system, had God planted firmly in their hearts, but it wasn't enough. In the end, neighbor turned against neighbor, and those who wouldn't join were killed and buried in the town cemetery.*

Of course, there were a few who didn't change, but simply gave in to the majority, or at least pretended to give in. Folks like Jaspar Hendricks, who not only had God in his heart, but was just too damned old and set in his ways. He watched the town change like summer to fall, and quietly blended in with the rest.

All the animal deaths had been a just a minor side effect to Cain, and the town's folk no longer had any reason to care. Their minds were infected with a dark disease that left them hopelessly changed into different people.

Here was a town that only the insects and people could survive the invisible touch of the book, a town where one foolish mistake could be your last.

7

It was noon, and Drew was sitting on the sofa talking to Jonathon. Ashley was watching cartoons on Swapp's television, and Jenny was in the kitchen. Drew could hear water running in the sink and the banging of dishes. The sun burned high in the cloudless sky, but the heavy curtains blocked most of the rays. A swamp cooler was mounted in the ceiling in the hallway, and it provided a nice current of cool air throughout the house.

"So you think you can get close enough?" Drew asked.

"Easy - as far as I could tell, from walking to the library and around town a little, most of the men are keeping on eye on the outskirts of town, where we would be most likely to try to escape. These guys aren't experts, they're gun-toting farmers looking for an excuse to shoot someone. This is the last thing in the world they'll expect."

"One thing I meant to ask you. Those people, those... witches... is there any chance of them showing up looking for the book?"

"We can't even be sure they still exist. Remember, this was a long time ago, something only historians know about."

"And us."

"And us. How are the girls holding up?"

"Ok, so far. And our friend is a little grouchy, but otherwise fine."

"Cool. Hang tight, my friend, tonight's the night. Talk to you soon."

"Hey Jonathon?"

"Yeah?"

"Thanks for sticking you neck out for us. I owe you big time."

"Hey, remember, you're helping me, too. So we're even. Let's just pull this thing off, and we can celebrate later."

Drew hung up the phone, and leaned back, rubbing his eyes. The smells of scrambled eggs and toast wafted in from the kitchen, and his stomach grumbled impatiently. Old memories drifted back....

Sunday mornings they always had a big breakfast. He could smell sausage and eggs from the kitchen. Rose would be barefoot in her robe, and pretty soon, if he didn't get up, she would have to drag him out of the bed. The sun was up, and the rest of the world had started without them, but it didn't matter. This was a day to slow down, to stop and realize just how good life was. And maybe after breakfast, they could lie in bed and make love; the rest of the world could wait....

Drew felt the familiar sadness in his heart, a void filled with loneliness and pain, and then he felt a hand on his shoulder, and looked up into Jenny's concerned face.

"Hey, you ok?"

"Yeah, I was just thinking." He put his hand on hers and gently squeezed it.

"I heard you talking to Jonathon, and I wanted to tell you thanks, too. Without you, I don't know what I'd do." She leaned over and kissed him on the cheek.

Her touch warmed away his sadness, melted away the icy void in his heart, and inside he thought: *Fuck you, Rose.* He wanted at that moment to put his arms around her, to keep her safe from harm, to protect her from the bogeyman that was haunting her thoughts.

And then his cell phone rang from inside his jacket, which was slung over the back of the sofa. They both looked at each other, realizing the inevitable. Ashley glanced over at the both of them as if to say: *Are you going to answer that, or what?*

Drew pulled the phone out of his jacket, pushed *talk*, and put it to his ear. Jenny could hear Cain's tinny voice issuing into Drew's ear.

"Hello, Drew Townsend."

"What do you want?"

"Why don't you stop this nonsense, and tell me where you're at?"

"I told you, I'm not that stupid," Drew said, and then something occurred to him. "I might be willing to go for a little trade." Jenny shook her head, mouthing the word: *No!*

Drew held his finger up in the air: *Hold on a minute....*

"What kind of trade do you propose, Drew?"

"I meet you somewhere, you let Amanda go, and take me in her place."

"How very noble of you, Drew. Your sister would be proud."

"So you'll do it?"

"Sounds reasonable enough to me. Why don't you meet me somewhere, and we'll discuss it?"

"I'll call you later, and let you know where and when."

"I'll be waiting for your call."

Drew hit *end*, and put the phone back into his jacket pocket. He stood up, walked around the sofa, and saw Jenny standing in the kitchen doorway, her eyes glistening with tears.

"You're not really going through with that, are you?" she asked.

"Oh, hey, I'm sorry," Drew said, rushing over and taking her in his arms. "I thought I could get Cain out of that church just long enough for Jonathon to steal that book. I'm not gonna leave you."

"You promise?" she asked, looking into his eyes.

"I promise." He couldn't help but lose himself in the wet pools of her frightened eyes, the feel of her in his arms, and then he was kissing her, and the softness of her lips and face filled him with a wondrous new purpose.

They saw Ashley staring curiously at them from her spot on the love seat, and Jenny went over and picked her daughter up, hugging her tight.

"Are you hungry, sweetheart? Lets go eat."

As they walked by Drew, Ashley held out both hands toward him, and when Jenny moved her closer she put her little arms around Drew's neck and kissed him on the cheek.

"Wow, what was *that* for?" he asked, smiling.

"Because we love you," she said, and she hid her face against her mother's neck. Drew kissed her on the cheek, which produced an impish smile on the little girl's face.

As they were walking into the kitchen, they heard Angus Swapp's voice call out from his bedroom.

"Hey, bring me some of that food, I'm dyin' back here."

Jonathon called at two o'clock sharp, and Drew told him of his plan.

"But what if he hurts Amanda?"

"Oh, I'm sure I'll hear from him first. I'll just let him know that if he hurts one hair on her head, he'll never see his precious book again. Just hide that book well. You never know, he might come looking for you."

"Oh, I'm sure he will. I'll call to let you know I'm on my way. Just give me enough time to get over there."

"Good luck, man. And be careful. In and out," Drew said.

"In and out, my friend, in and out. He won't even know what hit him."

8

Drew took his cell phone into the kitchen. Jenny was leaning against the counter, rubbing her hands together nervously. Ashley lay sleeping on the loveseat, oblivious that the two had left the room. It was just after eleven, and darkness now prevailed over the tiny town of Oak Junction. Drew dialed, and listened to it ring several times before a gruff voice spoke: *"I was about to give up on you, Drew. Did you change your mind?"*

"To tell you the truth, I almost did. But, I can't let my sister go through this. You can take me, as long as you let her go." Drew was playing the part perfectly, but he also knew that Cain was doing the same thing.

"All right, Mr. Townsend, give yourself to me, and your sister can go. Where can I find you?"

"I'll meet you at the cemetery. And don't bring that sheriff with you. I'll go with you, and you let my sister go. Do I have your word?"

"You have my word, Drew. You made the right decision."

Drew hit *end* and put the cell phone on the kitchen table. He was expecting a call in a short while, a call from a very angry man, indeed.

Just west of the church, and due south of where Tower Road joined the Winder Farm, was a large cornfield in which a lone figure lay on the ground between two rows, watching for signs of life from the old building. Farther north, closer to the Winder Farmhouse, Hal Winder, or what was left of him, was hanging on his post after another long day in the hot sun. The corn that had been jammed into his mouth had fallen out as his face had slowly broken open and sloughed downward like a rotted pumpkin on Halloween.

Jonathon could see a faint glow through one of the windows on the backside of the church. The eye of the moon watched above, just a sliver away from being full.

A figure left the church, walking down the sidewalk toward the car parked in front. A car door slammed shut, and the Caddy's engine came alive. The headlights blinked on and peered straight ahead, and he suddenly felt as if the car could *see* him, even though he had worn black jeans and a black shirt to blend in with the night.

The car stayed in the same place for a short while, and the feeling of being seen grew ever stronger. He dared not move one muscle, dared not breath.

The lights swung to one side and swept across the field as the car turned around and went up Church Street. The red taillights seemed to shrink as the car turned east and headed toward town.

Jonathon left the protection of the corn, and ran as fast as he could to the church. He planted himself against the cool stone of the back wall, heart pounding more from fear than exertion. He moved to one corner of the church, and poked his head around the side. There was no sign of the Cadillac. If all went well, Cain would be on his way to the cemetery to meet Drew. Jonathon would have to make tracks fast.

There were two small windows of frosted glass at the back of the church - one was dark, but the other was lit up. This was the one he had seen from the field, the one he knew from experience to be the window to his father's old office.

He reached up and tried to push the window open, but it held fast. He tried the other window, which he knew to be a storage room, but had no luck there. Time was already running short; the light in the office window beckoned for him to enter.

He ran around to the front of the church, and right up to the double doors. He would have to walk right in through the front doors. He looked around to see if anyone was perhaps watching him from afar.

Got to hurry, no time to mess around. Just do it!

He grabbed one of the brass handles, and pulled, expecting it to be locked. The door effortlessly swung open. He went inside, overwhelmed with nervousness; he was trembling slightly, and had to fight the urge to turn around and bolt.

The old church still smelled of the furniture oil his father had always used to keep the pews polished. Now, there was also a thick, dusty smell everywhere. And there was something else, too, something so faint that it almost wasn't there: whispers. The church seemed to whisper, like a small breath in his ear. He reeled around and saw nothing out of the ordinary behind him.

Ok, Jonathon, your mind's playing tricks on you. Let's just get what we came to get, and get out of here pronto! And yet...

There was a definite wrongness here, a new life in the walls of this old church, a presence here that was feeding on the place like a cancer. A shudder ran down his spine, as the feeling of being watched was stronger than ever before.

He saw the pulpit where Reverend Mott used to stand as he spoke not just from his bible, but also from his heart. *God lives in this house, and in your hearts. Let him enrich your lives with his truth*, he remembered his father saying.

Light spilled out of the back hallway. Jonathon made his way down the hall and into the office. He was surprised to find it pretty much as his father had left it, except for a thin layer of dust over everything. As he started to dig through the desk drawers, he found himself thinking of all the times he and his father had sat in this room, talking about the meaning of life, and how the office seemed to glow with an innate quality that belonged only to them as they shared their deepest thoughts as father and son.

The drawers contained his father's old notepads, and stacks of notes for his sermons. And right next to some yellow #2 pencils that had been bundled together with a thick green rubber band was his father's bible. It was white bound King James Version, one that had seen many years of reading. He set the bible on the desk, and kept searching throughout the office.

The old bookshelf behind the desk still harbored all of Earl Mott's books on religion and philosophy. Jonathon was surprised to see they hadn't been destroyed, but on the other hand, they probably meant nothing to Cain, merely amounted to useless words on paper.

Jonathon opened the metal drawers in the filing cabinet one by one. His father didn't keep many files, just enough office supplies to keep him in the pink. His fingers made smudges in the dust on the front of the drawers. There were, in fact, smudges in the dust everywhere in the office, and Jonathon thought: *When he gets back, he's going to feel so violated and pissed off, his head will explode. Then, he's going to find out who was in his shit, and he will make sure they never forget him.*

How many minutes had passed? Five? Seven? Surely no more than seven. And every minute that passed put him closer to running into Cain face to face. He was trembling intensely now, the presence in the church whispering into his mind things he could not comprehend.

Where would he hide it? Or for that matter, how many places can there be for a book?

He sat down in his father's old office chair, an ancient model with plastic castors that rolled and heaved unevenly on the hardwood floor. He tried to imagine himself as Cain sitting at the desk, and rolled forward into the kneehole.

The castors squealed and thumped, and yet, there was another sound, one that just didn't ring true to his ears. He rolled the chair backwards, and then forward again. There was definitely a moment when there was hollowness to the wood as the castors clipped over a particular spot.

He frantically jerked open the desk drawers again, looking for one item he remembered seeing only minutes before. When he spotted the letter opener, he snatched it up and wasted no time pushing back the chair, and hitting the floor on his hands and knees. He tapped the heavy end of the opener over the wooden slats of the floor. Even though the floor was old, the supports under the slats seemed solid enough, until he hit a spot that produced a hollow quality that could have been nothing else but empty space underneath.

He jammed the pointed end of the letter opener into one of the cracks between two old slats of hardwood, and the first piece came right out, as did the second and third. In the dark space below lay a bundle wrapped in a piece of black velvet.

Jonathon gingerly picked up the bundle and unwrapped it. He only had to look at it once to know what he had found. It was bound in rough leather that looked as if it may crumble into pieces at the slightest touch. The paper smelled like old wood, and strangely enough, it smelled of fire. He wrapped in back up, then noticed something else in the bottom of the space, and pulled it out as well.

It was a tattered blue spiral notebook. He quickly flipped through some of the pages, then put it on top of the book, and on top of that, his father's old bible. On his way out of the church, the whispers grew louder, and the bundle under his arm grew warm.

And then he was outside in the fresh night air, and the whispers where left to talk amongst themselves.

9

Cain drove to the back of the cemetery, and parked next to the fresh graves. He got out and lit a cigarette, and leaned against the front hood. He stared at the August moon, blowing smoke into the air and watching it drift and dissipate as it wafted upward.

He looked at the dark bulges in the earth, all this death and failure because of a little human weakness. This was exactly what he was counting on Mr. Drew Townsend to do, show his weakness, his pity for his sister, and when he gave himself up, Cain would bury him alive as punishment for fucking with him.

The minutes ticked on. The thought never occurred to him that someone might be invading his space, digging into his secrets, to be so bold and foolhardy as to risk going near his church without permission. And it was just impossible for him to know what was going on in a person's head over the phone. It was something Cain never thought about - it was a *weakness*.

Cain began to walk among some of the older graves. He kicked over a couple of headstones. Then his patience grew thin, and he pulled Amanda's cell phone out of his pocket, found Drew's number, and hit *send*. Anger rose inside him as he heard Drew's voice.

"Hello?"

"I thought we had a deal, Drew. Have you changed your mind?"

"I thought I would think it over longer," Drew said nonchalantly.

"Don't fuck with me, Drew Townsend! I might just take care of little Amanda a day early!" He paced back and forth in front of the Caddy, the muscles in his jaw pulsing with anger.

"I wouldn't do that if I were you, Cain. Not if you value you precious book."

Cain stopped cold in his tracks. "What are you talking about?"

"You heard me, Cain. I've got your book right here in my hands, and if you so much as lay a finger on Amanda, you'll never see this book again."

Cain let Drew's words sink in. How could he have been so stupid as to let someone take him for a ride? The whole thing became crystal clear as he heard Drew's final words: *"Go on, if you don't believe me. Hurry home to your little church, Cain. Sorry I won't be there, though, I had to run. Nice little place you got, though."*

Cain hit *end*, and stuffed the phone into his pocket.

He got in the car and shot out of the cemetery at breakneck speed, going south on 5th Avenue, wheeling around the corner at Church Street like a madman, which was essentially how he was feeling at that moment, for he would have stopped for nothing, not even a pedestrian crossing the road, so blind he was in his fervor to get back to the church.

For a moment he thought he was going to lose control around the bend at the west end of Church Street, just before the church, but he somehow managed to maintain control, squealing to a stop at the curb in front of the church.

When Cain ran inside the church, he immediately knew something was amiss; there was a different odor in the air, the odor of a *person*, of different clothes altogether. It felt as if the church had been turned inside out for the whole world to see, much in the same way a person feels coming home to find his house burglarized.

And when he discovered the opening in the floor right before the knee hole in the desk, he clenched his hands tightly, fingernails digging little half moons into the palms of his hands, and his eyes turned black as he loosed an inhuman scream coursed with the black hatred that had ruled him for so long. He dashed out of the office, down the short hallway, and past the rows of pews, into the night. He ran behind the church, searching across the open field, trying to catch sight the person who had invaded his territory.

He knew he was acting foolish, but he had never anticipated *this*. It was something he could never tell to anyone. But, he would *have* to tell Craven if he wanted help to get his book back. What he would *not* tell Craven was that without the book, his days on Earth were numbered.

As soon as Jonathon was out of the church, he clutched the bundle of books to his chest, and ran like hell. He went north, toward Tower Road. The barbed wire fence that demarcated the Winder property came up fast, *too* fast, and he stopped just in time to prevent himself from running headlong into the jagged wire.

He set the books through the wire to the other side, then propped a foot up on one strand and jumped over. He ran pell-mell through the corn, anxious to widen the distance between him and the church.

As soon as he crossed Tower Road, he veered right, heading east toward 1st Avenue. Here, he stopped short of the street. He would have to cross behind his neighbor's house to reach his backyard. Seeing no lights on at the house, he made a wild dash past his neighbor's backyard and into his own yard, where he almost went sprawling.

Safely inside the house, he locked the back door, and leaned against a wall to regain his breath. His lungs burned for air, and he choked and gasped from the dryness in the back of his throat. It took several minutes before his breathing calmed to a normal rate.

But the race wasn't over yet; he had to find a place to hide Cain's property soon, for Cain could show up at any moment and find his book here, which would mean certain death for Jonathon. He raced around the house, looking for the perfect spot. Finally, he found a suitable place for the book, and about five minutes later, someone banged on his front door.

Cain!

Jonathon grabbed a beer from the refrigerator (something he never indulged in, but he had decided tonight would be a good night for it) and popped it open, taking a long swig, which burned his throat on the way down. He opened his front door, still stealing drinks from the beer.

Cain stood on his front doorstep, looking very disturbed and slightly disheveled. He glared hatefully into Jonathon's eyes, watching for the tiniest hint, the blink of an eye, or quick look to the side, anything that might tell him that this man, whom he had wanted to kill in the first place, had stolen his book.

He's trying to dig into my head...

In his mind he replayed over and over again the vision of the creature that had taken his mother's life, her soul. He kept thinking: *The ritual, the ritual...*

Jonathon burped loudly, and said, "Mr. Cain, hi. What brings you out here this time of night?"

"I don't know, Jonathon, why don't you tell me?" Cain said, walking inside the house. He stared coldly at Jonathon as he passed him, then whirled around in the middle of the living room to face him.

"It's the funniest thing," Jonathon said feigning a mild intoxication, " but I thought the ritual was *tonight* - got drunk and everything. Turns out it's *tomorrow* night. Boy, I need to lay off the sauce." *Keep it up, boy, you're doing fine.*

"Jonathon, someone broke into my church tonight and stole a very important item from me. You wouldn't know anything about that, would you?"

He looked Cain squarely in the eyes. "No sir, I don't know anything about that. Would you like a beer, Mr. Cain?"

"No, Jonathon, I do *not* want a beer."

"It's too bad about mom and pop, isn't it? I don't understand why I was so mad at first, but now I see. It's all for the better, right?"

Cain was taken aback by Jonathon's sudden change of heart. His features relaxed, and he did a very surprising thing - he walked over and put his arm around Jonathon's shoulders.

"You're right, Jonathon, it *is* all for the better. I'm very glad to see you've finally come around. When this whole messy business is over, we really must get together and talk, what do you say?"

Jonathon went dead serious. "You know, I would really like that, Mr. Cain."

"Then I'll look forward to seeing you tomorrow night," Cain said, and went for the door. Jonathon followed him out onto the front porch, and shook his hand.

He watched as Cain climbed into his car and sped away, disappearing around the corner on 1st Avenue. He went inside, closing the door behind him. He felt like he was in a dream. "That didn't just happen," he said to himself, and picked up the phone.

Drew answered the phone after one ring. "Hello?"

"I got it. And our friend was just here poking around. He thinks I had a change of heart. It was almost *too* easy."

"I told him I had the book," Drew said. *"Told him if he even touched Amanda the wrong way, he would never see his book again. He thinks I was inside the church tonight."*

Jonathon said, "Thanks buddy, that was the icing on the cake. Now I'm going to do a little research. I'll talk to you in a couple of hours."

Jonathon hung up the phone and went to the refrigerator. But, it was not another beer he was after; what he wanted was in the *freezer*. Funny thing was, when he pulled the book out of the freezer, it still felt warm.

If Harvey had spent only a few more minutes in the cluttered field by Randolph Street, he would have seen a figure leave the church and run toward the cornfield to the north. But then again, he may not have seen any such thing, for his mind was too pickled and filled with psychotic thoughts of murder; but not just murder. He had traveled over that line where murder was much too benign for his crumbling thought process. His mind had created a world filled with unspeakable acts that before had, even to him, seemed too inhumane to consider.

Now, as he stumbled around in the darkness, the fantasies in his mind grew ever larger, and he had a new reason for finding his runaway wife. One that had nothing to do with money, or heartache. It had everything to do with punishment.

He looked up high at the August moon, and saw it waver in his vision. He was near the woods north of Zeb's station, and stopped to take several deep breaths. He decided that if he *were* to find Jenny, he would have to slow down quite a bit on the booze. Unfortunately for her, this had no affect whatsoever on his unstable mind. Once he found her, there were so many things he wanted to do to her. And he would make the little girl watch, just to make sure she knew better that to try and run again. After all, he had *plans* for that little girl.

Eventually, he found himself passing directly in front of Angus Swapp's house. He had a wild impulse to walk right up to Swapp's front door and ask the farmer if he had seen Jenny anywhere around the area. The inclination quickly passed, but left him with a few afterthoughts while he walked home. *Maybe I'm going about this all wrong. Maybe tomorrow night, during the ritual, I could do myself a little window peeking. Couldn't hurt. After all, everyone will be gone, won't they? All except you know who. And we could have ourselves a little party. One-two, you know who.*

That night Harvey dreamt that he found Jenny at the edge of a cornfield. She pleaded with him, and he silenced her pleas by putting his fingers tightly around her throat and squeezing as hard as he could. She gawked up at him, her eyes bulging from her bluing face, tongue sticking out from between her fading lips. Then her face changed, and to Harvey's chagrin, he was looking down at his own unshaven face, and greasy hair, and he let go, letting himself drop to the ground. The other Harvey looked up at him and said, "You're a dead man."

Harvey woke up soaked in his own urine. He got up, threw the sheets off the bed, and went promptly back to sleep.

10

Jonathon took the bundle into his father's old den and placed it on the desk. He made sure the curtains were closed, then turned on the green desk lamp he had given him one year for Christmas. He took the white King James bible and put it in the top drawer, along with his father's neatly arranged notebooks, pens, pencils, and the many different bookmarks he gave away to the kids at Sunday school. Some had scenes depicting Noah and the Great Flood, while others showed John the Baptist baptizing robed people in a river. Most though, were of Jesus himself: Jesus teaching, Jesus at the Last Supper, and Jesus on the Cross.

He closed the drawer, and sat down at the desk. He slowly began to unwrap the old velvet material, and there, almost sparkling in the glow of the lamplight, was the death's head he had read about. It gleamed as if it were brand new, this gold forged from another time. Jonathon was almost sure the cover was made of some kind of animal skin, dried just enough to turn black, but no further. It seemed the book had not aged in over six hundred years. John Holland's words replayed in his mind: *Not by fire or water or blade....*

Could he have meant the book? Looking at the book, it seemed logical. He thought: *The book cannot be destroyed. Not by fire or water or blade.*

The smells he had encountered in the church were much stronger now. Raw wood had been pounded into a pulp suitable for the spine and the covers, but as for the pages, he could not quite place the material, nor did he have any idea of what would have been used for ink that long ago.

The other smell was there, too.

Fire. That's definitely fire. Did someone try to burn the book? Not by fire or water or blade.

Jonathon lightly ran his fingertips over the rough material, and quickly pulled away, startled by the odd static sensation he felt shoot through his fingers. He stroked it again, absorbed in the sensation of electricity in the tiny hills and valleys on the surface of the book.

He pulled the cord hanging from the lamp, and the den went dark. He then ran his fingers over the book again. He saw tiny blue sparks arc from the book to his hand, the residual color shoot up the back of his hand in quick, electrical flashes.

He switched on the lamp again. If it was true about the book - everything from John Holland's journal to the accounts of Albert Pennygood and his secret society of witches- and indeed it seemed every bit true now - then Cain might very well be the one who was supposed to unlock the book's secrets, and he must never be allowed to possess the book again.

Jonathon opened the book and slowly turned the pages, studying the ancient text and pictures drawn on each page. Every now and then, from the corner of his eye, he seemed to catch a glimpse of gold. A tiny flash here, a slight sparkle there, but close examination of the pages revealed nothing.

The book's playing tricks on me. It's got a mind of its own, but it can't hurt me. I grew up with a man of God, and this book can't affect my beliefs or me. Or can it?

Jonathon had never seen such a collection of vile creatures and drawings. Even the text itself seemed beyond human. These were true angels of Hell, especially the large drawing of the beast that ruled over the Desert of Blood. He knew this thing existed, he had seen it up close, in the field by the old Willard place.

A sense of foreboding came over him as he looked through the pages, a sense that this book was at the center of something vaster that what was happening now, something more terrible than even Cain.

A short while later, he wrapped up the book, set it aside, and then began to examine the old spiral notebook. As he began to read the handwritten text, the whole purpose of the notebook became clear (and this book *had* aged. It wasn't very old, but old enough for the paper to be curling up at the corners, some of the ink fading).

It's a translation! Holy shit, he managed to translate most of it into Modern English.

The more he read, the more he became convinced that Cain did not know the true nature of the book. At the back of the notebook was a handwritten chart with all the dates of the full moons for that year.

The very last page had another translation that read:

Beware all ye untrue bearers of the book, for in the Dark One's name shall ye honor the full moon, lest ye become an abomination unto the earth, never again to see the light of day. Hark Bearer! For if the light of Him should bear upon thou skin, ye will become as ashes in the wind, scattered to the ends of the earth.

Jonathon smiled at this last revelation.

...ye will become as ashes in the wind....

Cain was caught between a rock and a hard place, and running out of time.

11

When Cain first read from the book over a year before in his Sioux City apartment, the last thing he expected was for his world to be turned upside down. He lost track of all conscious thought, and when he woke up, the first thing he saw was the blood red sky of Dundayin. He was lying on a very hot patch of sand, and didn't even realize he had changed until the ground near him burst open and the thing from the book rose up in front of him.

He scuttled backwards on his hands and feet; only they weren't the same hands and feet he was accustomed to. He felt the misshapen form of his head and tried to scream, but his deformed mouth wouldn't speak for him. "No! This isn't what I wanted!" he shrieked in his mind.

The creature before him spoke back to his mind.

"But you are not the true bearer of the book, Cain."

"I thought it was mine. All I wanted was power, but not this."

"And power you shall have. But did you think there would be no price for this power? You have something that does not belong to you, something you don't understand, and for that, you must answer to me. You will bring me a living soul with each full moon, for it is here that I feed on the souls of the living for sustenance."

Cain gazed around him, and realized he wasn't alone. As far as the eye could see, across the sands of this vast desert, were living corpses on the sand, their blood oozing slowly out of the different wounds on their bodies, soaking in small puddles in the sand.

"But look at me! I can't go back like this!" Cain yelled up to the beast.

"And you won't. You are too valuable to me to leave you like this. But heed my warning: Disappoint me, and you will become as you are now. Now go back to your pitiful little life, Cain"

Cain woke up back on his sofa sleeper, drenched in sweat. In the blink of an eye, he had set the course for the rest of his life, however long that may be.

Part 4
The Night of Cain

1

Ronnie Taylor had lived in Oak Junction his whole life, and had spent much of it working at some of the local farms, making money almost as fast as he could spend it for a good bag of dope. At twenty years old, and living in the basement of his parent's house (girls had to be snuck in through a window - his folks would not hear of him bringing tramps into the house), his future seemed less than favorable.

So on the morning of the ritual, when Sheriff Craven phoned the Taylors and told them he had a little job for Ronnie to do, they readily agreed. There would be money involved, not for Ronnie, but for his parents.

"Will he be coming back, Sheriff?" Mr. Taylor asked Craven, to which the sheriff calmly and matter-of-factly replied, "No sir, I wouldn't count on seeing him again." To which Mr. Taylor replied, "Great. I've been meaning to do some remodeling in the basement, maybe put in a bar."

Several hours after Jonathon had called Drew and Jenny from the library to tell them what he had found, the Taylors told their only son that Sheriff Craven had a job for him to do, and although he was a little reluctant (he and the Sheriff weren't really the best of friends), the prospect of making an easy hundred bucks sounded pretty sweet.

"And get cleaned up," Mrs. Taylor told him. "You don't want to look like a bum."

Ronnie put on an old pair of jeans the sported ragged holes along the crotch and ass, a stained tee shirt, and a pair of Nikes he had stolen from a neighbor's back porch. This was as good as it got for Ronnie Taylor, as good as it was ever going to get. His parents knew it, Sheriff Craven knew it, and so did Cain.

The last thing he did was brush back his thick red hair, which hung loosely around his shoulders, and let the screen door slam behind him as he started hoofing it for the church, where he was supposed to meet Craven. He knew that was Cain's church, but he tried not to concern himself with it too much.

Mr. Taylor, who was grabbing a beer from the fridge when Ronnie left, almost jumped out of his skin when the screen door slammed against the doorframe. He hated the sound of it, in fact, could not stand the sound of his good for nothing son slamming the fucking screen door every time he left, day in and day out. If he had to hear that fucking sound one more time, he would go through the roof. But he would have to take this one time in stride, bite the bullet, and he sat down at the kitchen table to drink his beer, and enjoy the tranquil solitude of a warm summer afternoon.

It was going to be a wonderful day.

Ronnie walked down Church Street West, the church rounding into view as followed the southward bend in the road. The church looked much older then he remembered; the white cross was gone, and the paint on the bell tower was flaking off, revealing weathered wood beneath. Even the main structure looked changed. Pieces of mortar had crumbled off from between the stones, and now littered the ground below the dusty windows. The sun had parched the grass, once a lush green.

ISheriff Craven's cruiser was parked at the curb in front of the church, right behind Cain's long black Cadillac. Ronnie stared uneasily at the tinted windows as he walked toward the small sidewalk that led to the entrance. *Somebody could be in that fucking thing watching me, and I wouldn't even know it*, he thought, as he grasped one of the brass door handles and pulled. He turned his attention away from the Cadillac just in time to see a meaty fist appear in front of his face a split second before it put out his lights.

"*Wake up, sleeping beauty*", a voice said. Ronnie opened his eyes, and tasted warm blood in his mouth. He tried to talk, and winced at the sharp pain in the side of his face where Craven had broken his jaw. He moaned and tried to put a hand to his injured jaw, and discovered that his hands were handcuffed behind the straight-back chair he was sitting in. He saw Cain staring at him from behind the desk, like a hungry animal contemplating dinner.

"No," Ronnie said groggily, moaning loudly as the broken bones in his jaw, which were hanging loosely just under the skin, ground together in a bright burst of pain.

"Don't try to move or speak, it'll just make it worse," Craven said. Ronnie gawked at the black spider that was crawling across the top of Cain's (Reverend Mott's) desk.

"Oh come now, Ronnie, you're not afraid of a little spider, are you?" Cain asked, his mouth twisted wickedly up at one corner. Cain's eyes were unnaturally dark, and Ronnie's heart pounded as he tried to read those eyes.

The spider was small, but had a bulbous abdomen that throbbed and pulsed, and Ronnie's eyes grew wide as Cain picked up the spider. "It's absolutely harmless," he said, and placed the spider on Ronnie's leg.

Ronnie tried to scream, but cried out in pain instead, his eyes filling with tears. He tried to dislodge the spider from his leg, but it held tight.

"Don't move, or it will bite you," Cain said.

Ronnie's eyes rolled wildly as he watched the spider crawl up his leg, and stop near his shirt.

"What about you, Sheriff, are you afraid of spiders?"

"Personally, I hate the fucking things, but I'm not afraid of them, either. But then again, I'm not the one with a spider crawling up my pant leg, now, am I?" Craven laughed out loud, and Cain smiled, crossing his arms over his chest, and sat on the edge of the desk.

"I love your sense of humor, Sheriff," he said.

The spider was on the move again, and Ronnie could feel its legs through the thin material of his tee shirt. The muscles in his chest went rigid as he tried to prevent the spindly legs from touching the skin. The muscles in his jaw tensed, and he screamed in pain.

"I told you not to move, you idiot," Cain said. "Now listen to me. You are going to help us with a little problem we have. Are you listening?"

Ronnie nodded, but managed not to scream, and his face turned an ugly red as the ball of nerves in his face sent thunder coursing into the side of his face.

"That's good, very good. The thing is, we have a stranger roaming around town, and he's taken it upon himself to steal something very valuable from me. So you, my friend, will go to him, and set him straight. And you will return to me with the location of my book."

Ronnie had been trying so hard to concentrate on what Cain was saying, that he failed to notice when the spider moved all the way up to his shoulder. He could just see its legs from the corner of his eye, and then it was gone.

Something touched his neck. He tried to stay as still as he could, could feel his blood racing in his veins, pumping shots of pain into his face.

Eight hairy legs touched his skin ever so delicately as the spider worked its way to his face, where it paused on his tightly squeezed lips. He closed his eyes against the pain, the terror, and he heard Cain's voice for the last time say, "Closing your mouth won't help you now."

And then it was in his nose, wiggling frantically as it forced its way in deeper, to the inner workings of his skull. Ronnie screamed, no longer focused on the pain in his cheek, for there was a new threat, and a new pain, digging and clawing its way into his head, and fresh blood ran from his nostrils. He screamed one last time, then felt something *give*, like the snap of a rubber band, and could no longer feel anything.

His eyes were still wide open as he stopped breathing, and his head flopped backwards, mouth agape, oblivious of any pain.

A few minutes later, his right eye softly burst open, depositing its fluid onto his cheek, and the thing that had once been a normal spider crawled out from under a flap of the eye. Craven watched all this indifferently, then looked at Cain.

"Very good," Cain said. "Now to the business of Mr. Townsend."

"That was a very foolish thing to do, Drew," Cain said. Drew stood in the living room, peeking through the curtains at the front of the house. The place looked deserted. At the back of the house was more corn, cut off at an angle by River Road, which was actually an access road between Swapp's farm and the Despain farm just to the north. The coast there was clear as well, the neighboring farm too far away to be of any concern to the current residents of the Swapp farm. But Drew kept a constant vigil at the windows just the same.

Drew held the cell phone to his ear, throwing Jenny a cautionary look as she stood in the kitchen doorway listening to Drew.

"I wouldn't call it *that* foolish. After all, I have your book. All you have to do is let Amanda go, and I'll let you have your book back, simple as that," Drew said. "And I've been looking through your precious book, and I get the feeling that you need it more than you're letting on."

"*No matter what happens, your sister will die, Drew. Think about it. And in the end, I* will *have my book back.*" Cain's voice was calm, audacious, but Drew knew that the man on the other end of the line must have been wearing the face of abhorrence; fists clenched tightly, and ready to kill at the drop of a hat.

"Think about *this*, Cain. If my sister dies, I will leave this town and go as far away as I possibly can. I will make it my life's work to keep this book away from you. You see, I've been doing a little reading in your notebook here, and I have a feeling that if you don't get this book back by, say, midnight tonight, then something very, very bad is going to happen."

"*Don't kid yourself, Drew. You don't know what you're dealing with.*"

"I want to see my sister now, you asshole! Where is she?"

"*She's fine, Mr. Townsend. You'll get to see her tonight, at the ritual. Amanda's the guest of honor, you know.*"

The line went dead. "He hung up," Drew said, and set the phone down on the end table next to Swapp's old black phone.

"Do you think he's buying it?" Jenny asked.

"Oh, I'm sure he thinks I have the book now, but he's playing the whole thing down. I think if we hold out long enough, stretch this thing out to the last minute, he'll wait for his book. We're really going to have to put all of our heads together to pull this off, because you can bet your last dollar than Cain plans on killing us all."

Jenny walked up to Drew, put her arms around him, and leaned her head against his chest. She could hear the steady thrum of his heart. *The beat of a good heart*, she thought.

"Mommy, I want another sandwich!" Ashley demanded from her perch at the kitchen table. Jenny had found some fresh lunchmeat and bread in Swapp's refrigerator, which was quite surprising, considering the condition of the rest of the food. Most of it was left to waste, but obviously Angus Swapp *did* eat occasionally, and kept fresh staples to live on. A darkening mold had begun to spot the inside of the refrigerator door, the man had no qualms about *where* he kept his food, and even as hungry as they were, they were still somewhat hesitant about eating anything that came out of *that* refrigerator, but in the end, sheer hunger had ruled the day.

While Jenny started making sandwiches for Ashley and Drew, a tiny black spider was attempting to force its way out of one of the holes in the receiver of Drew's cell phone. At first, just a thin leg probing around, then several legs, pulling the rest of its tiny frame out into the open. Finally, the tiny black bulb popped out, and the spider rolled once on the surface of the phone, then gained its legs and scurried across the table to a corner, where it crawled over the edge, disappearing underneath for a moment before reappearing on the table leg. It moved quickly down the leg and onto the faded brown carpet.

Here, it hesitated, contemplating its next move. Then it was on the go, crawling across the deadly space of carpet in front of the kitchen doorway, where discovery would mean certain death in the form of a very large and heavy shoe. But today, it would go unnoticed, even from the roaming and curious eyes of a child.

It continued down the hallway until it reached the master bedroom, where Angus Swapp had again dozed off (Drew for the life of him could not figure out how a man tied in his position could sleep so easily) after eating a breakfast of eggs and toast at gun point. The door was closed, but the spider slid easily enough under the crack, and entered the room.

Drew washed his sandwich down with a glass of fresh water from the tap; there was a half gallon of milk in the refrigerator, but the due date had passed by a week, so that was out of the question.

I guess we should make a couple for our friend in there," Drew said, and Jenny nodded, pulling out the last three slices of bread.

"Well, one, anyway," she said, peeling off several slices of lunchmeat and laying it on the bread.

Drew opened a cabinet door above the sink, which housed Swapp's collection of liquors and wines (mostly the cheap stuff), reached up, and carefully retrieved his .38. The brown satchel was in one of the larger cupboards, with Jenny's gun tucked away with the money. They had both agreed that while keeping a gun nearby was necessary, it was also necessary to keep the guns at a safe distance from Ashley. They had already talked to her about the danger, and she did not seem likely to try touching one of the guns, but leaving a weapon like that laying around was an accident waiting to happen.

"Do you need help?" Jenny asked, giving him one of her looks that were beginning to melt his heart. It was during those moments that he had often wondered what it would be like to make love to her. He smiled and took the sandwich. "No thanks, I think I've got it covered." He smiled at Ashley, who smiled back through a mouthful of sandwich, and went into the hallway.

He turned the doorknob and started to say, "Ok Swapp, time for a little...." But as the door squeaked open, Drew heard an odd sound, something totally different from the hinges of the bedroom door. He started as if someone had snuck up behind him and yelled *boo!*, and the sandwich fell from his hand and thudded to the carpet in two pieces.

He stared dumbstruck at the sight before him.

2

Harvey woke up in a bedroom that was blasting hot. He looked around the room with bloodshot eyes, and a ten-ton weight on his head. He sat up in bed and ran his hand through his hair. He was naked except for his underwear, which was stained yellow from his own urine. He couldn't recall taking off his clothes the night before, but he vaguely recalled something about the sheet, which was lying in a heap at the foot of the bed. He could smell the urine from the bed, but it drew a blank in his head. He stood and walked on less than stable legs into the living room, where he switched on the small window mount air-conditioner that he had installed in the side window a year before.

He walked into the heat of the kitchen, and pulled a cold beer out of the fridge. A bottle of aspirin sat on top of the fridge, and this he opened, popping four tablets into his mouth and chasing it down with beer.

After two beers, he was feeling more like his old self again. After four, he was starting to feel *really* good. After six, and a glass of warm whiskey, that warm cozy feeling rose up inside and gave him new strength. His head cleared, and he thought about Jenny. Then he recalled the dream he had the night before, and it left him with a strange sensation, as if it was trying to tell him something.

I'm going to find you tonight, you bitch, and when I do, you're going to wish you had never met me, oh yeah. Don't worry about the girl, though, I'll take real *good care of her.*

The funny thing was, Harvey was right - he *was* going to find Jenny, and it would be a night that one of them both would remember forever. In fact, it would be a night the entire town would remember.

Around the corner and a block away from where Harvey stood wearing nothing but a pair of dirty underwear in a heat drenched kitchen, Sheriff Frank Craven was just returning from Oak Junction Cemetery, where he had deposited Ronnie Taylor's corpse into a shallow grave.

He unlocked his office for the first time that day (these days the Sheriff kept no *real* schedule, just showed up whenever he felt the need), and began to fill out the various forms he needed to file with the county in order to keep up appearances. They were the ones who signed his checks, and in return they had to make sure that the Good Sheriff was doing his part by flagging speeders and other assorted wrongdoers in order to add his fair share of revenue to the state.

And while he *did* manage to keep up on a fair share of his duties, his fair share of revenue had seriously declined over the past month. To make up for that, Cain had a seemingly endless supply of money at the Good Sheriff's disposal. So he filled out phony reports and forms, and mailed the originals to the county, coupled with whatever funds he had collected, and filed the copies just like normal. As far as the county was concerned, the Good Sheriff was doing a stand-up job in his part of the state.

He opened the inside door to the booking area, which was always hot, that day being no exception. The Oak Junction Sheriff's Office was equipped with central air, but the booking area had only one vent, which was almost as good as none at all, so the inside door had to be kept open most of the time.

When he went into the back, he found Amanda Townsend sitting on her bunk, sweat running down her forehead.

"Should cool off in here pretty soon. You want something to drink?"

She slowly nodded her head. Craven went back to the front area, and she heard him dropping coins into the pop machine, heard the can tumble down into the catch at the bottom. He returned with a can of Coke, and handed it between the bars. Amanda stood and approached the bars, but just as she was reaching for the can, Craven pulled it away.

"Just want to let you know, you might as well consider this your last meal. After tonight, you and your brother will be food for the worms." Craven suddenly went quiet, and handed the can to Amanda. She took it, and asked, "What do you mean, my brother?"

"Never mind," Craven said. He set the Coke on the floor next to the bars and left without another word. She heard his hushed voice as he talked on the phone, but she could not make out the conversation. If she would have been able to hear Craven, she would have heard him trying to explain to Cain how he had accidentally let it slip that her brother was somewhere in town.

What about my brother? Is he here? Why isn't he here with me? Or maybe that's the thing; they don't know where he is. Drew....

3

Drew instinctively took one step back, but couldn't pull his eyes away from what he was seeing. Swapp was staring blankly at him, with the one good eye he had left anyway, but Drew knew he was already dead. His head rocked back and forth like a marionette on strings.

The thing that was clamped to the side of Swapp's head looked like a huge black spider, or what *used* to be a spider. Only this thing was slightly bigger than a basketball, with a throbbing sack that seemed to have a point at the end that stabbed blindly at the man's shoulder.

The spider had planted one long leg deep into Swapp's other eye socket, and another into his mouth, and these two legs kept yanking his head back and forth while it continuously chomped at a bloody hole in the side of Swapp's head with a mouth bearing two large, white fangs. Its other six legs were wrapped around the other side of his head. Drew noticed that all the legs had a little spur at each of the leg joints. One of the legs on the other side of his head sunk its way into his right ear with a liquid *crunch!* as it forced its way inside.

But Drew's gaze kept returning to the mouth, and its unnatural, yet familiar shape. It didn't dawn on him what he was looking at until it turned and looked directly at him - with eight human eyes. It's mouth opened and closed with sickening intakes of air, and there was actually a tuft of dark red hair on the crown of its head like some bizarre new-wave haircut.

My God, it's a man...or was a man, Drew thought as he gawked at Ronnie Taylor.

The thing shrieked, released itself from Swapp, and dropped to the floor. Drew caught one more glimpse of its nightmarish face as it scrambled across the floor toward him, then he slammed the bedroom door shut.

It bounced once against the door, and a second later he heard it scuttle away. Then he heard glass breaking. He slowly turned the knob and pushed the door open, a crack at a time. He saw Angus Swapp's corpse, still tied to the chair, the one eye glaring at him, mouth open in a silent scream. The hole in the side of his head had broken through the skull, and a part of his brain was protruding out of the gap.

He opened the door a little farther, cool air from the cooler flowing past him. The lower section of the window was a jagged hole, the thin curtains flailing out around its edges. Drew shut the door and ran into the kitchen.

"Take Ashley, and get into the living room!" he said. Jenny could tell by the look on his face that his was no time for questions. She snatched the little girl up and ran into the living room with Drew. They stood in the middle of the room, Drew pointing the .38 out in front of him, head cocked to one side.

They all jumped as a crash came from the kitchen, broken glass raining down on the old kitchen linoleum.

"Stay here," Drew said, advancing to the kitchen doorway. Behind him, Ashley said, "Mommy, I'm scared!" and clutched her mother tighter.

The spider stood amidst the broken shards of glass from the window in the back door, its bulbous abdomen pulsing behind its eight glaring eyes. It scurried frantically, trying to get at Drew, but its legs only scattered glass everywhere, giving Drew the time he needed to point and fire.

There was a loud pop like a firecracker as the gun discharged, the closed quarters making it louder than it really was, and at the same time Ashley screamed from the living room. One of the thing's legs separated from its body and slid across the linoleum, and a thick, dark green fluid oozed from the stump. The thing shrieked, and Ashley again screamed from the living room, this time joined by Jenny. It was surprisingly agile, for it then leapt up and out the hole in the window.

"Shit!" Drew said, rushing over to the window and looking out through the hole. The spider was gone, but there were spots of the goo leading along the back of the house.

"Drew! Are you ok?" Jenny called from the living room.

"I'm ok," Drew said, as he ran into the living room. He went straight for the window, and peered between the curtains. The spider was crawling across the sun-baked dirt toward the barn, tripping itself up as it tried to accommodate for the missing limb. When it reached the barn, it clawed at one of the doors until it opened slightly, and vanished inside.

"It's in the barn, I have to go after it," Drew said.

"No, don't go," Jenny said. "You might get hurt! Whatever it is, just let it go!" Ashley had her arms around Jenny's neck, staring at Drew with tearful, frightened eyes.

"I have to go. That thing could come back after us. Or worse yet, it might try to get back to Cain, and I have a feeling that's exactly what it's supposed to do. We can't let Cain know where we're at," Drew said.

"But what if someone sees you outside?" Jenny said, grabbing the sleeve of his shirt.

"That's a chance I'll have to take," he said. He went into the kitchen, and returned with the Glock. "Here, hang onto this until I get back."

Jenny sat Ashley down on the sofa and took the gun in one of her shaking hands. "Please be careful," she said.

"Don't worry about me, just look after you and Ashley. I'll be right back." He went back into the kitchen, his shoes crunching on the broken glass as he unlocked the back door and left, closing it behind him.

Jenny peeked through the curtains, and at first saw nothing. Then she saw Drew running toward the barn and the empty stable (it wasn't *quite* empty, though - one more horse lay rotting inside one of the stalls, half consumed by maggots). Then he, too, vanished inside the barn. Jenny bit her lip and waited.

When Drew went outside, he followed the spots left by the spider to the corner of the house. He stopped to let his eyes adjust to the blaring sunlight, mindful of any movement at all. Then he ran full-bore to the barn, stopping just inside so his eyes could adjust to the gloom.

Spikes of dusty sunlight shot through the sides of the barn, illuminating it with a golden glow. The old tractor regarded him silently. To his right were empty stalls, and to his left he saw greasy machine parts and tools scattered against one wall. His eye fell upon a pitchfork, and it occurred to him that firing the gun in the barn might draw unwanted attention. He slid the .38 into a back pocket of his jeans and picked up the pitchfork, hefting it in his hands, feeling the weight of it.

Sunlight striped across him as he slowly walked to the middle of the barn, wielding the pitchfork like a hunter might wield a rifle. He surveyed the barn, but saw no sign of the spider. He stood as still as possible in the quiet of the barn.

A sound reached his ears, a sound so small and indistinct that he couldn't even place the direction it was coming from. He heard it again, this time louder. A peculiar hissing, like a leaky air hose at a gas station.

A glob of the dark green fluid smacked the floor next to his shoe.

Drew thrust the pitchfork upward, felt it hit something solid, and he looked up to see the thing hanging above him by a silky thread, several prongs from the pitchfork buried in its face. He swung it away from him, could feel the weight of the thing as it disconnected from the forks and flew across the barn, thumping against one wall and falling to the floor.

Drew walked over to the black mass, which was laying near a wooden crate that had an oily rag draped over the top of it. Drew used the pitchfork to turn the spider over; its legs were curled in around itself, and the pitchfork had skewered three of its eyes, but the remaining five stared emptily ahead. Fluid ran from the deep stab wounds in its head.

While Drew was examining the spider, its legs twitched violently, and he brought the pitchfork down hard on its head, and he heard something brittle inside snap. There was no more movement from Ronnie Taylor's abnormal spider form.

But when he had brought the pitchfork down on the spider, he had also whacked into the box that was pushed snugly against the wall. The oily rag had fallen off, revealing faded red diamond labels on the front and top of the box that read: DANGER-EXPLOSIVES.

He thought, *Holy shit, is that what I think it is?*

He gingerly lifted the cover from the box. He knew what it was as soon as he saw it. At the bottom of the box were a dozen sticks of dynamite, and by the looks of them, they were fairly new. He picked up a stick and held it in his hand. The red paper had a waxy feel to it; it was the first time he had ever been this close to a stick of dynamite. He set it carefully back with the rest, and stood up.

Drew thought about the dynamite for a long time before replacing the cover. Ideas started to form in his mind, to gather momentum. He found a cardboard box and some electrical tape, and returned to the house. While he and Jenny cut out squares of cardboard and taped them over the broken windows (he did Swapp's bedroom alone. "You just don't want to see that," he had said), he told her what he had found in the barn, and what he was thinking of doing.

"You're crazy," she said, shaking her head.

Over the next hour and a half, Drew's cell phone rang every ten minutes. "We'll just let him sweat it out," Drew said, and Cain was, in fact, sweating it out. The church reverberated with his screams and curses, as he stormed around the church, breaking things apart with his mind. The first two pews on the right-hand side of the main isle lay canted at odd angles, split down the middle by Cain's angry rampage. There was a huge crack running up the south wall of the church, separating rock and mortar in a wide fault. But it wasn't benches or walls he wanted to destroy, it was Drew Townsend. He was going to tear his head open like a grapefruit, and he would make sure the whole town, including his sister, would get a good view.

But, buried deep in Cain's anger was something he dared not admit was even there, but it was, nonetheless, floating around at the back of his thoughts like the face of some unknown ghostly emotion trying to break out of the darkness and into the light - fear.

He had somehow failed with the spider, and now the hour drew late. Without the book to summon the beast, all that was left were mere parlor tricks. He remembered the night he was taken to Morgoroth's realm and shown what he would become, should he fail. The more powerful he grew, the more that particular memory seemed to fade away, like old newsprint. Now, it was fresh and clear again, what had once seemed so implausible had now manifested itself into something very real and horrifying, even for Cain.

You have something that does not belong to you, something you do not understand, and for that, you must answer to me.

The beast's words echoed through his thoughts, poured into his veins like ice water. And for the first time in a long time, he truly did feel fear.

His cell phone had rung so many times, that it almost didn't click in Drew's brain that *Swapp's* phone was ringing. He snatched it out of its cradle, and put it to his ear.

"Hello?" he said, as if he had no idea who the person on the other end might have been.

"Drew, it's me, Jonathon. What's wrong?"

"Boy, am I glad to hear from you," Drew said, nodding to Jenny. He relayed to Jonathon everything that had happened since they last talked, and Drew's cell phone again began ringing on the end table. "See? You hear that? He's been trying ever since he sent that monster here to kill us."

"Yeah, I hear it. Maybe he's getting desperate. But he must have some *power left without the book.* But I don't think it's much. As long as we avoid him until tonight, that is."

"Why would a guy like Swapp have dynamite, anyway? Isn't that kind of strange?" Drew asked.

"Not really," Jonathon said.*" I've seen farmers use it to clear land - to blow up tree stumps, and that kind of thing. It's pretty common in an area like this."*

"Makes sense, I guess, but I had something else in mind," Drew said, and spelled it out for Jonathon, including Jenny's thoughts on the idea.

"She's right, you are *crazy. But it's probably our only chance. Cain won't be expecting it. You realize this is one hell of a risk we'll be taking, right? We might all end up dead."*

"Hey, just like you said, in and out. He won't know what hit him."

"I hope you're right, my friend, I hope you're right."

4

Night had fallen outside of Harvey White's house, and night had also fallen over any rational thinking that he had left. He had not showered before getting dressed, had merely pulled on a pair of dirty jeans and a tee shirt. His face was covered in a thick layer of stubble, and his unwashed hair stuck out in all directions. He didn't seem to notice the aroma of urine rising off his body as he moped from room to room as if he were catatonic, just a shell of a person on automatic pilot.

In one hand he carried the steak knife he had used to cut up Jenny's blue blouse, and subsequently the rest of her clothing. In the other hand he carried a bottle of whisky, of which he had consumed half between beers. Eventually, he gave up on the beer and stuck to the hard stuff as he orbited around the house, dragging through the scattered remains of Jenny's clothes, which he had strewn everywhere as a testament to his anger. He walked into the kitchen, pulverizing the broken glass a little bit more each time he trampled over it.

He was waiting for that magic moment when the night had finally consumed the day, leaving the town dark and empty. It would be his private time alone with the world.

Can't let them see me, because they'll all think I'm crazy. They'll throw me in the loony bin for sure, because they just don't understand. But I'll make them understand....

He took a long hot drink from the whiskey bottle. It hardly burned anymore.

...You can't do that to a man. You can't just up and leave the man you love all alone, the man who has given up everything for the sake of a woman. I'll show Cain, and that fucking Sheriff. I'll drag her in a piece at a time if I have to, but I'll show them.

Harvey went into the bathroom to urinate, and saw the face in the mirror, the face of the dead man who kept watching him with those silent, bloodshot eyes. *You are dead,* a little voice in his head whispered.

Not bothering to flush the toilet, he walked into the kitchen, and slurped more of the whiskey down the numbness of his throat. He capped off the bottle, and put in a cupboard.

He would need something to celebrate with when he got home later.

5

Amanda heard the sound of a key being forced into the deadbolt on the outside door of the booking area. Somebody walked in and hit the fluorescents. They blinked on with an electric hum, and she sat up in her bunk as she heard Sheriff Craven's police issue shoes thumping down the short hall to the cells.

"Get up," he said, "the party's about the begin." He unlocked the cell door and swung it open.

"Where are we going?" Amanda asked from her bunk.

"If you don't get up right now, I'll break both of your arms and tie them into a pretzel around your fucking head. Now, GET UP!" he boomed, going into the cell. She quickly stood, but it was too late; Sheriff Craven slapped her face with a heavy hand, and she cried out as she fell to the floor.

"Now, get up and turn around. I don't have all fucking night," he said, pulling a pair of handcuffs from his belt. She stood and turned around, putting her hands behind her back. The side of her face burned like a sunburn.

"Out we go," he said.

She walked past him, smelling the after-shave bath he must have taken earlier that day. The door to the parking lot was wide open, she saw the darkness outside and hesitated, earning her a massive shove against her back from the Good Sheriff. She almost stumbled onto her face, but managed to keep her balance all the way out to the cruiser.

He opened the rear door, and she climbed in, sliding over before he could deliver another shove. He slammed the door shut, went around to the other side of the car and got in. He backed away from the building, and drove around to the front along the thin driveway at the east side of the structure.

He drove east on Broadway, and then south to Main, which from their position was the closest way to reach Old Farm Road. At the edge of town, cars parked along both sides of the street, and Craven had to honk at the various throngs of people as they walked down the middle of Old Farm Road toward the abandoned Willard place.

Amanda watched in horror as faces appeared at the window, scowling at her with both disdain and curious excitement. Some just sauntered down the road as if in a daze, smoking and drinking beer, paying no heed to the cruiser that flowed past them.

"Is my brother here in town?" Amanda asked.

Craven grunted, and said, "Won't be for long."

She fell silent again as they approached the field. A young man with a pony-tail and glasses was standing next to the barn as they pulled up in front, and he said something and winked as she sat in the back seat, waiting for Craven to get her out. Although she couldn't hear what he was saying, she was almost sure he had said her name.

Amanda.

She tried to maintain her composure, but she was perplexed by the strange man with the ponytail. Craven got out and opened her door, motioning for her to get out of the car. She slid out with some difficulty, and Craven slammed the door shut and grabbed one of her arms with his fist, leading her away.

Amanda was frightened and confused at the spectacle before her. The east end of the field was milling with what looked like every single person in town. They were laughing and drinking, and the air buzzed with chatter.

At the west end of the field was a large, open area; she saw the post that had been driven into the earth, saw the ring of torches surrounding it, and she was suddenly filled with dread. A figure in black stood inside the circle, his long black hair blowing in the mild breeze. He had streaks of gray running through his hair - he looked older than she remembered. When they entered the clearing, several people pointed at her, and a cheer rose from the crowd.

"Hello, Amanda," Cain said solemnly.

High above, the full moon glowed in all its glory, signaling the start of yet another ritual.

Harvey walked across the field next to Cain's church, ignoring the darkened building as he worked his way toward Hal Winder's farm. Winder was good and dead, which suited Harvey just fine because he never did like Winder anyway. In fact, Harvey absolutely *hated* everyone in town, including Cain. And he would kill anyone he ran into. As if to emphasize this, he made wild slashes at the air as he walked along, stumbling occasionally over loose rocks.

The Winder farmhouse loomed up in the moonlight, and he was reminded about the night before, when he had stood in front of Swapp's house. He knew it must have been wishful thinking, but the urge to actually go up to the house had been overwhelming at first. His mind told him that she could be in *any* house, but he felt as if he had passed something up out there.

And, of course, there was the dream. He could almost see her bluing face hovering in front of him, her tongue stinking out like a kid like blowing a raspberry. That had been near a cornfield. The association was undeniable.

Harvey walked up to the front door and found it unlocked. He boldly walked inside, flicking a light switch. The power was still on, and the room lit up; apparently the power company was still under the impression that Hal Winder, a long time customer with an outstanding payment history, would be sending in a payment soon.

But Winder was hanging from a pole in the middle of a cornfield, and as they say, you can't get blood from a turnip. It wouldn't be until after the second delinquent notice that the power company would send a man out to disconnect the power. But until then, the juice would continue to flow to this residence, and Harvey White was going to take full advantage of this overlooked bit of information.

He went from room to room, sure he was going to discover Jenny and Ashley hiding in one of the rooms, huddled together in a corner like scared rabbits. But all he discovered was that others had been there, as well. A lot of the furniture was gone, and there were impressions on the living room floor that revealed where furniture had once sat. In one bedroom, the blankets had been torn from a bed, leaving only a stained mattress. On the floor next to it was a used condom left by a couple of horny teenagers from town.

Empty beer cans decorated the floors, along with squashed cigarette butts. In one back bedroom, someone had burned a large hole in the blue carpet in the center of the room. It reeked of urine. The general destruction of the house meant nothing to him, raised no flags in his conscious. He simply finished his tour, urinated on the blue carpet, and turned off all the lights.

He stepped outside and closed the door behind him. He heard the distant cheer of the crowd in the ritual field. He started walking south toward the woods, with his next destination already mapped out.

Angus Swapp's farm.

6

Jenny watched nervously as Drew bundled four sticks of dynamite together with the rest of the electrical tape. Ashley was in the living room watching TV.

"Are you sure that stuff's safe?" she asked, looking at the bundle in Drew's hands.

"I'd feel a hell of a lot safer if somebody else was doing this," he said, opening the back door and carrying the dynamite outside. He put the bundle in a duffel bag and set the makeshift bomb on the ground next to the house, and went back inside. "We'll just leave it there for now."

Both of their guns were now on the kitchen table. He picked up the Glock and handed it to her. "I want you to keep this with you until I get back. Don't put it down for anything. If someone comes in the house, shoot to kill." He put the .38 into his back pocket.

She set down the gun and wrapped her arms around his neck. "I'm afraid you won't come back," she said. "The thing is, I...I *need* you to come back."

"I'm going to take you away from all this, I promise," he said. He kissed her, then went to the kitchen door and turned around. "Just be ready to go at a moment's notice." He winked and she half-heartedly smiled, and then he was gone.

She locked the door, picked up the gun, and went into the living room. She was too wired to sit down, just stood there biting her lip.

Come back, Drew. Please, God, Bring him back.

Drew ran across River Road, carrying the old duffel bag he had found in a closet at Swapp's house. Inside were the four sticks of tightly wrapped dynamite. He felt strangely out of sorts, as if he were another person altogether. But on the other hand, he *was* another person. He had fallen into a new life, and a new love, by coming to this town, and he was now on his way to have a showdown with a very dangerous man.

He climbed a barbed wire fence and vanished into another farmer's cornfield.

Out on the old Willard property, in a dry, trampled field littered with dead cornhusks and empty beer cans, the residents of Oak Junction waited impatiently for the ritual to begin. The dark side of human nature had bloomed from a mere seed into a full-blown disease, twisting and tumbling through their veins, always thirsty for more. They wanted to see something that used to cause them to turn away in revulsion, but now held them transfixed, unable to look away.

This was tainted ground they stood upon, these souls that were now beyond redemption, and it was as if they had traveled back to a time and place where it would have been commonplace to condemn someone to a public stoning, or burn them at the stake.

But, these lost souls were unfamiliar with such rituals of the past, only the ritual of the here and now, the one for which they had unknowingly forsaken their former lives, their former *selves*.

Your souls are no longer your own....

And the man responsible for purging them of their former lives now stood before them in the firelight at the head of the field, a man who had gained a terrible power, and yet was losing the strength to use that power a little bit at a time. Yes, he was the bearer of the book, but because of his ignorance he was also the bearer of this burden that he knew not how to invalidate. He was slowly paying the price for his greed, and now he was going to pay an even bigger price, for without the book, his power paled, weakened.

But the blackness in his heart would not let him give in to the fear; he kept it at bay, even now as a silvery moon glowed in the night sky and hundreds of people waited nearby with their anxious eyes always returning to the figure in black.

For the time being, the figure in black paid no attention to the onlookers. He seemed to be looking off past them into the woods beyond, as if sensing something they did not. He went over to the sheriff and said quietly, "Keep your eyes and ears open, he could be anywhere." And then, "What time is it?"

"Eleven-forty-five," Craven said. He had no idea of the significance or urgency of that question.

Craven stood behind the post to which he had handcuffed Amanda, trying not to look too conspicuous as he spied for any sign of the young man he had run out of town two days before. Of course, there was also the matter of the woman, Harvey White's wife, who had disappeared with her daughter on the night of the last ritual. But, that was the drunk's problem. Moreover, Cain had made it clear that if the problem weren't taken care of, things would get nasty for Harvey White.

Amanda was all too aware that she was the center of attention, and she tried to avoid eye contact with those who weren't talking or drinking, but simply watching her with great interest.

"You had better hope that you're brother is still around, my dear, and ready to do business," Cain said, stroking her cheek with the backs of his fingers. She turned her head to the side in evasion of his touch, and he grabbed the sides of her face with both hands, forcing her to face him. "You cannot even imagine what is about to happen to you," he snarled.

Cain turned to the crowd and waved his arms in the air. "People! My friends! Quiet yourselves!" They grew silent, all eyes trained on him. "I have a little matter I must attend to before we can begin. And I must have silence. I will kill the first one who speaks." He glared at the crowd and saw no takers. He crossed his arms over his chest and paced around in the ring of torches, his black overcoat spreading out behind him, the flickering of the flames playing on his features.

"Drew Townsend, I am waiting!" he called out in no particular direction. "You will bring my book to me now, or Amanda will suffer dearly!" He stopped, and turned his head from side to side, seeing nothing but the muted crowd, and the dark woods beyond. "Drew, you are running out of time! Return it to me now!"

The town's folk watched and listened, oblivious that Cain was actually the one running out of time, and that without the book, there would be no ritual. But, there *would* be something very interesting to see, and very soon.

"Ok, Mr. Townsend, you leave me no choice but -"

A voice called out suddenly, cutting Cain off mid-sentence. A voice strong and clear, rising somewhere from the woods to the north. Heads craned to see who was doing the speaking, but the figure was well hidden for the moment. Cain looked in the direction of the voice, frowning deeply. Amanda instantly recognized the voice; it was the voice of the person who had always been there for her when they were kids, the person who had always stuck up for her, looked out for her. Her eyes opened wide as she strained against her bonds.

"Cain! Leave her alone! I have your book!" the voice called from its hiding place.

7

It didn't take Harvey long to reach Swapp's property, as his pace had quickened with his determination. In the woods, the darkness seemed to have corrupted his vision, and he bumped into several trees, which only added fuel to the fire. In the corn, it was much easier, especially with the full moon casting its dim light over everything.

He soon saw the blurry lights of the house ahead, its shape, which looked out of focus until he came closer. There were lights on inside, but all the curtains were pulled - except on one window, a smaller one to the right, the lower half of which was blotted out altogether.

This window he approached first, and he saw that cardboard had been fastened over a hole in the window.

Had that been there before? He couldn't quite recall.

He moved up closer, heard the crunch of glass under his feet and saw the jagged edges of glass protruding from the frame. He lightly touched the cardboard with one hand. The light in this room was dim, emanating perhaps from a crack under a door. Putting one ear close to the window, he listened...and heard soft voices.

Harvey crept up onto the porch, stopping as a board moaned under his weight, then, stepping over the spot, went to a large picture window that glowed in a soft green light. He tried to find a crack in the curtains, even the tiniest little hole, but there was nothing. A wave of dizziness swept over him, and he had to lean against the house until it abated.

He slowly pulled open the screen door, the hinges releasing a small but nonetheless alarming squeal. He squeezed his hand into the crack and gave the doorknob a quiet jiggle. A voice from inside the house froze him on the spot. It echoed in his head with a familiarity and understanding that started his blood pumping.

"Mommy!" a tiny, muffled voice exclaimed. Then: "Shhhh!"

Harvey's mouth widened with a sinister grin as he descended the porch, going past the broken bedroom window to the side of the house. He accidentally poked the palm of his hand as he tried to retrieve the knife from his pants pocket, could even feel the warm flow of blood, but he ignored it, suddenly overcome with anticipation.

Jenny!

Ashley!

He went into a frenzy, slashing the knife at the air, grunting with excursion as he sliced it back and forth in front of him. When this little spell subsided, he peeked around to behind the house. More windows, also covered with drapes. He kept close to the house as he made his way to the back door. There was a small kitchen window above him, and he could imagine Jenny peering out into the night, unaware that right below her the bogeyman was stalking her.

Harvey's bloody hand felt sticky on the wooden knife handle. He hesitated as he saw yet another broken window, this one on the back door. There was no screen door here, only a door with a large pane of glass on top, now broken out and covered with cardboard. He tried the doorknob, heard a little gasp from inside. They knew he was there.

It was time to go in and take care of business once and for all.

"Let her go, Cain, and you can have your book!" Drew called from the trees.

"Return my property to me," Cain replied.

"Not until you let her go." Silence.

Everyone watched this little drama unfolding, afraid to make a sound lest it should provoke Cain's anger. Cain turned to Sheriff Craven and said, "Bring her to me." The Sheriff undid the handcuffs and led Amanda over to Cain. The flames flickered and sparked all around them as they stood in the middle of the circle. "We can't disappoint these folks, Mr. Townsend. They might become unruly. They came here to see a sacrifice, and that is what they shall see!" he yelled out to the crowd. They roared in approval, and Cain raised his arms, abruptly silencing them.

"We shall need a replacement, Sheriff." Cain's gaze swept from person to person, their eyes filled with terror. "You. You will do fine," he said, pointing at the red head standing at the front.

Betty Atwood realized with horror that he was pointing at her. Her mouth fell open. She shook her head in denial.

"No. No, Mr. Cain. Please not me. Just take that worthless bitch," she said, pointing to Amanda, who took an involuntary step backwards. Cain grabbed her arm, jerked her closer to him, and looking directly into Betty's eyes said, "The problem is, her I need. *You* are suddenly the *worthless* one. Sheriff?"

Sheriff Craven strode around the perimeter of the circle; his face fixed on Betty, a woman with whom he had shared his bed with countless times, a woman who had in the blink of an eye become utterly worthless to the Good Sheriff.

"No, Frank! Tell him! Not me, please!" she cried, backing away from him. Hands latched onto her from behind, and she saw all the malevolent glares of those who were holding her. She struggled to break loose, but she was caught in a spider's web of groping hands.

Craven's face was cold, expressionless, as he walked up to her and grabbed one of her arms. "NOOOO!" she screamed, and fell to her knees. Craven grabbed a big handful of her hair and began to drag her toward the circle of torches. So relentless was his strength that she had to scramble to avoid being dragged all the way by just her hair. She began sobbing hysterically as the sheriff lifted her up and shoved her against the post. He handcuffed her hands behind her, and then stood in front of her.

"Shut up, bitch," he said calmly. He backhanded her across the face, which left her reeling against the post.

"Hang on to her, Sheriff," Cain said, handing Amanda over to him. Craven took her out of the ring, holding her arms behind her. "I must ask for quiet," he said, and again silence consumed them. Betty Atwood looked as if she was trying to focus on something, anything at all, failing miserably.

"All right, Drew, here is your little Amanda. Now bring me my fucking book!"

A figure emerged from the trees, and slowly the man came into view. He was wearing a jacket and carrying a tan duffel bag. As he came closer, Cain saw the stern look on his face, his determined strides, and suddenly coming face to face with the person who had caused him so much trouble stoked the terrible anger that Cain lived with every day.

Drew stopped about ten feet away from the flames surrounding Cain.

"Drew!" Amanda cried, trying to escape Craven's iron grip.

"Is this what you plan on doing, killing everyone in town? What's going to happen when you run out of people, huh? What then, Cain?" Drew stood with his hands at his sides, one hand holding the bag containing the dynamite. He had no intention of using it at that moment; he only wanted to buy time, lead him along, to make Cain think his book was inside the bag.

"There is no need for me to kill everyone in town, Drew. Not when I have troublemaking fools like you around."

"Maybe so, Cain, but sooner or later you'll be taking them one by one for your ritual, and you'll have no one to control, will you, Cain? Or should I say *Lucas*?" Faces turned to look questioningly at Cain, who was caught off guard by the mention of his name.

"ENOUGH!" Cain said, his eyes growing wide and feral.

Drew suddenly jerked and, dropping the bag at his feet, clutched his head with both hands. He screamed and fell to his knees.

"Drew!" Amanda sobbed, still trying to break free from Sheriff Craven.

"Now, you are going to pay dearly, Mr. Townsend," Cain said.

8

Once again Ashley was sitting quietly on the sofa in her tiny jacket, waiting for the time to come when they would be leaving, as on the night when they had fled their own home. She sensed the urgency in the air, sensed it in her mother, who was pacing nervously around this stranger's house (Angus Swapp still sat tied in his chair in the bedroom with the door closed to spare anyone going to the bathroom across the hall from having to see him) with a gun in one hand.

She heard a creak from the other side of the front door, sat up straight and alert, eyes pinned on the door. She heard the jiggling and saw the slight motion of the doorknob.

"Mommy!" she said, pointing at the door as Jenny came in from the hallway. Jenny went up to her daughter and gently put her hand over her mouth. "Shhhh!" She bent over and whispered in her ear, "Go in the bathroom and lock the door! Don't turn on the light. Just wait for mommy there, ok? Don't be afraid, honey. Hurry!"

Ashley ran down the hall and into the bathroom, gazing curiously at the bedroom door, behind which the weird man had grown strangely quiet. She put the lid down on the toilet, closed and locked the door, and was encased in darkness. She sat on the toilet, and waited.

Jenny listened at the door, but heard nothing. She went to the kitchen doorway and stood there, listening to her own heartbeat. Something caught her attention, and it was then that she saw the doorknob on the back door twist slowly back and forth. She let out an involuntary gasp as her breath caught in her throat. One word, plain and clear and dreadful, popped into her mind: *Harvey!*

It can't be, it just can't be! she told herself. *Oh God, don't let it be him, please, don't let it be him!*

She shook uncontrollably as she turned around, first looking down the hall, then into the living room, then back to the kitchen. The gun quivered in her hand. She ventured into the kitchen, and stopped just short of the back door with its cardboard patch over the window, unsure of what to do next.

Ashley! Go check on Ashley!

That last got her going; she whirled and made for the doorway, but as she rounded the corner, she stopped dead in her tracks. She was paralyzed, unable to move or speak at the sight of the figure standing in the hallway next to Angus Swapp's open bedroom door.

"Hello, Jenny. Long time, no see," Harvey said.

The pain in Drew's head was excruciating, as if a metal clamp was squeezing his skull to the point when at any moment it would burst like a melon. He was no longer aware of his surroundings; sight became a smear of color, sound a nonsensical buzz in his ears. And somewhere amidst all this he kept thinking: *Please, let it end, just let me die!*

But then it *did* end. He didn't hear the person across the field near the barn calling to Cain, distracting him so he might stop this agonizing pain, he just knew that it suddenly stopped, not slowly or gradually, but immediately like it had never been there.

He fell to the ground, and then got to his knees, shaking his head to clear his vision. He felt something warm on his lips, tasted the blood that was running from his nose.

"Cain, stop! He didn't take your book, *I* did!"

Cain spun around at the sound of the voice. Amanda recognized the man by the barn, the one who was now talking to Cain. It was the man who had winked at her and mouthed her name as she sat in the back seat of Sheriff Craven's cruiser.

"It's true. I have your book right here," the man said, holding up a large book for all to see.

"Is this some kind of game, Jonathon?" Cain said.

"No game, Cain. I took your book," the man said from the other side of the field. Amanda wasn't sure what to think of this individual, only that he was somehow connected to Drew, and that they were indeed playing a very dangerous game with this sadistic man.

The people of the town gawked at the man, unable to believe that he had had the nerve to steal something from Cain, to risk being the next to participate in the ritual. And like Amanda, they did not know what was happening here, only that they would do whatever it took to protect Cain.

"What did you hope to accomplish," Cain asked, shrugging.

"Oh, I don't know. I just thought maybe I could learn a few things from it."

Cain opened his mouth to say something, closed it again as his mind reminded him of something he had forgotten about.

The time.

Beware all ye untrue bearers of the book, for in the Dark One's name shall ye honor the full moon, lest ye become an abomination unto the earth, never to see the light of day again. Hark Bearer! For if the light of Him should bear upon thou skin, ye will become as ashes in the wind, scattered to the ends of the earth.

Cain remembered this all too well, had lived by its rule, and the warning from the beast known as Morgoroth:

"But you are not the true bearer of the book, Cain."

"I thought it was mine. All I wanted was power, but not this."

"And power you shall have. But did you think there would be no price for this power? You have something that does not belong to you, something you don't understand, and for that, you must answer to me. You will bring me a living soul with each full moon, for it is here that I feed on the souls of the living for sustenance."

Cain looked around, and realized he wasn't alone. As far as the eye could see, across the sands of this vast desert, were living corpses on the sand, their blood oozing slowly out of the different wounds of their bodies, soaking in small puddles in the sand.

"But look at me! I can't go back like this!" Cain yelled up to the beast.

"And you won't. You are too valuable to me to leave you like this. But heed my warning: Disappoint me, and you will become as you are now."

He remembered how his gaze had fallen on his horrifying new skin, how appalled he had been, and how frightened he was as he laid in the sand of that ungodly place, the beast towering over him.

"Bring me that book!" he screamed. "Quickly!"

Amanda watched as a man from the crowd ran over to the person holding the book, saw the person hand the book over, and then the other was running at breakneck speed toward Cain, who snatched the book from the man and shoved him aside. The man left the circle of flickering light, and walked panting back to those who were watching.

The wicked smile Cain had as he grabbed the book quickly faded once he had it in his hands. He hefted the book several times, held it close to his face. He ran his fingers over the surface, which should have been rough, but was now smooth. This book was shiny, and smelled of spray paint. The gold death's head looked as if it had been stenciled on. A look almost like panic spread over his features as he opened the book and saw an eight by ten portrait of Earl Mott staring him in the face.

A fucking photo album!

Cain hurled the photo album to the ground (when it hit the ground it popped open to a page boasting old family photos, with a very small Jonathon Mott), pointed to the man on the other side of the field, and said, "Get h -"

He could not finish the sentence. In a field in the middle of Iowa, filled with the lost and hateful souls of this small town now standing under a bright August moon, the clock struck midnight. The first lightning bolts of pain shot through Cain's body.

"NoooOOOH!" he screamed into the nighttime, his voice already changing, becoming the guttural growl of something else altogether. He hitched violently, and began tearing at his clothes as if they were crawling with fire ants.

Just getting to his feet, Drew's vision was finally clearing up, and the first thing he saw was Cain rolling around at the feet of Betty Atwood, trying to get his boots and pants off, a strange half-naked figure moaning and snarling within the ritual torches.

Amanda felt Sheriff Craven's grip on her arms loosen as he watched the transformation taking place before them. She looked over at Drew, saw that he had picked up the duffle and was now groping behind his back for something.

With all eyes on Cain, including the man who was now just barely keeping his grip on her, she saw the window of opportunity open, and without hesitation took it. She brought her right leg up behind her as hard as she could muster, felt her foot connect with Craven's crotch. This produced a throaty grunt from the Good Sheriff as he released his grip on her arms, and she fled from his grasp. He made one feeble attempt to grab her, and fell to the ground, both hands at his wounded package.

Amanda threw her arms around Drew and said, "Thank God, you're all right. Can we get out of here now?"

A few of the onlookers were coming toward them, their faces masks of hatred and vengeance at what was happening to their leader. Drew finally got the .38 out of the waistband in the back of his jeans, pointed it at the advancing party.

"Don't even fucking think about it!" he said. They stopped in their tracks.

"Look what you did to him!" one man said to Drew, but Drew was already leading Amanda away from the field. They passed by the sheriff, who seemed to be gathering himself together, and Drew said, "Get his gun, sis."

Amanda said, "Gladly," and unsnapped the holster strap and removed his huge service revolver.

They both took one last look at Cain. He was lying motionless, naked and face down in the dirt. People started gathering around Cain's limp form, and Betty started bellowing for someone to get her off of that goddamned pole.

Suddenly, the doors to the old Willard barn burst open, a truck flying out amidst the pieces of barn door exploding out in every direction.

"What the hell is *that*?" Amanda asked.

"That would be our ride," Drew said, as they hurried toward the access road at the top of the ritual field.

9

"What's the matter, cat got your tongue?" Harvey asked.

She couldn't speak, not just yet. She had wondered if it had been Harvey outside the house, even *expected* it, but the Harvey she had expected was a different man, an arrogant, selfish man. This man standing in the hallway was one in the throes of advanced mental and physical decay.

He stank of sweat and urine, more strongly of the latter. Fresh blood was soaking into his shirt at the shoulder, blood from a deep gash he had received from one of the shards of glass lining Swapp's bedroom window as he crawled across the sill. In one hand he held a large steak knife, its wooden handle smeared with the blood from his wounded hand. His oily hair stuck out in curly licks, and his face was an overgrown garden of stubble. But what frightened her the most were his eyes.

His eyes were...*disturbed*.

"What happened to *him*?" Harvey asked, tipping his head at the body in the bedroom.

"Harvey, I..."

"Oh well, no matter. He's good and dead now, right?"

The bathroom door. He was standing next to the bathroom door, just a few feet away from Ashley. *Don't look at the door!* she thought.

"Why did you run away from me, Jenny? I'm your husband, you know, and a wife should honor her husband. It really hurt me...right here." He put his hand over his heart and produced a little pout.

And then took a step forward.

Jenny took a step back, almost into the kitchen. "I-I was scared, Harvey. I didn't know w-what to think anymore. Everyone in town is... I just wanted to get away for a while."

"Everyone in town is fine, Jenny. I mean, really. You had me worried sick. And I was worried about you, too. And Ashley. I just didn't know if you were ok."

Another step forward.

She stepped back, and was now standing on the faded kitchen linoleum.

Stay quiet, Ashley. Dear God, don't say a word, honey.

Harvey looked like he was on the verge of tears, and this caused a slight pang in Jenny's heart, a sliver of sorrow for this man. After all, she *had* loved this man, bore his child. And although she no longer cared for him, did she really want to hurt him?

"I just wanted to make things right for you and Ashley." Another step forward. He was just outside the kitchen doorway. "Don't you believe me?"

She stepped back again, and tried to muster up the strength to stand up to this man, and make him go away.

"I believe you, yes. But things are different, now. I think you need to get on with your life, Harvey, and forget about Ashley and me. I want you to leave, Harvey."

But now he was standing in the kitchen, spotting the linoleum with the blood from his shoulder.

Jenny thought she would gag if she had to smell him for much longer.

"You want me to...go away?" he asked, blinking.

"Yes, Harvey. I want you to go away. I'm not a part of your life anymore, can't you see?"

His arms went limp. He hung his head down so she could no longer see his face. Jenny's fear of this man was gone now, and only compassion remained; she could see he was in pain, suffering and degraded, and she knew in her heart what his final end would be, but she did not want to be around to witness it.

"Please, Harvey, just go away. For your own good, go away."

He stirred, slowly raised his head.

And she saw his was not a face of pain or suffering.

His was a face of hatred and insanity. A face of evil.

Of death.

His lips curled back from yellowing teeth, eyes burning with an internal sickness.

"I'm going to cut you up into a million fucking pieces and eat your heart raw, you fucking tramp!"

Her compassion, her sorrow - both were gone now. She saw that face, the face of the man who had murdered Paul Mayfield, the man who had so coldly hit her to the ground like a stray dog, the man whose final destination she knew would be right here in this kitchen.

Just before he came at her, she remembered something she and Drew had talked about: *"I said, 'Fuck you, Rose!', and I felt better than I had in a long time." Drew was actually smiling now.*

"*You said it out loud?*" Jenny asked, smiling at the very thought of it.

"*Yep. Out loud. I'll tell you what, it's great therapy. You should try it.*"

Harvey raised the knife high in the air, and walked toward her. Jenny pointed the Glock at him.

"You can't shoot me, Jenny, you don't have the guts," he said.

It's great therapy, you should try it.

"Fuck you, Harvey!" Jenny said, and pulled the trigger.

10

No one seemed to notice, or didn't care, that Jonathon kept glancing down at his wristwatch. Everyone was looking at the book he was holding up in the air (an old family album he had spray painted black before cutting out his own stencil to make the jawless skull on the front), including Cain, who was too far away to see. It was all too simple; he could have been holding just about anything, and Cain's followers wouldn't have known the difference.

He tried to stall as long as he could, but when he saw what was happening to Drew, he could wait no longer. The man who ran up and grabbed the book from him said, "You're gonna die," then ran off holding the photo album in both hands.

Another glance at his watch. Close.

He saw Cain look at the book, and then hurl it to the ground. Saw him point at him, and begin to say something, then stop.

Midnight.

He heard Cain scream and start performing some bizarre dance, tearing his clothes off. Everyone was watching Cain now, the time was almost right. As soon as he saw Amanda Townsend plant her foot into Sheriff Craven's balls, he turned and ran for the barn. He looked over his shoulder, and saw two men chasing after him, but he had gotten the jump on them. He reached the barn long before them, and slipped inside.

His father's Ranger was parked inside, had been since earlier that day; it was too dark to see, but all he had to do was go forward until he bumped into it, then work his way around to the driver's side and open the door. The dome light illuminated the cab, and he jumped inside, turning the keys that were already in the ignition. The engine came to life, and Jonathon stuck it in drive, flooring the gas.

The two men that had been chasing him reached the barn doors just in time to be plowed into by the Ranger. Pieces of the old barn doors exploded outward, hitting one of the men in the face and breaking his nose before he disappeared under the truck. Jonathon felt the truck bounce as the man's body rolled underneath.

The other man was knocked into the air, and landed on the windshield of Craven's cruiser face first.

Jonathon had both hands glued to the wheel, staring straight ahead. He paid no mind to the men he had just run over; there just wasn't time to consider what he had done. He turned onto the access road, and went north.

Up ahead he saw Amanda helping Drew to the road. She had a huge revolver in her hand. He skidded to a stop beside them, reached over and opened the passenger door.

"Get in," he said calmly. Amanda helped Drew into the truck, and climbed in beside him. "Hang on," Jonathon said, and spun the truck around, spitting gravel everywhere.

They went south, past Sheriff Craven who was staggering across the field now, yelling something, and waving his arms. He would eventually reach his car and discover a surprise on his windshield.

People were trying to crowd the road, but Jonathon only went faster, and they scattered as the Ranger roared past. Jonathon saw Cain's naked form lying motionless in the ring of torches, surrounded by his followers.

"Let's get the hell out of Dodge," Drew said.

Most were too afraid to enter the circle, except for Sheriff Craven and the man who had delivered the phony book to Cain. Craven stood next to Cain's body, ignoring Betty's pleas to be released. The other man knelt down and put the flat of his hand on Cain's back.

"Mr. Cain, are you ok?" the man asked. He gave Cain a little shake. "Mr. Cain, can you hear me?"

There was a little movement in the body. The man looked up at Craven and said, "I think he's still alive." Then he screamed as a thin, bony spur shot out of Cain's back and into the palm of his hand, protruding out the back of it about six inches.

He grabbed his wrist with his other hand, and tried to pull his hand off, but the small, jagged nodules on the sides prevented it from moving upward more than half an inch.

"Sheriff, help me!" he cried, watching the thick blood ooze from the hole in his hand onto Cain's back.

The body stirred, and another spur poked out farther down the spine.

Craven bent over and used both of his big hands to grab the man's fingers and wrist. "Here it comes," Craven said, and ripped the hand off the spur. The fishhook nodules tore the hole open to twice its previous size, and the man screamed bloody murder at the raw pain in his hand.

Another spur shot through the skin, which suddenly began to split open along the center of Cain's back. Holding his ruined hand, the man walked out of the torchlight, where he promptly fell down and passed out from shock.

Craven instinctively backed out of the circle, out of harm's way. The crowd of onlookers drew closer, their faces solemn in the flickering torchlight.

"Frank, please let me go," Betty pleaded, but Craven paid her no mind.

Cain's skin seemed to bubble just beneath the surface, changing shape and color. Betty listened in horror as the bones in Cain's limbs broke and snapped into pieces like twigs, his arms and legs stretching out long and thin. Fingers and toes stretched into spindly extensions tipped with deadly black claws.

His body elongated, and she could hear the bones in his spine *popping* apart; he now had a full set of the jagged spurs running down his back. She could actually hear the bones clicking together as they mended themselves, forming a whole new body.

Cain raised himself up on his crude elbows, screamed like an animal as all of his raven black hair fell off into a pile below him as if the barber

had just given him a haircut, and his baldhead turned a mottled gray like the rest of him. Two spurs like horns popped up above his forehead.

Cain was up on his feet before Betty could blink an eye. Her mouth started to tremble as she looked at the thing standing before her.

Cain was now very tall and spindly, his elbows and knees thick bony knobs under the gray skin. He had the face of a devil, his overly large mouth upturned in a sick grin filled with needle-sharp teeth, over a long pointed chin. His nose was a shriveled nub. And his eyes…oh, she couldn't bear the sight of those eyes. They were an intense yellow with a black slit down the middle like that of a cat. His ears were now pointed as well, sticking up to the top of his head before reaching slightly outward.

He spread his teeth apart and hissed, a long black tongue wagging out at her before recoiling back inside his mouth.

Cain looked over at Craven, who stared breathlessly at what Cain had become. The look had intelligence, recognition, and

Craven knew then that Cain was not dead. He was just wearing a different skin.

Cain looked back at Betty.

"M-Mr. C-Cain?"

With one quick motion of his talons, he slashed her face open to the bone in four parallel cuts, taking out one eye and splitting her nose in half. She screamed, the skin on her face split apart, blood pouring from the exposed flesh.

Cain shrieked at the full moon, then turned his attention to the town's folk. Many backed wordlessly away from the circle, while others turned tail and ran. Cain *bounded* over the torches, slashing out as he landed among the fleeing bodies. He jumped to and fro, stripping flesh from all he touched. Screams filled the night air, screams of fear and pain as people fell maimed and bleeding in their tracks.

And still Cain pushed on, leaping maniacally from person to person.

Somewhere among all the mayhem stood Jaspar Hendricks, Oak Junction's oldest resident. He had witnessed too many bad things over his long life, but nothing so macabre as this field of slaughter.

Cain landed directly in front of Jaspar, one bloody claw pulled back, ready to strike. Jaspar looked calmly into the face of evil; he had not lived so long by running. And at his age, fear no longer mattered - if he was going to die, he would die, one way or the other.

But his charmed life prevailed, and Cain turned and bounded away, this time toward Old Farm Road.

Sheriff Craven watched the lithe creature swallowed by darkness as it went down the lane in great strides, leaving the ghastly scene behind. Most of those who had stayed put survived. The rest were dead or dying, or running pell-mell across the field.

When Craven reached his cruiser, he found a man's body pressed into the shattered windshield. Another lay at the entrance to the barn, surrounded by bits of wood from the doors. He pulled the corpse off the windshield, letting it flop to the dirt next to the car. He got inside and began kicking out the windshield in great, heavy stomps of his shoes. It broke from its seal and went sliding across the hood and off the side of the car.

He started the big engine, and headed down Old Farm Road, forced to drive slow as the wind was forcing tears from his eyes, making it difficult to stay on a straight course. But as frustrating as it was, he kept moving.

11

Harvey was still coming toward her when the Glock discharged, sending the bullet into his forehead and out the back of his skull, taking a large chunk of brain and bone and hair with it. Incredibly enough, he was still standing. The force of the impact had knocked his head back, but he managed to lift it forward again, allowing a river of blood to pour from the bullet hole down between his eyes to his chin, where it dripped onto the floor.

His mouth dropped open, and she thought he was going to say something, but all he could produce was a gurgle from his throat. He fell where he stood, staring at the cabinets where the satchel of money was hidden. A pool of blood grew around his head.

She opened the cabinet door closest to her, withdrew the satchel, and put the gun inside. Harvey's body was blocking her way, and she had to step over him to escape the kitchen. She imagined one bloody hand reaching up and grabbing her ankle, pulling her down into his clutches. Although she knew it impossible, she nonetheless shuddered as she passed over his body and made for the bathroom door.

She set the satchel on the carpet and tapped on the bathroom door and said, "Open the door, honey, it's mommy." She saw the light go on from under the door, and Ashley fumbling with the doorknob. She opened the door and Jenny scooped the little girl up in her arms. Ashley threw her tiny arms around Jenny's neck. "Are we going now, mommy?"

"Yes, honey, in a minute. But first I need you to close your eyes real tight for me." The last thing she wanted Ashley to see was her father lying dead on the kitchen floor. A sight like that, in the condition he had been in, could traumatize her for a long time. Jenny carried her into the living room.

"Mommy, why do I have to close my eyes?"

"Never mind, dear, just keep them closed for me. Promise me."

"I promise."

A vehicle was pulling up in front of the house. A second later, she heard the front screen door open, and Drew came through the front door. "No time to waste. Let's go," he said, then noticed the corpse just inside the kitchen doorway.

"Don't ask. Not now," she said, and he nodded.

She followed him outside, Ashley cradled in one arm, carrying the satchel with the other hand.

"Thank God, you're ok," she said.

"Hurry, get in. We'll have lots of time later."

She saw the blood drying on his face, and exclaimed, "You're hurt!"

"I'm all right, really. Right now, we just need to get out of here, and fast."

They went around to the other side of the truck, where Jonathon was holding the door open for them. She climbed in next to Amanda.

They smiled at each other, and then Jonathon was talking.

"There's no room in the cab. I'll ride in back, you drive," He said to Drew, grabbing the duffel bag from the floor of the truck.

"You're crazy man. C'mon, we'll squeeze in somehow."

"It won't work, Drew," Jonathon said. "It's too dangerous with all of us packed in there like that. I'll be fine. Just get us out of here!"

Drew looked at him solemnly for a moment, then retrieved his .38 from the cab and handed it to Jonathon. "Watch yourself," he said, and got into the truck. Jonathon climbed into the back and settled down against the cab.

A shriek tore into the night, like the sound of a madman losing what little sanity was left in his sickened head.

"What the hell was that?" Jenny asked, clutching Ashley tighter to her breast.

"That would be Cain. And by the sound of it, he's really pissed off."

Drew put the truck in drive, and gunned the engine. The truck spun around in the dirt, spewing dust and rocks at Angus Swapp's house, and flew toward River Road. Jenny looked over her shoulder through the cab's rear window and saw Jonathon trying to keep with the motion of the truck, almost losing his balance several times.

River Road intersected with 1st Avenue south, just past the point where it left town on its way past Zeb's to the highway. And it was before that intersection that the devil would catch up with them.

They barreled down River Road, which was dirt and gravel from end to end, headlights pooling on the road in front of them. No one spoke, just waited. Waited to see if they were really going to get out of this town alive, or if their efforts would turn out to be futile. Their very lives seemed to be hanging by a thread, and their silence only reinforced that notion.

Drew saw movement from above, a flick of a shadow perhaps, and then Cain landed heavily on the hood of the Ranger. Amanda and Jenny started screaming at the same time, Jenny holding Ashley's face against her as Cain's face appeared in the windshield. Drew jumped back and almost lost hold of the wheel. The truck rocked slightly to one side, but he quickly regained control.

The long, black tongue came whipping out of Cain's mouth, and suddenly he was up above them on top of the cab. They heard him scrambling across the metal roof, and Jenny turned in time to see Cain land in the truck's bed near the tailgate.

He turned and faced Jonathon with his flaming yellow eyes.

"Jonathon!" Jenny called, but she didn't think he would hear her anyway. Amanda had turned and saw the horror advancing on Jonathon. Drew only had time to glance in the rearview, but it was long enough. He had to keep moving.

Still sitting against the back of the cab, Jonathon raised the .38 and fired into Cain's midsection. Cain let loose an ear piercing screech and disappeared over the tailgate.

"He got him, he got him!" Jenny said.

"You think that killed him?" Amanda asked.

"I don't know," Drew said, "but I wouldn't count on it."

1st Avenue South loomed ahead. Drew slowed down to take the turn, still had to grasp the wheel as tightly as he could while the truck slid sideways before jetting forward again.

Two spotlights mounted on the front of the building lighted Zeb's station, and they were now turned on, illuminating a wide area around the pumps. Moths circulated around the hot lights. The inside of the station was dark as they pulled up next to the pumps and skidded to a stop.

Jonathon jumped from the back of the Ranger and ran to Drew's door. The window was down, and Jonathon wasted no time with what he was about to say.

"Get out of here, now. I'll take care of the rest."

Drew was stunned. "What are you talking about? We agreed we would blow this place and get the hell out! *All* of us!"

"It won't work, Drew. He'll just keep coming until he catches us. One of us has to stay behind to make sure the job gets done, and that's me."

"You can't mean it, Jonathon."

"Look, you were never meant to be a part of this," Jonathon said. "I need to do this."

"What are you talking about?"

Another shriek sounded nearby.

"Go!" Jonathon shouted. "He's coming! Get the fuck out of here!"

Drew reached out the window and put a hand on Jonathon's shoulder. "Thanks, man. I'll never forget you." He put the truck in drive and they sped away. Jonathon looked up at the moon, and then ran over to the gas pumps. He unzipped the duffel bag, pulled out the bundled dynamite, and laid it next to one of the pumps. He put his hands behind his back and waited for Cain.

The road to town wound off into the dark. The full moon coasted silently across the clear summer sky.

There was movement ahead, a shape coming into view, loping along in big strides. Closer he came, until Jonathon could see his malevolent features focused right on him.

Easy Jonathon, he thought, *let him get closer.*

As Cain took his last leap at him, Jonathon could see dark fluid oozing from the bullet wound in his chest. He saw Cain's lips pulled back, revealing his deadly set of pointed teeth, saw his eyes opened wide with murder.

Cain was almost on him when Jonathon pulled the .38 from behind his back, fired at the dynamite, and kept firing to be sure he hit the mark. The second shot did the trick; Cain had nearly reached Jonathon when Zeb's station was swallowed by fire.

And then Jonathon and Lucas Cain were swept away.

12

They felt the concussion beneath their feet, heard the blast. The girls had turned around to watch through the cab's rear window. Drew glimpsed in the rearview the bright yellow-orange bloom over the station.

Good luck, Jonathon, he thought.

Two men ran out into the middle of the road, and started waving them down. One of the men had a rifle cradled over one arm.

"Get down!" Drew shouted, and floored the gas. Amanda and Jenny ducked as low as they could, Jenny trying to cover Ashley with her own body.

The two men dashed out of the way barely in time to avoid being squashed by the Ranger. Drew heard something like a rock hitting the tailgate, another ricocheting off his door just below his window.

They reached the highway and, slowing down just enough to prevent a rollover, Drew made the turn. They were heading south toward home.

About five miles north of Oak Junction a state trooper was parked at a small turn-off, drinking coffee from a thermos while he watched for potential speeders. He almost dropped the plastic lid filled with the hot liquid onto his lap when he saw the pillar of fire rise into the black sky somewhere south of his position.

"Holy shit," he proclaimed, and grabbed the mike from his radio.

13

Zeb's station was demolished, along with Zeb himself, and the official report that Sheriff Craven later filed would list the incident as an accident due to negligence on the part of the owner.

"So no one else was hurt?" a state trooper asked Craven.

"No, just old Zeb. Damn shame, too. I liked the old guy. Everybody did. But to be honest, I told him time and time again that one of these days he was going to blow himself up if he didn't quit drinking and smoking so much. I'd say he fell asleep with a lit cigarette, or something close. Careless, just plain careless."

By the time the first fire engine arrived, half the town, including Sheriff Craven, had gathered to witness the event. Now, there were two fire engines and the paramedics (an ambulance stood by in order to remove any remains of Zebediah Brown, should there be anything left), and the area was thick with smoke, and clogged with hoses and firemen working to control the fire amidst the flashing lights from the emergency vehicles and police cruisers.

The two paramedics went through the crowd, checking for any injuries. There were four state patrol vehicles (not to mention Craven's damaged cruiser, which was parked up the road a ways - he didn't want to have to explain the missing windshield), one of which belonged to the trooper that was talking to Craven.

The chaos continued for hours, and eventually the crowd began to drift away. There were only a couple of people left to see the firemen pull Zeb's charred corpse from the wreckage. It would be daylight before the last of the firefighters left Oak Junction, leaving behind a huge, blackened hole in the ground surrounded by a wide area of debris from the destruction.

The smell of burnt rubber and gasoline was strong. The station was no longer standing; it was a mound of burnt wood and broken glass. Zeb's cooler and its contents had been scattered among the ash. There were tools and old tires and engine parts. His wrecker lay on its side about twenty yards from its spot next to the station, its tires melted, hull scorched. Its days were behind it now.

But, before the men who were trying to control the blaze left, before the state troopers finally exited Oak Junction in their dusty cruisers, another casualty of the blast was discovered in the woods north of the site.

A figure walked among the trees, all but invisible under the cover of the woods. Here, the moon was barely visible through the foliage. The figure heard harsh breathing, and stopped. He turned to his right, following the sound until he found the source. And there, nestled in the fallen leaves and overgrown ivy, was Cain. Or what was left of Cain.

He looked up with his single remaining eye at the figure bending over him, and wiggled around in a panic. Upon closer examination, the figure discovered that most of Cain's extremities had been blown off in the explosion. He had been a strong, powerful creature, but his thin limbs just could not withstand the force of the blast. They were mere stumps now, except for one arm (his right, which had been away from the center of the blast), which was still almost half there. His flesh was burned and blistered, and smelled horribly unnatural.

The figure knelt down and put his arms under Cain's trunk; it was considerably lighter now that the arms and legs were gone. He lifted him up, and Cain protested with growls. He opened his maw and his tongue darted out, but now the tip was burned completely off. Ignoring him, the figure walked off through the trees, carrying Cain in his arms.

The full moon blinked through the treetops as they made their way to the northern end of the woods. They entered a small field, and in the moonlight the figure could see that Cain's good eye now had a dull glaze over it, as if it were slowly going blind.

Their destination lay straight ahead, dark and abandoned on the edge of the moonlit field. The figure took Cain inside the Fellowship of God church and carried him through the inky blackness to the pulpit, where he laid him on the floor.

Cain lay alone while the figure went to switch on the main lights. Cain closed his eye against the glare, grunting as pain shot into his skull.

The figure returned to his side, and inspected what was left of him. Cain's gray skin was blackened, peeling in spots, his left eye burned completely out of its socket. A tiny puddle of dark fluid had formed under him from the bullet wound, and minute amounts oozed from his stumps; his wounds had been all but cauterized by the intense heat.

Cain cautiously opened his eye and saw the blurry figure standing over him. When his vision cleared, recognition set in, and he began to wriggle about with fright. It was incomprehensible, but here he was in the flesh. The figure standing there was...

Jonathon?

Jonathon Mott stood next to Cain's dying form, a knowing and confident look on his face. He was completely naked, his skin smudged from ash (the explosion had burned off all of his clothing), but otherwise unscathed. His long brown hair hung loose over his shoulders.

"Surprise, surprise, Lucas. You don't mind if I call you Lucas, do you? I didn't think so."

Cain opened his charred lips and moaned.

"This must be quite a shock for you," Jonathon said, "but you had it coming. After all, the book belongs to me, always has. I'll tell you all about it, Lucas, but let me get cleaned up and dressed. Of course, I'll need to borrow some of your clothes. Anyway, I get the feeling you won't be needing them anymore."

Jonathon walked away, vanishing down the small hallway that led to his father's old office and the small room that had been converted into a bedroom years before his father took over the church.

A short while later, he returned.

14

As soon as he put his hands on the book, Jonathon knew something was different about it. It wasn't just a book, but a living thing, filled with a vibrant energy the seemed to flow into him like hot liquid.

But, it wasn't until he got it home that he discovered the true *purpose of the book. While he explored the pages, and Cain's translations, the book filled him with a strange sense of tenure and wisdom, almost as if he was already familiar the book.*

But it made no sense.

He assumed that the book could not affect him, though, he being the son of a reverend, raised in a house of morals and prayer, but his way of thinking was quickly changing. It got to the point where he didn't care if the book affected him, nearly wanted *it to affect him.*

And then there were the little flashes of gold on the pages. He thought his eyes were playing tricks on him, or perhaps the book was playing its own sort of tricks. But after he called Drew and told him what he had found out, he went back to the book.

The twinkling of gold again caught his eye; only this time it was no trick. Words formed on the pages, words of gold. And the words were of Modern English, quite understandable.

As the revelation appeared to him, he saw tiny wisps of smoke curling up from underneath the book, and when he looked at the front cover he saw the source of the smoke: the death's head. Smoke was emanating from the gold symbol, dissipating in the air and giving off a sulfurous smell. And then his skin was burning, and when he lifted up his tee shirt he was not surprised to see a thin trail of smoke also rising from the death's head branded on the center of his chest. Now there was no doubt - there was a grand purpose to all this, and he was at the very center of it.

The book truly belonged to him.

And he truly belonged to the book.

He undid his ponytail and began to read the words that were undoubtedly written with Lucifer's own hand:

The prophecy must be fulfilled. You, the one known as Jonathon, son of a holy man are the chosen one. The book has reached its final destination. It has traveled to the ends of the earth and back, and into the hands of the one called Cain, who, in his greed and ignorance, delivered the book into proper hands.

I am the shadow in your mind, the thorn in your heart, the fire in your blood. You shall deliver me unto mankind to spread my tyranny, and I will take my place as ruler of man.

I shall send the descendants of the others unto you, and they will soon gather with you, and your number shall be 13. The sky will open and release the winds of hell onto earth, bringing with it the demons of the apocalypse.

Mankind will fall, only those who take the dark path will survive. Those of a righteous heart and soul will die, and suffer in torment in a living hell on earth. It is inevitable.

Hark my words. The false bearer of the book is dangerous, and will try to kill you. He must be destroyed. In time, you will be more powerful. You will be merciless. And you will stand by my side as the harbinger of death.

You will forsake everything that has been dear to you, for you will possess such knowledge and power that nothing will stand in your way.

The day and year has been chosen. Fulfill the prophecy.

Jonathon's body suddenly flowed with fire, and he was blinded by an intense whiteness. Images appeared, flying past quickly, filling his mind with horrors and atrocities that he never imagined could exist. There were destitute landscapes filled with thousands of people running, screaming as great winged beasts soared overhead, spewing fire down onto the masses. Millions of heads mounted on posts. People being tortured and torn apart, the agony inhuman and yet exquisite, climactic in its rapture.

The images, the pain, the suffering.

The ecstasy.

He watched as Lucifer's words wavered and faded away, leaving no sign of ever being there. The date of his mission had not been on the page. He simply knew it.

In his last act of humanity, he decided to let Drew and the others go free, for they would be instrumental in stopping Cain. They would have only one week to live, though, but he would keep his secret from them.

There was still the matter of Cain to attend to, and there could not be distractions. He was not strong enough to battle Cain as of yet, and Cain could not be killed by any normal means. He would have to be prevented from the performing the ritual, thereby changing him into something that was vulnerable to attack.

He would tell one person, though, the last person on Earth that Cain would suspect of being a traitor: Sheriff Frank Craven.

He called the Good Sheriff the following morning, and told him he had something very important to tell him, something that involved Mr. Cain, and would he please meet him at the barn on the old Willard property.

Jonathon drove his father's Ranger out to the Willard place, planning on parking it in the barn. When he opened the two large doors, however, he got a big surprise. Drew and Amanda's cars were parked at the back of the barn. He smiled to himself, climbed into the truck, and backed it into the barn. There was plenty room.

He got out of the truck, and leaned against the front hood, waiting for Craven to show up. He looked around the interior of the barn. The wood walls were rotted through in places, and it smelled damp and musty. There was also another smell, equally as strong and familiar as all the other smells in the barn; the odor of rotting bird corpses brought back memories of when he was young, finding the occasional dead bird in a field or under a tree, with that same smell in the air. Here in the barn, the heat from the sun had slowly baked the dead birds, intensifying the smell that much more.

He heard a car pull up in front of the barn, so he walked out into the morning light to meet with the sheriff. Craven got out of his cruiser.

"What's this all about, son?" the sheriff asked.

"Come into the barn," Jonathon said, "and let's talk."

"I don't think it's such a good idea, you going in there."

"I already know about the cars, Sheriff. I know about a lot of things. But there are a few things you need to know." Jonathon walked into the dankness of the barn, followed by Craven.

Once inside, Jonathon said, "I need to talk to you about Cain."

"What about him?"

"His time is up, Sheriff Craven. He needs to go," Jonathon said gravely.

"You're really asking for trouble, Jonathon."

"Fuck you."

Craven was taken aback. "What the hell did you say?"

"You heard me. Fuck you."

"I think we need to pay a visit to Mr. Cain," Craven said.

"We're not going anywhere, you fat fuck."

That was all the prompting the sheriff needed - he threw his fist squarely at Jonathon's face, a punch that should have broken his nose and maybe knocked out a few teeth. But instead of smashing into Jonathon's face, his fist smashed into something like solid steel. Jonathon didn't budge, didn't even blink an eye.

The Good Sheriff dropped to his knees next to the Ranger, groaning in pain and holding his injured hand, his face turning beet red.

"The book won't allow you to harm me, Sheriff. After all, it was mine all along. So, are we ready to talk?"

Craven nodded.

"Good. As I mentioned before, Lucas Cain has to go. Now, some friends and I have devised a scheme to get rid of him once and for all, and when we are through, they will be allowed to leave. The girl you are holding in the jail, her brother, Harvey White's wife and child. It's the least I can do for them for helping me. Understood?"

"Yes, but...the book..."

"Never mind the book for now. Are you with me on this?"

Craven nodded again. "Yes, I'm with you."

"Ok, this is what we're going to do," Jonathon said, offering a hand to the sheriff.

Cain was none the wiser that night when he asked the sheriff for the time, and the sheriff told him 11:45, five minutes slower than the actual time. Jonathon figured the extra five minutes would be enough, along with Cain's anxiety about getting back the book. He would be easy to string along.

The one thing Craven didn't count on, though, was the swift kick to the nuts he received from Amanda Townsend. When midnight struck, and Cain began to change, he purposely loosened his grip on the girl, sure that she would take flight from his grasp. Obviously, she felt that she needed a little extra assurance.

And he practically handed over his gun before the girl took it, knowing fully well he had a shotgun in the trunk of his cruiser that he planned on using to kill Cain if worse came to worse.

When the fugitives fled in the truck, Cain following close behind, Craven brought up the rear to make sure things went smoothly. Cain had fallen prey to a conspiracy, though, and in the end, he lost.

15

Cain had blanked out, and now was slowly returning to reality, again finding himself under the control of a young man whose parents he had ruthlessly killed. His body was a mass of burning pain, and he now wished for Jonathon to end it so he could be free of the suffering.

The Lost Grimoire had ruined his life from the very beginning, had *used* him, only to leave him for dead. Now, with the morning sun rising outside these very walls, he could not have felt more vulnerable.

For if the light of Him should bear upon thou skin, ye will become as ashes in the wind, scattered to the ends of the earth.

Jonathon entered the room, wearing nothing but a pair of Cain's blue jeans. Cain could see the telltale brand on Jonathon's chest. Barefooted, he paced the floor next to Cain as he spoke. "You know, you really shouldn't have messed with something you knew nothing about, Lucas. When you play with fire, you get burned." He stopped and faced the thing on the floor, his voice growing angry as he spoke. "You're nothing, Lucas, nothing at all. All you ever were was the insignificant little errand boy who delivered my book. That's right, *my* book. It's funny, but I never knew who or what I really was until I got the book. I lived in ignorance my whole life, believing in my father, and his disillusioned God.

"It's too bad you won't be around to see the end, but it's probably better that you don't. In one week's time, twelve others and myself will gather to summon the demons of the Apocalypse. Darkness will veil the Earth, and mankind will fall into oblivion. The Dark One will take his rightful place on Earth, and I will be a master of the multitudes. Earth will be the Kingdom of Hell." He stopped talking, and knelt down by Cain's leg stumps.

"But enough of this talk. All of this means nothing to you, now. It's time for you to make your departure." He grabbed the stumps, stood, and began dragging him toward the back door. The devil man pounded his head against the floor, growling in denial and fear. At the rear entrance to the church, Jonathon dropped Cain's stumps and opened the door.

"What a nice day it is, wouldn't you agree, Lucas?"

Jonathon hauled him out into the sunlight, and Cain immediately howled as his skin started to smoke. His one good eye burst open, and his skin melted off his bones like wax, quickly turning to ash. Now he was silent. His bones also fell into little piles of ash, which the morning breeze began to carry away.

Without another word, Jonathon went back inside the church.

When Cain woke up, he was back in his old body. He opened his eyes, expecting to see bright sunlight. Instead he saw a deep red sky filled with black clouds. Startled, he sat up and looked around him. A landscape littered with the undead, suffering and bleeding, forever bleeding, forever feeding the hungry beast.

Dundayin!

The ground rumbled and shook, and Behemeth/Morgoroth rose from the sand at his feet. Cain tried to scuttle backwards with his hands and feet, but Behemeth snatched up both of his arms and tore them from their sockets. Cain cried out in agony as blood spouted from his wounds into the sand.

The beast watched him screaming, and finally tore his tongue from his mouth and ate it. Blood gurgled in Cain's throat. He fell to the sand convulsing violently and on the brink of eternal insanity.

16

"Do you think Jonathon is still alive?" Jenny asked Drew, who was biting into a bagel. It had been a week since their escape, and they had heard nothing on the news of Oak Junction. Drew took a sip of his coffee.

"I don't know. I just hope he made it somehow."

Jenny sat down at the kitchen table across from Drew. Golden morning sunlight poured through the window over the sink. Another beautiful day.

"I just can't help thinking about him," she said sullenly. "I mean, he *did* help us get away."

"And we'll never forget it, either. I promise." He took her hand in his and gave it a gentle squeeze.

Clouds suddenly obscured the sun, and the room went dim. Drew got up and went to the window. Thunderheads were rapidly filling the sky. *That's odd*, he thought. The wind picked up, howling around the eaves and whipping the curtains on the kitchen window.

"Whoa, looks like we're in for one hell of a storm," Drew said. "We better close all the windows. You check Ashley's room."

Jenny went into Ashley's room, and the little girl had awakened from her nap. "What's wrong, mommy?"

Lightning flashed, and a second later thunder literally shook the house. Jenny heard Drew exclaim, "Wow, what the hell was that?" from another room in the house.

"It's ok, honey, just a storm on the way."

Indeed, there was a storm on the way, one *hell* of a storm.

END

ABOUT THE AUTHOR

David Rhodes currently resides in Provo, Utah. He claims that the frequent nightmares he feared as a child eventually captivated him, and kindled his fascination with all things dark and mysterious. He insists that the scariest things in our world are people.